FINAL JUDGMENT

A LOU MASON THRILLER

BY

JOEL GOLDMAN

Praise for Joel Goldman's Novels

Motion to Kill

Michael Connelly and Lee Child recommend the Lou Mason Thriller Series!

"Lou is a fascinating protagonist . . . fans will set in motion a plea for more Lou Mason thrillers."

—*Midwest Book Review*

"The plot races forward."

—*Amarillo Globe News*

"Lots of suspense and a dandy surprise ending."

—*Romantic Times*

The Last Witness

"Fast, furious and thoroughly enjoyable, *The Last Witness* is classic, and classy, noir for our time, filled with great characters and sharp, stylish writing. We better see more Lou Mason in the future."

—Jeffery Deaver, author of *The Vanished Man* and *The Stone Monkey*

"*The Last Witness* is an old-fashioned, '40s, tough-guy detective story set in modern times and starring a lawyer named Lou Mason instead of a private eye named Sam Spade. There's a lot of action, loads of suspects, and plenty of snappy dialogue. It's a fun read from beginning to end."

—Phillip Margolin, author of *The Associate* and *Wild Justice*

Cold Truth

"Wanted for good writing: Joel Goldman strikes again with *Cold Truth.* Kansas City trial lawyer Lou Mason doesn't shy away from the hard cases. Always working close to the edge, he worries that he 'was taking the dive just to see if he could make it back to the surface, gulping for air, beating the odds, wishing he had a reason to play it safe.'"

—*Kansas City Star*

"Joel Goldman is the real deal. In *Cold Truth*, Lou Mason goes his namesake Perry one better, and ought to make Kansas City a must-stop on the lawyer/thriller map."

—John Lescroart, best-selling author of *The First Law*

Deadlocked

"In his fourth novel, attorney-turned-author Joel Goldman delivers a well-plotted legal thriller that takes an insightful look at capital punishment and questions of guilt. *Deadlocked's* brisk pace is augmented by Goldman's skill at creating realistic characters and believable situations. Goldman is among the legion of strong paperback writers whose novels often rival those in hardcover."

—Oline H. Cogdill, *Orlando Sun Sentinel*

"A certain death penalty case and execution is the catalyst in Joel Goldman's legal thriller *Deadlocked*. The fourth Lou Mason case is the best and most thought provoking and when the action starts it is a real page turner delivered by a pro."

—*Mystery Scene Magazine*

"Lou Mason's best outing . . . very satisfying and highly recommended."

—Lee Child, *New York Times* best-selling author

Shakedown

"Here's why . . . mystery lovers should put *Shakedown* on their nightstands: Goldman, a 'nuthin' fancy' kind of writer, tells a story at a breakneck pace."

—*Kansas City Star*

"Goldman's surefooted plotting and Jack Davis's courage under fire make this a fascinating, compelling read."

—*Publishers Weekly*

"*Shakedown* is a really fine novel. Joel Goldman has got it locked and loaded and full of the blood of character and the gritty details that make up the truth. Page for page, I loved it."

—*Michael Connelly*

"*Shakedown* is a chillingly realistic crime novel—it's fast-paced, smartly plotted, and a gripping read to the very last page. Joel Goldman explores—with an insider's eye—a dark tale of murder and betrayal."

—*Linda Fairstein*

The Dead Man

"A masterful blend of rock-solid detective work and escalating dread. *The Dead Man* is both a top-notch thriller, and a heart-rending story of loss, courage, and second chances. I loved it."

—Robert Crais, *New York Times* best-selling author

"*The Dead Man* by Kansas Citian Joel Goldman is a rock-solid mystery with likable, flawed characters. I would have enjoyed it even if it had not been set in Kansas City, but scenes such as Harper looking out over Brush Creek or eating in the Country Club Plaza added to the pleasure."

—*Kansas City Star*

"*The Dead Man* is one of those rare novels you will be tempted to read twice: the first time to enjoy, and the second to appreciate how Goldman puts the pieces together. The hours spent on both will be more than worth it."

—Joe Hartlaub, Bookreporter.com

No Way Out

"Sleek and sassy, *No Way Out* is a page-turner that keeps going full speed until the very end."

—Faye Kellerman, *New York Times* best-selling author

"Goldman spins his latest yarn into a clever, complex tangle of chain reactions between six families of characters whose lives are intertwined by blood, grief, lust, desperation and even love. The fun, of course, lies in the untangling . . . If you like to blink, you may want to skip this novel."

—*435 South* magazine

FINAL JUDGMENT

A LOU MASON THRILLER

BY

JOEL GOLDMAN

ISBN: 0989859908
ISBN-13: 9780989859905

NOVELS & SHORT STORIES BY JOEL GOLDMAN

THE LOU MASON THRILLERS

Motion To Kill

The Last Witness

Cold Truth

Deadlocked

Final Judgment

THE JACK DAVIS THRILLERS

Shakedown

The Dead Man

No Way Out

THE ALEX STONE THRILLERS

Stone Cold

Chasing the Dead

THE DEAD MAN SERIES BY WILLIAM RABKIN & LEE GOLDBER

Freaks Must Die

SHORT STORIES

Fire in the Sky

Knife Fight

For Stephanie, Pam & Mark. Welcome to the family.

CHAPTER ONE

THERE WAS A dead body in the trunk of Avery Fish's Fleet- wood Cadillac. Not that he didn't have enough problems already. He was late for a meeting with his lawyer, Lou Mason, and the assistant U.S. attorney, Pete Samuelson. They were negotiating a deal for Fish's body and soul like they were haggling over a used car, both sides selling him "as is."

Fish knew how it would go. Mason had briefed him the day before, telling him he'd better be on time.

"Why not just strip me down to my shorts and check my teeth like I was a horse being sold by the pound?" Fish asked.

"Because you're too old and ugly," Mason answered, grinning. "The feds wouldn't buy and I'd be stuck with you."

Fish waved his hand at Mason's joke. "So what kind of deal am I going to get?"

"You're charged with mail fraud. I'll offer twelve months suspended with probation, which is a downward deviation from federal sentencing guidelines, and a hundred thousand dollars in restitution for the people the government says you swindled."

"Like I've got that kind of money."

He didn't deny his guilt. He just wanted to know what he owed, figuring he was negotiating with his lawyer as well as the Justice Department. Mason ignored Fish's complaint, knowing that Fish had the money or could get it, just as he had gotten the money to pay Mason's fee.

"This is your first conviction. You're not a young man. Samuelson will want eighteen months of real time and more money, maybe two hundred and fifty grand, plus a fine. Probably the same amount, maybe a little less."

"What are the chances I'll get probation?"

"Not good unless you've got something else to offer besides money and remorse."

"Like what?"

"Someone you could give to them. Someone who has bigger problems than mail fraud."

"You mean inform on someone? I'd rather go to jail," Fish said.

"The government calls it cooperation. Judges are very impressed by it and nobody would rather go to jail."

"Such a future." Fish rubbed the top of his bulging stomach. His heartburn could eat through sheet metal. He appreciated Mason's precise explanation. First conviction. Not first indictment. He shouldn't complain. Not at his age. But he couldn't help it. "Spending my golden years as a bankrupt federal snitch. Acch! What a life."

"Beats the hell out of stripping to your shorts and having your teeth checked by some Aryan Brotherhood inmate who thinks you remind him of the uncle that molested him when he was a kid," Mason had told him.

Now this, Fish thought to himself, as he stood in the parking lot of his synagogue in south Kansas City, the weekday morning service just finished. The air was damp and cold, the day raw and typical for February. The pavement and the sky were the same flat gray, just like the body in the trunk. He should have gone to Scottsdale for the winter like everybody else.

The dead man was naked and wrapped in a sheet of clear plastic that made him look like a prehistoric hunter left frozen in ice a thousand years ago. The limbs were tight against the torso, their skin unblemished by any visible wounds.

Fish's briefcase was in the trunk. He didn't need it for the meeting with the lawyers. In fact, there was nothing in it besides the latest issue of Fast Company with an article he wanted to read, especially now, titled "How to Make Your

Own Luck." But, carrying the briefcase gave him a more substantial look. Like he was a businessman, not some gonif caught with his nuts in the wringer.

Which he was. Gonif, Yiddish for thief, was a word that defined itself as much by its pronunciation as its meaning. He liked the guttural way it rolled off his tongue, straight from the back of his mouth like he was throwing it at someone.

His briefcase was tucked underneath the dead man. Fish worried that the poor bastard had bled onto it even though the body was wrapped in plastic. He didn't want to walk into the meeting with the U.S. attorney carrying a briefcase with a bloodstain painted on it like a bull's-eye. He left it where it was and closed the trunk.

He was seventy-three years old. He had a wife who referred to herself as his ex-wife on the slight technicality that they'd been divorced for twenty-five years. Like that mattered. He had two daughters who didn't talk to him unless they had to and four grandchildren who never stopped.

He was thirty-five pounds overweight. He had plantar fascitis in both feet and chronic pain in both hips. He had a lumbar disc at the base of his spine that bulged like a teenage boy's dick at his first skin flick and chest pain that woke him at night like the devil was slipping a blade between his ribs. But he didn't complain. That was life. The odds favored a man like him having problems like these.

But a dead body in the trunk of his car on the day he was to bargain his life away in a comfortable conference room at the Federal Courthouse—that didn't defy the odds. It beat the living daylights out of them.

Fish didn't realize he was sweating until he slid into his car. And he was sweating and breathing as hard as a racehorse on the backstretch. Certain of what he'd seen, he still didn't want to believe it. It was too awful to be true, but it was. In spite of the cold, he turned on the air-conditioning, gripping the leather-wrapped steering wheel until he cooled down and could breathe normally.

What are the odds? A dead body in his trunk. Blinking the sweat from his eyes, he squinted, remembering when he'd last opened the trunk. It was the night before when he'd gotten home from meeting with Mason. The briefcase had been on the front seat of the car, the magazine already in it. His dry cleaning had been in the trunk. He'd taken the laundry out and left the briefcase in its place.

He'd stayed home the rest of the night. Gone to bed early. Slept all night except for the three times he'd gotten up to go to the bathroom. His car had been parked in front of his house, the garage crammed full of junk he'd been meaning to throw away since his divorce.

Had to have been during the night. He lived on a quiet street. Hell, it was a historic district! That's how quiet it was. Most of the neighbors were old like him, the houses even older. No young kids coming home late to interrupt some killer who had turned Fish's car into a drive-by drop-off for dead bodies. If the killer had bothered to ask, Fish would have told him that there was a twenty-four-hour Goodwill drop-off a mile away.

During the night was a better bet than while he was in the synagogue, even if there were only a handful of cars in the parking lot belonging to the ten people who showed up for the morning service. It was still dark when he arrived a few minutes before seven that morning. The service lasted forty- five minutes. The rabbi had buttonholed him for another fifteen minutes afterwards, making him late for his meeting with the attorneys, asking him how things were going with his case. His legal problems weren't a secret. The media and a city full of gossips had taken care of that.

He set aside the odds against a dead body showing up in the trunk of his car. It had happened. The odds had gone from astronomical against to one hundred percent in favor. Fish's next bet was on when it happened. The odds favored last night while Fish slept. He didn't have time to figure the odds on the harder questions. Who was the dead man? Who killed him? Why did the killer pick the trunk of his car?

Fish didn't want to know the answers to any of these questions, certain that he was better off not knowing. It had nothing to do with him anyway. The body in the trunk was his bad luck. That's all.

He had to be downtown in fifteen minutes and he was thirty minutes away. He couldn't leave his car in the parking lot without arousing suspicions at the synagogue. He couldn't leave his car at home and take the bus downtown because he didn't know where to catch the bus or even which bus to take if he did.

As he considered his options, the idea of parking his car with its decaying cargo at the Federal Courthouse wasn't as bad as he first thought. The parking lot was across the street from the courthouse. It was secure, regularly patrolled by the U.S. Marshals' deputies who were responsible for courthouse security. No one was going to break into a car in that lot. It was cold enough and the corpse was fresh enough that the body hadn't started to smell. Mason had told him that the meeting with the U.S. attorney shouldn't take too long, though he could expect some fireworks as the attorneys postured for one another, doing their peacock dance. Fish hoped the meeting was more a formality than anything else.

Good, he thought to himself. Things work out if you give them a chance and work the right angles. That had always been his philosophy. He took a deep breath, put the Cadillac in gear, and tried not to think about the body in the trunk.

CHAPTER TWO

FISH WAS IN sales. Buy, sell, trade. He didn't always own what he sold. He didn't always pay for what he bought, and he didn't always have what he traded. These were business risks that he managed through the next buy, sell, or trade.

His entire life had been a teetering Ponzi scheme in which he had to make the next deal just to stay a step ahead of the last one. Not that he was in Bernie Madoff's league, not by a long shot. Now there was a gonif. Fish admired Madoff for his balls, but even he had cringed at the scope of the devastation Madoff had caused, rationalizing his own crimes as minor offenses that had left a few people short a few bucks, nothing they couldn't recover from.

The U.S. attorney had indicted Fish for mail fraud stemming from a vacation time-share scam. Fish had assembled a loose network of third-rate condos in Orlando and Ft. Lauderdale, promised below-market prices for theme park and cruise packages, and bundled the pitch in a slick, glossy, four-color brochure. He bought a mailing list of likely marks and mailed them his solicitation. He got so many takers that the properties were oversold and double-booked. People complained that they couldn't book their time-share or that, when they did, their unit was already occupied when they arrived.

He made a killing, using the proceeds to pay off the most vociferous of the complainers, until one outraged customer told the story to his next-door neighbor, who happened to be a secretary at the Kansas City office of the FBI. And the rest was commentary.

It wasn't difficult or sophisticated. A good scam never was. It depended on people who would jump at deals that were too good to be true. Fish counted on them to forget the flip side of the axiom that such deals almost always were.

For Fish, life was a game in which everyone was a free agent. Winners anticipated the responses of the other players. Winners took advantage of better information. Winners made hard choices.

Losers reacted based on imperfect information and wimped out when their losses got too high. That's why most people who complained about their time-shares settled for getting less than one hundred percent of their money back. Fighting harder wasn't worth the effort. Fish knew that.

He was reconciled to being the loser in the game with the U.S. attorney. He admired Mason for not conning him. The government's case was solid. The feds had been sniffing after him for years. They were going to take him down. Cutting a deal wasn't wimping out. It was the only rational decision. The body in the trunk presented an entirely different problem. He had no idea how to get rid of it without being implicated in a murder he didn't commit. He could stop at police headquarters and invite a homicide detective to take a peek. Given his present circumstance with the Justice Department, he doubted the cops would buy his "beats me" answer to the questions they would ask.

He could tell his lawyer, but he knew what Mason would tell him. Go to the cops. Maybe good advice for another day, but definitely not today.

By the time he pulled into the courthouse parking lot, Fish was convinced of two things: He had to get out of there with a signed deal as fast as he could, and then he had to take care of the dead body on his own.

He'd have to get a new car as well. He couldn't take the chance that a latent hair of the murder victim would one day be scraped out of the trunk while he stood around shrugging his shoulders like the old Jew in the joke about why Jews have such short necks. "I don't know," Fish said to no one, shrugging and smiling to himself. Don't lose your sense of humor, his mother always told him. He pictured her for a moment as he walked toward the courthouse, smiling without reason.

Fish met Mason in the hall on the eighth floor. He was leaning against the wall, arms folded across his chest, when Fish got off the elevator. Fish hurried toward him, hands outstretched.

"I'm sorry I'm late. The rabbi grabbed me after services this morning. Everything with him is another sermon. He wouldn't let me go until I told him he'd have to call the FBI and tell them I hadn't jumped bail."

Mason shook his hand. "Don't worry. Samuelson is running late too. His secretary said he'd be another twenty or thirty minutes. There's a lot of hurry up and wait in the practice of law."

Fish pulled off his topcoat, and laid it across his arm. He looked out the eighth-floor windows at the panoramic view to the south, focusing on the parking lot below. He spotted his car tucked into a space at the back of the lot. Someone parked next to his Cadillac, got out, and walked toward the courthouse without so much as a backward glance. Fish exhaled loudly, unaware that he'd been holding his breath.

Mason asked, "Are you okay, Avery? I've got mold in my refrigerator that looks better than you do."

Fish wiped his brow. More sweat. "How should I look? I work all my life and I'm about to get the penitentiary instead of a pension."

"There's a bathroom down the hall. Splash some water on your face. Straighten your tie and pinch your cheeks for some color. You look like death warmed over. I want Samuelson to see the grandfather not the gonif."

Fish smiled. That's why he liked Mason. No bullshit and a sense of humor. It didn't hurt that he was a member of the tribe, a fellow Jew. When it was crunch time, his people always took care of one another.

Forty minutes later, they were ushered into a conference room by Samuelson's secretary, who apologized again that her boss had been delayed by an emergency in another case. She apologized a second time that there was no coffee, closing the door and leaving Fish and Mason alone.

The conference room was small and had no windows. Pinpoint beams of light aimed at them from miniature floodlights buried deep in ceiling canisters. Mason sat in one of the black leather chairs ringing a circular table. Fish paced, brushing his hand along the surface of the table.

"Samuelson," Fish said. "He must be a young guy."

"Around thirty, I'd say. How did you know?"

"This conference room. It's for minor leaguers. You want to impress somebody with the might of the federal government, you get the big room with the picture of the president on the wall and a couple of flags in the corners. Maybe one of those big bronze seals with the eagle on it. I'd say Samuel son doesn't carry a lot of weight around here if this is the best conference room he can get."

"Don't be insulted that you didn't get the big-shot treatment. There's a price for that, and it's paid in jail time and money. Better to be a low-profile defendant in a low-profile case with a young guy still learning his way around."

"Yeah, yeah, yeah." Fish smoothed the lapels on his suit jacket, hiking up his pants and tugging at his shirt collar. "If I'm right, then why is he keeping us waiting? What's with this baloney about an emergency in another case? I know it's the government we're dealing with here, but don't they have to try to run on time for Christ's sake?"

"Avery, you got someplace else you've got to be today? Something more important on your schedule than this? Sit down, take a breath, and relax. These things always take longer than they should. We're going to get a deal you can live with. It may not be perfect, but it will beat the hell out of taking this case to trial. Trust me."

"Don't get me wrong." Fish sat heavily in one of the chairs, leaning back, then forward, gripping the table with one hand, drumming his fingers on the surface with the other. "I'm not looking for a trial. I just want to get this over with and get out of here."

CHAPTER THREE

THE DOOR OPENED and Pete Samuelson breezed in, dropping his file on the table. He was tall, thin, and bald with a shiny forehead that jutted out like the granite face of a cliff, his eyes chiseled out of the rock like half-hidden caves kept in perpetual shadows regardless of which way he turned. He may have been thirty, but there was no exuberance of youth in him. He was a grinder. A humorless lawyer committed to working endless hours rigidly enforcing the law. He was a perfect prosecutor.

"Busy day?" Mason asked.

"Yeah," Samuelson answered, biting the word and his lower lip at the same time. He opened Fish's file, picked up a sheet of paper, and studied it for a moment as if he were the only one in the room.

"Pete," Mason began, stopping when Samuelson raised his hand.

"Okay, here's the deal," Samuelson said, putting the page back in the file and closing it. "Your guy is dead-nuts guilty.

We've got his promotional pieces promising people they'd get everything but laid. We've got wiretaps of the owners of the vacation properties telling him they couldn't handle anywhere near the number of time-shares he was selling and him telling them it didn't matter so long as he collected the money from the dumb schmucks. Dumb schmucks is a direct quote, by the way."

Mason leaned forward across the table, cutting the distance between him and Samuelson in half.

"My guy's name is Avery Fish and he's sitting right here, in case you hadn't noticed. He's not a terrorist or a dope dealer or a bank robber. He's a grandfather and an active member of his synagogue who's never been convicted of a crime. We're not here to argue about your case against him. We're here to make a deal."

Samuelson turned to Fish. "Mr. Fish, I meant you no disrespect. I just want you to know that I can put you away for a long time, maybe the rest of your life depending on your health. You've got a good lawyer, but not even he is good enough to keep you out of the penitentiary if we don't make a deal right now in this conference room. Do you understand that?"

Fish had a sudden image of Pete Samuelson wrapped in plastic in the trunk of his car. "I'm an old man, Mr. Samuel- son. Don't worry. You scared me. Talk to my lawyer."

Samuelson nodded and reopened his file. He took out the page he'd already studied and slid it across the table to Mason. "Eighteen months, two hundred fifty thousand in restitution and a fine for another two-fifty."

Mason ignored the page in front of him. "Let's go, Avery," he said, standing.

Fish looked at Mason, eyes wide. "Go? Where? We aren't done. We haven't made the deal."

"We haven't made the deal, but we are done. Mr. Samuel son is too proud of his case. He thinks he can bully you into taking a deal that's no worse than you'd get at trial, where he's got no better than a fifty-fifty chance at a conviction. He'll be lucky to get the wiretaps into evidence, and I'll bet when we start digging, we'll find out that he made a sweetheart deal with those people in Florida to testify against you in return for their own time-share out of jail. Let's go."

Fish didn't move, but he did sweat. A moist layer that bubbled onto his brow as his skin paled. His breath came in quick bursts. "I want to make a deal. Now," he managed.

Mason had told Fish that this could happen when they met the day before. He predicted that Samuelson would come on hard and that they would respond by walking out, counting on Samuelson to back up rather than tell his boss that he blew the negotiations. The government's case was strong but not invincible. Mason bet that Samuelson had been given orders to get rid of the case. No one liked sending old men to jail. Fish was supposed to follow Mason out the door, not fold and beg.

"You're a smart man, Mr. Fish," Samuelson said, the first hint of a smile leaking from the corners of his narrow mouth.

"Fortunately, he's got a smarter lawyer," Mason said. "If you want to negotiate, we'll negotiate. But you can save the take-it-or-leave-it crap for somebody else. If my client wants the deal you put on the table, he'll have to get another lawyer, and you know as well as I do, no lawyer is going to tell him to take that deal. I'm not selling him out. Avery, get your ass out of that chair!"

Fish pushed himself away from the table, still holding on to it. He rose, picking up his coat, his round shoulders sagging as Mason opened the door.

"Okay, Mason," Samuelson said. "You made your fee speech. Everybody sit down and you tell me what you're looking for."

Mason nodded at Fish, who collapsed into his seat. Mason remained standing, one hand on the doorknob. "No jail time. Twelve months suspended with probation. A hundred thousand in restitution and a seventy-five-thousand dollar fine."

"You're not sitting down," Samuelson said.

"Not until I know if we're in the ballpark."

Samuelson ran his hand over his bald head, Mason catching the glow of sweat from his shiny pate. He had been right to call Samuelson's bluff.

"Same ballpark, but still a long way from home plate. Sit down. I can't do probation."

"He won't pay what you want without probation. That's not negotiable."

"Fine. I'll give you something else that's not negotiable. Money doesn't buy probation."

There was a knock at the door before Mason could answer. Dennis Brewer opened it, not waiting to be invited in. He was the FBI agent on Fish's case: a tall, broad-shouldered, middle-aged man wearing an expensive dark suit and a flat expression on his ruddy face. The first time they met, Brewer had made it clear to Mason that he had more important things to do than screw around with a small-time con man like Fish. He shot the cuffs of his shirt to make the point, his gold cufflinks with diamond centers catching the light. Mason wanted to ask him, Who's your daddy?

Brewer took two quick steps to Samuelson, bent down, and whispered in Samuelson's ear, cupping his hand to shield what he was saying. Finished, he stood, giving Fish a hard stare.

"You're certain?" Samuelson asked Brewer.

"Absolutely," Brewer answered. "Another emergency?" Mason asked. "Take your time." Samuelson frowned, the little light in his eyes dimming.

"Not necessary. We're done. Our deal is off the table." "Done? Why?" Mason asked. "There's a dead body in the trunk of your client's car."

CHAPTER FOUR

CLIENTS NEVER TELL their lawyers everything. Mason knew that. Expected it. He tried different things to encourage their candor. He worked hard to build rapport that translated into trust. He provided a sympathetic audience of one ready to receive confessions without passing judgment. He extolled the sanctity of the attorney-client privilege, assuring his clients that their darkest secrets would remain locked in his ethical vault.

But he knew better than to be disappointed or surprised when a client held something back. It was a self-protective human impulse, the remnants of a primordial survival instinct. Knowledge is power. Confession is weak. Truth is a commodity to be bartered for freedom.

Avery Fish had raised the bar for holding back to new heights. A dead body wasn't easy to overlook or ignore. One parked in the trunk of your car was positively unforgettable, however unmentionable.

Samuelson and Brewer left them in the conference room, Brewer telling Fish to stay put until the police arrived. Mason cracked the door open a moment later. A deputy U.S. Marshal stared at him from the hallway, motioning him back into the conference room with one hand, the other resting on the butt of his service weapon.

Mason closed the door and turned to Fish, who was slumped on the table, his head on his folded arms.

"I've got at least fifty questions I could start with," Mason said.

"Do me a favor," Fish mumbled. "Pick an easy one."

Mason needed answers before the cops arrived. There wasn't time for Fish to fall apart. Regardless of what Fish said he knew, the cops would assume that he knew more. Mason had to get a feel for the truth, which he assumed was somewhere between what Fish would admit and what the cops would suspect.

"Sit up and look at me."

Fish lifted his head, his eyes glassy as if Mason had woken him from a drunk, strands of thin white hair drifting over his brow. He rubbed his meaty hands across his jowls, pulled off his glasses, and massaged the corners of his eyes.

"Okay, already. I'm sitting up. I'm looking at you. Ask your fifty questions."

"Whose body is in the trunk of your car?"

"I don't know."

"How did the body get there?"

"I don't know. I didn't put it there."

"How long has it been in your car?"

Fish took a deep breath and clutched the edge of the table with his hands. "It wasn't there last night when I got home around six o'clock. It was there this morning when I left the synagogue."

"You knew there was a body in the trunk of your car when you drove downtown?" Mason asked, not certain he'd heard Fish correctly.

Fish nodded with a sigh, avoiding eye contact with Mason.

"Avery, I'm not being critical here, but why didn't you call the police instead of parking a dead body at the Federal Courthouse?"

Fish leaned back in his chair, crossing his arms over the top of his belly and forcing his considerable stomach outward an inch or two like a blowfish puffing itself up to ward off attackers.

"That question I can answer, Mr. Smart Guy Lawyer. After services this morning, I opened the trunk to get my briefcase, only the body was on top of it. You told me not to be late and even though I thought this was a good excuse, I didn't think the U.S. attorney would agree. Besides, a dead body is hard enough for an average citizen to explain and these days I'm not exactly an average citizen. So I kept my mouth shut, hoping you would get me out of here in a hurry. Then I'd figure out what to do. I was going to ask your advice, if it makes you feel any better."

Mason let out a breath. "It always makes me feel special when my client drops an asteroid-size shoe on my head in the middle of negotiating a plea bargain."

"Your head?" Fish asked, coming out of his chair. "Your head? Listen, boytchik, it's my head that's going to nestle into a prison pillow every night for the rest of my life. Not yours!"

"You can count on that if you keep me in the dark! The U.S. attorney figures I either knew about the body and didn't say anything or that I have no control over you. Either way, my credibility takes a hit, and when that happens, your penitentiary frequent-guest points start stacking up. So make me really feel better. Tell me who it was."

Fish fell back into his chair. "I told you. I don't know."

Fish's voice was suddenly reedy; his burst of anger evaporated, a fearful desperation taking its place. Mason liked him and wanted to believe him. He wasn't a terrorist, bank robber, or dope dealer. He was a gonif, a swindler, a con man, and he was good at it, having made a nice illegal income for a long time. That required a fair measure of charm, which Fish had in abundance, and an easy capacity to lie about anything to anyone. Mason hoped his client wasn't lying to him now.

"Man or woman?" Mason asked.

"Man."

"Okay, fine. You didn't know him. What did he look like?"

Fish shrugged. "Not much. He was white. Probably around six feet, like you. Nothing special."

"His face, Avery. What did he look like?"

Fish answered slowly, his hands covering his eyes before he dropped them in his lap in surrender, the memory too fresh, the day's events piling up. "He didn't have one."

"C'mon, Avery," Mason said, annoyed that Fish would try to play him. "If you knew the victim, the police will eventually figure that out."

"Somebody cut off his head. And his hands," Fish whispered, the words catching in his throat as tears spilled from his red-rimmed eyes.

CHAPTER FIVE

THE HOMICIDE DETECTIVES went easy on Fish at first, as if he was a lesser victim of the crime and not a suspected killer. They commiserated with him about his grisly discovery, practically apologizing for their questions.

The two detectives, Kevin Griswold and Tom Cates, both white men in their late thirties, were lean, fit, and earnest— brothers under the skin with Pete Samuelson. Mason wasn't fooled by their demeanor and trusted that Fish wasn't either. Pious grandfather or old con man, Fish was their first and best suspect.

Fish stuck with the story he'd told Mason, which boosted Mason's confidence that Fish was telling the truth. That he was afraid to call the police because he'd be late to his meeting with the U.S. attorney bordered on the improbable. Not because it wasn't possible, but because it made Fish look so bad. Such confessions carried with them the ring of truth, especially when Fish could have easily claimed that the body in the trunk was news to him.

"So your lawyer here, Mr. Mason," Detective Griswold said. "He told you not to be late for your meeting with the U.S. attorney. That's why you didn't call the police when you found the body." Fish nodded. "That's right, Detective. You understand I'm not blaming my lawyer. When I saw the body, I didn't know what else to do. All I could think was to come here and talk to Mr. Mason."

"And you told your lawyer there was a dead man in the trunk of your car?" Griswold asked.

"With no head or hands," Detective Cates added, shaking his head sympathetically. "And your lawyer says let's take one crime at a time. Make a deal with the U.S. attorney and then clean up the mess in your car. Is that about it?"

Mason ground his teeth at the way the questioning had developed, uncertain whether to be angrier with his client or the cops. Fish had led the detectives away from him and directly at Mason, making Mason an accomplice in a cover-up just in case the cops didn't buy Fish's protest of innocence. He'd done it with disarming skill, making the cops think it was their idea, not his. Mason bet Fish could have sold both detectives time-shares in Florida.

Mason couldn't let Fish answer the last series of questions without waiving the attorney-client privilege. The moment Mason instructed Fish not to answer, the impression Fish was leaving would be embossed in the cops' minds. Yet Mason had no choice.

"Forget it," Mason told the detectives. "You know better than to ask my client what he and I talked about. He told you what he knows. He found the body in the trunk this morning. His actions are understandable and not illegal."

"The law says you're supposed to report dead bodies, not hide them, Counselor," Griswold said, ratcheting up the tempo for Mason.

"Within how many hours?" Mason asked. "He found the body after breakfast. It's not even lunchtime. You want to charge him with failure to report, write it down. If you think you can prove that this fat old man killed whoever is in the trunk, then cut off the victim's head and hands and drove around town with the leftovers, just say so. Otherwise, we're leaving."

Detective Griswold said, "We'll have a warrant to search your client's house in a couple of hours. Tell him not to go home and clean house before we get there."

"You want to search my house?" Fish asked, standing and putting on his topcoat. "Be my guest. Search all you want. You don't need a warrant. Just wipe your feet so you don't track up. The last time the FBI searched my house, they left a mess. My housekeeper yelled at me for a week after that."

Mason drove to Fish's house. Fish rode with him, the detectives following behind. He had agreed with Fish's offer of a voluntary search. It was another indication of Fish's innocence. Or, from the cops' perspective, it was proof that

Fish committed the murder somewhere other than at his house. Either way, there was the risk that the cops would find something to incriminate Fish in the murder or in an unrelated offense.

"Don't worry. My house is clean," Fish said, reading Mason's mind.

"A good housekeeper is hard to find," Mason said.

Fish chuckled, a dry sound from deep in his throat. More regret than amusement. "I do have a good housekeeper and they are hard to find. But we both know that's not what we're talking about. I didn't kill that man. I have no idea who he is or how he wound up in my trunk. It's my bad mazel, my bad luck. That's all. So don't worry."

Mason smiled. Fish had a way of comforting people, putting them at ease. He sprinkled Yiddish words into his conversations with Mason, a subtle reminder of their Jewish kinship, leaving the Yiddish out of his patter with gentiles.

Mason's Jewish upbringing had been at the hands of his aunt, Claire Mason, who had raised him after his parents died in a car wreck when Mason was three. Claire had abandoned ritual and cultural Judaism, but faithfully practiced the commandment to heal the world with a law practice devoted to the underdog.

Avery Fish was the polar opposite of Mason's aunt. He was devoted in his observance of ritual, attending daily services, keeping kosher and observing the Sabbath and the many holidays on the Jewish calendar. Yet he was a crook.

Mason had asked him about the obvious contradiction the first time they met. They were in Mason's office, a one-room layout above a bar called Blues on Broadway in midtown Kansas City. Fish was candid about his guilt and worried about whether he would be able to keep kosher from a prison cell.

"I grew up in a very observant home," Fish explained. "I studied Torah with my father every Shabbos. I learned to chant all the prayers and the different melodies of the service. The rituals became my rituals. It never occurred to me not to be an observant Jew."

"That part I understand," Mason said. "What I don't understand is the government's indictment of you for mail fraud and the arrest-dodging track record you've compiled when you're not praying."

Fish shrugged his shoulders, his chin disappearing into the folds of his neck. "It's not a perfect world and I'm not a perfect man. But I know who and what I am. God knows too. One day, He and I will settle up."

Mason shook his head, uncertain whether Fish was being honest about his imperfections or merely hypocritical about his faith. Mason's own life was not without contradictions.

He defended people accused of crimes, yet had sometimes crossed the line in their defense, leaving others dead or ruined. But his clients had been vindicated, the guilty caught. Who was he to judge Avery Fish? What would he do when it was his turn to settle up?

CHAPTER SIX

MASON PULLED UP in front of Fish's house. There were two police cars in the driveway and two more parked on the street. A contingent of cops waited at the front door. Neighbors watched from their windows, a few braving the cold for a better view from their front yards.

Fish quickly took in the scene, groaning as he got out of the car. "Oy, the tsoris I've got!"

The detectives, uniformed cops, and forensics crew spent four hours combing through Fish's house. They moved every piece of furniture, rolled up every rug, opened every cabinet, drawer, and closet. They unscrewed air-conditioning vents, poked their heads and shoulders into ventilation shafts, and swept the concrete basement floor for any sign of freshly poured cement. They rattled the radiators, jimmied the floorboards for loose panels, and crawled through the attic. They raked the dead leaves that had piled hard against the house and they wormed through the boxes, old clothes, and other leftovers crammed to the ceiling in the garage.

Griswold and Cates took turns glaring at Fish, who sat at the kitchen table reading a book whose cover promised that a short history of nearly everything lay within its pages, oblivious to the whirlwind around him. Mason had neither Fish's patience nor his attention span and followed in the wake of the searchers, taking a silent delight in their growing frustration.

By mid-afternoon, the party was breaking up. The cops had bagged hairs, fibers, and threads so they wouldn't go home empty handed, but they hadn't carried out a head or hands packed in ice or buried in dirt. They hadn't found any bloodied butcher knives or surgical instruments with bits of flesh and blood clinging to the sharp edges.

The search had been a bust, and Mason read the results in Griswold's slumped shoulders and Cates's pursed lips as he dragged on a cigarette, the two of them huddled at the curb next to their unmarked Crown Victoria.

Mason knew that it was a mistake to treat the detectives as interchangeable parts. Though they were partners and were cut from the same physical mold, there had to be differences between them, and Mason needed to know what they were beyond which one would play the good cop and which one the bad cop. Did one of them have a chip on his shoulder? Was one of them too lazy to dig out the facts? Could he trust either of them?

He hadn't seen enough of them to know the answers to these questions. Griswold had given him a business card. His first name was Kevin. Cates hadn't offered one, though Mason overheard someone use his first name—Tom. Griswold wanted to make an impression. Cates didn't care. It wasn't much, but it was something.

"All in and all done?" Mason asked them, the air frosting his breath.

"Yeah," Griswold said.

"For now," Cates added, the red tip of his smoke weaker than the threat he was trying to make.

"Don't be so disappointed. There are lots of other places to look for the killer."

"Maybe," Griswold said. "But I'm still thinking this is a pretty good place."

"Come back any time. We're always open. Just call ahead and bring a warrant next time. Only the first search is free."

Cates flicked the butt to the ground, grinding it with his heel and turning to his partner. "Let's get out of here."

"Hang on," Mason said. "It's my turn."

"For what?" Griswold asked.

"I let you talk to my client. I let you march through his house without a warrant like Sherman marched through Georgia. The gate swings both ways. I want some information."

Cates gave Griswold a look that said, Forget it. Griswold answered with a raised hand. "Gate swings both ways, Counselor. You remember that."

"If I don't, Detective, I'm sure you'll remind me."

"Okay," Griswold said. "Ask."

"Who found the body?"

"U.S. Marshals deputy patrolling the parking lot with a dog. The dog was trained to sniff out bombs but still had a nose for dead meat," Griswold said.

Mason kept a poker face, not wanting to dip into Griswold's callous pool. "Any blood in the trunk of the car?"

"Nothing obvious. Won't know for certain until forensics gets their test results back."

"Cut a guy's head and hands off, the body is going to bleed until the heart stops. Make a hell of a mess. Which means he was killed somewhere else and his body dumped in the car," Mason said.

Cates smiled. "You do brain surgery too?"

Mason ignored the dig. "Any signs of wounds to the body?"

"Nope," Griswold answered.

"Rigor?"

"Full," Griswold said.

"So the victim had been dead at least six to twelve hours. Maybe longer with the cold temperatures. The fatal wound was probably a gunshot or blow to the head, right?"

"Or broken neck, or strangled or poisoned or smothered or half a dozen other ways you can kill someone without leaving marks on the body, especially if you cut the head and hands off," Griswold said.

Mason nodded. "Lot to think about."

"You do that," Cates told him. "Tell your client to think about it too and let us know what you come up with. Make it a lot easier on us cops if you lawyers and defendants would solve these murders for us. Make it even easier if your client just confesses."

"Can't do that," Mason said. "Then you would have to go back to working the midnight security shift at Walmart."

Cates took a step toward Mason, but Griswold cut him off. "Okay, kids. That's enough for today." He turned to Mason. "You want it this way, you can have it this way. We'll be on you and your client twenty-four/seven. You want it the other way, remember how that gate swings."

CHAPTER SEVEN

Mason studied the well-maintained block as the detectives drove away. Not one of the houses was less than sixty years old. All of them hewn from a rock-solid architecture featuring stone and brick, wide front porches, and detached garages at the rear of long, narrow driveways.

The houses sat on lots raised above street level, giving neighbors comfortable perches beneath broad spreading oaks and elms. More trees lined the street. Stripped of their leaves by winter, they were bare stout sentries. Mason imagined them in the summer, their leafy branches forming a protective canopy over the pavement.

Cars were parked in driveways and at curbsides in front of many of the houses. Fish's car would not have been out of place. Nor would it have been the only one the killer could have chosen. Streetlamps dotted the block, offering enough light in the dead of night to discourage a killer in search of an anonymous random place to abandon a body. Looking at the block, Mason saw what the cops saw. The killer had picked Fish's car for a reason.

Fish lived on Concord Avenue in the Concord Historical District. The District was one long block that ran east from Main Street to Wornall Road on the west. Mason never knew it existed until he met Avery Fish even though it was a mile from his own house. Access from Wornall Road to Concord was from Fifty-second Street directly across from the entrance to Loose Park.

Mason couldn't remember ever having driven down Fifty-second Street or Concord despite his many visits to the park. He'd grown up in Kansas City and was always surprised when he found pockets that were new to him. They were the city's secrets.

He found Fish still sitting at the kitchen table still reading the same book. Fish glanced up at him before returning to the pages

"Must be some book," Mason said.

Fish laid the book down. "It's about the origins of life and a lot of other things. The author says it's an incredible long shot that life exists at all and that the odds of any one of us even being born are even longer."

"Does that make you feel lucky?"

Fish shrugged. "Makes me feel religious. But, if you're asking me, I could use a little good luck. No?"

"More than a little. I don't think the cops found anything, but that doesn't mean they won't keep looking."

"So what were they going to find? I didn't kill that poor schlimazel."

"Did you leave your car unlocked last night?"

"I'm sure I didn't. I always lock it, but it's easy enough to break into. All you need is a long piece of stiff wire. Slide it in between the door and the frame along the window and then push it against the lock button and that's all there is to it."

"Voice of experience?"

"I've locked my keys inside the car more than once. There's another button that opens the trunk."

"Let's hope the killer didn't know that and jimmied the trunk. Maybe scraped the paint or left some other evidence of forced entry."

"The police can't seriously think I killed that man!" Fish said, smacking his hand against the table.

"They can and they do and they'll keep thinking that until they come up with a better idea."

"So what happens to me now? What about our deal with the U.S. attorney?"

"Everything is on hold until the prosecuting attorney decides whether to charge you with murder."

"U.S. attorney, prosecuting attorney—how am I supposed to keep all the lawyers straight?" Fish asked, slumping in his chair.

"Pete Samuelson is the assistant U.S. attorney. He's federal and he wants you on the mail fraud charge. Patrick Ortiz is the prosecuting attorney. He's state, not federal. He'll decide about the murder charge."

Fish let out a long sigh. "Samuelson. Mr. Federal Attorney. You were right about him."

"What do you mean?"

"I cheated people out of their dream vacations. I admit that. So I'll pay them back and they'll take a vacation next year instead of this year. I'm an old man. Why send me to jail for something like that? There must be something else that they want."

"You keep telling me that you're just an old man," Mason said. "What do you have to offer the government?"

Fish stood up, laying a heavy hand on Mason's shoulder. "You don't get to be an old man in my business without finding out a few things. Go ask Mr. Samuelson what he wants so I don't have to die in jail."

CHAPTER EIGHT

Mason didn't run back downtown to ask Samuelson what it would take to get probation for Fish. It was the right question but the wrong time to ask it. Cases were like relationships. Some Mason had to push along and others came to him if he sat back and waited. This was one to wait for.

Fish's trial date on the mail fraud charge wasn't until late June. Winter had yet to breathe its last. March Madness was a month away. The first pitch on opening day was even more remote. The NBA play-offs would still be going on when Mason picked the jury that would decide Fish's fate. If he tried to put the plea bargain back on the table now, Samuel- son would think he was too anxious to deal.

Mason also knew that Samuelson wouldn't make a move until he knew what was happening with the murder investigation. The corpse in Fish's trunk could lead to valuable information for Samuelson. Samuelson would want a direct feed from the police.

Griswold and Cates would want the same from the FBI.

The Bureau's file on Fish could be a rich source for motive and the identity of the murder victim.

Mason knew that neither law enforcement agency would get all that they wanted from the other because the relationship between cops and the FBI was dysfunctional on a good day. With every reason to work together, they usually didn't unless forced.

Cops thought the FBI didn't know their ass from third base when it came to investigating street crime. The Bureau was equally certain that the police were too far behind the twenty-first-century law enforcement curve to ever catch up. Their sibling rivalry only got worse when a turf battle broke out, and Avery Fish guaranteed such a conflict.

The feds would try to leverage Fish's mail fraud charge if they thought Fish knew something they could use to nail someone else. The cops might want Fish for murder. Neither would give up the prize for the other. Both would designate a liaison with the other to coordinate their investigations, either Griswold or Cates for the cops and probably Dennis Brewer for the FBI. Each liaison would talk with the other just enough to keep up appearances, exchanging scant information and less trust.

All of which was good news for Mason, who believed in the military salute—confusion to the enemy. That's why Mason spent the next morning cleaning off his desk instead of bird-dogging Pete Samuelson or nagging Griswold and Cates for information.

He had mail to open and answer, motions to file and respond to, bills to collect and pay. It was the life of the solo practitioner. He was a one-man band and it suited him just fine. He'd practiced law in other firms, large and small, but settled into his own practice five years ago. He liked the freedom to pick and choose his cases, knowing that he could hold a partners' meeting in a phone booth or bathroom.

Technology allowed him to get by without a secretary. His Aunt Claire, who had raised him from the age of three, had insisted that he take typing in the eighth grade, the single most useful course he ever took. That was before computers replaced slide rules as the indispensable educational tool.

Mickey Shanahan had been the only person on Mason's payroll, working as his legal assistant. Mickey had hated the job title, preferring wingman because it had more Gen-X appeal. The position was currently open since Mickey had joined the staff of Josh Seeley when Seeley was elected the previous November as Missouri's newest United States senator. Mickey hungered for a career in politics like a junkie with a jones on.

Abby Lieberman, Seeley's chief of staff, had hired Mickey. Mason carried his own pained longing for Abby. They had been in love, still were as far as Mason was concerned. Abby didn't deny it. She just said love wasn't enough to overcome Mason's penchant for violent cases.

She could accept that he defended people charged with heinous crimes, but she couldn't live with the violence that poured out of his cases and into his life and hers. More than that, she couldn't understand why he so willingly dove into the dark water floating around his cases. He couldn't explain something to her that he scarcely understood himself.

He hadn't seen Abby since they had dinner just after the election in November, four months ago. She'd told him she was moving to D.C. Driving home, he had turned on the radio, catching Tina Turner asking, What's love got to do with it? The lyric stuck with him, surfacing whenever he thought of Abby. He shoved the song out of his head one more time and refocused on the stacks of paper littering his desk.

One of the things Mason liked most about his law practice was its sheer unexpectedness. The uncertainty of where the next case would come from, the unpredictability of the story the client would tell him, the jaw-dropping impact when most of it turned out to be true. None of which prepared him for the knock at his door.

"It's open," Mason called out, looking up from his desk.

Vanessa Carter opened the door, standing in the frame, waiting a moment to be certain that Mason recognized her. She was black, handsome though not beautiful, with a close- cropped Afro flecked with traces of silver. She was neither slim nor thick, but solidly midlife, dressed in a conservative navy suit, a long winter coat slung over one arm.

The last time Mason had seen her was in her chambers. She had been Judge Vanessa Carter then, a conservative judge on everybody's short list for promotion from the state trial court to the federal bench, and she had been presiding over the murder case of Wilson "Blues" Bluestone, Jr.

Blues was Mason's closest friend, landlord, and tour guide to the world of violent dispute resolution. At the time, he was being held without bail for a murder he hadn't committed. Mason had asked for a gangland favor to pressure Judge Carter into letting Blues out on bail so he could help Mason find the real killer.

The favor was given and Mason cleared Blues's name. Judge Carter quit the bench the day she released Blues, rumors trailing her like poisonous vapors.

The last thing she told Mason still haunted him. She would have granted bail anyway.

In the years since then, she had quietly rebuilt her career as a private judge specializing in mediation and arbitration, a low-cost alternative to expensive civil litigation. The practice provided a second career for retired judges, and Judge Carter had gradually won a significant following with her balanced handling of cases.

Mason had taken comfort in her success, his guilt assuaged but not forgotten. He handled a few civil cases from time to time, and when the parties elected alternative dispute resolution, he'd always managed to convince the opposing lawyer to select someone besides Judge Carter. While Kansas City may seem like a small town to those who didn't know it, it was more than large enough for Mason not to have crossed Judge Carter's path since that last hearing in her chambers.

He looked at her now and didn't know what to say. She filled the void.

"We have a problem," she said.

CHAPTER NINE

"I'M BEING BLACKMAILED," Vanessa Carter told him.

She threw her coat onto Mason's sofa, draping it over a stack of files Mason was storing against the cushions. She angled one of the low-slung round-backed chairs in front of his desk, sitting down with enough authority that Mason nearly rose and said, Good morning, Your Honor.

His clients always began by telling him they had a problem. His problem was helping them with their problem, but that didn't make them the same problem. Their problems came down to freedom or prison, sometimes life or death. His problems were always legal, strategic, and pragmatic. Keep the client free or, at least, off death row. And get paid.

Vanessa Carter announced that she and Mason had a problem like it was a shared burden. Her simple declaration demanded his next question, one that hovered over his heart, taunting the long scar that dressed his chest. He suspected the answer, even knew what it had to be, but had to hear her say it.

"By whom?" he asked. His pulse quickened as he struggled to remain neutral.

"Somebody at Galaxy Gaming."

She said it like she was pronouncing sentence on Mason, her words hitting him like a term of twenty-five years to life. There was no statute of limitations on some debts and Mason's had just been called.

Galaxy Gaming had purchased the Dream Casino three years ago. It was a riverboat cash cow docked on the Missouri River at the spot where Kansas City had been born more than a hundred and fifty years earlier.

Galaxy had purchased the Dream from the estate of Ed Fiori, the grantor of the gangland favor Mason had used to force Judge Carter to free Blues. Mason had always suspected that Fiori had secretly recorded his request for Fiori's help. Whether it was audio or video Mason didn't know, but he knew it didn't matter.

After Fiori's death, Mason had worried that the casino's new owners would stumble across the tape, hoarding it until they needed a return favor, explaining to Mason the laws of inheritance that governed secret sins. When no bent-nose pit boss with a Jersey accent knocked at his door over the next couple of years, Mason's fears had begun to recede.

Sometimes, he indulged in the fantasy that he'd gotten away with it, just as many criminals got away with their crimes. Other times, he reminded himself that he had had no choice, would do it again if he had to, and would deal with the consequences when the time came, increasingly hopeful that it never would.

But it had and the fact that the messenger was Vanessa Carter bound the moment in the irony that so often shrouded trouble and justice. The ripple in his pulse spent itself as he forced his hands to loosen their grips on the arms of his chair. He was a lawyer and lawyers made their living untying shrunken knots. Get at it, he told himself, nodding at Judge

Carter, unable to think of her without the honorific.

"Tell me about it," he said.

"I was hired as an arbitrator in a sexual harassment case. The plaintiff is a woman named Carol Hill. She worked as a blackjack dealer at the Galaxy Casino and claimed that one of the supervisors harassed her. The hearing was last week. I took the case under advisement and told them I would have a ruling in thirty days. Yesterday a man called me. He didn't give me his name and I think he used something electronic to disguise his voice. He said that if I didn't rule in Galaxy's favor, I was finished."

"How could he make that happen?"

She glared at Mason like he was a simpleton. He returned her stare, forcing her to lay it out. She drew a breath and squared her shoulders.

"He said he had a tape recording of me agreeing to do a favor for Ed Fiori when I was still on the bench. I told him he was a liar. He played the tape for me over the phone."

Mason caught the first cracks in her judicial demeanor as her voice quivered and her eyes blinked. She swallowed hard, a momentary spasm tightening the muscles in her neck. He gave her a minute to regroup.

"He wasn't lying," Mason said.

"No, he wasn't lying," she said, her voice solid again, her eyes steady and clear. "On the tape, Fiori tells me to release Wilson Bluestone on bail or my son's gambling debts would be collected the hard way. I asked Fiori why he cared what happened to Bluestone and he said that he didn't but Lou Mason did."

Mason sat completely still, absorbing Judge Carter's explanation. The shoe was dangling, but it hadn't dropped. The law was built on fine distinctions. Shades of intent, percentages of fault and knowledge, real or imputed, can save a life or cost a fortune. Enough of the truth can carry the day even if it isn't the whole truth and nothing but the truth.

The blackmail tape was of a conversation between Judge Carter and Ed Fiori, not between Mason and Fiori. Mason's name was used, but, without the tape of Mason's conversation with Fiori, it was a secondhand indictment. He made himself breathe.

"Blackmailing you doesn't make any sense. If Galaxy is that worried about the case, they would just settle it."

"They tried. The plaintiff and her lawyer want blood, not money."

"Why come to me? Why not just go to the police?"

"Because, Counselor," she began, drawing out the words like Mason had attention deficit disorder, "we both know that the tape is legitimate. If I go to the police, I compromise myself. I've done that once and I won't do it again."

Mason ignored her reminder of his complicity. If he didn't say it out loud, maybe he could keep ducking it.

"We both know that any legal action I could take would have the same result. What do you expect me to do?"

"I expect you to take care of it and I don't care how you do it. You put me in this box."

"You could have said no when Fiori called you."

"You don't have kids, do you?" she asked. Mason shook his head. "How about someone you love?"

Mason nodded.

"Do you love her enough to die for her?" she asked. Mason nodded again. "Then don't ask such fool questions."

"I'm only a lawyer. I can't get an injunction against the blackmailer, even assuming I can find him. You should hire somebody else."

Judge Carter rose, gathering her coat from Mason's sofa, not taking her eyes off him.

"If I have to hire someone else that will be one more person who will know what happened. I don't think you'd like that. Besides, I'm not hiring you. I'm telling you. Ask your friend Mr. Bluestone to help. He's as much a part of this as you are. Between the two of you, I'm certain you'll think of something."

Judge Carter was blackmailing him and there was nothing he could do about it. What had been her problem when she walked in the door had swiftly morphed from a shared burden to his problem. He came around from his side of the desk.

"I'll need your file on the arbitration."

Judge Carter opened her purse and handed Mason a flash drive. "The attorneys scanned everything onto this drive. It's all there—exhibits, testimony, everything." She didn't shake his hand, thank him, or wish him luck.

He stood in the center of his office, watching as she walked briskly down the hall without a backward glance, past Blues's empty office and down the back stair that led to the parking lot at the rear of the building. He palmed the flash drive, knowing at last what it was like to hold his life in his hands.

CHAPTER TEN

MASON SPENT THE day reading the arbitration file. Carol Hill signed an agreement when she was hired to submit any claims against Galaxy Gaming to binding arbitration. That was okay with her. She needed the job and couldn't imagine having to file a claim anyway.

The process was private, quick, and cheap when compared to the courts. Employers liked it because there was no jury that might have either the good sense or bad judgment to sock them with a bell-ringing verdict.

Her case was a garden-variety story of sexual harassment. Charles Rockley, her supervisor, had hit on her until it hurt. When he wouldn't stop and her complaints to management were ignored, she sued.

Rockley started with compliments about her appearance, for which she thanked him just to be polite, even though his remarks made her nervous. He was her boss and she didn't want to offend him. It wasn't long before he escalated to suggestions that she wear tighter, low-cut tops to show off her shape to the customers. She demurred, reminding him that the casino provided modest uniforms for dealers, buttoned to the chin, saving the cleavage outfits for the cocktail waitresses. Rockley had laughed, explaining that he was just imagining how she would look for him.

Next he began asking her out. Just drinks after her shift, he told her. Then it was how about a late dinner, maybe a weekend getaway if she was interested. Each time she declined, explaining that she wasn't interested and, besides, her husband wouldn't like it.

Rockley kept at her, finally summoning her to his office one night after she finished dealing, telling her it was time for her to meet the meat. She was afraid she'd lose her job and gave in to him. Afterwards, consumed by guilt, she told him never again. He gave her a bad performance review and put her on probation.

That was Carol Hill's story as summed up by her lawyer, Vince Bongiovanni, in his closing argument. Mason knew him by reputation. He was the hotshot plaintiff's lawyer of the month, knocking off companies for big bucks when their employees played grab-ass with the wrong person. Each victory attracted a new wave of clients. No human resources manager looked forward to an invitation to one of Bongiovanni's courtroom parties.

Galaxy Gaming's lawyer was Lari Prillman. Employers liked being represented by a woman lawyer in sexual harassment cases because of the not-so-subtle message they hoped it would send. Some of our best friends are women. We even hire them as lawyers. Besides, if we were the creeps the plaintiff says we are, no self-respecting woman—not even a lawyer—would defend us.

Lari Prillman had taken advantage of that misplaced wisdom for twenty-five years, building a successful boutique practice devoted to the defense against claims made by the Carol Hills of the world. She parlayed her own good looks and charm in a male-dominated world, happily taking every advantage, God-given or otherwise. Though she could defend these cases in her sleep, she didn't, taking nothing for granted and screwing down every fact and inconsistency. She lived by the Al Davis rule—just win, baby.

She dismissed Carol's accusations and Bongiovanni's theatrics as the romance-novel fantasy of a disturbed woman looking for a way to distract her jealous husband from her own indiscretions. Carol was the aggressor and the sex was consensual. Rockley backed her up.

Worse yet, Carol was banging one of the bartenders, though Lari put it more delicately, forcing Carol to tearfully admit on the stand that she had been unfaithful to her husband. A fact that Carol had failed to share with him until Lari extracted it from her under oath before Judge Carter, her stunned husband watching as Lari dismantled his wife and marriage.

Bongiovanni protested Lari's tactics, claiming that Carol's indiscretions were irrelevant. He was right, but that was one of the wonderful things about arbitration. There were no rules of evidence, allowing both sides to throw mud. Even if she had strayed, he argued, that didn't make her fair game for someone who had the power to force her to submit or be fired.

Bongiovanni countered with corroborating testimony from a girlfriend of Carol's, who recounted how Carol had complained of Rockley's crude advances. He closed his case with the reluctant testimony of another supervisor, who admitted that Rockley had bragged that he was "getting some" from Carol Hill.

Lari Prillman had counterpunched with evidence of the girlfriend's prior conviction for forging a coworker's signature on a paycheck she'd stolen from the coworker. Then she cajoled the other supervisor to sheepishly admit on cross- examination that he had often bragged about his own mythical sexual exploits and had assumed as much about Rockley's story.

After reading the file on his computer screen, Mason charted the case on the dry erase board that hung on one wall of his office. The board was low tech, but it helped him put everything in perspective and allowed him to think in visual terms, picturing parties, witnesses, and lawyers. And it helped him find the pieces that didn't fit or that were missing.

This case was a deadfall, a push. There was no way to pick a winner from the one-dimensional lifeless transcript. That was not unusual. Judge Carter had heard the testimony live. She had observed the demeanor of the witnesses. She was in the best position to decide whom to believe.

One thing was clear to Mason. There was nothing in the case that would cause Galaxy Gaming to risk blackmailing Judge Carter. If Carol Hill won, Galaxy would pay her off, probably fire Charles Rockley, and move on. Galaxy's HR manager would conduct sensitivity training for the casino's employees. It was a cost of doing business. If Galaxy was blackmailing the judge, there had to be a reason unrelated to the lawsuit.

If Charles Rockley was willing to rape Carol Hill, he was probably willing to blackmail Judge Carter to keep his job. He was the obvious—and, for the moment, only—suspect.

Mason went back to the computer, pulling up Rockley's personnel file, printing the page with his home address and phone number. While he couldn't sue Rockley to make him back off Judge Carter, he was confident that Rockley would respond to Blues's powers of persuasion. Maybe, Mason thought, this would all work out after all.

There was only one thing that nagged at him. Rockley was such an obvious suspect. Just like Avery Fish, and Mason was certain that Fish was innocent.

CHAPTER ELEVEN

IT WAS AFTER dark by the time Mason finished reviewing Carol Hill's file. He stood in the bay window looking down at the traffic on Broadway. Headlights bounced off cars and curbs. A few people scurried along the sidewalk, ducking into doorways beneath neon lights, finding a bar to warm up in before heading home. The late winter chill gave them and the rest of the city a hunkered-down feel, everyone holding on against the cold, hoping that spring was just around the corner.

Mason hunched his shoulders, feeling the cold passing through the glass and into his bones, the wind tunneling past his window. Some of those people would camp out on bar stools and in booths in the bar one floor below where he stood. Blues on Broadway was a place where people came to order a draw and kick back to live jazz, the regulars hoping Blues was in the mood to play the piano.

Most of those people spent their lives walking a straight line that led from the delivery room to the mortuary with predictable, orderly stops along the way for school, jobs, marriage, kids, dreams, disappointments, and death. A handful, like Blues, made a conscious decision to stay off the track.

He was a full-blooded Shawnee Indian, taller than Mason, with jet-black hair, dark eyes, and copper skin that made no secret of his ancestry. He was all coiled muscle and sinew, never forgetting the survival skills he'd learned in the Army's Special Forces. After the Army taught him to be a killer, the Kansas City Police Department taught him to catch killers. He quit when he couldn't make his hard-nosed code fit with a bureaucratic approach to justice.

Since then, Blues had invoked his code as a shield or sword for those who needed it or deserved it. Mason had needed it more than once.

Along the way, Blues had learned to play jazz piano jamming in joints like the one he now owned. When he played, it was for himself. Anyone who could afford the price of a cold beer could watch and listen. That was fine with him. He paid no attention when people whispered their amazement that sounds so sweet could come from the hands of a man whose looks could kill.

Mason went downstairs and sat in a booth at the back of the bar waiting for Blues to finish playing a number that Mason didn't recognize. Three people listened from stools along the mahogany bar that dominated the room. Hank, a beanpole bartender, kept their drinks fresh. The customers clapped when Blues stood. He acted like he hadn't heard, joining Mason in the booth.

"Something new?" Mason asked.

"Yeah," Blues said. "I've been fooling around with my own stuff. Thought I'd try it out."

Mason shook his head. "I'll never understand how you can compose music. Do you hear the sounds in your head before you play the notes?"

"I feel them more than I hear them."

"Well, that makes it so much easier to understand."

"I saw Vanessa Carter going up the back stairs earlier today. What's she want with you?"

"It's what she wants with us."

He summarized his conversation with Judge Carter and covered the highlights in Carol Hill's file, keeping his voice low even though Hank and the three customers were too wrapped up in an argument over which college team had the best point guard to pay any attention to them. Blues listened, completely still, his face a mask.

"You think it's this guy Rockley?" he asked when Mason finished.

"Makes sense. He's the guy with the most to lose. Galaxy can't be happy about the case, but there's nothing there to make them take a chance like this."

"So if Rockley's just a supervisor, how does he know about the tape of the conversation between Fiori and the Judge? And how does he get ahold of it so he can play it over the phone for her? That's not the kind of thing Galaxy is gonna leave lying around in the employee lunchroom."

Mason chewed his lip, annoyed that he hadn't considered Blues's questions. "I don't know, but it makes sense to start with him. We can't just call up Al Webb and ask him which one of his employees is a blackmailer."

"Who is Al Webb?"

"General manager of the Galaxy. I read his testimony from the arbitration. He made Rockley sound like the employee of the year."

"How long has Rockley worked for Galaxy?"

"About a year," Mason answered. "Same as Webb."

"So Rockley wasn't around when Galaxy took over the boat, which means that he couldn't have stumbled across the tape when he was cleaning out Fiori's office. If Rockley made the call to the judge, somebody else had to have told Rockley about the tape."

"It's not just the tape of the call between Fiori and Judge Carter. That tape implicates me, but it doesn't convict me. It's the tape of the conversation between me and Fiori that we've got to find, if it exists."

"And the people who know about it."

"That too."

"There aren't any small problems, are there?" Blues asked.

"Nope. Just big opportunities," Mason said.

"Still gets back to Rockley for now."

"He's the guy with the most to lose in the arbitration. Galaxy loses, they pay off and move on. Rockley will probably be out of a job."

"So we go pay Rockley a visit and help him redirect his life."

Mason shook his head. "It's better if you go by yourself. Keeps me one step removed from Rockley."

Blues leaned back in the booth, his hands on the table, long fingers spread wide. "You can't dodge this thing forever. You did what you did. You're going to have to deal with that."

Mason drew a deep breath, letting it out. "I know. It's just a little tricky to figure it all out at once. I can't just step up to the plate, turn myself in to the cops and the state bar disciplinary office, without leaving Judge Carter hanging out again. She deserves better from me."

"That's a pretty sharp sword to fall on, anyway."

"I'll do it if I have to. A blackmailer is never satisfied.

Maybe the only way to finish it is to go public. Take away the threat of being exposed. Besides, like you said, I did what I did."

"Don't order your sackcloth and ashes yet," Blues said. "There's other ways to take care of this."

CHAPTER TWELVE

MASON ROWED EIGHT thousand meters Thursday morning while it was still dark. He kept his rowing machine in the dining room, taking advantage of the double windows to watch the hardy souls who jogged down his block. Yellow light from streetlamps caught the reflecting tape stuck to their running clothes as they passed, leaving puffs of frozen breath visible in their wake.

His exercise routine alternated between running and rowing, not only because of the cross-training benefits, but to avoid boredom. He had played rugby until a few years ago when it became too hard to get out of bed the morning after a vicious scrum. Conceding that he was forty-three, he gave up the game, staying in shape with his current routine.

His house was in a tony neighborhood nine blocks south of the Country Club Plaza, Kansas City's answer to New York's Fifth Avenue, and two blocks south of Loose Park, a micro-scale alternative to Central Park. Kansas City didn't claim to be the Big Apple of the Midwest, but it had long ago shed its cow-town image.

He lived in an area that was home to the upwardly mobile who were certain they'd arrived. Many of the people who lived there were fighting the same battle against time that he was, convinced that if they ran another mile they would live another day. Mason figured eight thousand meters was at least as good an investment.

His Aunt Claire had given the house to him and his ex- wife, Kate, as a wedding present. He'd grown up there with Claire, but the house had worked better for him and his aunt than it did for him and his wife. When Kate moved out, Mason refurnished the dining room with the rowing machine. Abby banished it to the basement, Mason hauling it back up when she left town, his love life defined by its location.

His dog Tuffy, a German shepherd–collie mixed-breed anti-watchdog, did three laps around the rowing machine before settling in front of the flywheel, enjoying the breeze from Mason's labors.

The sky was rounding out to a gunmetal gray by the time he got out of the shower, dressed, and started scavenging for something that would pass for breakfast in his kitchen. He spread the Kansas City Star on the kitchen table while he chewed a nutrition bar that promised him more than it could possibly deliver.

There was a teaser above the masthead about an article in the Style section on how to make tomorrow, Valentine's Day, special. Mason had bought a card for Abby, signed it, stuck it in an envelope, and then thrown it away. He didn't want to be like the nutrition bar and promise Abby something he couldn't deliver.

An hour later he was in his office, behind his desk, staring at the dry erase board. He used circles, broken and solid lines, boxes, triangles and any other geometry he could think of to link the people and facts of a case, making room for what he knew or suspected and taking stock of what he didn't know or feared. He studied the resulting graffiti, searching for a pattern that illuminated the answers to the five questions— who, what, where, when, and why. Before retreating to his desk chair, he circled Charles Rockley's name and drew a solid line to nowhere, punctuating it with a question:

Who told Rockley about the tape?

Blues was right. If Rockley had only been employed at Galaxy for a year, he couldn't have known about the taped conversation between Ed Fiori and Judge Carter unless someone else at Galaxy had told him. Double-checking his reasoning, he pulled up Rockley's personnel records from the arbitration file and reviewed Rockley's employment history, comparing it to his testimony at the hearing.

Rockley was thirty-eight years old. He graduated from Ohio University with a business degree and worked a series of middle-level management jobs in unrelated industries before being hired by Galaxy a year ago. He was divorced and had moved around a lot, no job lasting more than a few years. Galaxy hired him to be a shift supervisor for blackjack dealers, a position that required more middle-level management skills than it did an understanding of when to hit on thirteen.

Rockley's résumé was that of a flat-liner, someone who had topped out early, substituting lateral moves for advancement. He was an invisible employee, never leaving a mark or a memory. Asked at the hearing why he'd moved from job to job, he answered that each new job was a better opportunity. It didn't look that way to Mason, but it was an innocuous answer that Vince Bongiovanni, Carol Hill's lawyer, didn't challenge.

In her defense of Galaxy, Lari Prillman underscored something that was missing from Rockley's employment history. He'd never been the subject of a complaint for sexual harassment. He was, at least on paper, a model—though decidedly undistinguished—employee.

Rockley's deposition testimony read like the milquetoast image Mason gleaned from his personnel file. He gave polite, simple, and direct answers to the lawyers' questions, refusing to take Bongiovanni's bait and fight with the opposing lawyer. Mason could practically see him looking Lari Prill- man squarely in the eye as he denied Carol Hill's allegations with a carefully calibrated hint of outrage at her accusations.

All of which made Mason's question—Who told Rockley about the tape?—all the more compelling. Rockley was the kind of guy who would never be in the loop on something so sensitive. There was nothing apparent in his past or present to explain why anyone at Galaxy would share with him the explosive information about Judge Carter or Mason.

Perhaps, Mason speculated, he'd stumbled onto it, realized its value, and decided to blackmail the judge to save his job. If so, Mason had grossly underestimated Rockley's paper persona. Maybe Rockley was one of those guys who showed up at work one morning with an assault rifle and mowed down half a dozen coworkers before the cops shot him, leaving the survivors to scratch their heads and comment what a quiet guy he had always been.

Re-examining the dry erase board, Mason highlighted the names of Al Webb, the casino's general manager, and Lila Collins, the HR director. Mason assumed that Webb was more likely than Collins to know about the taped conversations, but he relocated their names to the end of the line reaching from Rockley's.

That was all Mason could do until he heard from Blues. He had no doubt that Rockley would talk to him. When Blues wanted information from someone, he rarely came up empty. The greater risk was what Rockley would do after Blues finished with him. Blues would motivate him to keep his mouth shut and make another career move, this one out of town. Mason was certain Rockley wouldn't be missed at Galaxy.

If Rockley could point the way further up the food chain at Galaxy, Blues would make him draw a map. Mason would add that information to the dry erase board, knowing it was only a beginning. Rockley had to be the loose end of the thread, not the beginning.

He wasted ten minutes throwing darts at the target hanging on the wall across from his desk, arcing high lob shots, not paying attention to where the darts landed, just passing time. He had other cases to work on, but couldn't muster his concentration. If the blackmail scheme blew up in his face, he'd be charged with corrupting a public official. He checked the Missouri Criminal Code. It was a Class C felony punishable by a sentence of up to five years in the state penitentiary. The statute of limitations hadn't run.

He'd also lose his law license and, for the moment, that prospect chilled him as much as prison. Claire had motivated him to become a lawyer, though in the early years of his practice she had often chided him that he didn't have the fire to become the kind of lawyer she had become. Someone who battled for the underdog, someone who was passionate not only about the law but about justice, sometimes squeezing justice out of a legal system too often reluctant to dispense it.

Claire had eased up on him since he had opened his own practice, spending most of his time defending people accused of crimes. Regardless of their station in life, they were always underdogs when compared to any state or federal prosecutor. Though now she teased him that he was finally showing some promise, he'd learned one fundamental truth about himself: Being a lawyer was who and what he was. Take that away from him and Mason wasn't certain what would be left.

CHAPTER THIRTEEN

HE DRIFTED THROUGH the rest of the morning, walking two blocks down Broadway to a diner for a greasy cheeseburger at noon. The cold didn't bother him. It had settled in his bones since Vanessa Carter's visit.

The phone rang at three o'clock that afternoon. It was Pete Samuelson.

"What can I do for you?" Mason asked him.

"Why don't you and Mr. Fish come back downtown and we'll talk. That is, if he doesn't have any more dead bodies in the trunk of his car."

"Does that mean you've decided to take our offer?"

"I can't do that while the murder investigation is pending."

"Then we don't have anything to talk about."

"Actually, we do. If your client agrees to cooperate with us, we may be able to help him."

"How are you going to do that?"

"Just bring him downtown. Tomorrow morning. Eleven o'clock."

Samuelson's offer meant that he might know enough about the corpse in Fish's trunk to exonerate Fish but that he hadn't shared that information with the cops. If he had, the cops would have already given Fish a pass. That meant that the feds were holding out on the cops. It also meant that the feds were conducting their own investigation of a crime that was not in their jurisdiction.

Detectives Griswold and Cates weren't the kind of cops who would give Mason a heads-up if they no longer considered Fish a suspect. Nor would they tell Mason if Mason called and asked them. They would enjoy letting Fish twist while the investigation ran its course.

Mason picked up his phone, dialing Samantha Greer's cell phone number from memory. She was a homicide detective with whom Mason had had an on-again, off-again relationship for a couple of years before Mason met Abby. Since Abby left town, Samantha had done her best to fill the void in Mason's social calendar. Lately she had lost some of the fire that had first attracted him. Working homicide could do that, gradually sucking the life out of you until you ended up alone and drunk. That hadn't happened to Harry Ryman, a veteran homicide cop who was Mason's surrogate father, because he had Claire. Samantha didn't have anyone.

He still enjoyed her company but couldn't give her the commitment she wanted, feeling guilty that he was stringing her along. The reason was the answer to the question in Tina Turner's song. Love had everything to do with it. Somehow, they'd defied the odds against ex-lovers remaining friends, though Mason wondered whether that reflected Samantha's wistful optimism that they would eventually end up together if she just hung in there.

"Detective Greer," she said, answering on the first ring.

"Feeling official?"

"Feeling beat. Long night on a domestic abuse case that finally hit the finish line. The husband divorced his wife with a baseball bat."

"Buy you a beer?"

"Business or pleasure?"

"Business first. My client, Avery Fish, a corpse, and your buddies Griswold and Cates."

"That'll take two beers. Davey's Uptown Rambler Club. Meet you there at six."

CHAPTER FOURTEEN

Mason ran into Blues in the parking lot behind Blues on Broadway. The potholes that Blues had filled the previous summer had returned, the asphalt giving way to the freezing, wet winter. The left front tire of Mason's SUV rested in one crater, tilting it like a sinking ship. Only one of the two halogen lamps Blues had installed to light the back of the building was working. Blues was a much better piano player than he was a property manager.

The parking lot was narrow, bordered by an alley that ran between the buildings that fronted Broadway and a string of old, three-story apartments one block to the east that backed up to the other side. The high walls on both sides kept out light and warmth except when the sun was directly overhead, the urban terrain making a cold, dark night colder and darker.

They leaned against Mason's SUV, Blues nearly invisible in a black leather jacket, Mason cupping his hands, blowing on them for warmth. Mason hadn't seen or talked with him since their first conversation about Rockley.

"Any luck?" Mason asked him.

"Zero."

"Try his house?"

Blues's expression didn't change, even though Mason knew it was a stupid question the moment he asked it.

"Three times. Lives in an apartment up north. His mailbox is full. Nobody has seen him. But we're not the only ones looking for him. One of the neighbors told me someone else came around yesterday."

"Get a name?"

Blues shook his head. "I asked if he left a business card. The neighbor said no. Cops, FBI—always leave business cards. PIs almost always leave business cards."

"So who doesn't leave a business card?"

"Somebody who wants you for the wrong reason."

"Is Rockley still working at Galaxy?" Mason asked.

"I don't know. I called Galaxy and asked for him. The operator connected me to his extension and I got his voice mail. It said leave a message and I'll get back to you. I called back, said I got his voice mail but it was important that I talk to him right away. The operator transferred my call to a woman named Lila Collins."

"She's in charge of HR," Mason said.

"Or bullshit. She told me that she wasn't permitted to release any information about employees. Talked like he still worked there."

"Did she ask you who you were or why you wanted to talk to Rockley?"

"Not a word. It was like she was waiting for the call. Made her little speech and hung up without saying goodbye."

"What do you think?"

"I think Rockley's hiding out until Judge Carter issues her ruling and Galaxy is helping him do it."

"That fits with our theory that Rockley had help with the blackmail. What now?" Mason asked. "I'll keep looking." "You've got a bar to run and I'm not paying you." "You paid me in advance three years ago," Blues said.

CHAPTER FIFTEEN

Davey's Uptown Rambler Club was at the corner of Thirty- fourth and Main, an intersection that was either seedy or had character, depending on your attitude toward bars, porn, and vacant storefronts. Davey's was on the southwest corner. Ray's Playpen was on the northwest, offering sexual novelties but no sex. The vacant storefronts were across the street on the east side of Main.

Further north were Crown Center, the Liberty Memorial, Union Station, and the Crossroads Art District. To the south were Thirty-ninth Street and Westport Road, two east–west arteries that had harnessed urban cool into successful restaurant and retail lifelines capturing the uptown flavor Davey's claimed as its own. The waves of progress washed out before reaching Davey's and Ray's corner of the world. They didn't mind and neither did their customers.

A large unlit neon sign that hung on the north side of Davey's offered parking behind the bar. Mason used the rear entrance, following a short, dimly lit hallway past the john and into the bar. There was a large room to his right with a couple of pool tables, games in progress on both; the players were using their cues to balance themselves more than to make a shot.

Davey's was long and narrow, three booths on Mason's left toward the front, two round tables with stools in the center and the bar covering the wall on his right. A collection of bleached cow skulls and gold-painted ceramic cherubs hung above the rows of whiskey bottles behind the bartender.

The regulars manned the stools along the bar, nursing their beers. A television tuned to ESPN, the sound off, hung from the ceiling. One of the round tables was occupied by five guys unwinding on their way home. Mason caught enough of their conversation to know they were lawyers, nodding at their looks of recognition when they saw him. Mason accepted that he had a high profile, but he didn't play off it.

Samantha Greer was waiting for him in the front booth, her back to him. The lawyers' conversation softened as he passed, one of them saying hello and asking how it was going, Mason answering good enough, wishing it was.

He slid into the booth across from Samantha. She was midway through her first beer, tipping the bottle toward Mason.

"You're late. I had to buy my own."

"Better to owe you than cheat you out of it." Mason reached across the table for her hand, squeezing it until she squeezed back a little too tightly. "Thanks for coming."

"Couldn't resist. Never could."

They had known each other for four years. The first two years were marked by meteoric sex fueled more by need and loneliness than anything else. Recognizing it for what it was, they made mutual promises that they weren't making any promises. Mason had kept his promise, but Samantha wished she'd never made hers.

"You changed your look," he said.

She fingered hair that hung just past her chin. She used to be blond. Now she was some metallic copper shade.

"Cut it and colored it. I needed a change of pace. You like it?"

"Looks great," he said, meaning it, glad to see a bright flicker in her green eyes.

Samantha finished her beer. "I bought the first round. Might as well stick with the program."

He watched as she walked to the bar and bought two more bottles. She had a compact body, muscled enough to take down a suspect, soft enough to fit nicely against his, the memory indelible. He hadn't seen her much while he was with Abby. Her hair wasn't the only thing that had changed. Crow's-feet stretched from the corners of her eyes, and there was a resignation in her face that was at war with the determination he'd once found there. He did some quick math. She was forty, or nearly so. Her birthday was this time of year, though he'd forgotten the date.

"Nice place," Mason said, gesturing with his bottle when she returned. "You a regular?"

She shook her head. "I figured we should avoid a cop bar or Blues's place. Not likely we'll see anyone here who gives a crap if they see us together."

"Who would care?"

"Griswold and Cates, for starters. They know our history. They'd assume that I was talking to you about their case, telling you things I shouldn't tell you."

"Will you?" he asked, leaning back in the booth.

She twirled the neck of her bottle in one hand, flicking condensation off with the other. "No. I'm a cop. It's not my case. I won't screw it up for them."

"Then why agree to meet me?"

She dipped her head, took a sip from her beer. "It's good to see you."

"It's good to see you too, Sam."

They sat for a moment, neither of them talking, the silence building to an awkward crest. Mason had called her to ask her to do exactly what she wouldn't and shouldn't do. She had said yes in the hopes he would do what he could but wouldn't do. At least their disappointment was mutual.

Mason broke the silence. "Hey, let's get some dinner."

She shook her head again. "Can't. I've got to finish up the paperwork on that domestic case. Take a rain check?"

"Sure. How about next week—Tuesday?"

He understood the message in her refusal. She was available, but not just so he could use her as an inside source. Dinner was a way of saying she was right, admitting that she deserved better from him.

She brightened again. "Tuesday would be great," she said, getting up. "There is one thing I can tell you."

"What's that?"

"Griswold and Cates still don't know who the victim is, but they like your client for it anyway."

"Why, other than where the body was found?"

"Because it works and cops like that better than anything else."

CHAPTER SIXTEEN

Mason told Fish he would give him a ride to the Federal Courthouse on Friday morning. Fish protested it wasn't necessary even though the police had impounded his Cadillac as evidence.

"I rented a car. A white Taurus. A schlepper's car," he had explained when Mason called the day before to tell him about the meeting.

"There's nothing wrong with a Taurus," Mason said.

"I'm a successful businessman. It's no car for a successful businessman."

"Can you fit a body in the trunk?"

"Very funny. All right. You can pick me up. Be here at ten."

"The meeting isn't until eleven. It won't take an hour to get downtown."

"Look at it this way. If being a little early is a crime, we'll be in the right place."

A minivan was parked in the driveway when Mason pulled up in front of Fish's house on Friday morning. He glanced in the windows as he walked up the driveway, noting the car seats inside. When Fish opened the door, Mason heard squeals of laughter coming from the living room. Fish smiled, clapped him on the back, and pulled him toward the noise.

Four toddlers, three boys and a girl, were chasing each other in circles until they crashed in a heap on the floor before jumping up and doing it again, breathless, giggling and glowing. Scraps of brightly colored wrapping paper littered an Oriental rug in the center of the room.

Two women, whom Mason took to be the mothers of the children, sat in chairs on one side of the room, their arms and legs tightly crossed. One wore jeans and a sweatshirt, the other a warm-up suit. They shared the same dark hair, thin faces, and tightly pinched mouths that pronounced them as sisters. A small pile of toys was bunched beneath each of their chairs, out of harm's way.

Mason stood on the edge of the living room as Fish waded into the gang of kids. Their laughter reached an upper octave as they swarmed on Fish's legs, one grabbing each knee, the others flinging their arms around his ankles. He carefully shook one leg at a time, casting them off in another game that was repeated until he made his way to an easy chair opposite the two women.

He tousled each child's hair, hugging them in turn, and sent them off with gentle pats on their bottoms. Satisfied, they dove under their mothers' chairs, retrieved their toys, and raced up the stairs.

"My daughters, Sharon and Melissa," Fish said.

Mason crossed the room, shaking one hand at a time. "I'm Lou Mason, your father's lawyer."

"I'm Sharon," said the woman who was wearing jeans and a sweatshirt.

"We know who you are," Melissa added, tugging her warm-up suit around her as if the temperature had dropped when Mason entered the room.

Sharon gathered the wrapping paper off the floor, disappearing into the kitchen. She returned wearing a winter jacket and carrying another over her arm. She handed it to Melissa, who had laid out four tiny parkas with mittens clipped to each sleeve in a line on the floor.

"You don't have to leave," Fish told them. "My lawyer's early. We've got plenty of time, don't we, Lou? Besides, the kids are having fun."

"Sure," Mason answered. "There's no rush."

"I've got a full day, Dad," Melissa said, straightening the parkas again. She stood and ran her hands through her hair.

"Me too," Sharon said.

"But you just got here," Fish said.

"We've been here long enough," Sharon said.

Fish let out a deep sigh. "Is it so awful?"

Sharon cocked her head at her father, bit her lip to keep from answering, and walked to the stairs, calling the kids instead. Melissa glanced around the room, looking for anything else that hadn't been packed up as if she were checking out of a hotel room.

"Dad," Melissa said. "We've been through this. Sharon and I agreed to let you see the kids. You've seen them."

"I'm your father and you treat me like I'm a monster."

Sharon said, "We know what you are, Daddy. It wasn't good for us, and in the end it won't be good for our kids. Especially now with this whole dead-body thing."

"Tell them, Lou," Fish said. "Tell them that I didn't kill anybody. I just want to spend time with my grandkids."

"Stop it!" Melissa said, covering her ears with her hands. "I can't take any more of this."

The four children galloped down the stairs, skidding to a halt in front of their jackets. They bent down, slipped their arms in their coat sleeves, and flipped them over their heads. Fish spread his arms wide and they rushed into his embrace.

"Now!" Sharon said to the kids, clapping her hands. "Let's get going."

Fish followed them to the door, watching until they drove off. He turned around. "They're my kids," he said to Mason with a shrug. "What are you going to do? I'll get my coat."

They walked down the front steps towards Mason's car. Fish waved to a man across the street picking up his newspaper at the end of the driveway. The man returned Fish's gesture with a tentative half-hoisting of his arm, not certain what to make of his newly notorious neighbor.

Fish and the decapitated corpse had made a media sensation, catching the attention of the cable news networks forever hungry for the next titillating case. Mason had given Fish strict instructions to refuse all comment. Mason limited his remarks to a firm assertion of Fish's innocence coupled with a reminder of Fish's full cooperation with the authorities. The media beast was barely satisfied with those crumbs. They would be back at each stage of the case: when the body was identified; when an arrest was made; when the preliminary hearing was held; when the defendant farted.

Although Avery Fish had been identified as the prime suspect according to an unidentified source close to the investigation, he acted as though he didn't have a care in the world since his near meltdown in the U.S. attorney's office. Except when confronting his daughters, he was buoyed by instinctive optimism and reflexive good cheer. His faith rested in the firm belief that he could sell everyone something. All he had to do was figure out what they wanted. He repeated his cheerful wave to his neighbor.

"Good morning, Morty," he bellowed across the street. Morty hurried back inside as if he was afraid Fish's greeting was contagious. Fish climbed into Mason's SUV, huffing with the effort. "Sanctimonious son-of-a-bitch, that nogoodnik Morty."

"Friend of yours?"

"Cheats on his wife and his taxes and then treats me like I've got the plague."

"These are the times when you find out who your friends are."

"All my friends are dead. And you met my daughters."

"What about their mother?"

"My girls like me better than their mother does. We got divorced twenty-five years ago. Not that I blame her, or the girls for that matter. No one would confuse me with Father of the Year, making the kind of living I did. But those grand- kids are my second chance. You get me out of this mess and maybe my family will give me a break."

"Is that why you told me to be an hour early?"

"I just wanted you to know. That's all," Fish answered.

"We'll see what Pete Samuelson has in mind."

"Tell me again what he said."

Mason repeated the conversation, adding his commentary at the end. "I talked to a homicide detective who's a good friend. She said that the body hasn't been identified yet. The only way Samuelson can help you is if he knows something that eliminates you as the killer."

"He wants to trade that for something from me?"

"That's what it sounds like. What do you have that he wants?"

"I don't know, but I don't think I'm going to help him."

"Why not? You're facing a prison term for mail fraud and a possible murder charge. You should be willing to do back flips naked down Broadway if we can make a deal with Samuelson that gets you back with your grandkids."

"Listen to me, boytchik. Samuelson is playing a game with us, but I'm much better at these games than he is. If Samuelson has proof I didn't kill that poor bastard and he doesn't turn it over to the police, he's the one who will end up behind bars. Once he tells you that he has that kind of information, he has to give it up. So why should I give him something in return when I'll end up with it anyway?"

"So what will you tell him?"

"I'll tell him no. At least to his first offer. That's never the best offer anyway."

CHAPTER SEVENTEEN

Samuelson's secretary ushered them into a large conference room. Unlike the bleak room from earlier in the week, this one had windows that looked north over the Missouri River, past the downtown airport and halfway to Iowa. A picture of the president hung on one wall.

This time there was a pot of hot coffee and half a dozen bottles of water arranged on a credenza beneath the Great Seal of the United States. The secretary promised that Samuelson would be right there and he was, appearing at her side as she finished uttering his name.

"Thank you, Evelyn," Samuelson said, dismissing her. "Gentlemen, thanks for coming down on such short notice," he added, beaming his best government smile at them and taking a seat near the head of the long, rectangular conference table.

Mason grabbed a bottle of water and sat in a chair across from Samuelson with his back to the windows. Fish, a wry grin creeping from the corners of his mouth, walked the length of the room as if he was measuring it, stopping to admire the view from the windows, before sitting next to Mason.

There was a sharp knock at the door. Mason looked up as Kelly Holt walked in carrying a thin manila folder. She stood next to Samuelson, her smile polite and professional. Her piercing blue eyes held him in check as she studied his reaction to seeing her for the first time in five years.

"Hello, Lou," she said.

"Kelly," he managed, coming to his feet and nearly knocking over his water bottle.

Her hair was a rich brown now instead of the dark blond she had when he'd first met her early on a summer morning after he had fallen asleep on a lounge chair at a resort in the Lake of the Ozarks in southwest Missouri. She was a sheriff then, having quit the FBI, driven out by accusations she'd walked on the dark side with her dead partner, who had also been her lover. She woke him to tell him that the senior partner of his law firm had been found murdered during the firm's annual retreat.

They had nearly fallen in love, but Kelly left to heal wounds that the murder investigation had torn open. Mason had reached out to her a few times afterward until she finally stopped returning his calls. He let go, deciding that what they'd felt came more from what they'd been through than what they had meant to each other. Circumstantial lust, he called it to lessen the loss.

"Agent Holt told me she had worked with you on a case when she was away from the FBI," Samuelson said.

"I didn't know you had gone back to the Bureau," Mason said to Kelly.

"A few years ago," she said.

"And you've been in Kansas City all this time?"

He couldn't suppress the surprise in his voice but hoped he didn't sound hurt that she hadn't called or, worse that he didn't sound like a whining ex-boyfriend who'd been dumped. He didn't know what he would have done if she had called. His relationship with Abby was the real deal. Circumstantial lust didn't figure in the equation. There was no room for old flames no matter how intensely they had once burned. Even now, he hung on to Abby though he knew she was drifting away from him. Still, the instinctive response of I can't believe you didn't call rippled through him.

"Occasionally. Special assignments."

The door swung open again before Mason could ask if she was taking Dennis Brewer's place and before he could assess what her involvement might mean for Fish or for him. An older black man dressed in pinstripes, his shoulders square and his pace more like a march than a walk, joined them. Samuelson didn't salute, but he did stand. Mason and Fish followed suit.

"Roosevelt Holmes," the man said, introducing himself and repeating the handshaking ritual.

He didn't mention his title—United States attorney—because he didn't have to. Mason knew who he was. Appointed two years ago, he'd established a reputation as a tough administrator who let his frontline lawyers, the assistant U.S. attorneys, make deals and try cases. He was a policy maker, not a trial lawyer. He got personally involved in cases that required the prestige or approval of his office or of his commanding officer in Washington, D.C., the attorney general.

Holmes had been an Army JAG lawyer before entering private practice. He'd given up his position as managing partner of a large downtown firm to take the U.S. attorney's job. He knew how to give and take orders, and none of his assistants had any doubt about who was in charge.

Holmes was there so Mason would know that Fish's case was no longer a small-time matter entrusted to a wet-behind the-ears assistant U.S. attorney. Samuelson was the messenger, but the message came from the top. The price of poker had gone up. Mason glanced at Fish, whose eyes danced as he shook Holmes's hand.

"This is a very impressive conference room, Mr. U.S. Attorney," Fish said. "The government treats you well."

"The government treats everyone the same, Mr. Fish," Holmes answered. "Fairly and justly."

"I couldn't ask for anything more than that."

Holmes sat at the head of the table flanked by Samuelson and Kelly on his right and Mason and Fish on his left. He pursed his lips, folded his hands together, and turned to Samuelson, giving him a barely perceptible nod.

"Yes, sir," Samuelson said and cleared his throat. "The Kansas City Police Department has requested the FBI's assistance in identifying the body found in Mr. Fish's car. Agent Holt is directing the response to that request and has been designated as our liaison to the homicide investigation."

Kelly took her cue, opening her manila folder, drawing Mason's eyes to her hands. No rings. Still. He remembered how confidently those hands had gripped a shotgun and how tightly they had held him. Her crisp voice brought him back.

"The body was decapitated and the hands were amputated, which eliminated identification by facial features, dental records, and fingerprints. That made it difficult to identify the victim but not impossible."

Mason listened as much for what Kelly said as what she didn't say. If the killer wanted to be certain that the body wasn't identified, he wouldn't have left it in Fish's car. He'd have hidden it where no one would ever find it. If the feds couldn't explain why the killer dumped the body in Fish's lap, they didn't know as much as they wanted him to think they knew.

Samuelson picked up where Kelly left off. "The police provided us with a DNA sample the morning the body was discovered."

"The Bureau maintains a DNA database," Kelly added, their presentation tightly choreographed. "We found a preliminary match. A complete analysis won't be finished until next week, but the prelim has a ninety-five-percent confidence level."

CHAPTER EIGHTEEN

THEY LET THAT bit of news hang in the air like a come-on in a singles bar. Fish leaned back in his chair, arms contentedly draped over his belly. Mason sat up straight. Fish was right. If the feds had information to exonerate Fish, they had to give it to the cops. If the information somehow incriminated Fish, they had to turn that over as well.

"I'm sure you've already shared that news with the police," Mason said.

"Actually, not yet," Samuelson said. "We just got the information yesterday. Agent Holt has been very busy, but I'm certain she'll get together with the detectives as soon as she can."

"You had time to invite us over to play Let's Make a Deal, but you're too busy to call the police and tell them whose body was in the trunk of my client's car. Things must really be hopping down here," Mason said.

Roosevelt Holmes raised one hand an inch off the table, stopping his subordinates from responding.

"Mr. Mason, you'd be surprised just how much things do hop down here. In fact, we can make just about anything or anyone hop, skip, or dance. You keep that in mind." He glanced at his watch and stood. "You'll excuse me. I have another meeting," he said and left.

"This must be good," Mason said. "Your boss wants us to know he's behind whatever you're about to offer, but he wants the plausible deniability that comes from not being here when you offer it. Makes it lonely in the middle."

Samuelson leaned back in his chair, confident in the support from his boss.

"We will tell the police the identity of the victim. However, we do have some flexibility regarding when and what else we tell them because of an ongoing investigation being conducted by our office and the FBI. That's where Mr. Fish comes in. We'd like his help. If he agrees, we'll tell you what we know."

"You'll have to tell us what this other investigation is about and what you expect my client to do," Mason said.

Samuelson shook his head. "I can't do that without an agreement in advance that we have a deal. It's too sensitive."

"And if he refuses to sign on for a secret mission too secret to tell us what it's about up front, you'll let him be prosecuted for a crime you know he didn't commit? Do you really think you can get away with that?"

"Let's be clear about a couple of things," Samuelson said. "We may know who the murder victim is, but we don't know whether Mr. Fish is innocent or guilty. We won't interfere with that investigation and we won't set up your client to take the fall for a crime he didn't commit. The murder is the state's problem. Our concerns are at the federal level."

"Mr. Holmes promised that you would treat me fairly and justly," Fish said. "So you'll tell the police the name of the dead man, who, by the way, I didn't kill. When the police find out who the man was, they'll realize I had nothing to do with it. So why should I be interested in your investigation?"

"There's very little we can tell the police without compromising our investigation and we aren't prepared to do that. But what we can tell them won't be helpful to you," Samuel- son said.

Mason came out of his chair and leaned over the table. "How do you think this will play after I hold a press conference about your strong-arm tactics?"

Kelly stood, planting her palms on the table, squaring off against Mason and letting him know that the past was past. "Take your seat, Lou."

Samuelson said, "I'd take her advice, Mason. Nothing you could tell the press will change Mr. Fish's problems. He will be charged with murder and he will be convicted of mail fraud. Now mail fraud may not sound as bad as murder, but I guarantee it won't help him with the jury in the murder case."

Fish reached for Mason's arm, tugging on his sleeve and gesturing for Mason to speak to him privately. Mason leaned toward Fish.

"The name," Fish whispered in his ear. "Just get the name."

Mason nodded, took his seat, and waited for Kelly to stand down. "You can turn the screws all you want, but at least you've got to give us the name. We've got to have something to go on besides faith in your compassion for my client. If we can do business, we will. If not, we'll take our chances."

Kelly gave Samuelson a look. "Your call," she told Samuelson, who nodded at her. "Fair enough," Kelly said. "Charles Rockley was the man in the trunk of Mr. Fish's car."

CHAPTER NINETEEN

Cheating spouses deny infidelity with facile deceit. Con men nimbly tap-dance around implausibility. Criminals beat lie detector tests with steady breathing and beta blockers that control the involuntary tremors of a lie. Their survival depends on practiced deception. They are ready when the gun sounds and the games begin.

Mason was good, but not that good. Vanessa Carter had knocked him off track. Kelly Holt had resuscitated dormant memories he thought he had discarded. He hadn't expected either woman to leap from his past into his present, though he managed to keep his game face on.

But writing Charles Rockley's name on the toe tag for the corpse in Fish's trunk took his breath away. It was like finding his pants down around his ankles in front of a disappointed audience. Certain that his eyes were bugging out as if he had a runaway thyroid, he wished for a sudden palsy that would subdue the quivering muscles in his face. Mason barely heard Fish say he didn't know anyone by that name.

Kelly pulled a photograph from her file, sliding it across the table to Fish. "Do you know this man?"

It was a grainy color photo taken during the day in front of an apartment building. The man was tall and broad, his features well known to Mason though he was a stranger to Fish. Blues was the man in the picture.

The photograph shook Mason out of his stupor. "Where did you get this?" he asked before Fish could answer.

"That's not important," Kelly said.

"The hell it's not!"

He quickly saw the alignment of the planets. The FBI had Rockley's apartment under surveillance. Kelly recognized Blues in the photograph. She knew that Mason represented Fish and that Blues did Mason's investigative legwork. Once the FBI identified Rockley's body, she assumed that Mason had sent Blues to Rockley's apartment because he knew that Rockley was the murder victim, something he could have learned only from Fish. The last piece was easy. Fish knew because he had killed Rockley.

It was obvious, logical, and wrong, but Mason couldn't tell them why. If the FBI gave the photograph to the cops, school was out. Fish would be indicted. Blues would be subpoenaed and forced to testify. Blues could tell the truth and exonerate Fish. Or he could lie and save Mason.

Kelly looked at Mason, her eyes flickering with regret, though Mason knew her sympathies were misplaced. She turned toward Samuelson, a silent gesture telling Mason that it was out of her hands.

"We'll let you talk privately," Samuelson said. "When you're ready, call my secretary at extension two-two-one."

Fish waited until they left before picking up the photograph, pointing it at Mason. "You know this man?"

Mason took a deep breath, got up, and walked to the windows, leaning against the glass. For a moment, he wondered if he could push hard enough to force the glass from the frame. He already felt like he was falling.

"I'll get you another lawyer."

Fish swiveled in his chair toward Mason. "Why do I need another lawyer? Who is this man?"

Mason looked at Fish, hands in his pockets. "It's complicated."

"What's so complicated? You know this man and you don't want to tell me who he is or how you know him. Tell me and we'll see how complicated it is."

The practice of law was about lines. Some of them were bright. Some of them were blurred. Either way, lawyers made their living on the margins. Mason shook his head, unable to squeeze more room from the tangled lines wrapped around him. His problems with Vanessa Carter and Charles Rockley created the mother of all conflicts of interest for his representation of Avery Fish.

He couldn't represent Fish any longer, but he couldn't tell Fish why or anything else that might come back to haunt him. As much as he liked Fish, he had to assume that Fish would ultimately do what every other defendant in a tight spot does. Make a trade. Mason didn't want to end up as the player to be named later. Still, he knew that Fish would eventually learn that Blues was the man in the photograph.

"His name is Wilson Bluestone, Jr. People call him Blues. He's a friend of mine."

Fish shrugged. "This friend of yours, did he kill Rock- ley?"

"No."

"Then why does the FBI have his picture and why do I need a new lawyer?"

"The picture was taken outside Rockley's apartment building. The FBI must have had Rockley under surveillance. Why, I don't know. You need a new lawyer because that photograph means I have a conflict of interest that prevents me from continuing to represent you."

Fish hauled himself from his chair, his face reddening with the effort. "So you've got another client you'd rather represent than me?"

Mason looked at Fish, surprised at the hurt in his eyes. "Believe me. If there was any way I could, I'd much rather represent you."

Fish took Mason by the arm. It was a comforting grip, as if Fish realized that Mason was caught between things worse than conflicting clients.

"Don't quit on me so easily. I need you. Tell Mr. Samuel- son we'll get back to him next week."

"I don't know. I don't think there's a way around this."

Fish patted Mason on the cheek. "There's always a way. Our people haven't survived for over five thousand years by giving up. You think about it. Call Samuelson. Tell him to have a nice weekend."

Mason left word with Samuelson's secretary that they were leaving and that he didn't need to talk with her boss. When she insisted on transferring his call to Samuelson, he assured her that wasn't necessary. He and Fish were standing at the elevator when Kelly Holt caught up to them.

"Lou," she said, arms folded across her chest. "We need to talk."

Mason gave her a faint smile. "Next week. I'll call you."

"Now," she said, leaving no room for negotiation.

The elevator arrived. Fish stepped in and turned around toward Mason. "Talk to her. What could it hurt? I'll wait for you downstairs," he said as the elevator door closed.

CHAPTER TWENTY

"OKAY, I'M LISTENING," Mason said.

"Your client needs to take this deal," she said.

"Deal? What deal? Help out with some mysterious investigation that's too top secret to tell us about? Give me a break."

"It's important and your client is in deep trouble."

Wearing slacks and a waist-cut jacket over a blouse, Kelly could have passed for anyone from a soccer mom to an executive on casual day. The give-away was in her eyes and jaw, where there was no give. He studied her, remembering their past. She was tough then, letting her guard down a little but not enough that he could say he ever really knew her. Her wall was up again and their past was forgotten. Mason waited as one of the elevators opened again and several people got out, brushing past them.

"It's always important when the government wants to trade lives," he said. "My client needs more time to think it over."

"There isn't a lot of time. What can I tell you to make it easier for him to decide?"

"Other than the details on what you want him to do?"

"Other than that."

"Okay. Why did the FBI have Rockley under surveillance?"

"We didn't."

"C'mon, Kelly," Mason snapped. "We both know that Blues is the guy in that photograph and that's how you tied Fish to Rockley."

"That doesn't mean we had Rockley under surveillance."

Mason cocked his head, surprised at her insistence. Then he remembered Blues telling him that someone else had been snooping around Rockley's apartment, talking to neighbors, without identifying himself. The FBI always left business cards.

"So where did you get the picture?"

It was Kelly's turn to hesitate. She glanced around to make certain no one else was within earshot.

"It was attached to an e-mail we intercepted."

"It's hard to get a warrant to intercept e-mail. It's even harder to get a warrant to hack into someone's computer and search their stored e-mails. This must be some big case you're working on."

"The Patriot Act makes it a lot easier."

"Are you telling me that Rockley was mixed up with terrorists?"

"The Patriot Act isn't limited to terrorists."

Mason knew she was right. The Justice Department had taken advantage of its new powers in a wide range of cases that had nothing to do with terrorism. The ACLU and criminal defense bar had complained, but no one had heard them. The Bill of Rights was eroding against the tide of better safe than sorry.

"So if Rockley wasn't a terrorist, who was he?"

"A murder victim," Kelly said.

"Who just happens to pop up in an overnight DNA search? I don't think so. You have any idea how long it takes me to get DNA results in a criminal case? Months. Every criminal defendant in America wants his DNA tested. There aren't enough labs to run all the tests and nobody gets results, even preliminary results, overnight."

"We're the FBI. We don't have to wait."

"I don't buy that. I don't think you tested the murder victim's DNA sample, ran it through the Bureau's database, and just got a lucky match, all in less than twenty-four hours. The only way you could have gotten the results that fast is if you knew who you were looking for. I think you tested the sample against Rockley's DNA because you already had his on file and you suspected he was the murder victim. So who the hell was Rockley?"

Kelly shook her head. "You haven't changed a bit. Still too smart for your own good. Just don't wait until it's too late to make up your mind."

CHAPTER TWENTY-ONE

Mason told Fish about his conversation with Kelly as they drove through downtown. People walking to lunch clutched their hats and scarves against a chill wind that whipped along at street level, channeled by office towers reaching for the high arched ceiling of thick clouds overhead. Fish listened without asking questions or offering any comments. The rest of the drive was a quiet one.

"It's not about me. It's about you," Fish said when Mason pulled up in front of Fish's house.

"What's that supposed to mean?"

"That photograph. The one with your friend in it that means I need a new lawyer. That FBI agent—what was her name?"

"Kelly Holt."

"She was showing that picture to you, not to me."

"What makes you say that?"

"The two of you, there's some history there. I can tell by the way you looked at her. Am I right?"

Mason hesitated. "Yeah, we were involved in a case five years ago."

"So you were involved. Does she know this friend of yours, Mr. Blues?"

"She does."

"Then it doesn't matter if I know who he is since you already do. She wanted to see your reaction."

"I wasn't exactly cool."

"You nearly plotzed. Some poker player you are."

"Maybe she wanted to see if you would lie about knowing Blues."

"Why would I tell a lie that could be so easily exposed?" Fish asked.

"Crooks tell bad lies all the time."

"Not me. It's bad for business."

Mason looked at Fish. The old man had been grinding away at Mason's problem, considering it the way a con man would. What's the angle? What doesn't fit? Where's the hook?

"You still need a new lawyer," Mason told him.

"What will the government think if you quit?"

Mason shrugged. "That you didn't pay me."

"If that was the case, you would have already quit. What else?"

"That we disagreed over the deal they offered. You wanted to take it and I wouldn't go along. Or maybe that you were going to perjure yourself on the witness stand."

"I don't think so. No. Your FBI agent, Miss Holt, she will think you quit because of the picture of your friend, Mr. Blues. She will think you know too much about Rockley to be my lawyer. That's why this is all about you, not me."

Fish was analyzing his case like the con man he was. That didn't mean Fish was wrong, but it meant Mason had to understand Fish's approach.

"What makes a good con?" Mason asked.

"Two things. The con man has to have better information than the mark and the mark has to want to believe the con."

"That's why this is about you and not me. Blues used to be a cop. He helps me with some of my cases. Kelly Holt knows that. She thinks you knew that Rockley was the murder victim because you killed him. You told me, and I told Blues and sent him to Rockley's apartment. It's what she wants to believe. If she shows that photograph to the cops, they'll agree with her. She's wrong, but I can't tell her why."

"So you think she's trying to con both of us so that I'll take this cockamamie deal they've offered."

"That's the best I can come up with."

"And Kelly Holt wants to believe I killed Rockley, but you're the one with the better information."

"That's me."

"And you won't tell me what it is. So who's conning whom?" Fish asked.

Mason looked at Fish, realizing that there was something else that made a good con. The mark had to trust the con man like a penitent trusts a priest. Mason fought the temptation to trust Fish. He was torn between wanting to tell him and worrying that he'd already told him too much.

"I'm sorry."

"Sorry is for losers. And you're no loser. Come for dinner on Sunday. Six o'clock. We'll talk some more."

"There's nothing more I can tell you."

Fish climbed out of the car, holding on to the door as he leaned back in. "Trust me, we'll find something to talk about, eh, boytchik."

Mason spent the rest of the afternoon looking for the path of least resistance to the truth about Charles Rockley. He was certain of one thing. The story laid out in Rockley's employment records didn't jibe with someone whose DNA was at the top of the FBI's unidentified murder victims pile. The FBI's DNA database was for convicted felons and suspected terrorists, not middle managers. Mason shifted his focus to proving that Rockley's résumé was phony.

He pulled up Rockley's application for employment at the Galaxy Casino on his computer. It listed the names, addresses, and phone numbers of five prior employers.

He picked up the phone and started dialing, betting that the companies were either out of business or had never heard of Charles Rockley. An hour later he was done. All five were still open for business. All five confirmed that Rockley had worked for them, just as Rockley had written on his application to Galaxy. All five gave him glowing references and said they had been sorry to see him go but had understood that he had to take a better job.

It didn't make sense, but that didn't matter. No con artist, not even the FBI, could get five different companies in five different states to lie about a former employee.

He studied the names on his dry erase board, looking for someone who would talk to him. Al Webb was the manager of the Galaxy Casino. Lila Collins was the HR director. Both knew Rockley. Carol Hill knew Rockley well enough to sue him for sexual harassment. Once word got out that Rockley had been murdered, their lawyers would wire their jaws so tight they'd have to learn sign language.

Mason was about to give up on the dry erase board as an oracle when Blues came into his office carrying two cold bottles of beer. He handed one to Mason and retired to the sofa with the other bottle.

"Happy Hour," Blues said.

"Except I'm not happy." He set the beer on his desk and leaned forward in his chair. "Charles Rockley is dead."

"Then you ought to be happy if he was the one blackmailing Judge Carter."

"Not if he was also the dead man in the trunk of Avery Fish's car and not if the FBI has a picture of you outside Rockley's apartment."

Blues nodded. "I can see how that wouldn't make either one of us happy. What's the story?"

Mason laid out the day's events, glad to have another perspective. Blues was a bloodless problem-solver even though his solutions were often bloody. He didn't get hung up on sentiment or regret, which enabled him to see things others didn't and do things others wouldn't. When Mason finished, Blues walked to the dry erase board, picked up a red marker, and circled the name of Carol Hill's husband, Mark.

"I'd say this cat is one seriously pissed-off motherfucker," Blues said. "And I'll bet you he doesn't have a lawyer to shut him up or a friend who gives a shit."

Mason grinned. "A man like that needs at least one friend."

"Two would be even better."

CHAPTER TWENTY-TWO

CAROL HILL'S LAWYER, Vince Bongiovanni, had asked her typical softball questions at the arbitration about how wonderful her marriage had been until Charles Rockley started harassing her. It was a standard tactic designed to elicit sympathy.

Mason knew it was lost on Vanessa Carter, who was more likely to find sympathy in the dictionary between shit and suicide than in a plaintiff's well-rehearsed tears. Especially after Galaxy's lawyer, Lari Prillman, shredded Carol's warm and fuzzy story, ripping out the last thread with Carol's admission that she'd had an affair with one of the casino bartenders.

In addition to its marginal value as soap opera, Carol's testimony had included enough information for Blues and Mason to track down her husband, Mark, who worked at the GM plant in the Fairfax Industrial District and did his drinking at a bar not far from the plant called Easy's. That's where Blues and Mason found him just after six o'clock either winding down from the week or winding up for the weekend.

Easy's was a one-room cinderblock dive with no windows, blue lights, and bar stools worn to the nails. Friday after work was prime time and the bar was full of men who had traded hard hats for cold beer. A jukebox pounded out country music, love-gone-bad songs sending some men home and others back to the bar. Two waitresses worked the room, their hard-bitten faces offering no comfort. The bartender, a dirty towel slung over his bony shoulder, made change and conversation.

Blues shouldered his way to the bar and paid ten dollars more than the price of two beers, the heavy tip a fair price for a line on Mark Hill. He navigated back to Mason, who was standing near the door, squinting while his eyes adjusted to the perpetual dusk.

"That's him," Blues said, aiming his bottle at the man sitting on a stool at the far end of the bar, shoulders hunched, head down. "Bartender says he's a mean drunk. Likes to mix it up."

Hill was husky, broad in the shoulders, heavy in the gut. He was wearing a barn jacket that padded his shoulders, giving him an even more rounded look. Mason guessed that he was in his mid-thirties, though he looked older. Probably been working the same assembly-line job long enough to be bitter, more so after his wife humiliated him.

He finished his beer, shoving the mug away from him, a silent signal to the bartender for a refill. He chased it with a shot of whiskey, wiping the back of his hand across his mouth. He was drinking at a steady pace that would blind him before the night was over. No one talked to him. Even in the crowded bar, people kept their distance. The bartender had him pegged.

Mason slipped through the crowd, rested his elbow on the bar next to Hill, and waved a twenty-dollar bill at the bar tender. Blues lingered a step behind him.

"A shot and a beer for my friend," Mason said.

Hill turned his head toward Mason. "I know you?"

"Nope," Mason said, taking a draw on his bottle.

"Then you ain't my friend, so why you wanna buy me a drink?"

His eyes were glassy and his speech was slow, more suspicious than slurred.

"Because I want to talk to you."

Hill narrowed his eyes, turning away. "I buy my own drinks."

"Don't you even want to know why I want to talk to you?"

"Don't give a rat's ass. Fuck off."

"It's about Charles Rockley."

"Don't know him," Hill said, rapping his empty mug on the counter to summon the bartender.

"Sure you do. He's the guy at Galaxy that screwed your wife—not to be confused with the bartender she was banging."

Hill slumped toward the bar as if he'd been slapped. Mason took the fake and didn't see Hill reach inside his coat, barely catching the flash of steel as Hill whipped a knife at his throat.

Blues grabbed Hill's wrist as he cleared his jacket, twisting it until Hill dropped the knife on the bar. Mason scooped it up, closed the blade, and slipped it into his pocket. The bartender made a point of looking the other way. If anyone else noticed, they kept it to themselves. Blues was right. Hill didn't have a friend who gave a shit.

Blues leaned in against Hill's face, still gripping his wrist. "Let's get some air."

Mason and Blues flanked Hill, impersonating three buddies ready to hit the road. They hustled him out to the parking lot and up against the side of Mason's SUV. Blues frisked him, nodding to Mason that he was unarmed. Mason climbed into the backseat from the driver's side as Blues shoved Hill in from the passenger side, slamming the door shut.

"Who the fuck are you guys?" Hill asked.

"Just a couple of sailors on leave looking for a good time," Mason said.

"Bullshit! Lemme go," Hill said, reaching for the door, changing his mind when he saw Blues on the other side.

"We'll let you go just as soon as we're done talking."

"Well, I got nothing to say to you, asshole. So if you and your buddy are gonna bust me up, let's get it over with."

Mason believed him. The booze couldn't mask the resignation and resentment in Hill's voice. He'd been kicked so many times he expected it. The best he could hope for was to get in a few licks of his own before someone turned out his lights.

"We just want some information about Charles Rockley, and don't tell me you don't know who he is or my friend will get very annoyed."

Hill peered out the window at Blues, who stared back before turning around and blotting out the window with his back. He looked at Mason, who gave him no room.

"What do you want to know?"

"All I know is that Rockley worked at the Galaxy and harassed your wife. She sued him. Fill in the blanks."

"That fucking cousin of hers, the smartass lawyer. It was his idea."

"You mean Vince Bongiovanni? Your wife's lawyer?"

"Yeah. Vince said he was dying to pop the Galaxy on account of what happened after Ed got killed."

"Ed who?" Mason asked.

"Ed Fiori. He owned the boat when it was called the Dream Casino. Got himself killed a few years ago. Hell of a thing. Galaxy bought the boat out of Fiori's estate. Vince said they screwed Ed's family on the deal."

"Why does Bongiovanni care what happened to Ed Fiori?"

"Who the fuck knows? They're all related. Carol and Vince are cousins; Fiori was their uncle. Anyway, Carol bitches to Vince that this guy Rockley is coming on to her at work. Won't take no for an answer. Vince says how bad is it? Carol, she says it's bad, but it ain't so bad. Vince says the worse it is the more it's worth. Next thing I know, she says the guy raped her. Vince, he says ka-ching."

"What did you say?"

"I said I'm gonna cut Rockley's nuts off. Vince tells me to sit tight 'cause there's more than one way to get money out of a casino. So I go along like a dumbass and she makes a fool out of me at that hearing when that bitch lawyer gets her to admit that she was hosing one of the bartenders all this time I'm wantin' to kill Rockley to protect her honor. Fuck her and the bartender and Rockley! You satisfied?"

Mason nodded. "Almost. When was the last time you saw Rockley?"

Hill tugged at his chin, stalling. "At the hearing. Guy's a punk. Him and me ended up in the head at the same time. He sees me and grabs his crotch. Tells me you want some, come get some. Vince showed up or I woulda popped the little shit."

"How about Carol? Did she run into him at work after the hearing?"

"She's been off since before the hearing. Too much mental anguish," Hill explained, not hiding his sarcasm.

"You don't buy her mental anguish?"

"Hey, I'm buying whatever Vince and Carol are selling long as I get my share of the money."

Carol's claim against Galaxy included a claim on behalf of her husband for loss of consortium, a quaint legal term that meant loss of a spouse's services caused by the defendant's wrongful conduct. Services was loosely translated as sex. How frequent before compared to how frequent after. Then put a price on it. Carol testified that she and Mark screwed like rabbits until having sex with Rockley made her hate to be touched. Lari Prillman asked how she found the time when she was spending so much of it shacked up with the bartender. Mason doubted Mark would see a nickel for loss of his wife's services even if Judge Carter weren't being blackmailed. Rather than break that news to Hill, Mason changed subjects.

Lari Prillman had never identified the bartender by name during the hearing. Mason thought that was unusual but attributed it to Galaxy's desire to avoid dragging another employee's name into the case. Carol Hill didn't volunteer her lover's name, which made sense to Mason.

"The bartender. You ever get his name?"

Hill's face reddened. "Johnny Keegan."

"How about Keegan? You going to cut his nuts off?"

Hill looked away from Mason as his eyes filled. "I'm done talking. Lemme outta here."

Watching Hill die a little more made Mason feel ashamed for kicking him when he was down. "Sure. Sorry we hassled you."

"Right. You and everybody else."

Mason opened the door, got out, and stood aside. Hill slid out, drawing his coat around him. Mason couldn't tell if the tears on Hill's checks were from the booze, the cold, or the pain. Hill brushed them away and headed for his truck.

CHAPTER TWENTY-THREE

Blues and Mason watched from the front seat of Mason's SUV as Hill floored his pickup and slalomed past parked cars on his way out of the lot. Turning sharply into the street, the truck fishtailed and clipped the front end of a sedan parked across from the bar. The impact spun Hill around until the two vehicles were nose to nose.

A man with a weight lifter's build and a mop of blond hair hanging down his neck jumped out of the driver's side of the sedan at the same moment Hill poured out of the pickup, the two of them trading shouts. Hill swung at the man, who stepped inside the punch, landing a left-right combination that put Hill down in a heap, the man standing over him, still cursing. A second man, smaller and wirier than his partner, got out from the passenger side, pulling the driver away before checking on Hill.

"What do you think?" Mason asked Blues.

"The guys in the car were looking for someone. Let's wait a minute and see if they're public or private."

"Hill could be hurt."

"Looks okay to me."

The passenger helped Hill to his feet, brushed him off, and leaned him against the pickup. The driver slammed his hand on the hood of the sedan, pointing to the front left fender that had been crushed into the tire, disabling the car. He yanked a cell phone from his belt, punched a number, and yelled some more.

A moment later a second sedan pulled up and another man got out. He stepped into the glare of Hill's headlights, his block-cut head and shoulders suddenly familiar to Mason.

"Son of a bitch," Mason said.

"Friend of yours?"

"Dennis Brewer. He's the FBI agent handling Fish's case. He interrupted my meeting with Pete Samuelson to tell us that they'd found a body in the trunk of Fish's car."

"You recognize the other two?"

"No, but they look more private than public to me."

"I doubt the Bureau has a side gig helping stranded motorists. What are they doing here?"

"Two choices," Mason said. "Watching Hill or us. The feds already tied Rockley to you and me, but that's because I represent Fish. Maybe they found out about Carol Hill's lawsuit and decided to talk to her husband just like we did."

"Hard to believe they're as smart as we are."

"You've got a point. I don't remember seeing them at the last Mensa meeting."

"Still doesn't make sense. Rockley's murder is for the local cops. Why is the FBI on it?"

"Kelly Holt told me that they got the picture of you outside Rockley's apartment when they intercepted an e-mail that had the picture attached to it. Pete Samuelson wants Avery Fish to help with a government investigation he wants to keep a secret. Dennis Brewer shows up on Mark Hill's tail. I may not be the sharpest knife in the drawer, but my guess is the feds are investigating Galaxy."

"Which means that Rockley wasn't just a guy who couldn't keep his zipper zipped."

Mason nodded. "That's what I thought when the FBI made an instant DNA identification. Then I checked out Rockley's prior employers and they all vouched for him."

"Something was hinky with Rockley. I don't care who vouched for him. And, we still don't know if the FBI is watching Hill or us."

"Let's try the back side of the bar. Maybe there's another way out."

"Forget it. They already saw us with Hill."

"You want me to wave as we drive by?" Mason said.

"It never hurts to be polite."

Blues took his cell phone out of his pocket.

"I thought you hated those things," Mason said.

"I do. They're like an anchor wrapped around your neck. Doesn't mean I won't use one, especially one that takes pictures. Take it slow and I'll get a set of mug shots."

He lowered his window, resting his arm on the door, hiding the phone in his hand, the camera lens peeking between his fingers.

"Tell them to smile," Mason said as he put the SUV in gear.

"Brewer was backing up those guys. Let's see if someone is backing up Brewer. Just drive by like it's none of our business. If no one else picks us up, they're probably babysitting Hill. If we find a friend, we're it."

Mason eased the SUV out of the lot, crawling past the accident, Brewer and the two other men turning their heads away from them. Mason laid on the horn, chuckling as they whipped around toward the SUV, letting Blues snap their pictures in full piss-off mode.

"Nice," Blues said.

Mason had a straight shot for almost a mile before he would have to make a turn, plenty of time for a third crew to play catch-up. The neighborhood was industrial except for an occasional bar or convenience store. It was lightly traveled and well lit, making it an easy stretch of road on which to find someone. Mason took his time. Six blocks later, another sedan fell in behind them, keeping its distance. The driver was alone.

"Bingo," Blues said. "There's a traffic light coming up. Let it turn yellow, speed up like you're going to run it. If the car stays on us, stop at the last second and we'll get another picture."

Mason gunned the SUV. The trailing sedan matched him, then quickly closed the gap, giving up any pretense of stealth. The light blinked from green to yellow when he was half a block away. Mason pushed harder before slamming on the brakes, skidding to a stop half a length into the intersection as the light turned red. The sedan screeched and shimmied, nearly kissing his bumper before it stopped.

"Anybody you recognize?" Blues asked, not turning around.

"Yeah," Mason said, looking in his rearview mirror. "Kelly Holt." He watched as she smacked her palm against the steering wheel and fumbled with something on the seat next to her.

"Old home week."

"Yeah. Maybe I'll just invite her over for dinner."

Mason got out of the SUV, walking toward her as she opened her door, meeting him halfway.

"I'm taking Blues back to the bar and then I'm going home. You remember how to get there?" he said.

"That's not the point." She folded her arms like a vise across her chest.

"Sure it is. Since you know where I'm going, you don't have to follow me. You can meet me there."

"What you're doing is really stupid," she said.

"Which part?"

"All of it."

"Can't be any more stupid than expecting my client to help you with an investigation too secret to tell us what it is."

"You've got to trust me," Kelly said.

"I never had a client with that much faith. Besides, I know that you're after Galaxy, so you might as well tell me what you want from my client."

Kelly glared at him. "You can't possibly know that."

"No? Well, you can't instantly identify Rockley's DNA if he's spent his whole life bouncing from one company to another counting how many sick days he's got left. Rockley worked at Galaxy. You monitored someone's e-mail and snagged the picture of Blues. I haven't figured out the rest of it, but I will."

She held his gaze, not giving ground. That steeled look was one thing about her that hadn't changed since they first met. There was no backing down in her. Not then, not now.

"I'll talk to Samuelson on Monday," she said. "Maybe we can work something out."

Mason saw no reason to tell her that Fish would have a new lawyer on Monday. "See you around the ballpark," he told her.

CHAPTER TWENTY-FOUR

IT WAS PAST eight o'clock when Mason stopped in his office. He had three voice messages. The first was from Vince Bongiovanni, who left his cell phone number and a promise that his call was important enough to return as soon as possible even if he didn't say why. The second was from his Aunt Claire inviting him to dinner on Sunday.

The third was from Rachel Firestone, a reporter for the Kansas City Star. Though they began as adversaries, each using the other to advance a case or a story, they'd become close friends. For a time, she backed off covering his cases to avoid any questions about her objectivity before deciding that she was a good enough reporter to know when to draw that line.

When Rachel told her editor that she wanted to resume covering Mason's cases, he noted the rumors about their relationship and questioned whether she should write about someone she was sleeping with. When she showed the editor a picture of her girlfriend, the editor made a snide remark about lesbians who really wanted to change teams. It was his last official act. Her new boss told her he trusted her judgment but to remember who signed her paycheck.

Mason replayed her message to be certain he'd heard it right.

"Hey, babe. It's me. I got an anonymous tip that the body found in Avery Fish's car was some guy named Charles Rockley. I checked it out with the cops, who did their no comment thing, but I got the feeling it was news to them. Since when does someone leak the ID of a murder victim and leave the cops out of the loop? Call me. I'm on deadline."

The phone rang before Mason could return any of the calls. It was Vanessa Carter.

"Where are we?" she asked.

"At the end of a long day and a longer week," Mason said, glancing at his calendar. "Happy Valentine's Day."

"Don't waste your humor on me, Mr. Mason. I asked where we are."

Mason let out a deep breath and pinched the bridge of his nose, knowing that the story would be on the front page of tomorrow morning's paper. "Charles Rockley is dead. Someone killed him, chopped off his head and his hands, and dumped the body in the trunk of a car owned by a client of mine named Avery Fish."

"I'm aware of Mr. Fish's case. It's been all over the news. There's been no mention of the identity of the victim."

"You can read about it in tomorrow morning's paper."

Judge Carter didn't respond. Mason heard her breathing softly and steadily. In judicial parlance, she had taken his information under advisement before issuing a ruling or, in his case, another ultimatum. He knew better than to interrupt.

"Charles Rockley wasn't the one," she finally said.

Mason realized that she was avoiding any mention of blackmail. Having once been burned by having her phone conversation recorded, she was not taking any chances.

"How do you know?"

"I just received another call."

"Tell me about it."

"He asked why I hadn't issued a ruling. I reminded him that I had until March tenth, which is thirty days from the end of the hearing. He said they wanted the decision not later than a week from today, the twenty-first. I told him that wasn't possible, that I had other cases besides this one. He said that this case was the only one that should matter to me and that they wouldn't hesitate to convince me of that."

"Where are you?" Mason asked.

"At home."

"Is there someplace else you can go until this is over?"

"I will not be run out of my home and I will not have my life ruined again, Mr. Mason. Do your job. Make this go away."

"It's not that simple."

"It's your tangled web, Counselor. Do whatever you have to do or I will," she said and hung up.

Mason put the phone down as Blues opened the door to his office.

"What?" Mason asked, exasperated by the new deadline.

"Don't shoot me, man. I'm only the piano player." Blues handed Mason prints of the digital photographs he'd taken. "The light was bad and the angle wasn't great, but at least I got their faces."

Mason studied the photographs. Blues had caught them in an unguarded moment, their faces screwed up in surprise. He didn't recognize the two men in the car Mark Hill had struck. All three were wearing heavy jackets over jeans or khakis. Nothing with FBI stenciled on the back.

Mason dropped the photographs on his desk and pointed to the phone. "That was Judge Carter. She got another call and a new deadline for her ruling. A week from today or the tape makes the top forty."

"I guess that rules out Rockley as the blackmailer."

"Not necessarily. The way she described the call, it sounds like more than one person is involved. The caller kept referring to 'they,' not just to himself. Rockley could have been one of them. On top of that, I got a message from Rachel. Someone leaked the news that Rockley was the guy in Fish's trunk."

"Only the FBI and the killer knew Rockley's identity and the killer sure as hell isn't going to call the Star. Why would the Bureau leak it before they told the cops?" Blues asked. "Why go out of their way to make them look bad?"

"Beats me. Plus, I also had a message from Vince Bongiovanni to call him as soon as possible. Even left me his cell phone number."

"What time was that call?"

Mason checked the log of calls stored in his phone. "Seven p.m."

"We left Hill at close to seven. Brewer and his buddies didn't look like they were in the mood to let him call his lawyer so it's probably not about that."

"I never told Hill who I was and I doubt he recognized me," Mason said. "Brewer could have told him, but he wouldn't have had any reason to. I think Vince got the same tip Rachel did. Makes me wonder why."

"When did Rachel call?"

"Seven-oh-five."

"That fits and it explains one other thing."

"What's that?"

"Why Bongiovanni is waiting for you downstairs. He's in the back booth."

CHAPTER TWENTY-FIVE

JURIES LIKE DIFFERENT kinds of lawyers. Patrick Ortiz, the prosecuting attorney, was a rumpled everyman, the kind of lawyer jurors imagined going bowling with or having over for chili. Mason was a street fighter, ready with a killer cross-examination or a devastating one-liner, but always ready. He was the lawyer jurors wanted to represent them if their life was on the line.

Vince Bongiovanni had the chiseled chin, penetrating eyes, and smoky cool that made women want to take him home and men want to be his pal, hoping some of what he had would rub off on them. He was tall, sandy-haired, and trim and dressed like the million bucks he routinely racked up in fees. One local magazine did a feature on eligible bachelors and labeled him the total package.

"Hey, Lou," he said, as Mason slid into the booth opposite him. "Buy you a drink?"

"I'll pass. Sorry I didn't return your call earlier. I just got your message."

"Don't worry about it. I figured I might catch you here. Nice place."

Mason looked around. Myles Cartwright's trio was playing mellow sounds on the small stage, the drummer and bass player taking their lead from Cartwright's piano. The music complemented the soft buzz of conversation. Some people came to hear the music, others just to be near it.

"Your message said it was important."

Bongiovanni nodded. "It is important. I understand you represent Avery Fish."

"It's been in the papers."

Bongiovanni grinned. "You kill me, man. You get more ink than I do."

"Ah, but you get the big bucks."

"Somebody's got to do it."

Bongiovanni delivered the practiced punch line, grinning again. Mason didn't envy Bongiovanni's success. He'd learned the hard way to stick to the cases that suited him best. He dabbled occasionally in representing plaintiffs, always coming back to the higher stakes of life and death.

"Might as well be you," Mason said.

"Might as well. I got an anonymous tip that the body found in your client's car has been identified."

Mason could understand a newspaper getting an anonymous tip. The tipster got off on seeing his story in print. Feeding the news to the lawyer who was suing the victim smacked of inside baseball. He wondered who would gain by leaking to Bongiovanni.

Mason saw no reason to deny something that would be reported in the morning paper. He'd only look foolish if he did. However, that was no reason to tell Bongiovanni anything else. Bongiovanni would eventually find out what had happened between Mason and Mark Hill, but that would be a tap dance for another day. This was the time to listen.

"I heard that too."

"Guy named Charles Rockley. You know him?"

"Never met," Mason said.

"You didn't miss anything. He worked at the Galaxy Casino. In his spare time, he sexually harassed a client of mine, a woman named Carol Hill. I sued him and the Galaxy. The case was arbitrated last week in front of Judge Carter. We're waiting for a ruling."

"That's good to know. The cops think Fish had something to do with Rockley's death. I'd like to talk with Carol about Rockley."

Bongiovanni leaned forward in the booth. "I already talked to her. She had nothing to do with it."

Mason figured it had been little more than an hour since Bongiovanni was tipped off about Rockley. That wasn't much time to cross-examine Carol Hill about the murder and hustle down to Blues on Broadway to wait for him.

The timing made him wonder if Bongiovanni had known Rock- ley had been murdered before he got the tip.

The quick denial of Carol's involvement raised, rather than lowered, Mason's suspicion. He hadn't considered Carol as a suspect until her lawyer assured him she wasn't one. Mason could picture Mark Hill angry and drunk enough to kill Rockley especially if his wife egged him on. None of that led to the trunk of Avery Fish's car. Still, Bongiovanni's assurance of Carol's innocence gave Mason an opening.

"I'm glad to know that. Then she won't mind talking to me."

Bongiovanni hesitated, rubbing his palm against his bottle of beer. He frowned long enough to convince Mason that his indecision was rehearsed. "I'll make her available, but I want whatever you come up with on Rockley."

"Why? Your case is over. Mine is just beginning."

"My case is a toss-up. Rockley claimed to be a choirboy, said my client was lying. Carol took some hits on cross- examination. If I can get something good on Rockley, I'll ask Judge Carter to let me add it to the record before she rules."

Mason remembered Judge Carter's comment that Carol and her lawyer were out for blood, not money. He knew that lawyers and clients often changed their appetite after the harsh realities of the courtroom set in.

"Why not settle?"

Bongiovanni tightened his jaw. "Not a chance."

"You said it was a close case. Sometimes a bad settlement is better than a bad verdict."

"Carol is family. This isn't ever going to be one of those times."

Judge Carter's assessment had been dead-on. If the case was a toss-up, Bongiovanni's deal made sense except for one thing. The better his case got, the harder it would be on Judge Carter to rule in Galaxy's favor. Still, Mason needed whatever he could come up with on Rockley, and Carol Hill was as good a place to start as any. He had to talk with her as soon as possible while putting Bongiovanni off until after the blackmailer's deadline.

"I'll keep you in the loop, but I may not have anything for a while. Depends on how much cooperation I get from the cops or from Galaxy. The sooner I can talk with your client, the sooner I can start putting something together."

"How about tomorrow morning? We can meet at her house."

That was the last place Mason wanted to meet, imagining her husband wandering out from the bedroom with a hangover. He shook his head.

"My office. Ten o'clock."

"Done. I'll bring the bagels," Bongiovanni said.

"One other thing. Who do I talk to at Galaxy about Rock- ley?"

"Forget it. You'll have to go through Galaxy's lawyer, Lari Prillman, and there isn't enough heat in hell to melt her heart." He stood, clapping Mason on the shoulder. "A Jew and an Italian on the same team. Look out, world."

Mason waited until Bongiovanni cleared the front door of the bar before he called Rachel Firestone.

"What do you know about Charles Rockley?" she asked him.

"Just because you have caller ID doesn't mean you don't have to say hello."

"Hello and I'm on deadline. My editor said if you don't give me something on Rockley we might as well start sleeping together since I won't be any good to him anyway."

Mason preferred the old Rachel, the one he could confide in, trade tips with, and not worry about what was on or off the record. He couldn't give her the whole story because he didn't know which pieces might come back to haunt him.

"Your message was the first I heard about the victim's identity. I'll talk to the cops on Monday and give you what I can," he said.

"That's it? This guy is murdered, butchered, and dumped in the trunk of your client's car and you've got nothing? I don't believe it."

"Best I can do," Mason said.

"I wouldn't brag about it," she told him.

CHAPTER TWENTY-SIX

MASON STAYED AT the bar, hoping the music would soothe the tension in his neck and shoulders, finally leaving close to midnight. It had been a long day. He felt like a fighter who had spent eighteen hours in a crouch. He hadn't taken a beating, but his instincts told him one was coming and he didn't know if he could stay covered up long enough to avoid the knockdown.

He lived in the middle of a block of houses that were statelier and better cared for than his, as were the people who lived in them. His neighbors barely tolerated him, resenting the turmoil that too often followed him into their quiet acreage. He tried to ignore their conscious disregard for him though it had begun to gnaw at him.

He'd lived there all his life, first while being raised by his Aunt Claire, then during the few short years he was married to Kate, and now for the seven years since, when he'd lived there alone. Abby Lieberman hadn't moved in, though she'd spent enough nights there to qualify for Gold Guest status until she found herself agreeing with the neighbors.

He understood Abby's reasons for leaving and his neighbors' reasons for wishing that he would follow. Whether it was stubbornness, inertia, or a blind willingness to sacrifice what he wanted for what he needed, he'd not been able to change. He couldn't resist lost causes, last chances, or dark water.

When Abby left for Washington and took Mickey Shanahan with her, his world shrunk, its population reduced to Claire; her longtime boyfriend and retired homicide cop, Harry Ryman; Blues; and Rachel. Now he was playing dodgeball with Rachel, wincing as he imagined her redheaded fury when she discovered he'd been holding out on her. Everything felt smaller and isolated—his office, his house, and especially him.

Heading for home, he thought about driving south and west into the Kansas-side suburb of Leawood, where Judith Bartholomew lived with her husband, her children, and her mother, Brenda Roth, but decided against the late-night drive. He'd only recently pried from a very reluctant Claire a slice of his tarnished family history. Mason's father had had an affair with Brenda when Mason was a small child. His parents had died in a car wreck that had its genesis in their illicit relationship.

Growing up, Mason had idolized his father though he knew that his memories were manufactured, his father dying too soon for honest ones. He didn't know much about his father's life except that his father had gone to college; met and married his mother; tried his hand at a couple of different businesses before settling on insurance; and that was about it.

He hadn't needed the details to craft his family myth, imagining his father as a strong, silent hero, resolute and doomed though unaware of his fate. Claire had a picture of the three of them, his father wrapping one arm around his mother, the other arm draped over Mason, who hugged his father's leg. The picture fed his childhood fantasies of what might have been, all of them dependent on the legend he'd imagined about his father.

The remnants of his myth had given way to the harsh reality that his father had cheated on his mother. He wondered how his father had justified the betrayal, knowing that it didn't matter then or now. His father had crossed a line; his parents had been killed by the implacable rule of unintended consequences.

Sifting Claire's revelation, he couldn't shake a queasy wonder about Judith Bartholomew. He'd seen her outside her house. From a distance, he thought that she bore a soft resemblance to him, perhaps real, perhaps imagined in the knowledge that she was born at a time when his father and his mistress could have conceived her. He still longed for his father, to understand him and to forgive him. Perhaps, even to redeem him. He wondered if Judith Bartholomew was part of that.

Mason knew that he too had crossed a line, breaking the law when he had asked Ed Fiori to strong-arm Judge Carter. He hadn't used those words, hiding instead behind euphemism and rationalized need. Now the words and the reasons didn't matter; only the consequences did. Redemption was too remote a prospect at the moment. He just wanted to survive.

A car was parked across the street from his house when he pulled into the driveway, the windows fogged, the motor running. Two men got out as he waited for his garage door to open. They walked toward his car, their hands in plain sight and empty, their faces red in the glow of his taillights. It was the homicide cops, Griswold and Cates.

The garage door rose. Mason parked, killed the engine, and took his time. Cates lit a cigarette and started for Mason's car. Griswold took his arm, telling him something Mason couldn't make out, though it was enough to make Cates wait a little longer. Mason thought about hitting the remote for the garage door, letting it slide back down the rails as if he hadn't noticed the cops. It would have been worth it just to see Cates swallow his cigarette. He got out instead, meeting them on the driveway.

They wore dark suits and tan overcoats left open for quick access to the guns they wore under their jackets. Their shift had ended a while ago and the late hour showed in the sag of their faces. Cates had beer breath. Griswold had mustard on his white shirt. They were working Fish's case off the clock, meaning they were close to arresting him or that it had gotten personal.

"Place is a mess or I'd invite you in," Mason told them.

Griswold nodded. "You're a compulsive smart-ass, Mason. Not that we mind. Sometimes you're even halfway funny."

"Like midnight on Valentine's Day?"

"Not yet."

"It's been a long day. Give me a minute to get warmed up," Mason said.

"We got an ID on the body in your client's car," Cates interjected.

Mason doubted they had camped out in front of his house just to tell him that.

"I'm listening."

"Charles Rockley," Cates said. "What do you know about him?"

"You think my client killed him and you expect me to answer that question? I should be asking whether you've got anything that links my client to this guy."

Griswold put his hand on Cates's arm again. "It's late, we're all tired. You could do your client some good if he's got any reason for us to believe he's not connected to Rock- ley."

"You're right about that, only I haven't had a chance to tell him about Rockley. But you didn't wait here just to tell me about Rockley. Monday would have been soon enough. What do you want?"

"We want anything you've got on Rockley," Griswold answered, sticking to his story. "We know he worked at the Galaxy Casino."

Cops didn't ask a suspect's lawyer for information on the victim unless they really had nothing to go on or they thought the lawyer was dumb enough to help them out. Mason rejected both possibilities, knowing the cops would get to the point when they were ready.

"That's not much. A lot of people work at the casino. You'd do better to talk to them."

"This guy worked there too, only he isn't talking," Cates said, handing Mason a photograph of a man lying on the pavement, the side of his face pressed against the ground, his one visible eye wide open, the back of his head blown away. The time and date stamp in the bottom right hand corner said the picture had been taken two hours ago.

"Who is it?" Mason asked.

"Thought you might know," Cates said.

"Why would I know him?"

"He had a piece of paper in his hand with your name and phone number on it."

CHAPTER TWENTY-SEVEN

THIS WASN'T THE punch Mason had been expecting, though it rocked him. He had no explanation and couldn't think of one he'd be happy about. He studied the picture more closely. A man who dies naturally and peacefully looks like he's sleeping, not dead. Take the same man, excavate his skullcap with a bullet, and you get a death mask his mother wouldn't recognize. Mason shook his head at the cops. Griswold's expression was flat. Cates flashed a devil's grin through cigarette smoke.

"I give up. Who is he?" Mason asked.

"A bartender at the Galaxy name of Johnny Keegan," Cates said. "Why would he have had your name and number?"

"Beats the hell out of me."

"With luck, it might," Cates said. "Let us know if you think of something. Monday is soon enough."

"Help me out," Mason said. "When did it happen?"

Cates was halfway down the driveway, his back to Mason. Griswold watched him go. "He doesn't like you."

"Occupational hazard. How about you?"

"Doesn't matter. All I want to know, are you part of the problem or part of the solution?"

"You'll be the first to know."

"Glad to hear it. Keegan finished his shift at the casino at eight o'clock. His body was found in a vacant parking lot about a mile away around nine-thirty. So, you still got no idea why he had your name?"

"I wouldn't have known him if he bit me on the ass."

"I hear you lawyers are into that," Griswold said. "Better watch out Keegan doesn't get you from the grave."

Two Galaxy employees murdered in one week was unusual enough. That they were both linked to Carol Hill was even more unlikely. That they were both linked to him was the trifecta of bad karma. Every rock turned over in this case uncovered something that made him look like a coconspirator.

Griswold and Cates suspected that Mason had known about the body in Fish's car. They had said as much when they first interviewed Fish.

Kelly Holt suspected that Mason knew Rockley was the murder victim since he had sent Blues to check out Rockley's apartment. She assumed that meant Fish was guilty, and she and Pete Samuelson were relying on that to pressure Fish to accept their offer of cooperation.

Now that they knew Rockley was the murder victim, the cops would find out about Carol Hill's lawsuit as soon as they talked to Al Webb and Lila Collins. It wouldn't take long for them to catch up to Mark Hill, who would happily spill the story about Mason and Blues bracing him in the parking lot at Easy's. Even though Mason and Blues hadn't identified themselves, the cops would make the connection from the descriptions Hill would provide.

Add Johnny Keegan to the mix, put Mason's name in his hand and a bullet in his head, and stand back. Mason was lucky the cops didn't take him downtown.

The truth was worse than what either the cops or the FBI believed. He could explain everything, make it all go away, and qualify for his civic duty merit badge. All he had to do was give up Vanessa Carter and himself. Then he realized how much worse the truth really was. If the cops found the tape of him asking Ed Fiori to blackmail Judge Carter and figured out that Rockley or Keegan were linked to the tape, Mason would shove Avery Fish from the top of the list of murder suspects.

Mason nearly tripped over Tuffy as he walked into the house. The sleeping dog yawned, rolled over, and opened one eye at him before going back to sleep.

He turned the light on in the kitchen, sat at the breakfast table, and massaged his temples, wondering if he could trade places with the dog. The message light on his answering machine was blinking. He pushed the play button and closed his eyes.

"I'm coming home for a few days. My plane gets in at ten, tomorrow morning. It would be nice if you could pick me up. Happy Valentine's Day," Abby Lieberman said.

"Perfect," Mason said to the dog. "Just perfect."

Mason wandered through the first floor of his house, stopping in the living room. The dining room table had been transplanted there to make room for his rowing machine. He sat at the head of the table, lights off, staring out the picture window at the street. Griswold and Cates had hit him with the photograph of Johnny Keegan's body hoping he'd slip and give them something they could use. Mason had taken the punch but disappointed them.

He didn't blame them for trying since Keegan had left this life clutching a scrap of paper with Mason's name on it.

Turning over the possibilities, Mason suspected that Keegan must have known about Mason and Judge Carter. He and Rockley could have been partners in the blackmail scam.

That scenario raised more questions. Was Keegan about to call Mason when he was killed? If so, why? Maybe Keegan had been planning to put the squeeze directly on Mason, leaving Mason to wonder if the killer was a homicidal guardian angel who had killed Keegan to protect Mason.

There was something else that didn't fit. Keegan was a bartender. Rockley was a middle manager. How did two guys from the rank and file get their hands on something as explosive as the tape of Ed Fiori's conversations with Vanessa Carter and with him?

Remembering that Mark Hill had all but blamed Rockley and Keegan for ruining his life, Mason pegged him as the early favorite for double-murderer of the week. If he was right, Carol Hill could be her husband's next victim.

He had been ready to convict Carol of being her husband's accomplice the minute Vince Bongiovanni assured him of her innocence. One murder later, Mason was worried that she was the third name on her husband's hit list. Not that those two scenarios were mutually exclusive.

He marveled at how little it took for him to slap the labels of innocent and guilty or killer and next victim on someone he'd yet to meet. It was no surprise then that the cops and the FBI didn't hesitate to brand Fish on less information. He dialed Bongiovanni's cell phone.

"Yeah," Bongiovanni answered.

Music and loud voices made it hard to hear. "It's Lou Mason. Where's Carol Hill?"

"How the hell should I know? I'm her lawyer, not her nanny," Bongiovanni shouted over the din.

"Johnny Keegan's body was found a couple of hours ago. Somebody blew the back of his head into next week."

Mason listened to the music, waiting for Bongiovanni to answer. It was hard-driving country. He didn't figure Bongiovanni for honky-tonk. He knew his phone call would raise questions he didn't want to answer, but that couldn't be helped. Not if he was right about Mark Hill. The music faded to a low buzz, heavy on the bass. Bongiovanni had found a quieter place to talk.

"What do you know about Johnny Keegan?" he asked Mason.

"Enough to tell you that if he and Charles Rockley end up dead in the same week, you better be damn sure you know where your client is and it better be someplace her husband can't find her."

"Are you telling me that Mark Hill killed Rockley and Keegan?"

"I'm telling you to take care of your client. One other thing. I can't make it tomorrow morning. How about two o'clock?"

"I'll make it work," Bongiovanni said. "And thanks for the heads-up."

CHAPTER TWENTY-EIGHT

MASON RETRIEVED SATURDAY morning's newspaper from the end of his driveway as Tuffy chased scents around the trees in the front yard. The air was crisp, the sky a Neapolitan blend of orange, pink, and blue layers as the sun edged over the horizon, promising a mild day, a teaser for the coming spring.

The couple that lived across the street came out their front door wearing matching jogging outfits, the husband leading their chocolate Lab on a leash twisted around his fist. They turned down the sidewalk, ignoring him. Tuffy bolted for a sniff of the Lab. The neighbors reined their dog in, casting a venomous look at Mason for keeping such an ill-mannered animal as they picked up their pace, putting distance between them.

Watching them run away, he replayed last night's conversation with Bongiovanni. He had jumped to the conclusion that Mark Hill had killed Rockley and Keegan out of jeal ousy and risked disclosure of his problems with Judge Carter to protect Carol. Ten hours later, he wasn't so certain. Hill may have killed Rockley and Keegan, but that didn't explain why he chose Avery Fish's car as Rockley's casket. Without that missing link, it was hard to tie the two murders together.

Rachel Firestone hadn't connected the murders either. Her story on Rockley was front page, below the fold. It was straightforward although the slant edged toward sensational. She reported that the police couldn't confirm the anonymous tip she'd received concerning the identity of the murder victim found in the trunk of Fish's car. They acknowledged that they had sent DNA samples to the FBI for identification but said they had yet to receive a report.

Despite the cops' equivocation, the Star considered the tip reliable enough to print the story naming Rockley as the victim. That meant Rachel had corroborated it with the only source that could—the FBI. Yet the article quoted spokesmen for the FBI and the U.S. attorney as having no comment. A Police Department spokesman also declined comment when she asked him if someone had leaked the story to embarrass the department.

The story was more about the cops getting scooped than either the killer or the victim, since she had nothing to report about them. She capped it off by tying Rockley back to Avery Fish's trunk and the mail fraud charges pending against Fish, adding Mason's no comment to the litany of those who should know something but claimed that they didn't. Anyone reading the story would conclude that the cops, the feds, and the lawyers were either morons or on drugs.

The story on Johnny Keegan was on the inside of the Metropolitan section of the paper, reported without a byline, one of several blurbs about overnight crimes committed in the city. Mason took no comfort in that. Rachel and the cops would make the connection soon enough.

He put the paper down and scratched Tuffy behind her ears. He still hadn't figured out what he would say when Bongiovanni asked him again how he knew about Johnny Keegan and Carol Hill. He had until the afternoon to figure that one out. Plenty of time.

CHAPTER TWENTY-NINE

Kansas City International Airport was on the northern edge of the city limits on a broad, flat plain that confirmed every stereotype about Midwestern topography. It was so far from the center of the city that people arriving for the first time often thought they had boarded the wrong plane or that they had been hijacked en route.

Its saving grace was a design that put the gates practically on the curb, allowing people to meet their friends and family as they got off the plane. It was an anomaly in an age of draconian airport security in which wheelchaired grandmothers were nearly strip-searched and travelers were forced to walk a mile to find a familiar face.

The layout also resulted in tightly knotted clusters of people converging like a mosh pit in front of the door from which passengers emerged. Abby's flight was full, which meant that the area in front of the gate was clotted with people waiting for its arrival. Young children clung to parents or darted between legs, stepping on toes until they were put in time-out. Old parents clung to middle-aged children, waiting for their grandchildren. Lovers stood on tiptoes, craning their heads, anticipation arching their backs.

Mason leaned against the wall opposite from where the passengers would appear. Surveying the crowd, he realized he didn't fit in any of these categories; such was the limbo in which his relationship with Abby lingered.

When she stepped through the gate, smiling and waving at him through gaps in the crowd, his heart quickened. She was carrying a coat over one arm and wearing black slacks and a bright red sweater, the contrast perfect with her porcelain skin. His glimpse of her erased months of doubt even though she'd asked for nothing more in her phone message than a ride from the airport and offered less in return. All she had said was that it would be nice if he could be there to meet her. That was enough for him.

Blues had once asked him if he wished that Abby was the only woman he'd ever loved. He wasn't certain how to answer, not regretting all his past relationships, just the ones of which he wasn't proud. Finally he answered, telling Blues no, but he hoped she was the last woman he would ever love.

They wedged through the crowd, joining hands as people swirled around them. She looked up at him, her eyes expectant, the corners of her mouth crinkled in a sly grin. She let go of one hand, brushing her dark bangs off her forehead, giving her head a shake and thumping him lightly on the chest.

"It's okay. You can kiss me."

He leaned down, their lips brushing, her mouth slightly parted. "You look terrific. I'm glad you called," he said, still holding her hand.

"And why not? You're cheaper than a cab," she teased. "Let's get my bag."

He waited until they pulled out of the parking garage to ask if she had more in mind than a free ride.

"How long will you be in town?"

"A week. I'm meeting with people in the senator's Kansas City office and a number of locals—contributors, politicians, that kind of thing. Plus I'm doing some advance work. Josh is the guest of honor at a civic award dinner next Saturday night."

Mason noted that she referred to Josh Seeley both as "the senator" and by his first name, blurring their professional and personal relationships. Senator Seeley was married and Abby was no home wrecker. Still, Mason hadn't been able to shake his own jealousy when he'd seen them together. Real or imagined, their relationship bothered him. He hadn't made an issue of it, realizing that Abby's refusal to live with the violence that surrounded his cases posed the biggest threat to their future. He was surprised by her phone call and thrilled by her warm greeting, but he hesitated to read too much into either.

"Sounds like a busy week."

"All in the service of our constituents," she added with a laugh. "The Missouri Republican Party is having its annual Lincoln Day fund-raiser tonight at the Westin in honor of Abe's birthday. The senator will be shaking hands until his fingers fall off. I could use a date." She raised her eyebrows and smiled at him as if to apologize for the past. "I know this is short notice and it's okay if you've got plans."

"You're in luck," he said, tucking his smile into his cheek in a failed effort to play it cool. "I'm fresh out of plans."

"Great. It's black-tie and cocktails are at six. Pick me up at five-thirty. I'm warning you, though. My job means that I show up early and stay late."

"I can do that. What are you doing the rest of the day?

Are you going to write speeches, mend fences with the voters, or clean your apartment?"

Abby turned in her seat, her back against the door. The light in her eyes gave the sun a run for its money. "Whatever you want."

CHAPTER THIRTY

Abby's apartment was in a high-rise north of the Plaza. She had rented it before she moved to Washington, telling Mason that politics was too temporary an existence to give up her home address. Besides, she liked the view from her tenth-floor balcony. The Nelson-Atkins Museum of Art lay at her feet, its expansive grounds populated with sculptures by Henry Moore mounted in the shadows of giant shuttlecocks deposited on the lawn.

She closed the door to her apartment and wrapped her arms around him, pulling his face to hers. She eased back, her eyes moist, and then laid her head against his chest. They slow danced through the small living room to the bedroom, twirling and falling onto her bed, fumbling with each other's clothes, laughing at their clumsiness. They soon found a familiar rhythm, their lovemaking easy and urgent.

Afterward, she lay on her side molded to him, her hand drawn as it always was to the scar on his chest. She traced the raised line of flesh with her fingertip like it was the missing piece to a treasure map. He hoped she wouldn't ask if the knife wound still hurt, not wanting to ruin the moment with memories he knew still woke her in the middle of the night.

He draped his arm across her shoulder, avoiding the scar on her neck, remembering how she shivered whenever he touched it. The same man had stabbed them both, leaving wounds that bound them together and drove them apart. She raised her head and pulled herself to his chest, kissing his scar, leaving a tear behind.

"Whew," she said, sitting up and pressing her back against the headboard. "That's what I call a ride home from the airport."

He propped himself up next to her. “No point in asking for a tip, huh?”

She grinned at him. “Not unless you’re ready for a round- trip.”

“I left the meter running.”

“Save your strength. I’ll be here all week. I’m going to clean up.”

He lay in bed trying not to overanalyze the last two hours. He didn’t want to know whether it was love or lust or whether she missed him or was just lonely. They were adults with a history and, he hoped, lovers with a future. He heard the shower come on and joined her.

Winter always took a few days off in Kansas City, sprinkling the city with occasional days of unseasonable warmth. This was such a day, the afternoon warming into an imposter of summer. Abby and Mason had lunch on the Plaza, picked up Tuffy, and went on a long walk in Loose Park. People flew kites and picnicked. Some true believers spread blankets and sunblock, stealing a winter tan.

They walked the perimeter of the park, sat on benches in the Rose Garden, and guessed at the color of the blooms that would surface in the spring. He watched her, delighting in the way she chased the dog, and then laughed at him for trailing behind, teasing him about middle age. He was forty- three and she was thirty-seven.

“If you split the difference, we’re the same age,” he told her.

“Yeah, right,” she said, poking him in the arm and whistling at Tuffy. The dog crouched, tossed her head at Abby, and took off toward the pond that lay along Wornall Road on the east side of the park. Abby chased her again.

Mason caught up to them on the arched bridge spanning the south end of the pond. Tuffy sat between them, her tail thumping on the wooden slats. Abby leaned over the rail, watching geese stroke through the water, the sun painting gold the ripples they left on the surface.

Mason brought her up to date about the other people in his life. Harry’s eyesight was worse, not better. They called it macular degeneration for a reason. He’d given up driving and had gotten used to audiobooks, but that didn’t ease the frustration of a shrinking world. Claire was still waging war against the rich and powerful, filing lawsuits and serving subpoenas on behalf of her disadvantaged clients. Blues played piano at the bar on Wednesday and Friday and wasn't seeing anyone special. Rachel Firestone was chasing the ghost of Woodward and Bernstein, and she wasn't seeing anyone special either since breaking up with her girlfriend. Neither was he, he would have told Abby had she asked.

Washington, she said, was exciting and boring, though nothing about it bored Mickey Shanahan. The Senate was too clubby, almost calcified, but the aroma of power was intoxicating and everywhere. Josh Seeley was a freshman senator, meaning that he was in the outermost of inner circles. They were doing important work, but it was impossible to get anything important done. Politicians needed both hands, one to take the money and the other to scratch the backs of those who gave it. And, it was all about the money.

Her hours were too long for any real fun. She'd been to the White House but not the Smithsonian. She'd gone to parties at embassies but rarely to dinner with friends, of whom she'd made a few but no one special. "Sorry to hear it," he said, not meaning it at all.

They didn't talk about anything that threatened the fragile balance of a perfect day. She didn't ask about his practice, what cases he was working on, or whether anyone had swung or shot at him. He assumed that she knew about Avery Fish from reading the Kansas City Star, as keeping up from a distance was part of her job; but since she didn't ask, he didn't offer. He didn't ask about her relationship with Seeley, whether she had renewed the lease on her Kansas City apartment, or whether she wanted to get married as long as she was in town for a week.

Standing on the narrow bridge, they ran out of safe topics. He put his arm around her and she leaned in to him.

"Nice day," he said.

"The nicest in a long time."

"There aren't many days like this during the winter."

"Or ever."

"So..."

"So," she said, spinning away. "Let's not ruin it. Okay?"

Mason dropped Abby at her apartment and drove home, remembering as he pulled into the driveway that he'd forgotten his two o'clock meeting with

Vince Bongiovanni and Carol Hill. He called Bongiovanni's cell phone, leaving a lame message that something unexpected had come up and asking him to reschedule again. He left his cell phone number and told Bongiovanni to call as soon as possible. That was better than saying he'd spent the day thinking with his little head instead of his big head, though he imagined Bongiovanni would be more sympathetic to the truth than to his apology.

He had less than a week to find a way out of the wilderness Judge Carter had thrown him into, and blowing off a chance to meet with a critical witness was not the way to do it. That he had forgotten the appointment was either a measure of the hold Abby had on him or a sad commentary on his hormonal weakness.

His phone rang as he finished his second shower of the day. He stumbled into his bedroom, dripping and wearing a towel. He stubbed his toe against the dresser next to his bed and was cursing as he picked up the phone.

"Damn!"

"Such a warm greeting," Claire Mason said. "Much better than saying hello. I'll have to try it next time I want to impress someone."

Claire was his mentor and his conscience. She had raised him, shaped him, and kicked him in the ass when he needed it. Nearly his height, big boned, and strong, she had always been up to that task. She had an earthy sense of humor and was as devoted to him as he was to her.

Mason sat on the edge of his bed, rubbing his throbbing toe. "Sorry."

"Are you sorry that you didn't return my call from yesterday inviting you to dinner on Sunday or that you swore in my ear? Or are you just sorry in general?"

"All three, but I'm sorrier that I jammed my toe into the dresser as I was answering the phone."

"Apology accepted. If it's broken, tape it to the toe next to it. In the future, try wearing shoes or watching where you are going. Either one will work. Are you coming to dinner?"

"Sorry. I'm having dinner with a client."

"Two apologies in one conversation. You're getting soft. I hope the client is a nice Jewish girl."

"He's an old Jewish man if that counts for anything."

"Avery Fish?"

"The same." Approximately twenty thousand Jews lived in Kansas City, far too many for everyone to know everyone else, but few enough that it didn't take long to find someone who did. "You know him?"

Claire didn't ask Mason about his cases, understanding the boundaries of client confidentiality. If he asked for her advice, she offered it. Though Fish's case had received a lot of press, she hadn't mentioned it to him.

"I haven't seen him in years."

"He's an interesting guy. In a lot of ways, he's the opposite of you."

"Really? How so?"

"He goes to the synagogue every day, keeps kosher, and doesn't work on the Sabbath—all those things you don't have time for. But he's a crook. You spend every waking moment trying to heal the world but wouldn't make a collect call to God even if He'd accept the charges."

"If that's how I have to be compared to Avery Fish, I'll gladly accept that comparison."

"I gather you haven't missed him all these years. Why not?"

"He's not to be trusted and doesn't deserve you as his lawyer. Let's leave it at that. I'd rather you were having dinner with a nice Jewish girl."

"That's tonight. Abby is in town."

"Good. Try not to screw it up this time."

CHAPTER THIRTY-ONE

THE WESTIN HOTEL was part of the Crown Center complex stretching from Twenty-seventh Street north to Pershing, filling the blocks between Main Street on the west and McGee on the east. Crown Center had been the brainchild of Hallmark Cards, one of Kansas City's homegrown success stories. The company headquarters were already there so it had made perfect sense to develop the surrounding area into an office, hotel, and retail center. It was a solid pocket of commerce between downtown and the Country Club Plaza. The nearby Union Station and the lofts and art galleries of the Crossroads District provided eclectic neighbors.

The hotel was massive and upscale, geared to conventions and other large gatherings. Its signature feature was a three- story indoor waterfall cascading through a faux rainforest. The Missouri Republican Party had booked four adjoining ballrooms on the third floor for its Lincoln Day lovefest. The undulating perimeter of the expansive foyer outside the ballrooms overlooked the indoor Amazon. Escalators rose from the lobby to the ballrooms, cross-cutting the tropical landscape.

It was still early when Mason and Abby arrived ahead of the guests and dignitaries. Her counterparts on the staffs of the state Republican Party and the other elected officials scurried about tending to last-minute details. Servers dressed in white waist-cut formal jackets stood in a half-moon circle listening to final instructions from their supervisors. In a far corner, a Dixieland band tuned up.

Abby looked elegant in a shimmering black dress woven with flecks of silver. She pushed back the three-quarterlength sleeves.

"Duty calls. I'll catch up to you in a bit," she said and power walked toward a cluster of her compatriots.

Half a dozen bars had been assembled along the outskirts of the foyer. Three long tables dressed in patriotic bunting were aligned end-to-tend in front of the ballrooms. A team of attractive young women, evenly divided between blondes and brunettes, all possessing brightly bleached teeth, sparkling eyes, and distracting cleavage, waited behind the tables ready to dispense name tags that included the guests' names, company affiliations, political offices, or other designations of their station in life.

Mason checked the name tags beginning with the letter M, not surprised when he didn't find one with his name on it. Abby hadn't invited him until earlier that day and he was glad she wasn't so confident that she had ordered a name tag for him. He declined the offer of a Magic Marker and a blank tag, preferring anonymity.

He peeked into the ballrooms. Tables for ten were crammed together. Doing a quick count, he estimated there would be close to a thousand people. Satisfied it was a crowd he could easily get lost in, he found a bartender with a ready smile who twisted the cap off a bottle of beer like he was glad to do it. Mason parked himself within an arm's reach of his new best friend, gripped the icy bottle, and took a measured sip. It was going to be a long night.

The foyer gradually filled until it was a sea of men in black tuxes and women wearing designer gowns, the air filled with no-contact kisses and firm handshakes. Conversation buzzed around Mason, punctuated by laughs too loud for the jokes being told but perfect for the money being contributed. Such were the privileges of membership in the club.

Mason always voted but rarely contributed to campaigns, telling Claire it was risky enough to trust a candidate with his vote, let alone his money. Claire was a straight-ticket Democrat and chided Mason for failing to have any real convictions. He told her that he'd seen too many politicians with criminal convictions to put much faith in the political variety.

After a while, he abandoned his post and went to look for Abby. The place was thick with lawyers, more than a few throwing their arms over his shoulder telling him they were glad that he was there and that the party could use his support. He spun free of their grasp, telling them that he was freeloading and that no political party could long survive with him as a member. He saw no sign of Abby and gave up for the moment, making his way back to his friendly bartender.

"Mason! You're about the last person I expected to see here," someone said before he could get to the bar.

The voice came from behind him, though he had no trouble recognizing it. He turned around. It was Patrick Ortiz. Dressed in his tux, Ortiz had the clothes for the high rollers but couldn't shake the rumpled look that juries loved. He tugged at his bow tie, ill at ease in his outfit and his surroundings.

He was with a woman Mason assumed to be his wife. She was short, coppery skinned with bright eyes and dark hair. Her arm was wrapped comfortably over his, a plain gold band on her left hand.

"Business is slow. What better place to meet people likely to be charged with a crime than at a political fund-raiser?" He nodded to the woman, extending his hand. "I'm Lou Mason."

"I know," she said. "I'm Maggie Ortiz."

"My campaign manager," Ortiz said. "She makes me come to all these events."

"I tell him he can stay home if he doesn't want to run again," she said. "He loves to prosecute, but he hates to politick."

"But I'm getting used to it. There's the governor," he said, looking past Mason. "We better go say hello."

They were gone before Mason could buttonhole Ortiz and ask him if there was anything new on Rockley's murder. He didn't expect Ortiz to tell him, but he might learn something from Ortiz's denial. No didn't always mean no. The way it was said and the body language that went with it were like radio traffic and troop movements—intelligence to be analyzed.

The crowd surrounding Mason melted away as if the tide had gone out, the current depositing a cluster of fresh faces. One of them belonged to a man who looked to be in his early fifties, though his hair was too dark to be natural. His eyes flicked across the crowd, his long face a barely lined serpentine mask. The skin beneath his chin was loose, his neck weathered, the contrast exposing that he'd had a facelift that had taken ten years off his appearance if you didn't look too closely.

He was bony through the shoulders and sleek through the middle like a distance runner without the healthy glow; his skin was a subnormal chalk. His hands and fingers were elongated, as if he had stretched them while reaching for something—perfect for surgeons and stranglers. He ignored Mason, who read the man's name tag—Al Webb, General Manager, Galaxy Casino.

CHAPTER THIRTY-TWO

Feeling Mason's stare, Webb gave him a quick look and a dismissive nod. Mason knew the combination was code for I see you, but I don't want to talk to you. Mason responded with a broad smile and outstretched hand that said I know and I don't give a shit.

"I'm Lou Mason," he said, holding his ground until Webb shook his hand.

"Al Webb."

"At least they got your name tag right," Mason said, forcing the conversation. "They didn't have one for me."

Webb quit doing crowd reconnaissance and focused on Mason, taking his measure. "Maybe you weren't invited," Webb said with a wounded smile and a soothing voice.

The warm, rich timbre of Webb's voice surprised Mason and blunted the sting of his comment. Mason wondered if Webb had cultivated his voice to compensate for his bloodless countenance. Man-made or natural, Webb's voice was a weapon of mass deception.

"Actually, I wasn't. I'm a guest of someone who was invited."

"That's better than buying an invitation. Mine cost a thousand dollars," Webb deadpanned. He made it a charming self-deprecation, now drawing Mason close rather than pushing him away.

"I'd rather spend that kind of money at the craps table. I'll take my chances against the house over a politician's promise any day of the week."

Webb laughed. "Then you're the kind of gambler that keeps me in business."

"I thought it was the gamblers who can't resist betting on the long shots."

Webb shook his head. "Gamblers who play the long shots are either hopelessly optimistic or secretly suicidal. I don't understand them, but I'm grateful for them. Frankly, I wish there were more of them. Personally, I prefer the sporting player who understands the game. He accepts the odds, understands when he loses, and doesn't take too much credit when he wins. That's why he keeps coming back. The others don't last long enough."

Mason looked at him, the honey in Webb's voice dulling Mason's instinctively suspicious reaction to him. He was an unpleasant-looking man who'd added youth but not attraction to his appearance. His short dissertation on gambling sounded more like a parable about life than a beginner's guide to dice.

"You know who I am?"

"We don't sell newspapers in the casino, but I do read them. Were you looking for me or did you just get lucky?"

"Dumb luck. The only kind I have these days. One of your employees ends up dead in the trunk of my client's car and you and I end up at the same party talking about it. Are those odds optimistic or suicidal?"

"It doesn't matter since we aren't talking about it. I wouldn't take them either way."

"I'd like to talk to you about Charles Rockley."

"I don't blame you. But it's a police matter and I can't involve my company in your client's problems."

"Rockley was your employee. Doesn't that make his murder your problem?"

"We have hundreds of employees. Somebody is always getting married, getting divorced, getting sick, or getting well. Some of them die. We send them all a card."

"Who are you sending a card to for Rockley?"

Webb put one hand in his pants pocket, running his other hand across his chest and under his neck. "I don't know anything about his family. My HR director takes care of that."

"Sure," Mason said. "All those employees. Must be hard for you to get to know every one of them."

"It's part of my job. I do the best I can."

"But you knew Charles Rockley better than most because another one of your employees, Carol Hill, sued him and Galaxy for sexual harassment. Vince Bongiovanni told me all about it."

Webb blinked once, his only concession to the card Mason had played. "Then you should talk to Mr. Bongiovanni. He doesn't have to keep personnel matters confidential. I do."

"How about Johnny Keegan? Let's talk about him. What are the odds that two of your employees would be murdered in the same week and that one of them was having an affair with Carol Hill and the other one wished he was?"

Webb cocked his head at Mason, applying a thin smile, his voice dropping to a frozen register. "Too long for you to play them," he said.

CHAPTER THIRTY-THREE

WEBB WALKED PAST Mason before he could respond, the crowd swallowing him. Mason parsed their conversation, looking for what was meant even if it hadn't been said. Webb had a ready answer to Mason's questions about Rockley. No doubt the cops had been to see him and Webb surely had told them about Carol Hill's sexual harassment claim. All that made sense. And it made sense that Mason would take advantage of their meeting to ask Webb about Rockley. Webb could anticipate all that and be ready for Mason's questions knowing he'd have to answer them sooner or later.

Webb wasn't ready to talk about Johnny Keegan, although the cops would have tied Keegan back to Galaxy by now—probably talked to Webb, maybe even told Webb that Mason's name had been found on a piece of paper in Keegan's dead hand. They would have asked Webb what he knew about Keegan, Webb saying not much, that his HR director would send a card. Then, Mason wondered, why did Webb's temperature drop when he asked him about Keegan?

Unable to answer his question, Mason elbowed and shouldered his way past pockets of people, renewing his search for Abby. He reached the center of the foyer without finding her, pressing on toward the name tag tables. He was about to ask one of the young women if she'd seen Abby when he saw Lari Prillman pick up her name tag.

She was a head shorter than Mason; her harvest-colored hair was swept back, a stunning white gold and diamond chain cradling her bare neck. Her dress was off the shoulder, the look favoring her well-toned arms and slender frame. She was older than Mason, five to ten years, he guessed, but she hadn't conceded anything to the calendar. She looked fresh, full, and vital, carrying herself with the square- shouldered assurance of a woman who knew it. Mason had never met her but understood the lasting impression she made on clients and jurors.

"You don't have one," she said to him.

"One what?" Mason asked.

"A name tag. I hate these bloody things. I can't pin it on a dress like this without stabbing my breast. Here," she said, returning the name tag to the woman who'd given it to her. "Save it for next time."

"I'm Lou Mason."

"Lari Prillman," she said, extending her hand.

"I know. I read your name tag."

He shook her hand. Her grasp was cool and firm, though she quickly let go.

"And I've read your press clippings. You represent Avery Fish. I would have been here earlier except the police stopped by to tell me that an employee of one of my clients was found dead in the trunk of your client's car. Is our meeting a coincidence or were you looking for me?"

"Your client asked me the same thing not ten minutes ago."

"Al and I are sitting at the same table tonight. I'll have to remind him not to talk to lawyers. What did you tell him?"

He smiled. She didn't. He cocked his head, tried the smile again. She didn't melt. He'd blown the chance to talk with Carol Hill earlier in the day, hadn't learned much from Al Webb, and didn't want to waste his chance with Lari Prill- man. Charm wasn't working. Pragmatism might.

"Our meeting is strictly coincidence, but opportunity is usually like that. Your client is too good a poker player to have told me anything. But you and I may be able to help each other."

She smiled at last. "Straightforward answers and a straightforward proposition. I like that. It's a little crowded here. Let's find someplace to talk."

Mason followed her through the crowd. She managed to greet and be greeted without slowing down as people made way for her. They took the escalator down two flights to the lobby, finding a pair of softly padded leather chairs angled on either side of a pie-slice-shaped table hidden in a far corner of the bar. A lamp muted by an opaque shade separated and shadowed them. They couldn't have had more privacy unless they rented a room.

"What did Al Webb really tell you?" she asked Mason.

"Not much. He said his HR director sends out lots of cards to the employees. You should tell him that doesn't count as a fringe benefit. I was hoping you'd tell me something useful about Charles Rockley."

"I'll tell you what I told the police. Charles Rockley worked for the Galaxy Casino for the last year. No one at Galaxy knows anything about his murder, and no one has ever heard of Mr. Fish."

"That's very helpful. Saves me the trouble of asking all those employees what they know about Rockley and my client. Must be a couple of thousand of them. The cops tell you about Rockley while you're getting dressed for the party and you manage to interview all of the employees and still make it here on time. That's good work."

She clenched her jaw, straining her makeup.

"I charge my clients too much money to screw around every time an employee gets into trouble, and I contribute too much to the Republican Party to spend my evening trading shots with you. A gaming company can't afford to be drawn into a murder investigation. I can't help you with yours. Nice to meet you," she said, and stood, ready to go.

"How about two murder investigations?"

She looked down at him, the color fading from her cheeks for an instant before she recovered. Her eyes narrowed.

"I'm listening."

"A bartender who worked at the Galaxy named Johnny Keegan was killed last night after he got off work."

She drew a short breath at the mention of Keegan's name. "The police didn't say anything about that."

"Imagine that; the police not telling a lawyer everything. You and your client should have a lot to talk about over dinner. Did you give the police Rockley's personnel file?"

"I told them we'd respond to a subpoena."

"Just the kind of cooperation the cops love. Make them jump through hoops. That's what you call not screwing around. You'll get a subpoena Monday morning for everything Galaxy has on Rockley and Keegan. They won't just draw you and your client into these murders; they'll shrink- wrap you in them."

She planted a hand on her hip. "If you've got something to say, get to the point. I paid for that rubber chicken dinner upstairs."

"Vince Bongiovanni told me that Rockley, Keegan, and Carol Hill were playing she loves me, she loves me not. Carol said loves me to Keegan and loves me not to Rockley. Rockley was a sore loser. Carol sued Rockley and Galaxy for sexual harassment."

"If you talked to Vince then you know I defended the case for Galaxy. The arbitration was last week. We'll have a decision next month."

"Then you know that Carol's husband is seriously pissed. Both boyfriends end up dead. It won't take the cops long to connect the dots."

"From what I read in the paper, they've already connected Rockley's dots to your client. Why do I care if he or the husband did it?"

"Sometimes the sure thing is a sucker bet. The cops are going to be crawling all over your client's boat and your office as soon as they can get a judge to sign the search warrants. I'd clear my calendar for next week if I was you."

She took her seat again and leaned toward him, the glow of the lamp softening her features. "What do you want?"

"I want to see those files before the cops do."

"Why?"

"Whoever killed Rockley dumped the body in my client's car. There may be something in them that helps me find out why."

"And how does that help my client?"

"It might not. I won't know until I see the files. If there's nothing in there that points to someone besides Carol Hill's husband, the cops will treat the whole thing as a cheap domestic drama. That's good for my client and it keeps Galaxy out of the mix except for the bad luck of hiring those losers."

"Then I should give the police what they want and tell you to piss off."

Mason smiled, this time drawing a venomous one from her. "Unless the cops are wrong about my client and the husband. Then it's all about Galaxy. We both need to know what's in those files."

"You forget. I already know what's in the files."

"You were defending a sexual harassment case. This is murder. Everything looks different."

She studied him for a moment, giving nothing away. If she knew about the conversations Fiori taped with him and Judge Carter, she wouldn't let him see the files. It would make more sense to cooperate with the police than give Mason access to anything. Especially after she found out that Keegan had died with his hand around Mason's name and phone number—something Mason assumed she would eventually learn.

"After dinner," she said. "Meet me at my office." She opened her purse, handed him a business card, and left him sitting in the shadows.

CHAPTER THIRTY-FOUR

By the time Mason got back upstairs, the crowd was streaming into the ballroom, people threading their way among the closely packed tables. Abby found him, her eyes wide, breathing like she'd just finished a set of wind sprints.

"I've been looking all over for you," she said. "Where have you been?"

"Makes us even. I was looking for you until I was buttonholed by another lawyer wanting to talk about a case. She dragged me downstairs to the lobby and held me hostage."

"She?" Abby asked, arching an eyebrow.

"Jealous?"

"If she wants you, she can have you," Abby answered, the gleam in her eye exposing the playful lie. "C'mon, I want you to meet someone."

The head table was set on a raised dais at the front of the ballroom. As Abby led Mason closer he recognized the mayor, a couple of city councilmen, a few state representatives, a congressman, the governor, and Senator Josh Seeley, most of whom were accompanied by their spouses. The highest-ranking office holders were at the center of the table with lesser lights strung out to the end. Patrick Ortiz and his wife were at the end of the table next to the stairs leading up to the stage. Mason clapped him on the shoulder as he followed Abby toward the senator and his wife.

Mason had never met Seeley. He hadn't purposely avoided it, but he hadn't pursued the opportunity either. Mason and Abby had still been together when she started working on Seeley's primary campaign. He'd told her that he was too busy when she invited him to campaign events, which was sometimes true. The rest of the truth was that he would rather have a tooth pulled slowly than stand in a crowd and shout slogans or be solicited for a contribution while chitchatting about core values over cocktails.

Later, when his relationship with Abby hit the skids, there were no invitations to decline. Instead, he watched her on television, hovering at Seeley's shoulder; throwing her arms around his neck on election night. Seeley was married, his wife a good-looking woman with high cheekbones and knowing eyes she burned into the back of her husband's head as he and Abby embraced. At least that was the way Mason read the scene. He suppressed his jealousy, hopeful that Abby wouldn't sleep with a married man, especially one who was her boss and a United States senator.

None of which made Mason look forward to the meeting that was about to happen. Seeley rose from his chair. He was taller than Mason, his silver hair, blue eyes, and dimpled chin straight out of central casting. Mrs. Seeley kept her seat, the temperature at her chair hovering at the freezing mark.

"Abby," the senator said, grasping her by the shoulders, then quickly letting go when his wife shot him a glance.

"Wonderful job on the arrangements, as always. Introduce me to your friend."

"Senator and Mrs. Seeley. I'd like you to meet my boyfriend, Lou Mason."

"Boyfriend," Seeley boomed, shaking his hand. "Good for you, Mason. I was worried that Abby was going to wither away in the service of my constituents."

Seeley had been a wealthy businessman before running for the Senate, his first shot at elective office. Some said he bought the election. Others said every candidate buys their election; Seeley just used his own money. Seeley was in his early sixties, the current Mrs. Seeley his second wife and ten years his junior. Mason wondered if she'd earned her position at the expense of the first Mrs. Seeley, making her naturally suspicious.

Mason didn't blame her, especially since Abby had never once introduced him to anyone as her boyfriend. It was a term he bet she hadn't used since the eighth grade, and her use of it now made him feel the fool, more so in light of their recent rocky history. She had brought him to the dinner to calm the fears of her boss's nervous wife. He didn't know whether the fears were justified, only that he wanted no part of this charade. He wondered if their afternoon delight had been part of the script or whether Abby had ad-libbed that to give her performance tonight the ring of truth.

He wanted to punch the senator in the mouth, yank Abby off the stage, and get the hell out of Dodge, with apologies to Mrs. Seeley. Abby slid her arm around his, squeezing it. He felt the plea in her grip and swallowed hard.

"Nice to meet you, Senator," he said, matching Seeley's grin and grip. Turning to Mrs. Seeley, he added, "A pleasure," and offered her his hand.

She looked up at him, her lips pursed. "You're the boyfriend?"

"So I'm told."

"Be careful what you wish for," she said and turned away.

Abby murmured to him as they walked to their table. "Thank you. I'll explain later."

He didn't reply because a formal dinner with one thousand of his closest friends was not exactly the time or place for a come-to-Jesus session with Abby. He chewed his food slowly so that he wouldn't drink as much as he wanted to, though getting drunk was more appealing than the chicken Kiev he was pushing around his plate.

Lari Prillman was the other reason he didn't get drunk. He surveyed the room, catching a glimpse of her at a table several rows away from his. Al Webb sat next to her, their heads tilted together, Lari pointing her index finger at his chest like it was a steak knife. He looked their way again somewhere between the salad and the chicken. Webb was gone.

He kept tabs on Lari throughout the evening but still maintained a passable line of small talk with the accountant sitting on one side of him while avoiding eye contact with Abby. Dessert was served at ten o'clock, the speeches moments away. Lari stood and looked directly at him as if she'd been watching him the entire evening as well.

"Is that her?" Abby asked.

"Who?"

"The woman who just gave you that look. Is she the lawyer you were talking with earlier?"

"I didn't realize you were paying such close attention."

"Since you've hardly spoken to me all evening, I've got to pay attention. What's eating you?"

Mason pushed back from table, dipping his chin, keeping his voice low. "Look, I don't know what's going on between you and Seeley..."

"Nothing's going on!"

Mason nodded, trying to read her, afraid that he couldn't. "I'm sorry. I've got to go. You'll have to take a cab home," he said, getting up.

She stood next to him, taking his hand. "Will you call me?"

He squeezed her hand and let go without answering.

CHAPTER THIRTY-FIVE

MASON PULLED LARI Prillman's business card from his pocket, pleased that her office was in one of the Crown Center high-rises. He could walk there, maybe even get back before the speeches were over and sort things out with Abby.

Lari was waiting for him outside the ballroom, a fur coat slung over one arm. She held it out to him so he could help her put it on. It was a polite gesture he couldn't refuse and a subtle reminder that this was her show, not his.

"I hope I didn't disrupt your evening," she said as they walked outside, the air sharp, the afternoon warmth an uncertain memory, distant stars lost in a fog of ground light.

"Not at all."

"Your friend didn't look too happy to see you go."

Mason let out an exasperated breath, the cold crystallizing, then vaporizing his frustration. "How do women do that?"

"Do what?"

"I told the woman I was with—her name is Abby—that I'd talked with a lawyer, a woman lawyer, earlier in the evening about a case. She saw you stand up and look at me, and she knows you were the woman. You take one look at her and tell me she isn't happy."

Lari laughed. "Women pay attention to things men don't."

"Like what?"

"The way a man looks at a woman or tries not to look at her; the way a man talks to a woman or avoids talking to her."

"You were paying attention, weren't you?"

"I pay attention to everything. That's why I'm letting you look at my files. I'll be surprised if I've missed something important. If I did, I'd rather know now than after the police have their look."

Her office was on the twenty-ninth floor, the name of her firm—Prillman & Associates—scripted in gold leaf on the double glass doors. She knelt to unlock the dead bolt at the base of the door. She steadied herself with one hand on the glass, nearly falling over when the door gave way before she could insert the key into the lock. Mason grabbed her by the shoulder, helping her steady herself. They stepped inside, stopping at the reception desk, listening to the silence.

"One of your associates working late?" Mason asked her.

"Not unless we're in trial, and we aren't."

"Do you have an alarm?"

She shook her head. "The building is secure. You have to sign in after hours and you can't get to our floor without knowing the security code for the elevator."

"Maybe the last one to leave the office today forgot to lock the door."

"That was me and I didn't forget."

"How much space do you have?"

"Four attorney offices. Mine is the corner office at the back. Two paralegal offices, secretarial stations, filing room, and kitchen. About twenty-five hundred square feet altogether."

"Room to roam. Let's call the security desk. Have them send someone up before we go wandering around."

Lari frowned, pushed out her lower lip, and patted him on the cheek. "Don't worry. If some creep is snooping around my office, he's going to find my shoe up his ass."

She dropped her fur over the back of a chair, marched past the reception desk, flipping light switches as she went. Mason glanced at the receptionist's phone, his attention drawn by a blinking light indicating one of the lines was in use. The light blinked off.

He caught up to Lari as she was halfway down the hall, pulled her to his side, and held a finger to her lips. She opened her mouth in protest and he covered it with his hand.

"Don't make a sound," he whispered, biting off the words, leaving no room for argument. "Someone is back there. They were using a phone and hung up when they heard us."

The lights she had turned on suddenly went off, plunging the corridor into darkness. The doors to the lawyers' offices were closed, shutting out any exterior light. The entrance to the file room was directly across from them, a black abyss.

A red pinprick of light bounced off Lari's forehead. Mason heard the muffled spit of a silencer as he yanked her to the floor in the same instant a bullet exploded above them, shards of drywall stinging their eyes.

Mason lay on top of her, his mind racing with their limited options. He raised his head to gauge the distance to the front door. Another bullet whizzed past his head, flattening him against her. Either the shooter was wearing night vision goggles or he was taking random shots. Mason lay perfectly still, trying to shrink the target. Lari didn't move, though he could feel her chest slamming against his, her hands balled against his sides.

Lari wasn't dressed for running, especially in a crouch while trying to evade gunfire. The shooter would assume they would run for the door and lay down fire in the hallway. It wouldn't take long to find them if they hid in one of the offices, and twenty-nine floors was a long way down even if he could break a window. That left the file room, which would also be a trap unless it had another entrance he could use to get behind the shooter. Even if he could somehow do that, he had a better chance playing blindman's bluff than taking out a killer with night vision.

With Mason shielding Lari's body as best he could, they snaked into the file room, the smooth linoleum floor easing their passage. He felt for an aisle between two rows of shelves. She belly crawled ahead of him, crouching at the end of the row. He knelt next to her, their eyes adjusted to the darkness enough that they could make out each other's faces. He touched her cheek and she held his wrist, her grip firm.

Mason heard footsteps trot down the hall, stopping where they had entered the file room. He couldn't find another way out without giving himself away. They were trapped at the end of the aisle.

He couldn't judge the line of sight from the hallway to their hiding place, but he could hear someone breathing; slow, steady, and controlled. A red beam danced overhead, methodically dissecting the rows of files, searching for them. They pressed themselves against the cool tile, desperate to blend into the darkness. The beam angled to the floor, fixing on a point inches from them. Mason spread himself across Lari, sweat running in his eyes, waiting for it to find them and the bullets that would follow, not moving, hating even to breathe.

Minutes passed before Mason realized the breathing and footsteps had disappeared from the hallway. He slid a thin file off the shelf and edged it toward the beam, deflecting the light without getting shot. He raised the file in the air, slowly waving it back and forth, tossing it to the floor with the realization of what had happened. The shooter had herded them into the file room so that he could pin them down and escape. The beam that had paralyzed them was probably from a laser pointer left behind, tying them up more securely than a square knot.

"Where's the fuse box?" Mason asked.

"Inside a utility closet at the far end of the hall."

He found the laser pointer wedged between files on a nearby shelf, leaving it alone in the unlikely event it carried the shooter's fingerprints. He found the hallway, turned to his right, and felt his way along the wall. Once inside the utility closet, he fumbled with the circuit breakers until he found the right one, shuddering with relief when the lights came back on.

He ran back to the file room, nearly colliding with Lari as she made her way toward her office, ducking past her and continuing on to the front door. He relocked the dead bolt and did a slow circuit of all the offices. They were alone. He found Lari sitting behind her desk, an open bottle of scotch in her lap.

"It's okay," Mason said. "He's gone."

"I thought we were going to die."

"It was our lucky day. He just wanted to get out of here without getting caught. He shot at us to force us into the file room and out of the way, not to kill us."

"Well," she said, hoisting the bottle to her lips and taking a drink. "He succeeded admirably."

Mason looked around. Her office, like the rest of the offices, appeared untouched. Nothing had been ransacked, no papers tossed like confetti in a wild search for something special. The computers hummed, unharmed and unhacked.

"We must have surprised him before he could find whatever he was looking for."

Lari set the bottle on her desk and stood, hands on hips. She was a bit unsteady, whether from fear or booze, Mason couldn't tell. She straightened her dress, walked across her office, and took down a painting that hid a wall safe. She spun the lock to the right, then to the left, and then back to the right. The door swung open. The small vault was empty.

"I wouldn't be so certain," she said.

CHAPTER THIRTY-SIX

"WHAT WAS IN the safe?"

Lari shook her head, moving slowly back to her desk, picking up the bottle of scotch as she sat down, cradling it to her bosom. "I don't know."

Mason leaned over her, one hand on her bare shoulder, the other on the scotch. He gently pried her fingers from the neck of the bottle, setting it on the desk out of her reach. Her skin was warm. She leaned her cheek against his hand. She was used to fighting battles with different rules of engagement. No wounds were mortal and money forgave all sins. No one had ever shot at her.

"Stick with me, Lari. Whoever did this is gone. If he took something from your safe, you've got to tell me what it was."

There was a framed photograph on her desk of two teenage girls, faces full of promise. She picked it up, caressing the images.

"I don't know."

"Does anyone else have the combination to the safe?"

"I'm the only one."

He took the photograph from her and swiveled her chair hard around toward him, leaning in close again. "Then how could you not know what was in the safe?"

She closed her eyes, summoning her courtroom muscle. She opened them with a glare that backed him off. Mason retreated, relieved at her recovery.

"A client," she began, hesitating as she assembled her answer, "gave me something to keep in my safe. I wasn't told what it was."

"You didn't ask?"

"I only asked whether it was anything illegal, like drugs. I was assured that it wasn't so I agreed to store it."

"Who was the client? Someone at Galaxy?"

Lari folded her arms across her chest. "You know better than to ask."

"You'll have to tell the cops. You might as well tell me."

"Who says the police have to know anything about this?"

Mason pointed down the hall from her office. "Someone broke in here, shot at you, and stole something belonging to your client and you're not going to report it to the police?"

"If my client instructs me to file a burglary report, I will, though I doubt that will happen. If my client didn't want me to know what was in my safe, I don't expect my client will want the police to know either. As for the burglary, I'll get a better lock. Maybe an alarm system as you suggested."

Mason sighed in surrender. "Have it your way. What about your files on Rockley and Keegan? I might as well have a look as long as I'm here."

She stood, still rocky but regaining command. "I'll be back in a few minutes."

Mason waited, taking in the view from the twenty-ninth floor. A long line of cars poured out of the Westin's parking garage. The party was over. Cabs waited in front of the hotel.

Mason pressed against the glass, wondering which one Abby was in.

Lari returned with two manila folders, one labeled Rock- ley, Charles and the other Keegan, Johnny. The name of the case to which the files belonged was printed on the side of the folders—Hill v. Galaxy Gaming, Inc. She handed them to Mason, reclaiming her desk chair while he paced and skimmed the files.

Keegan's file was thin enough to slide under the door. It contained an employment application and two performance reviews covering the year he'd been employed at Galaxy. The details were bland. Keegan was a single, thirty-fiveyear- old high school graduate who'd been born in San Diego, worked his way east in a succession of bartending jobs until he landed in Kansas City. Now he was dead and there was nothing in his file that explained why or a hint of anyone who would care to know. He even left unanswered the question on his application of who to contact in the event of an emergency.

Rockley's file was no more illuminating, especially since he'd already seen what was in it. He took his time reviewing the meager pages so as not to raise any questions in Lari's mind.

He was more impressed by what wasn't in the files than what was. There were no attorney notes, no cross-examination outlines, no cross-references to important documents or the testimony of other witnesses. The files were too clean. She had sanitized them for his review, showing him something without giving him anything. He handed the files back to her and decided to compare her view of the case to Vince Bongiovanni's.

"Ninety-five percent of all lawsuits settle," Mason said. "Why didn't this one?"

Lari shrugged. "It should have. The case is a push. Classic he-said, she-said. The woman usually gets the benefit of the doubt, which means my clients usually pay. Bongiovanni refused to negotiate. Said it was personal. I get paid either way, so we went to trial."

"Ed Fiori was Bongiovanni's and Carol's uncle. He told me that Galaxy screwed Fiori's estate when they bought the casino. I guess he saw Carol's case as a chance to get even."

"That's what he told me too. I could care less. It doesn't get personal for me. So," she asked, pointing to the personnel files, "who did it?"

"The way you sanitized these files they don't tell me anything. Let me see the stuff you pulled out and the rest of the files on Galaxy, and I may be able to tell you."

"It would be easier if I just gave you my law license and all my money instead. That's what Galaxy will want if I violate their attorney-client privilege."

"Beats the hell out of a bullet in the head and a burial in the trunk of a car."

"I told you. No one at Galaxy knows anything about Rockley and your client. Either your client killed Rockley or he's a victim of circumstance."

"You came within inches of being a victim of circumstance tonight. Next time may be different. The girls in that photograph will be proud to know that you died protecting the attorney-client privilege."

Color flared in her cheeks. She pointed to the photograph, then swung her finger at him. "My daughters know the battles I've fought to get where I am.

Their father walked out on us when they were little. They understand what it's like for a woman alone."

"Trust me," Mason said, sitting on the edge of her desk, towering over her. "They won't understand murder. Nobody does when it takes someone they love. Tell me what was in your safe."

Lari rose and brushed past him. She inspected the safe once more, reconfirming that the combination still worked. She ran her hand over the inside of the vault, erasing any doubt that she had been robbed. She looked at Mason, her face pale and quivering, her courtroom bravado evaporated.

He handed her the photograph of her daughters. Lari snapped it out of his hand, hiding it beneath her arms as she hugged her sides. She squeezed her eyes shut, cringing as if a bullet had found her, turning her head so he wouldn't see that a tear had escaped her defenses. He put a hand on her shoulder, but she shook it off, stepping around him and gently setting the picture back on her desk, her back to him. She took a deep breath, her eyes still on her daughters.

"A CD. I don't know what was on it. I never listened to it."

A cold chill flooded Mason's gut. "How do you know it was a recording and not data or copies of documents?"

"I don't, really. I just got that impression from my client. He called it a one-hit wonder."

Lari had been careful up to that point to refer to her client without even a gender reference. Corporate clients don't have a gender. Lawyers typically refer to the person they deal with at the company as their client.

Mason put his hand on her shoulder again. This time she didn't object, leaning against him for support.

"Tell me his name. I need something to work with. Just a name."

She picked up the photograph of her daughters again, cradling it in her hands. "Al Webb."

"When did he give it to you?"

She turned to him, close enough that he could smell the perfume on her neck and the scotch on her breath.

"During the hearing on Carol Hill's case. He said he'd call me if he needed it. It hasn't been out of the safe since then."

"Don't tell him about the robbery or the shooting."

"I have to tell him. The CD belongs to him."

"Maybe not. Call me if he asks for it. We'll figure out what to do then."

"I can't do that," she said. "He's my client. He gave me that CD for safekeeping."

"He gave it to you to hide it and you almost got killed for your trouble. You can't charge enough for that kind of work. Besides, I don't think he'll ask for it before the end of next week. I may have this figured out by then."

She pulled away from him, her eyebrows raised, her cross-examination instincts revived.

"You couldn't possibly know that unless there's something you aren't telling me."

He smiled at her. "That's the difference between men and women. We pay attention to different things."

On his way out, Mason stopped in the file room and plucked the laser pointer from the shelf. There wouldn't be a police report and, even if there were, he would bet against finding any fingerprints on the pointer. He turned the red beam off and dropped it in his pocket.

Walking back to the parking garage, he turned his coat collar up against a bone-chilling wind that now whipped between the office buildings. The unseasonable warmth from the afternoon had vanished, the swift and brutal change in weather a reminder that paybacks are hell.

CHAPTER THIRTY-SEVEN

IT WAS A measure of the way his weekend had gone that Mason was looking forward to having dinner on Sunday night at Avery Fish's house. Fish would try to talk him out of resigning and Mason would have to smile, clean his plate, and quit even though it was the last thing he wanted to do.

Defending someone on a murder charge was unlike any other attorney-client relationship. All clients put their trust in their lawyers, but saving an innocent man's life was the most sacred of trusts. No civil case could trump it, no matter the millions that might end up in his pocket. No mega- merger could match the stakes of life or death. There were times when Mason almost felt sorry for his legal brethren and their pedestrian practices. The burden of innocence and his duty to protect it sustained him as much as it weighed on him. Abandoning Avery Fish was contrary to everything Mason believed in, save one. He couldn't allow his problems with Judge Carter to put Fish at greater risk.

Nothing that had happened since Friday changed Mason's certainty that he had to withdraw as Fish's lawyer. Though he couldn't prove it, he was certain that the CD stolen from Lari Prillman's safe contained the blackmail audio tapes. Its theft confirmed that he had no choice but to quit. The CD was like a virus. He had to destroy it before it spread, though he had no idea who might have stolen it or where to look for it.

Unlike Saturday, Sunday passed without him being overcome by lust and longing and forgetting a meeting with a critical witness. Nor had the woman he loved used him as a shield from a jealous wife. And, best of all, no one had shot at him since sunrise.

He started the day with a punishing run, during which he revisited his day with Abby. He refused to give women credit for the exclusive ability to read a relationship, no matter what caught their attention. It didn't matter whether something was going on between Josh Seeley and Abby or whether the senator's wife just believed they were having an affair. Well, it did matter. He was too in love with Abby to pretend otherwise. But it mattered just as much that Abby had used him.

When he got back there was a message from her asking him to call so she could explain. Her voice was laced with a mix of impatience and regret that ate at him. He erased it without returning her call.

He showered, paid bills, and watched a college basketball game as he ate lunch. It was an enforced normalcy that failed to take his mind off everything that had happened in the last week. When he realized that he had no idea which teams he was watching and didn't care whether either team won, he turned off the television and gave up pretending that his life was normal.

He whistled to Tuffy and asked her if she wanted to go for a ride. She beat him to the car, paws on the door waiting to be let in. He lowered the front passenger window enough for the dog to stick her snout into the wind and turned up the heat to cut the chill from the cold air. He drove to Shawnee Mission Park, a vast expanse in western Johnson County.

Kansas City was more than the geopolitically correct unit of city government on the Missouri side of the state line it shared with Kansas. It was more than a sister to Kansas City, Kansas, a city that merged with Wyandotte County to form one governmental behemoth. It was an amalgam of cities and counties spread on either side of the state line in every direction, home to over a million and a half people of every clan and category ever imagined.

It was a place where people fought over who had the best barbecue and how much to spend on a new performing arts center. It was a place where people rooted for football Chiefs and baseball Royals and protested war in the name of peace. It was a place where some schools excelled and others struggled while too many kids got their education on the streets. It was a place like every other place—full of hopes and promises, some that soared and others that were crushed. It was Mason's home and he wore it like a second skin.

Locals knew the difference between living in Raytown, Missouri, and Leawood, Kansas, but residents of both would probably tell out-of-towners that they lived in Kansas City. It was simpler than giving a lesson in geography or bragging rights. Johnson County was one of the Kansas-side pieces in the bi-state kaleidoscope with demographics that made high-end retailers slobber all over themselves.

Shawnee Mission Park took its name from the mission set up in the 1800s to help the Shawnee Indians find the white man's religion. Blues rarely talked to Mason about being a full-blooded member of the Shawnee tribe, except to say that the Shawnee got the shaft and the white man got the mailing address. You could send mail to anyone in the twenty-plus cities located in Johnson County and address it to Shawnee Mission, KS, the one city that existed only in the minds of the Postal Service. There was no such place.

The park had miles of trails, a lake with a marina, and a leash-free haven where people turned their dogs loose for a wide-ranging romp, the occasional bump-and-run encounter with a good-looking dog-lover a side benefit for singles tired of the bar scene. Mason let Tuffy out of the car, interested in nothing more than a head-clearing walk while his dog wore herself out.

The cold was enough to discourage most people, pancake clouds layering an oppressive grayness on the day. Barren trees stood idly by, refusing to break the gusting wind. Frozen concrete ground hit back against his boots as he followed Tuffy up a slow rising hill, along the tree line and down toward a shallow inlet of the lake. He lost sight of the dog for a few minutes, picking up his pace until he saw her nose-to-butt with a golden retriever.

The golden's owner, her blond hair sticking out from beneath a ski cap, stood with her back to Mason. She turned toward him as he made his way the last few yards to the water's edge. He stopped for a moment, sucking in a cold breath when he realized that the woman was Judith Bartholomew. He'd only seen her a few times, always from a distance, but he'd thought often enough about the possibility that they shared the same father that he had no doubt it was her. He'd met her mother, Brenda Roth, just once. She wanted nothing to do with Mason, and he was confident that Brenda had never spoken to her daughter about him.

Mason was six feet tall, had dark hair, gray eyes, and a long, angular face. He'd broken his nose more than once, and his heavy beard cast a shadow on his cheeks and chin even if he shaved twice a day. Judith was no more than five- six, with a smooth, creamy complexion. Her eyes were hazel, her face more round than his. From a distance, he'd imagined, or wished for, more of a resemblance. Up close, he could see nothing that linked them, though he knew of many siblings who resembled one of their parents but not each other.

She smiled at him, though it was the kind of tentative smile reserved for strangers. There was no hint of recognition. His life was complicated enough at the moment without adding any new wrinkles.

"Your dog?" she asked, pointing to Tuffy.

"All mine."

The dogs finished sniffing each other and started chasing along the rocky beach. Mason stuffed his hands in his pockets, avoiding introductions.

"I haven't been here in ages. My kids were bouncing off the walls, the laundry was piled to the ceiling, and my husband was sleeping in front of the television. I had to get out of the house. Fortunately, my mother lives with us. I told her she was in charge and I kidnapped the dog."

The explanation was hurried as if she felt guilty leaving her domestic duties behind and wanted to be certain Mason knew she was only there to walk the dog.

He nodded. "Good to get away for a little while."

She gave him a closer look, her eyes wrinkling with concentration. "I'm Judith," she said, extending her hand. "Do I know you?"

Mason took her hand, disappointed he didn't feel some genetic connection. "I'm Lou," he said, glad that she omitted last names. "I don't think we've met. I just have one of those naturally familiar faces like the ones on the wall at the post office."

The dogs came back to them, tongues and tails wagging. She patted the golden, looked at her watch, and sighed.

"If I don't get back, my mother will send out a search party."

"Take it easy," Mason said.

"I'll do that," she said. "You know, you do have one of those familiar faces, but it's not from the post office. It will come to me."

"Let me know. I'll wait here."

"Funny and familiar. Not a bad combination," she said. "Let's go, dog."

CHAPTER THIRTY-EIGHT

Avery Fish could cook. He served Mason baked tilapia encrusted with cashews, wild rice, fresh green beans, and a spinach salad with mandarin oranges. Dessert was a persimmon cake.

"I've never had anything like that," Mason said of the dessert.

"That's because you can't get persimmons here. This friend of mine in California, her name is Patty, makes them and sends me one every year."

"Well," Mason said, pushing back from the table. "Tell Patty to put me on her list after you die. I wouldn't have guessed you were such a good cook."

Fish shrugged. "You live alone long enough and you learn to cook. When I was married, we'd have dinner every Sunday night with my wife's family. Kids running all over the place, people laughing and talking. It was a beautiful noise and the food was always good. So now, at least, I've still got the food."

They didn't talk about Fish's case during dinner. Fish waited until after they'd eaten and were sitting in the living room. He had brewed tea for Mason and strong black coffee for himself. The lighting was soft, casting a warm glow against the walls; the furniture sagged but not too much. The walls were decorated with family photos Mason hadn't noticed on his last visit. The house was like a favorite old sweater, a bit worn but too comfortable to trade in for a newer version.

"So, should I take this deal the U.S. attorney is offering me?" He held his cup of coffee beneath his lips, blowing on it.

"I'd rather you talk about that with your new lawyer."

"You're still my lawyer until I get somebody new. Am I right?"

Mason shrugged. "Technically, I suppose that's correct."

"Then we'll talk about my case first and your problems second. Who knows? By the time we're done, maybe both of our problems will be solved. What about this deal? I don't even know what it is they want me to do."

"They want you to help them with a case, but they won't tell us what it is or what you would have to do. That's not much of a deal. But, I may know what they have in mind. Charles Rockley worked for the Galaxy Casino. Late Friday night, the cops made a house call to tell me that another Galaxy employee named Johnny Keegan had been shot to death."

"Oy! When did that happen?"

"Friday night, sometime after eight. That's when Keegan got off work."

"Why did the police tell you about this Keegan? Surely they don't think I had anything to do with it."

Mason felt like he was tiptoeing through a minefield. He had to be careful that he didn't tell Fish anything that would raise questions he couldn't answer. The cops would tell Fish's new lawyer about Keegan. He wouldn't be surprised if Rachel Firestone picked up the story as well.

"When Keegan's body was found, he had a piece of paper in his hand with my name and phone number on it."

"Which gets us back to your problems while we're supposed to be talking about my problems."

"Exactly."

"This Keegan, did you know him?"

"Never met," Mason said.

"So why would he have your name and phone number?"

"The easy answer is that he needed a lawyer. I don't know most of my clients before they walk through my door."

"But you're uneasy with the easy answer and you can't tell me why." Fish blew again on his coffee as he took a sip.

"The point is that the two murders could be connected to the FBI's investigation. If they are, it means the FBI is after someone at Galaxy."

"I don't know how I can help the FBI. I'm no undercover agent. I'm a businessman. I sell opportunities to people who want them at discount prices. To do that, people have to trust me and be greedy enough not to look at the fine print. Who's going to trust me after I'm accused of being a thief and a murderer?"

"I don't know either, unless the feds are after someone at Galaxy who doesn't care if you are a thief and a murderer. Know anyone who fits that description?"

"No, and I've never been to the Galaxy. I never bet against the house and I always make sure I am the house. Did you read the story in yesterday's newspaper? That reporter— she's a nice Jewish girl named Rachel Firestone. Do you know her?"

"I do. We're good friends, as a matter of fact."

"Some friend. She called me on the phone Friday night. On Shabbos! To ask me if I'd like to explain how this Rock ley's body ended up in my car and did his murder have anything to do with the mail fraud charges against me."

Mason wasn't surprised that Rachel hadn't said anything to him about calling Fish. That was the new Rachel, he thought, remembering how much he preferred the old version.

"What did you tell her?"

"Nothing. Just like you told me. I was Mr. No Comment."

Mason had been so caught up in Saturday's whirlwind that he'd overlooked the most important consequence of Rachel's story. Pete Samuelson, the U.S. attorney, had offered to keep the photograph of Blues outside Rockley's apartment under wraps. He wasn't doing Fish a favor. He was using the photograph as leverage to persuade Fish to take their deal. Rachel's article said nothing about Blues, but the bad press was worse than the photograph.

"That article may have cost you the deal with the feds. It forced their hand with the cops. Now, they'll be under a lot of pressure to turn over everything they've got including the photograph of Blues. They can't take the chance of being accused of withholding evidence."

"I thought they didn't want the police to know about their secret investigation. If they turn over the photograph of Mr. Blues, won't they have to explain how they got it?"

"Maybe. That doesn't mean the explanation has to be true. It just has to be an explanation."

"So, I don't need another lawyer. See, I told you we could work this out."

Mason put his cup on the table next to his chair. "I'm sorry, Avery. I don't see any way around it. Things will only get worse for you when the cops get that picture. They'll want an explanation from you. You'll have to tell them that you couldn't have told me to send Blues to Rockley's apartment because you didn't know Rockley was the dead man or where he lived. If they believe you, they'll want an explanation from me."

"And you can't give them one. Am I right?"

"You're right. I can't. That's why I don't see any way around this."

"Then keep looking. I don't want another lawyer."

Mason shook his head. "I'm glad you feel that way, but I don't have a choice. I've got to get out."

"You can't quit without telling me why. It's not right. Besides, maybe I won't mind that you've got a conflict of interest. My whole life has been a conflict of interest and things haven't worked out so bad for me."

"You're divorced. Your daughters will barely let you see your grandkids. You're facing a federal felony conviction for mail fraud and a state charge for murder. What's so good about that?"

"Yes, but I can cook," Fish said. "And, I can think and I've been thinking about Mr. Blues and your problem, whatever it is. Someone takes his picture outside the apartment of this dead man, this Rockley. Mr. Blues works for you. He's your gumshoe. The FBI thinks you sent Mr. Blues to Rockley's apartment because I told you that Rockley was the dead man in the trunk of my car. How could I have known that unless I killed Rockley? Am I right so far?"

"On the money."

"But, I didn't kill Rockley so I didn't know who he was before or after someone put him in my trunk. That means you had some other reason to send Mr. Blues to Rockley's apartment. You say that Mr. Blues didn't kill Rockley and I assume that you didn't kill him either. So whatever is going on between you and Rockley has nothing to do with me. Still right?"

"Still right."

"Then what's the problem? I'll tell you what's the problem. You're in some kind of trouble because of this Rockley and you can't get out of it and represent me at the same time."

Mason looked at his watch. "It's getting late."

Fish narrowed his eyes. "You've got that right, boytchik. I've been in my share of tight spots. I know what it's like to get squeezed. Tell me what this is all about. If I can't help you, I'll get another lawyer. Don't worry. Everything we talk about is confidential anyway."

CHAPTER THIRTY-NINE

FISH SAT WITH his hands on his knees, his fleshy face pinched with seriousness, his eyes filled with worry. Mason sensed that Fish was as concerned about him as he was himself. Mason didn't understand this, but it made him want to answer Fish's questions.

Fish's pitch was tempting. It was the same one he'd made to Lari Prillman. She had turned him down and he needed to do the same to Fish. Though, if anyone would understand Mason's predicament without judging him, it was Fish. A con man's instincts may be just what Mason needed. Yet he couldn't forget that Fish was a con man, someone not to be trusted. Claire had warned him.

Mason stood and stuffed his hands in his coat pockets. "I'll call you tomorrow with the names of some other lawyers."

Fish leaned back in his chair, hands making a steeple on his stomach. "I expected more from you."

Mason bristled at Fish's comment. He shouldn't have cared what Fish's expectations of him were, but somehow he did.

"Why? Because of what you've read about me in the papers? I've had some high-profile cases, but that doesn't mean I leap tall buildings in a single bound."

"No. You don't look like much of a leaper to me."

"Then is it because we're both Jewish? Does that mean I'm supposed to treat you differently than any other client? It doesn't work that way."

"We Jews have to look out for one another. That's one lesson we've learned after more than five thousand years. But that's not it either. I expected more from you because of who you are."

"What's that supposed to mean?"

"It means I knew your father and he never would have given up as easily as you."

Mason felt like the air had been sucked out of Fish's living room. His head spun for an instant until he realized that he wasn't breathing. He'd never met anyone who had known his father besides his Aunt Claire. She hadn't talked much about him over the years except to assure Mason that his father had been a good and decent man. She stuck to that description even after Mason learned the details about his parents' deaths. She said his father had made a mistake and couldn't put things right and that Mason should leave it at that. Some things just couldn't be fixed, she had told him. His father's betrayal of his mother was one of them.

He knew his father only through photographs and Claire's limited references. He hadn't pushed for more, content to grow up with Claire as his mother and Harry Ryman the closest thing he had to a living father. He wasn't like an adopted child who decided to search for his birth parents to complete his identity. He had found Brenda Roth and Judith Bartholomew more by accident than design. Afterward, he confronted Claire, demanding to know more about how his parents had died. When she told him what had happened, he saw in Judith a possible link to his father, an indirect way to connect with him without confronting who he was. Fish was offering the direct route and Mason wasn't certain he wanted to go there.

Mason stared at Fish and started to breathe again. The old man smiled at him. "You knew my father?"

"Sit down and I'll tell you a story. You were what—three, four years old when your parents died?"

"Three," Mason said, sitting and leaning forward in his chair, hands wrapped around his cup of tea.

"Who took you in?"

"My Aunt Claire."

"A very disagreeable woman," Fish said, his hand raised to blunt Mason's reply. "I know, I know. You think she hung the moon. Maybe she did, but I guarantee the moon didn't appreciate it."

Mason laughed. "She is tough and she's not a member of your fan club either."

Fish perked up, arching the folds of skin above his eyes into canopies. "You told her about me?"

"She invited me to dinner for tonight, but I told her you got to me first."

"What did she say?"

"That you didn't deserve a lawyer like me."

"Hah!" Fish slapped his palm hard against his knee. "She's still the sanctimonious keeper of all that's sacred. Your aunt and I had a go-round or two. She never cared for me and I never lost sleep over her. What do you think? Do I deserve a lawyer like you?"

"So far. How did you know my father?"

"I met your father, mother, and aunt through the synagogue. I was on the membership committee and they were new members. You might say I took them in, made them feel at home—introduced them to other people. A few years later, I got into some difficulty with a few of my fellow congregants. They were unhappy with an investment I'd recommended and wanted to run me out of the synagogue for duping them. The bylaws said I could be kicked out for acts of moral turpitude, which, being very religious, these people defined by the amount of money they lost.

"The board of directors called a closed meeting to decide what to do. Your father found out about the meeting and asked to speak to the board on my behalf. No one else did. I had no idea he was going to be there. He just marched into the meeting and asked to be recognized. He was a tall man, your father, like you, and he had a quiet way of speaking that made people listen. The board members were so surprised, they didn't know what to do, but they let him talk. He said that he didn't know me that well but that I'd been kind and good to him and his family. He talked about how easy it was to get caught up in something that was never intended; how things could go wrong in an instant without anyone ever intending for that to have happened, and how all of us deserved a second chance so we could set things right."

The image of his father filled Mason with pride, restoring polish to a tarnished memory.

"What happened?"

Fish hauled himself out of his chair and picked up Mason's cup. "Refill?" Mason nodded. "I'll tell you what happened. Your father left the room. I told the board I would pay the people back and they let me stay. I never got the chance to thank your father. That was the night your parents were killed in a car accident. It was raining like hell when I drove home. Nearly had a wreck myself."

Mason was numb, his arms and legs pinned to his chair as Fish lumbered toward the kitchen and disappeared. The newspaper account of the accident said his father had lost control on a slick, wet road; that their car had crashed through a guardrail and run down an embankment, and his parents had been pronounced dead at the scene. The investigating police officer blamed his father, calling it intentional.

Claire had explained when he finally forced her to tell him the truth. His father had been having an affair with Brenda Roth. He tried to break it off and she accused him of rape. He was supposed to turn himself in to the police the next day. None of that ever made the papers. It was a different time in journalism.

Fish came back, carrying two steaming mugs, the mixed aromas of tea and coffee rousing Mason.

"What did you hear about my father after he was killed?"

Fish lowered himself into his chair, careful with his coffee, sipping it before he answered. "There are always stories, especially after a tragedy. People love them. When they tell enough of them about you, you stop listening. So, I don't listen and I don't remember. What I do remember is that your father took a chance for me when he had bigger problems of his own."

"Maybe was talking about himself when he stood up for you."

"Maybe he was talking about both of us. What matters is that he was there when no one else was. That was enough for me. I repaid the people who wanted to throw me out. I never had the chance to repay your father until now."

Mason paced the room, setting his cup on the mantel above the fireplace next to a photograph of Fish with his daughters and grandchildren. "Where are their husbands, your sons-in-law?"

"Always out of town on business. My daughters hated me for being gone all the time, then they married men who do the same thing."

"I thought they hated you because you were a con man."

"Of course they do. But people will forgive a lot if you are there for them when they need you. I never was."

Mason looked at Fish. He saw a lonely old man filled with regret who was looking for a way to balance the books even if the credits wouldn't match the right debits. He looked around the living room. It wasn't a storehouse of memories so much as it was a reminder of lost opportunities. He caught his reflection in a mirror hanging in the front hall. The low light and distance made his image shimmer and shift as if he might disappear in an instant only to materialize thirty years from now, heir to Fish's regret.

"There is a woman named Vanessa Carter," he began.

Fish listened as Mason told him about Blues, Ed Fiori, and Vanessa Carter. He interrupted occasionally with questions, grunted at some of the details, chuckled when Mason told him that Vanessa Carter would have granted bail for Blues anyway. He nodded with understanding when Mason explained again why the photograph of Blues outside Rockley's apartment made it impossible for Mason to continue representing him. He let out a long sigh when Mason finished, pushed himself out of his chair, and disappeared into the kitchen, coming back with a fresh cup of coffee.

"So, this conflict of interest you're so worried about—I don't think it's a conflict at all."

"Then you weren't listening. The FBI has to give the photograph of Blues to the cops sooner or later. When they do, the cops will be convinced you killed Rockley. I can't explain the photograph without turning myself in."

"So we'll find the real killer. Problem solved."

"We?"

"Yes, we. There's an angle to all of this that ties the blackmail and the murder together. We have a lot better chance of figuring it out if we work together. I'll take the U.S. attorney's offer. It's the only way to find out what they're up to. You have to stay on my case because that's the only way we can help each other."

"Avery, a lawyer has to put his client's interest above his own. I can't do that if I'm trying to save my ass and yours at the same time."

"Look at it this way—if you save one of our asses you've got a lot better chance of saving the other."

Mason looked down at Fish, whose wide body filled the chair as if he'd been poured into it. "You're taking a big chance."

"I don't think so. You trusted me with the truth. Who does that? It's good enough for me."

CHAPTER FORTY

MASON KNEW A lawyer who described his practice as juggling knives. Every case was a gleaming, razor-sharp blade arcing over his head, waiting for him to grab it and toss it back in the air before he caught the next one in his neck. Mason knew the feeling and the difference between their practices. If his friend took one in the neck, he bled his client's money. Mason and his clients bled the real thing.

Studying his dry erase board early Monday morning, he saw too many knives to possibly avoid them all. He wrote Galaxy Casino in the upper right-hand corner and Carol Hill in the upper left. Across the top, he wrote Vanessa Carter, connecting her name to both Carol Hill and Galaxy. On the left-hand margin he drew a line down from Carol Hill connecting her to Mark Hill, Ed Fiori, and, at the bottom, Vince Bongiovanni. He listed Charles Rockley, Johnny Keegan, and Al Webb in a vertical parade on the right-hand margin ending in the bottom corner with Lari Prillman. He filled in the bottom margin with Avery Fish in the center.

He stepped back from the board and realized what he'd left out. He wrote Lou Mason in the middle of the board, like a bull's-eye, then drew more lines, each one a dagger aimed at him. On the line between him and Vanessa Carter he wrote deadline Friday. He connected Ed Fiori, Vanessa Carter, Al Webb, and Lari Prillman to one another and to him with audio tape, then erased it using CD instead.

He wrote Why me? on the line connecting him to Johnny Keegan. He wrote Why Fish? between Fish's and Rockley's names. He finished by writing Get out on the line between his name and Fish's, then added Can't.

The exercise in visualization didn't produce any answers. It did make clear how little he knew and how little time he had to figure it all out. The answers wouldn't suddenly appear if he just sat in his office and waited for them. He closed the cabinet doors over the dry erase board and called Pete Samuelson.

"We're ready to make a deal," he told the assistant U.S. attorney.

"Outstanding. When can you come downtown?"

"You come here. Tonight, ten o'clock. We'll meet you in the bar downstairs. Just you and Kelly Holt."

"You've got to be kidding."

"What's the problem? Past your bedtime?"

"I don't get it. What's wrong with meeting in an office during business hours?"

"You don't have to get it. All you have to do is show up." Mason hung up before Samuelson could protest any more.

The phone rang an instant later. Samuelson's number flashed on Mason's caller ID.

"Quit bitching about working late. Just be there," Mason told him, hanging up before Samuelson could utter a word.

His next call was to Vince Bongiovanni.

"You better have a good reason for stiffing me twice in one day," Bongiovanni told him.

"What qualifies for a good excuse other than the truth?"

"For you, getting killed; for me, getting laid."

"I'll take your lie over mine. Look, I'm sorry. I'll tell you about it if and when I can, but that's not today. I need to talk to Carol as soon as possible. You name the time and place and I'll be there."

"I don't know what's going on here, Mason, but you're going to have to tell me. Frankly, I didn't mind that you didn't show up since I had an appointment with my personal trainer, but Carol went nuts. She wants to talk to you and I mean now."

"I'm ready. Where? Your office?"

"No, and not at your office either. She wants to meet you at the Galaxy."

"The casino? Why?"

"Not the casino. The hotel next to the casino. Room 1201. She's waiting for you."

"Are you going to be there?"

"Are you kidding? I'd have to get killed and laid before I'd let you talk to her alone," Bongiovanni said.

Gambling in Missouri was one of the all-time great public relations coups. Promoters promised quaint two-hour riverboat cruises with five-hundred-dollar loss limits. The voters said bring it on and the gaming companies did, transforming riverboats into permanently anchored barges of a hundred thousand square feet or more accommodating casinos rivaling those on any river or reservation in America. Time and loss limits gave way to billboards bragging about which casino had the loosest slots, each ad including a toll-free number for a gambling addiction hotline, written in microscopic print not meant to be read.

The slots were tight enough to finance hotels next door on dry land, the casinos improving on the Field of Dreams prophecy with their own—if you build it, they will come, even if you take their money. Mason had been to the casino when it was owned by Ed Fiori and called the Dream. He hadn't been back since Galaxy Gaming took it over and he'd never been to the hotel that adjoined the casino. It continued the Galaxy theme, splashing glitter-covered stars and other celestial bodies throughout, tempting customers to blast off.

When Mason arrived, the lobby was packed with a senior citizen group checking out after a weekend extravaganza. Mason couldn't tell the blue-haired winners from the gray- haired losers. He wound his way through them, finding the elevator and taking it to the twelfth floor.

He assumed that Johnny Keegan's murder had hit Carol Hill harder than Charles Rockley's, especially after his warning to Bongiovanni that Mark Hill was a prime suspect and Carol a potential target. His warning must have prompted her to move out of the house and into the hotel.

Mason wondered whether Carol knew why Keegan had Mason's name in the palm of his hand when he died, but the timing of Keegan's death made that doubtful. Mason and Blues had braced her husband at the bar in Fairfax just after six o'clock on Friday evening. Dennis Brewer, the FBI agent, and his buddies were working Hill over when Mason and Blues left the parking lot of the bar. Bongiovanni got his tip that Rockley was the dead man in Fish's trunk at around seven. He was waiting for Mason at Blues on Broadway a little over an hour later. Keegan was gunned down sometime after he got off work at eight while Bongiovanni and Mason were talking. The cops told Mason about Keegan at midnight and Mason broke the news to Bongiovanni after the cops left. Mason couldn't find any point in that time line for Carol Hill to connect him to Johnny Keegan.

CHAPTER FORTY-ONE

Room service trays stacked with dirty dishes and unclaimed copies of USA Today littered the hallway floor as Mason counted down room numbers, finding 1201 in an alcove at the end of the corridor. He knocked once and Bongiovanni opened the door, looked down the hall as if he was checking for anyone who might have seen Mason, then motioned him inside.

Room 1201 was a suite with a large living room, a mini- kitchen, and a bedroom separated from the rest by French doors. Carol stood at the living room window overlooking the casino and the Missouri River, dressed in a bathrobe, a towel around her head and a cigarette jammed in the corner of her mouth. A king-size bed was visible through the open French doors, the linens tossed as if Carol had slept either poorly or with a friend. It was a high roller's hangout, the kind the casino would use to reward guests with a track record for dropping big bucks. It was too rich for a blackjack dealer on leave for emotional distress.

"Lou Mason, say hello to Carol Hill," Bongiovanni said.

The morning sun broke against the window, the glare obscuring her features. She stubbed the cigarette out in an ashtray and met him in the center of the room, her hand trembling when she shook his. Fruit-scented soap and shampoo mixed with tobacco smoke in a sweet but trashy off-balance fragrance. Just out of the shower, her skin was pale and a bit rough, the kind of complexion that did better with makeup. Her mouth was small, and he thought her upper lip had been shot full of collagen until he realized it was swollen and that the dark yellow ring round her left eye was man-made. She was wearing a bulky white terry cloth robe that blunted her figure, though she moved enough beneath it that he could tell it was the only thing she was wearing. Stripped, scrubbed, and beat up, she was barely holding herself together. Mason was ready to award her damages for emotional distress, though he wasn't certain who was liable.

"I'm sorry about standing you up twice on Saturday," he said.

"It's okay," she said in a whisper, clearing her throat. "Gotta quit smoking," she said, coughing again.

"Get dressed, honey," Bongiovanni said. "I'll keep Mason company."

Carol nodded and closed the French doors behind her. Bongiovanni sat on an overstuffed couch, put his feet up on the coffee table, and gestured Mason to a chair.

"Nice digs," Mason said. "If this is a Galaxy employee benefit, tell me where to apply."

"Try inheritance. Ed Fiori was my uncle. Carol's too. We're first cousins. Our mothers were Ed's sisters. He owned the casino and the hotel, but you knew that."

Mason did know that. What he didn't know was whether Fiori had been close enough to Bongiovanni to have shared the story about Mason and Judge Carter. Fiori had been a little bent but not enough that he couldn't get a gaming license. Mason had never known who Fiori's lawyers were, but it made sense that he'd consult his nephew the lawyer even about things that were outside Bongiovanni's practice. Keeping things in the family was another way of keeping things quiet.

"I did know that."

"You were there when he was killed, if I remember right."

"I was," Mason said, not interested in talking about the details. "I'm sorry."

Bongiovanni waved his hand at Mason. "Hey, don't be sorry. You didn't kill him and the bastard that did is dead. Shit happens. But, I'll tell you what. There was a hell of a mess after he died. Soon as I heard, I raced down to the boat to secure his office before the cops showed up. I didn't know everything Ed was into, but I didn't want the cops to find out first. Found lots of interesting stuff. He even had one of those secret tape-recording setups, just like every president since Kennedy."

Mason studied Bongiovanni, trying to decide if Bongiovanni was playing with him, dangling a baited hook. If Bongiovanni had the tape, he wouldn't use it to blackmail Judge Carter to rule against his own client, especially since Carol was his cousin. Still, Mason thought he detected a glint in Bongiovanni's eyes and a curl at the corners of his mouth like he knew what he was doing and was enjoying it. Mason refused to bite, changing the subject instead.

"I'll bet you did. So, he left you the hotel?"

Bongiovanni laughed. "I was a nephew, not a son. But he did leave me the permanent use of this suite. Those bastards at Galaxy offered me a mint to give it up, but I told them to pound sand. We had to sell the casino and the hotel to pay the taxes on Ed's estate. After everything that happened with Ed, buyers weren't exactly lining up. Galaxy practically stole it, but we didn't have a choice. It eats their ass not to have this suite, though, and I love it."

Mason began to understand why Carol and her lawyer refused to settle. The lawsuit, whatever its merits, was about getting even.

"What happened to Carol's face?"

"I called her after you told me about Johnny Keegan. She was crying, hysterical. Mark had been out drinking—came home and beat the crap out of her. I picked her up and brought her over here."

"Did Mark give you any trouble?"

"I didn't see him. He left after he beat Carol up."

"Did she file a complaint with the police?"

"For what? To get a restraining order? I haven't seen one yet that will stop an asshole drunk like her husband from knocking his wife around."

"He can't hit her if he's in jail."

"He can't hit me if he's dead either," Carol Hill said.

CHAPTER FORTY-TWO

Carol had changed into jeans and a long-sleeved gray T-shirt. Her auburn hair was brushed and pulled back behind her ears. She'd applied a thin layer of makeup that dulled but didn't hide her black eye. Lipstick softened her swollen lip. She had large breasts and full hips. Mason guessed she had been a high school knockout. Twenty years later, she was spreading out. Her shoulders were round and sloped like someone was riding her back. She was shaken and sad but angry enough to threaten to kill the man who'd beaten her and may have also killed her lover.

"If anyone kills Mark, it isn't going to be you," Bongiovanni told her. "He's a moron who will piss the wrong person off sooner or later and your problem will get solved in a hurry. In the meantime, he's not worth throwing your life away."

Carol sat on the sofa next to Bongiovanni. "Vince says you think Mark killed Rockley and Johnny."

"Your husband was jealous of Keegan and mad at Rock- ley. Men have killed with less reason."

"How'd you know about Johnny and me?"

It was a question Mason had anticipated since he'd warned Bongiovanni about Mark Hill. He had no believable explanation besides the truth and he needed Carol to trust him if she was going to tell him anything. The trick was to tell her enough without telling her and Bongiovanni too much.

"Your husband told me. I represent a man named Avery Fish. Charles Rockley's body was found in the trunk of my client's car. I did some checking on Rockley and found out about your case against him and Galaxy. Since you were represented by an attorney, I couldn't talk to you without your lawyer's permission and lawyers usually don't let their clients say much to other lawyers. I thought I'd have better luck with your husband and I found him at a bar in Fairfax Friday evening."

"That dump called Easy's?"

"That's right."

"He was all beat up when he came home Friday night. Did you do that?"

Mason shook his head. "It wasn't me."

"I wish it was you. At least I could thank you. Do you know who did it so I can thank them?"

"Sorry. I can't help you," Mason said, the image of Hill taking a shot to the chin flashing in his mind. "I'd like to ask you a few questions."

She looked at Bongiovanni, who nodded at her. "Okay. What do you want to know?"

"When did you start seeing Johnny Keegan?"

She blushed, fidgeted with her sleeve, and answered in a quiet voice. "Not long after he started work there. For almost a year. We were always on the same shift. He bought me a drink one night when I was on break. We got to talking, kept talking, and that's what happened. He was real nice to me. I didn't care that he was younger than me. It was only a few years, and what difference does it make anyway if people are nice to each other?"

"Did Keegan and Rockley know each other?"

She looked at Bongiovanni again.

"It's okay, Carol. If he asks you something I don't want you to answer, I'll tell you."

"I saw them talking to each other all the time, but that doesn't mean they were friends. Johnny was nothing like Rockley. Johnny was sweet and good. He made me laugh. Rockley was dirt. He came on to me because he knew about me and Johnny. He said if I was giving it to Johnny, there wasn't any reason I shouldn't give it to him too. So he took it."

"Did you tell Johnny about Rockley?"

"Sure I did. Johnny was royally pissed. He said he'd take care of Rockley."

"Is that when you told your cousin Vince about Rock- ley?"

"Yeah."

"But you didn't tell him about Johnny, did you?"

She shook her head. "I knew Mark would go crazy and I didn't want to get Johnny in any trouble."

Carol had made the same mistake Fish had made when he decided not to tell Mason there was a body in the trunk of his car. She told her lawyer what she wanted him to know and hoped that what she didn't want him to know wouldn't matter. She was too naïve to realize that the first thing Charles Rockley would tell Lari Prillman was that Carol was having an affair with another Galaxy employee. Lari was smart enough to keep that card in her back pocket, waiting to play it until it would do the most damage. Her strategy may have worked too well. It may have cost Charles Rockley and Johnny Keegan their lives. Even as he considered the possibility, he still couldn't come up with a reason for Mark Hill to hide Rockley's body in Fish's car.

"Did your husband ever mention Avery Fish's name?"

"I don't think so. Not that I remember, anyway."

"Did your husband buy a time-share for a vacation in Florida?" Mason asked, searching for any possible connection between Mark Hill and Fish.

"That's real likely. The only vacation he ever took was on a bar stool."

"What about Keegan? Did he ever talk about getting away, taking a vacation with you to Florida?"

Carol's eyes grew wet and she wiped them with her sleeve. "He said he wanted me to leave Mark and that he would take me away. He said he was working on something big and he'd have the money so we could start over somewhere else. It was going to be more than a vacation. It was going to be a new life."

"Did he tell you what his big deal was?"

She sniffled and shook her head. "No. He just said it was okay if I lost my case because he'd have enough money for both of us. He said he was going away. I thought he would take me with him."

Mason leaned forward. "Carol, this is very important. Did Johnny act like he knew you were going to lose your case?"

Bongiovanni sat up as well, taking a keener interest in Mason's questions. Carol hesitated, looking at Bongiovanni, then at Mason.

"I don't know. All he said was it didn't matter. I thought I was going to lose anyway after everything came out about Johnny and me. I'm sorry," she said to Bongiovanni. "I know how bad you wanted to get Galaxy and I should have told you about Johnny. I'm sorry."

Bongiovanni put his arm around her, drawing him to her and comforting her. "That's okay, honey. The judge hasn't ruled yet. If we lose, we'll just get 'em next time."

Mason said, "One last thing, Carol. Did Johnny ever say that he needed to hire a lawyer?"

Carol pulled herself up, brushing off her T-shirt. "No. Why would he?"

"Because when the police found his body, he had a piece of paper in his hand with my name and phone number on it."

"And I'm guessing that you'd never heard of Johnny Keegan," Bongiovanni said to Mason.

"No, but he had obviously heard of me."

"Sounds like somebody went to a lot of trouble to make sure the two of you never met," Bongiovanni said.

CHAPTER FORTY-THREE

MASON LEFT THE suite accompanied by Bongiovanni. The elevator was empty as they rode down to the lobby. The hotel piped in Tom Jones singing "It's Not Unusual." It was too early in the day for lounge singers, but the lyric was on the money. Nothing in this case was usual.

"Do you really think Mark Hill flipped out and became a jealous psycho killer?" Bongiovanni asked.

"Most murders are committed close to home—not physically but psychologically. Spouses, lovers, friends, coworkers. Somebody or something gets off the tracks. That makes Hill the popular choice."

"But this isn't a popularity contest, is it?"

The elevator reached the lobby and they stepped into a throng of retired veterans checking in for their chance at something for nothing, many of them wearing caps with their service insignias on the bill. Mason led Bongiovanni away from the crowd.

"No," he said. "It's Sherlock Holmes and The Hound of the Baskervilles. It's about finding the dog that didn't bark. What time was it when Mark Hill came home Friday night and started smacking Carol around?"

"Carol said it was a few minutes after nine. She was watching some reality show that had just started."

"Keegan got off work at eight. The cops showed me a picture of his body they took at ten. That's not much time, but it's enough for Mark to have popped Keegan before he went home to work on Carol. He'll need an alibi once the cops connect him to Rockley and Keegan. That should take until about lunchtime today."

"But you don't buy it, do you?"

"I don't have a better idea, but there are a couple of things that don't add up. First, Rockley's killer cut off his head and hands and dumped the body in the trunk of my client's car. I haven't found anything to connect Rockley to my client and I don't believe in bad luck. Second, Keegan's body was left in a parking lot a mile from the casino still wearing his head and holding on to a piece of paper with my name and phone number on it. There's no pattern to the murders and I don't know any reason Keegan would have my name. It would help if I could find out more about those two guys."

"I've got Rockley's employment records from the arbitration. You're welcome to them."

"Thanks. Lari Prillman let me look at hers Saturday night. There's nothing in either one of them. I even called Rockley's previous employers. All five of them gave him great references—said he was a great guy, great employee, sorry to lose him."

Bongiovanni studied Mason, his mouth curling at the corners again. It was a look that said gotcha.

"Mason. I've been handling personal injury and employment cases for fifteen years. I talk to employers all the time. They're scared to death of lawyers and lawsuits. I'm lucky if they'll confirm someone actually worked for them. No employer says a word about what kind of employee the person was. You got five employers to give you a goddamn reference over the phone. That sounds like a barking dog to me."

"Yeah, but the dog is barking up the wrong tree. Each company was in a different city and there's no connection between them. How do you make that work? Besides, I have very good telephone manners."

"You ought to get a nine hundred number and start charging people. And another thing, you saw Prillman's files Saturday night and you called me bright and early this morning to see Carol. What did you do, call Rockley's former employers at home on Sunday?"

Mason realized his mistake. He didn't answer, waiting to see how far Bongiovanni would push with his next question.

"Okay. You don't want to tell me. Fine. Here's the way it looks to me. I got a phone call about Rockley around seven o'clock Friday night. First anonymous tip in my career. Very exciting. You called me after midnight, told me about Keegan, and warned me that Mark may go after Carol. This morning, you told Carol that you talked to Mark Friday evening and he told you that she and Keegan were having an affair. Am I right so far?"

"Right enough."

"You couldn't have called Rockley's former employers between Saturday night and this morning. You had to have done that last week. Which means that you knew about Rockley long before I did. The article in Saturday's newspaper made it look like the cops didn't even know Rockley was the corpse in your client's car until that reporter told them. Sounds like you have better sources than my anonymous tipster. Maybe your client told you. Frankly, I don't give a shit. I just want to know one thing. How did you make the connection to Mark Hill?"

Mason didn't answer because he didn't want to tell Bongiovanni the truth and he didn't have a lie that was good enough to fly under Bongiovanni's bullshit radar.

"Better not to tell me than lie to me, huh, Mason? I can respect that. Let me answer for you. You had no reason to connect your client to my client until you knew that Rockley was the corpse in your client's car. But that wasn't enough to get you to Mark Hill. To make that jump, you had to know about Carol's lawsuit against Galaxy. You didn't get that from me, so you had to get it from Galaxy. Now that's one big goddamn barking dog. So what the fuck is going on?"

Mason always reminded his clients that it wasn't their job to straighten out the opposing lawyer if he got the facts wrong or jumped to the wrong conclusion. Let him wander around in the wilderness until he figures things out or gives up, Mason told them.

"Woof, woof."

Bongiovanni stepped close to Mason, clipping his words. "Listen to me, Mason. Carol isn't just my client; she's family, which counts for a lot where I come from. I appreciate that you warned me about Mark, but don't hold out on me if there's something else I should know."

"You said that you found a lot of interesting things when you searched Ed Fiori's office after he was killed. Did you keep any souvenirs?"

Bongiovanni threw his hands into the air. "What's that got to do with anything?"

"The gate swings both ways. We may be able to help each other. You let me have a look at everything you took from your uncle's office, and I'll tell you what I know about Rock- ley."

Bongiovanni chewed his lip. "That's a pretty broad request. If you were asking me to produce documents for a lawsuit, I'd say you were on a fishing expedition."

"Maybe I am. What do you care so long as I've got Rock- ley and Keegan for bait?"

"That stuff is more than just interesting reading. You have any idea what you're looking for?"

"I'll know it when I see it."

"All right. Just remember this. Some of that stuff, if I let you see it, I'll have to kill you. You don't mind, do you?" Bongiovanni asked with a wry grin.

"I've got the same problem. I guess we'll have to trust each other."

"How's that going to work? We're both lawyers."

"What's the matter? Did you already forget about the Jew and the Italian?"

Bongiovanni laughed. "You are bent, Mason. I'll give you that. Look. I've got a deposition this afternoon. You come by my office tomorrow morning. We'll play another hand of liar's poker."

CHAPTER FORTY-FOUR

MASON CALLED LARI Prillman as soon as he got back to his SUV. "You still have Johnny Keegan's personnel file handy?" "Yes. Why?" "I'd like you to do me a favor. Call his former employers and ask for a reference." "Who needs a reference for a dead man?" "I do. Write down everything they tell you and call me back." A moment later his cell phone rang. It was one of the homicide detectives, Kevin Griswold. "Hey, Mason, your week off to a flying start?" "A-plus." "Glad to hear that. I'd appreciate it if you'd drop by.

We've got a few things we'd like to go over with you." "Sure. I can do that. Middle of the week be soon enough?" "Make me wait that long and I'll have to send someone to get you. My partner, Detective Cates, he misses you. Says he'd like it a lot if you got your ass down here right now."

"I can do that too."

Police headquarters was a monument to Missouri limestone and the public works projects of the Depression. It was on the east side of the downtown, one corner of a triangle that included City Hall and the Jackson County Courthouse. Homicide was on the second floor. An outer ring of cramped offices surrounded the detective's bullpen, a collection of wooden and metal desks older than a lot of the department's cold cases that had been shoved together to make sure no one had a private conversation about anything. There were three witness rooms down one hallway that ended with a lineup room on one side and a holding cage on the other.

Detectives on different shifts shared the same desks and offices, each one adding their own personal touches. Pictures of spouses and kids competed for space with those of boyfriends and girlfriends. The mismatched images fit in perfectly with homicide, where relationships often didn't made sense but usually explained everything.

Griswold and Cates were sitting at their desks when Mason arrived. Griswold, who was on the phone, waved Mason toward them. Cates swung his feet from the desk to the floor and brushed past Mason on his way to the interrogation rooms, not apologizing for stepping on Mason's foot. Cates was a little smaller than Mason, but he was looking for trouble. Mason knew better than to tease the bear on the bear's home court. Griswold hung up the phone, smiling and shaking his head at the same time.

"I told you Detective Cates missed you. Follow me." Griswold led him down the hall, past the witness rooms. Cates was waiting at the door to the lineup room. "Do me a favor before we get started. We're one short for a lineup.

Usually, we get one of the rookies to fill in, but everyone's out. Only take a minute."

The invitation made Mason uneasy. It was a reflex hesitation picked up from defending people after they'd been fingered in a lineup. Positive identification was rarely positive and often wrong. Five people who witness the same crime will tell five different versions from who did it to what they were wearing. Put someone who's been beaten, robbed, or raped behind a two-way mirror with a zealous cop at her elbow giving a nudge when the suspect steps forward and don't be surprised when she says, That's the one. Mason didn't want to be part of that process, but Griswold was giving him a C'mon, be a pal smile and Cates was giving him a What kind of pussy are you anyway? glare.

"I live to serve," Mason said, and stepped into the room, taking his place at the end of the row nearest to the door.

Five men were standing around, shifting their weight back and forth, glancing at the two-way mirror. Two of them were young and black, both with shaved heads, gold jewelry, and attitudes. A third was mid-thirties, Hispanic, short, and fat. The other two were white guys in their fifties, soft around the middle like desk jockeys killing time until their next heart attack. They were all casually dressed, from blue jeans to khakis, their clothing the only similarity to Mason.

A lineup was supposed to consist of a group of people who were neither so similar nor dissimilar as to prejudice the ability of the witness to accurately identify the criminal. A defendant picked out of a lineup that was intended to make him stand out from the crowd had a good defense that the lineup was rigged against him. Stepping into the room, Mason concluded that the lineup was aimed at the Hispanic. He was the one who clearly stood out from the others by ethnicity, age, and physical condition. Even if the victim identified the Hispanic, the lineup would be easy to challenge in court.

One of the black men tried to intimidate everyone else with his ghetto glare. The fat Hispanic studied the floor as if he was hoping to get a glimpse of his feet. The other three looked around, impatient and uninterested. Griswold's voice came over a speaker mounted in a corner. He told them to line up against the wall, take one step forward and back again when their number was called. Griswold was right. It only took a minute.

When they finished, Cates pointed Mason toward the nearest witness room, followed him inside, and closed the door. Cates was smiling so Mason didn't, figuring anything that made Cates happy shouldn't make him happy. A moment later, Griswold opened the door carrying a cup of coffee. He reached behind him with his free hand to close the door, but missed the knob. He grabbed for it a second time, the delay long enough for Mason to see Detective Samantha Greer escort Mark Hill from the other side of the lineup room.

CHAPTER FORTY-FIVE

Mason didn't know whether his glimpse of Samantha and Mark Hill was intentional or accidental. Either way, he didn't like it. That he'd been set up was plain, though the purpose was not. He decided to pretend he'd seen nothing and let Griswold and Cates spin it out for him.

The witness room was furnished with police chic: a wooden table with uneven legs scarred with initials and cigarette burns, metal folding chairs, and windows covered with chicken wire. The sun warmed the room and the wire, casting a checkerboard shadow on the surface of the table. Mason sat with his back to the windows. Cates stood behind him, leaning against the glass. Griswold sat across from Mason.

"Appreciate the help with the lineup," Griswold said.

"I'll waive my normal appearance fee."

"All smart-ass all the time," Cates said.

"And I thought you were just jealous of my good looks," Mason said without turning around.

Griswold raised his hands. "My kids aren't as big a pain in the ass as you two are. Give it a rest, why don't you."

Mason held up his right hand in a fist except for his extended little finger. "Hey, Cates. Pinky truce?"

"Asshole," Cates said, smacking Mason's hand. "This is a waste of time. Let me know when you get a good idea," he said to Griswold. "I've got better things to do."

"What can I do for you, Detective Griswold?" Mason asked after Cates left.

"You're like a cold sore with a personality, you know that, Mason? Annoying as hell but amusing on someone else. Don't tell Cates, but I liked the pinky truce."

"Your secret is safe with me. What do you want?"

"Answers. Information. A road map. We know that somebody killed Charles Rockley and left him in your client's car. Maybe it was your client and he was so busy playing let's make a deal with the feds that he didn't have time to get rid of the body. Maybe it was someone who wanted us to look at your client. You got any ideas who might want to set up your client?"

"I've got no idea. He's a nice old man. Doesn't bother anyone."

"Cut the crap for five minutes, Mason. From what I hear, your nice old man has been fleecing people all his life, including a bunch that isn't getting their Florida dream vacation."

"Those people aren't out enough money to kill someone and try to pin it on Avery Fish. Give me a break."

Griswold ignored the holes in his theory and changed tacks. "Why was Johnny Keegan carrying around your name and number when he got clipped?"

"Must have needed a good lawyer."

"You ever talk to him?"

"Nope. The guy was only a bartender. He couldn't have afforded me anyway."

"We talked to the manager of the Galaxy, guy named Al Webb," Griswold said, consulting the spiral notepad he carried in his shirt pocket. "Webb says Rockley got himself sued in a sexual harassment case over a woman named Carol Hill, who, it turns out according to Webb, was banging Keegan. How about that?"

"Shocks the conscience."

"Pissed off her husband, too, from what Webb told us."

"Then why wasn't Hill in the lineup instead of me?"

"We picked him up for questioning yesterday. He had a lousy alibi and a fat lip so naturally we ask him if Rockley gave it to him and that's why he popped him, plus the fact that Rockley was pawing his wife. He says he didn't kill Rockley. Says he was minding his own business, drinking his sorrows away at a bar in Fairfax last Friday night. Said he got into it with someone and that's how he got the lip."

"And you think I gave it to him and now you're going to arrest me for assault?"

Griswold gave him an indulgent smile. "Putting a lawyer away would be a public service, but we'll wait for something with real bite. We went to the bar to check on Hill's story. The bartender confirmed that Hill was there last Friday when two guys braced him. Said Hill pulled a knife on one of the guys and the other guy took it away from him and then they hustled Hill outside. One of the waitresses said she recognized one of the two guys from seeing his picture in the paper and on TV. Said his name was Lou Mason. So Detective Cates calls Hill and asks him if he'd like to press charges against the guy who beat him up. Hill says sure and Cates says we've got a suspect we want to put in a lineup."

"That lineup was bullshit and you know it."

"It was bullshit if we wanted to charge you, but not if we wanted to test Hill's story and get on his good side, being sympathetic and all that. Just because we like your client for Rockley's murder doesn't mean we're sitting around with our thumbs up our ass. Could be it was Hill. We needed you for the lineup. Guess what?"

"Surprise me."

"He didn't pick you even though we stacked the deck. What do you make of that?"

Mason was wearing the same jacket he'd had on Friday night. Hill's knife was still in the inside pocket. He wasn't going to get out of the witness room by denying what had happened in the bar. He pulled the knife from his pocket and laid it on the table.

"We didn't lay a hand on him."

"We?"

"Blues and me. We went to the bar to talk to Hill. He pulled the knife on me and Blues took it away from him. We went outside and talked. He left and wrecked his pickup on the way out of the parking lot. Ran into a car parked across the street. The driver got out and decked him."

"Blues as in Wilson Bluestone, the ex-cop?"

Mason nodded.

"They still talk about him around here. Not the way I'd like to be remembered. I don't suppose you got a license tag on the other car or that you can identify the other driver?"

Mason was following two of the cardinal rules he gave his clients. Only answer the question asked and don't forget that the guy on the other side of the table isn't your friend.

"No tag. Tall guy, blond, works out a lot."

"You're a big help, you know that?"

"Best I can do. Sorry."

Griswold shrugged his shoulders and leaned forward in his chair. "It's like this, Mason. We didn't find out that Rock- ley was the stiff in your client's car until a reporter called us Friday night. By then, you'd already been to see Mark Hill. So me and Cates wonder what led you to him and we can only think of one thing. You knew that Rockley was the stiff and you knew about the sexual harassment case. Al Webb says he ran into you Saturday night at some Republican Party blowout and that you knew all about Rockley, Keegan, and Carol Hill. When we talked to you Friday night, you claimed you never heard of Johnny Keegan. You starting to see the problems me and Cates are having with all of this?"

Mason had been leaning back in his chair, the front legs off the floor. He eased the chair down. Griswold's refrain was the same as Vince Bongiovanni's. The only thing they were both missing was the picture of Blues outside Rockley's apartment.

"You think the only way I could have gotten to Hill was if someone told me about Rockley, and you think Fish is that someone because he killed Rockley."

"Head of the class, Mason. That's right where you're headed."

"Except Fish had no connection to Rockley and he didn't kill him. Whoever did had his own reasons for dumping the body in the trunk of Fish's car. That was Fish's bad luck, period."

"If Fish didn't tell you about Rockley, who did?"

Mason met Griswold's gaze, then looked away and stood. He couldn't keep ducking Griswold's questions without inviting more suspicion. He was willing to trade partial answers for information Griswold might have.

"You really didn't know that Rockley was the murder victim before Rachel Firestone called you?"

"It's not your turn to ask questions."

"It is if you want any answers from me."

Griswold hesitated, tapping his coffee cup on the table. "No, we didn't know. Made us look like rookies."

"Who leaked Rockley's ID to the press?"

"Had to have been the FBI. Who else could it have been? We sent them the DNA sample."

"Did you call them on it?"

"Damn straight! I'm the liaison with the Bureau on this case. My counterpart is an agent named Kelly Holt. Good looking but cold. She said it wasn't them. But you knew it was Rockley before the Star came out with it, am I right?"

Mason hesitated but saw no edge in denying the obvious. "Yeah, I knew."

"When did you find out?"

Mason sighed. "Friday morning."

"Friday fucking morning! Who told you?"

"Kelly Holt."

Griswold stood and stepped toward Mason until their chins were almost touching. "Listen to me, Mason—and this is Griswold's gospel. Kelly Holt got her skirt dirty once before and they ran her out of the Bureau. No one seems to know how or why she got back in. She wouldn't have told you about Rockley without getting something in return. I'd be real careful before I put your client's life in her hands. You tell Fish that if he killed Rockley, he'll never get a better deal than if tells me all about it right now."

"And if he didn't kill Rockley?"

"Don't get in bed with Uncle Sam. They'll fuck you for sport."

"What do we get if we climb in bed with you?"

"A kiss in the morning."

CHAPTER FORTY-SIX

MASON KNEW ABOUT Kelly's history with the FBI, though it was Kelly's version—wrongfully accused and brokenhearted. He didn't know what had brought her back to the Bureau, into Fish's case, and back into his life. Griswold had his slant. The facts were the same. The slant was everything.

He assumed Kelly would play hard and play to win but that she knew where to draw the lines. She probably assumed the same about him, though her assumption would collapse if she knew what he'd done to Judge Carter. Maybe they didn't know each other as well as they thought. It was all in the slant.

Samantha Greer fell in alongside Mason as he walked down the stairs from the bullpen.

"Sorry about the lineup," she said.

"Don't be sorry. You were doing your job."

"I know, but that doesn't mean I like it. Especially when I'm working with Cates. That boy is a P-I-G pig."

"Animal House, right?"

"Yeah. I went out with this guy who claimed there was no situation in life that couldn't be explained by that movie. It was his philosophy and his religion."

"How inspirational. Was there a second date?"

"No. The guy was a total loser, but I rented the movie and, you know what, there's something to it. In fact, there's one line that works better than any of the others."

"Which one?"

"It's right after they wreck the fat kid's car, the one he borrowed from his older brother. One of the guys says to him, 'You fucked up. You trusted us.' Now there's a lesson."

"And the rest is commentary."

"Hey, are you buying me dinner tomorrow night or what? It's my birthday."

They stopped at the bottom of the stairs. Samantha ducked her chin and fingered the ends of her hair as a couple of detectives walked by, giving them a knowing glance. She was acting like they were kids on the playground and he was asking her out. Except it wasn't a date even if she thought it was. It was an obligation—one he wished he didn't have especially now that she was involved in his case and even more so since it was her birthday.

"I've been saving up. How about that Italian place in the Freight House? Meet you there at eight."

She smiled, but only enough to hide her disappointment that he didn't offer to pick her up. For an instant, he thought she was mouthing the line from Animal House.

"Sounds great," she said instead, giving his hand a quick squeeze before heading back up the stairs.

Mason stood on the sidewalk outside police headquarters. It was a cloudy day, cold enough to make him want to keep moving, but he jammed his hands in his jacket pockets and ignored the temperature, concentrating on Kelly Holt.

She'd told Mason about Rockley but denied that she'd leaked the information to the press when Griswold asked her if she had. Mason believed her since keeping the lid on Rockley's identity a while longer was part of her pitch to him and Fish. Pete Samuelson had nothing to gain by leaking the information. Nor would he have had any reason to tip off Vince Bongiovanni.

That left someone else in the U.S. attorney's office or the FBI as the source of the leak. Mason could come up only with one candidate. Dennis Brewer, the FBI agent who'd appeared on the scene after Hill clipped the sedan on his way out of the parking lot at Easy's. That was a card he'd play when he and Fish met with Kelly and Samuelson later that night.

Fish had persuaded Mason not to quit representing him. It was time instead, as Fish had put it, to get in the game. That meant telling the feds they were ready to play. They'd figure out what to do after the feds told them what they wanted from Fish. Mason had agreed, but told Fish that he'd prefer to know what game he was playing, who was playing it, and what the rules were. Fish had laughed.

"The name of the game," he had said, "was Fuck Your Buddy. Everyone was playing it and there weren't any rules. That's what makes it so much fun."

Mason had parked his car in a lot on the opposite side of City Hall. He crossed Oak and continued walking west on Twelfth Street, passing the courthouse just as Vanessa Carter came off the courthouse steps onto the sidewalk. He had his head down, and he nearly bumped into her. She was wearing a full-length black wool coat with a fur collar, a flat-brimmed hat cast to one side of her head, and dark glasses. He took a step back when he recognized her.

"Don't look so surprised," she told him. "They still let me in the Courthouse."

Mason struggled for the right thing to say. "Good for them."

"Good for me and good for you. I get a call now and then to fill in pro tem if one of the judges is sick. It's almost funny. They don't really know what to do with me. I was a damn good judge and everyone knows that, but the rumors about why I quit hang around like a bad smell. It's like they're letting me stick one toe at a time back into the water to make sure I don't clear out the whole damn pool."

Mason sighed, relieved that another piece of her life was falling back into place. "That's great. Really great."

"You better believe it is, and I'll be goddamned if I'm going to let some two-bit blackmailing piece of scum ruin it for me again." She took him by the arm, her fingers piercing his jacket. "I can't afford to lose this all over again. You've got to make this go away. I don't care what you have to do. Now, promise me," she said, holding his eyes.

He felt a greater responsibility for Vanessa Carter than he did for many of his clients, most of whom were guilty. Even the ones who weren't had usually done something stupid enough to make them suspects. They were in trouble because of what they had done. Even so, he worked the cops, the case, and the system to get them the best result he could. But Vanessa Carter was in trouble because of what he had done. That she could have told Ed Fiori no when he pressured her to release Blues on bail didn't matter. Mason had put her in the position of having to make that choice. That was his burden, not hers.

He nodded. "Whatever it takes."

When Mason got back to his office, there was a message on his voice mail.

"Lou, it's Lari Prillman. I called all of Keegan's former employers. Every one of them said he was a good employee they'd like to have back. One woman even cried when I told her he'd been killed and asked where she could send flowers.

Let me know if I can do anything else."

Mason saved the message and called her.

"Is that unusual?" he asked her.

"Is what unusual?"

"For employers to give out that kind of information about former employees. I thought they were too worried about getting sued to give references."

She paused before answering. "I admit it's not typical, but when I told them that Keegan had been murdered and that I represented his last employer, they didn't hesitate at all. Why should they?"

"No reason, at least not that I can think of. Do me another favor?"

"At my hourly rates, you can't afford my favors."

"Then charge it to Galaxy. Saturday night when we first got to your office, one of your phone lines was lit up. Whoever took the CD from your safe made a call. Check with the phone company. Let's see who he called."

"Since that may be a favor for both of us, I won't even charge you. I'll fax the records to you when I get them."

He stared at the phone after he hung up, debating whether to call Abby. He ran through the litany of reasons. He'd been unfair, too hard and too jealous. Josh Seeley's wife was probably guilty of the same behavior toward the senator. Maybe Abby hadn't chosen the best way to defuse Mrs. Seeley's jealousy, but that didn't mean their day together had been a sham. Abby just wasn't that type.

What griped him, and kept his hand from the phone, was that she hadn't told him what was going on and asked for his help. It was all about honesty, he told himself with puffed-up pride. Then he thought about Vanessa Carter and realized he'd never told Abby what he'd done to the judge. It was a lot easier to insist that someone come clean if it was their laundry instead of his. He chided himself for setting the bar higher for Abby than he had for himself, then dialed her number.

He was only partially disappointed when she didn't answer. At least he got to hear her voice ask him to leave a message. He told her he was sorry about Saturday night and that he had jumped to the wrong conclusion and wanted to see her again before she left town. He left his cell phone number and said that he had a late meeting with a client that night.

Just before he left his office, he opened the dry erase board and studied the hieroglyphics he'd written in an effort to make sense out of everyone and everything. Picking up a black marker, he wrote two words in large block letters across the maze of names, questions, and lines that connected them—ANIMAL HOUSE.

CHAPTER FORTY-SEVEN

Meeting Pete Samuelson and Kelly Holt at Blues on Broadway had been Fish's idea.

"All this mishegas about blackmail, anonymous tip-offs, pictures from cell phones, and intercepted e-mails, it's enough to give me a headache," Fish had said. "But, I'll tell you this much. In a noisy, crowded bar, it's hard to intercept anything. Besides, we've been to their place enough. Let them come to us this time."

Mason had suggested the late hour, explaining that Monday night was Jam Night, when local musicians crowded the small stage, drawing appreciative crowds that let the musicians know when they got it right. If they wanted the security of a noisy crowd, it was the perfect time and place.

"We'll be lucky to hear each other. No one could eavesdrop if they tried," Mason had said.

"Good, but what if one of them is wearing—what do they call those things?—a wire?"

"Avery," Mason had answered, "wires are what under cover guys wear. Besides, we're not confessing to anything. We're there to listen. They ask you to do something that even smells hinky, we'll get it in writing signed by their boss, Roosevelt Holmes. They want to use you, not entrap you."

After reassuring Fish, Mason told Blues about the meeting with Samuelson and Kelly.

"Where do you want me?" Blues asked.

"Someplace where you can watch."

"You want me to wire the booth, I can do it. They'll never know."

Mason thought about it, but remembered his conversation with Fish. "I'll pass. Samuelson might be green enough to stick his foot in his mouth, but Kelly's too smart for that. Besides, as good as you are, if Kelly found out, we're finished."

Blues hung a reserved sign on the booth that was farthest from the door and the stage and unscrewed the recessed lightbulbs above the table. The bar was lit with soft whites and pale greens that blended into a smokeless haze. He sat in the corner of the booth and looked out. With the overhead bulbs removed, the booth sunk into a shadow that was like a one-way mirror. It was as if he could see out but no one could see in.

Mason settled into the booth at nine-thirty and waited. His eyes adjusted to the dim light. He watched the people clustered around the bar, servers dodging between them.

The Myles Cartwright Trio was packed tight on the stage mixing it up. Sonny Freeman joined them, Myles on piano giving him a nod. Sonny was a short, skinny black man with bony shoulders and close-cropped hair, his face as shiny as the sax he carried. He was a Jam Night regular, always welcome. The crowd let him know it, saying amen as he wet his mouthpiece. He tapped his foot a few times to pick up the beat and laid down a track following Myles's lead, wrapping his notes around the others like clinging ivy.

People walked past Mason as if he wasn't there, not seeing him in the shaded booth. Blues, tall enough to see over his customers, roamed behind the length of the bar. He filled glasses and made change, his eyes on the door.

Mason caught a hitch in Blues's shoulder and a moment later Fish materialized at the booth, hanging his coat on a nearby hook. He was wearing dark slacks and a mock turtleneck shirt under a cardigan sweater. He looked like everyone's grandpa, but when he slid in across from Mason, grunting with the effort as his belly fought with the table, he gave Mason a hungry look, like a night prowler. He rubbed his hands together.

"So," he said, "you think they'll be early or late?"

"Why wouldn't they be on time?"

"On time is for marks. Early and late are for players. Early means they don't trust you and want to get a lay of the land. Late means they want to make you nervous. Are they coming? Are they not coming? Did they make you sweat?"

"What if they just get caught in traffic?"

"Cute," Fish said, pointing a meaty finger at him. "You don't want to pay attention, don't pay attention. They get caught in traffic it's because they don't care if they're late. You understand? You want to figure out a con, you start with the setup. Early, late—it's like choosing an outfit. It sends a message. You watch."

Mason looked at Blues, who dipped his head at the door. Mason checked his watch. It was ten straight up. Pete Samuelson found them at their booth, and Mason stepped out, switching to Fish's side. As he did so, Kelly Holt emerged from another booth, leaving a glass of wine and cash on the table as she walked toward them. Mason looked over her shoulder at Blues, who shook his head. He didn't know how long she'd been there, but it was long enough to prove Fish's point.

Samuelson was wearing a suit. He loosened his tie, but the effort didn't loosen him up. He twisted his head in every direction like he was waiting for a camera flash. Fish watched him fidget, his mouth locked in a patient smile.

Mason and Kelly studied each other. He offered her a wry smile slicker than a come-on, the shrug of his shoulders pretending they were just having a drink for old times. She cut him off with an icy look that said Nice try, but don't go there. He got the message, leaned back into the booth, and started the dance.

"My client is ready to make a deal. Tell us what you want," Mason said.

Samuelson cleared his throat. "It's not quite that simple."

"What's so complicated?" Fish asked. "You want me to do something, I'll do it. Whatever it is, as long as it's not dangerous. I'm too old and fat for dangerous."

"And," Mason added, "as long as it includes dismissal of the mail fraud charge."

"That's what makes it complicated," Samuelson said. "Before we found a body in Mr. Fish's car, we were arguing over jail time and dollars. Now you want us to dismiss the charges in return for what? Mr. Fish's cooperation? I don't think so."

"Look," Mason said. "My client is agreeing to work for you without having so much as a job description. He's the cops' number-one suspect for a murder he didn't commit, so getting rid of the mail fraud charge won't exactly make him sleep better at night. You want him, you got him. But you've got to give us something worth having in return."

Samuelson looked at Kelly, who leaned into him, whispering. He let out a sigh. "I'll take it to Roosevelt Holmes. It's his call."

"You do that," Mason said and slid his cell phone across the table to Samuelson. "Right now, or we can just order a round and enjoy the music."

Kelly snapped the phone off the table. "I'll work it out with Holmes myself. Is that good enough for you, Lou?"

Mason hadn't figured out the pecking order, but it was clear that this was more Kelly's show than Samuelson's. She wouldn't have made the offer unless she knew it was already done.

"Good enough. What's the deal?"

Samuelson pulled an envelope from his suit coat, extracted a piece of paper, and handed it to Mason. In the dim light, Mason had trouble making it out, but quickly understood what it was.

"What is it?" Fish asked.

"It's a plea agreement, also known as your get-out-of-jailfree card. It says you agree to assist the Justice Department with an investigation and they agree to fill in the blank identifying the investigation after you sign."

"What's that supposed to mean?"

"It means that you sign first and they promise later. After Kelly talks to Roosevelt Holmes."

"What if her boss says no?"

"Then we don't have a deal. They reserve the right to reinstate the charges if they aren't satisfied with your cooperation. If Roosevelt Holmes doesn't agree to dismiss the mail fraud charge, you don't cooperate and we're back to square one."

"Such a crazy business."

"Your tax dollars at work. Sign it."

Fish signed his name and looked away as Samuelson sealed the agreement inside the envelope, tucking it back into his jacket pocket.

"Thank you, Mr. Fish," Samuelson said. "Your government is grateful."

"For what? I haven't done anything yet and I don't see how I can. My name is all over the papers like a common criminal. Which I'm not. Thank you very much. So how can I possibly help my government that's so grateful?"

Kelly answered. "We are investigating a money-laundering operation. We want you to launder some money for us so we can trace where it goes."

"How much money?" Fish asked, perking up now that the game had begun.

"A hundred thousand dollars," Kelly said.

"I don't know anything about laundering money."

"We don't care what you know. We're interested in who you know," Kelly said.

"I don't know any money launderers either."

"Mr. Fish," Kelly said, "have you ever been to the Galaxy Casino?"

Fish shook his head. "Casinos are for suckers, Ms. Holt."

"Who bring a lot of money with them and leave it there," she said. "The manager of the casino is a man named Al Webb. You'll make contact with him and tell him you need to put a hundred thousand dollars away where the government can't find it until you get your legal problems worked out."

Mason bit the inside of his mouth at the mention of Webb's name. He couldn't tell whether the noose he was caught in was getting tighter or whether he was about to find a way to slip out of the knot.

"And this Webb character who doesn't know me from Adam," Fish said. "I suppose he's going to thank me for my business, give me a receipt, and tell me to come back tomorrow to pick up the number for my new Swiss bank account."

It was Kelly's turn to take an envelope out of her jacket pocket. It contained a photograph. She handed it to Mason along with a pen flashlight.

"Do you recognize this man?" she asked Fish.

Mason shined the light on the black-and-white photograph as Fish studied Al Webb's image.

Fish tugged at his face, struggling with a dormant memory. He picked up the photograph, his hands shaking with recognition. "It's not possible," he said.

"What's not possible?" Mason asked.

"It's the eyes. He's done something. Plastic surgery, I suppose. But, you can't change a man's eyes. But it's still not possible."

"Who is it?" Kelly asked.

"Wayne McBride. But he's been dead for ten years," Fish said.

"How do you know that?" Mason asked.

"Because," Fish said in a low voice, "he was my partner and I was a pallbearer at his funeral."

CHAPTER FORTY-EIGHT

"YOUR EX-PARTNER IS doing well for a dead man," Kelly said.

"But I was there," Fish said. "At his funeral. I sat with his wife, Sylvia. She cried like a baby."

"When was the last time you saw her?" Kelly asked.

"I stayed in touch with her for a while. The last time I saw her, she told me she was moving back to Minneapolis. She had a sister there who was dying of cancer. She went to take care of her. That was about six months after Wayne died."

"Her sister died a year later. Sylvia inherited the house and still lives there. She works for a telephone call center and lives a quiet, modest life. She hasn't remarried."

"I can't believe it. They had a place at Ten Mile Lake in Minnesota. Wayne was fooling around on his dock. He slipped, fell in the water, and got caught under the boat. Sylvia, she went looking for him. I'll never forget what she said to me. It was a nightmare. She kept calling his name. Finally, she looked down in the water and there he was. Staring back at her. Drowned."

Mason interrupted. "You're saying this McBride faked his death. How did he do it?"

"It wasn't difficult," Kelly said. "His wife called nine- one-one and identified the body when the paramedics fished it out of the water. The coroner ruled the death accidental. No questions asked."

"What about the body?" Mason asked. "Whose was it?"

"Mr. Fish?" Kelly asked.

"Who knows? He was cremated," Fish answered, thumping his palm on the table. "Such a putz, I was!"

"You?" Mason asked. "Why? How could you have known?"

"I couldn't have. It was a small funeral. Closed casket, which was fine with me. That's not what I mean. Wayne owed me fifty thousand dollars from a deal we closed a week before he died. He didn't have any life insurance. I felt sorry for Sylvia and I told her to keep the money."

Mason turned to Kelly. "How did you find out that Webb was really McBride?"

Samuelson held his hand up. "We learned about that in our investigation. What's important now is that Mr. Fish confirmed his identity."

"I don't like this," Mason said. "If Avery asks Webb to hide his money, Webb will know that his identity is blown. He killed one man to fake his death. I don't want Avery to be next."

"We don't know that he killed anyone," Kelly said.

"What about the body?" Mason asked.

"All we know is that the paramedics found a man's body in the water. We don't know whose it was. A lot of people drown accidentally. Because the body was cremated, we can't prove there was a murder."

"That's supposed to make me feel better?"

"We'll do everything we can to protect Mr. Fish," Samuel- son said. "Besides, Webb won't be able to resist a million dollars."

"I thought it was only a hundred thousand," Mason said.

"That's the bait," Fish said. "Am I right?"

Samuelson nodded.

"Make it a million one-hundred sixty-seven. Nobody has exactly a million bucks lying around. I'll tell him that I'll let him handle the balance if he can take care of me on the hundred. He won't try anything until he gets the rest of the money. That's the way these things work. You always bait the hook first."

"And we nail him before he tries anything with Mr. Fish," Samuelson said.

Mason looked at Kelly, who coolly met his gaze, silently telling him she would do her best but that she'd leave the guarantees to Samuelson.

"What about Rockley's murder?" Mason asked. "Your scheme does nothing for him with the cops and Patrick Ortiz."

Samuelson cleared his throat. "We'll make certain the state authorities are aware of Mr. Fish's cooperation."

"That's just terrific. But we need something more than a letter of recommendation for the judge to read at his sentencing."

"That's the best we can do," Samuelson said. "Our case against Webb has nothing to do with Rockley's murder. We can't interfere with that investigation."

"I still don't like it. Webb, or McBride or whoever he is, won't take the chance that Avery isn't setting him up. He'll figure Avery needs something to offer the cops and the FBI to stay out of jail. He'll want to know how Fish got to him.

There's no story Fish can tell him that won't make him suspicious."

"I'll call Sylvia," Fish said. "She knew it wasn't Wayne's body they fished out of the lake. She was crazy in love with him. She has to know that Wayne is still alive. I'll tell her I need her help hiding the money. I won't have to mention Wayne's name. He'll find me."

Samuelson beamed. Kelly looked at Fish with newfound respect and permitted herself a small grin. Mason shook his head.

"How was your relationship with Sylvia?" Kelly asked.

"Like brother and sister. She was always after me to lose weight."

"Don't do this," Mason told Fish. "It's too dangerous. They can't make the murder charge against you and we can beat the mail fraud."

Fish put his arm around Mason's shoulder. "Such a good lawyer I've got. He tells me to take the deal before he knows what it is. Then he tells me not to take it after he finds out what it is. And I'm paying for this advice."

"You told them you'd cooperate as long as it wasn't dangerous. This is too dangerous."

Fish shrugged. "Danger is a relative thing. When you're an old man like me, there's nothing as dangerous as going to sleep at night. Who knows if you'll wake up the next day? I'm not so worried about my former partner. He likes money too much. And, when Miss FBI Holt says she'll take good care of me, I believe her."

"You don't think Webb will be suspicious?"

"Of course he'll be suspicious. People in my business are always suspicious. We don't trust anybody. He'll think I'm conning him, but he'll go along to see how it plays out."

"And you? Why are you doing it?"

"It's what I do." He turned to Kelly. "I assume you have Sylvia's phone number."

"She's in the book," Kelly said as she wrote the number on a napkin and slid it across the table to Fish. He studied it and grunted.

"Same old Sylvia."

"What do you mean?" Kelly asked.

"She liked to play a lottery where you had to pick seven winning numbers. She'd always pick three pairs of two numbers. Each pair added up to the same number and the seventh was that number. Like sixty-three, twenty-seven, fifty-four, and nine. Each pair adds up to nine. Get it? Now, look at her phone number. It's 445-3628. Break it down—forty-four, fifty-three, sixty-two, and eight. It's the same pattern."

"What's your point?" Samuelson asked.

"Sylvia never won the lottery, but she's still playing her system. I'll bet she even requested the phone number. When I call, she'll think she finally won."

CHAPTER FORTY-NINE

SAMUELSON AGREED TO be at Fish's house Tuesday morning at seven-thirty to place the call to Sylvia McBride before she left for work. He objected at first, wanting to use his office. Fish patiently explained that Sylvia probably had caller ID and would be suspicious if Justice Department flashed across the readout on her phone.

They left together, Samuelson helping Fish with his coat as if he were wrapping a fragile package. Fish played along, winking at Mason and letting Samuelson guide him by the elbow through the crowd. For effect, he added a deep cough that echoed like a parent's worry on Samuelson's furrowed brow.

"Fish will have that kid washing his car and cutting his grass before this is over," Mason said to Kelly.

"Cut him some slack. He graduated first in his law school class."

"Then I'm sure he'll do a great job with Fish's lawn. Buy you a beer?"

Kelly crinkled her nose. "Long day. Maybe we can catch up when this is over."

Mason shook his head. He was more interested in their present than in their past. Detective Griswold's warning about Kelly may have been nothing more than the usual collegial backstabbing between cops and feds, but that didn't mean he was wrong. Kelly had left the FBI under a cloud, though the Bureau wouldn't have taken her back if there was any doubt. Mason was certain of one thing. Their past was past. He couldn't count on any favors from Kelly, especially if she was playing him in an elaborate game in which his client's life was a chip to be tossed into the pot.

"I wasn't thinking of catching up. We weren't going to make it and we both knew that. You did the right thing breaking it off."

Kelly leaned against the booth, her hands folded together on the table, her face cool. "I'm glad you feel that way, especially now that we both have our jobs to do."

"I am a little curious about one thing."

Kelly's mouth twitched in a quick smile. "Really? Only one?"

Mason shrugged. "Maybe one or two. Why did you go back to the Bureau?"

"Unfinished business, I suppose. I didn't leave on my own terms the first time. I'd been accused of something I didn't do. I thought I could leave the accusation behind. But it didn't work that way, even after I was cleared. It was like I could hear them whispering about me no matter how far away I was. I had to go back to show them they were wrong."

Mason could have closed his eyes and imagined Judge Carter making the same speech. She wanted to silence the whispers too, except she was guilty, even if Mason had entrapped her.

"Are they still whispering?"

"A few of them always will. I just don't listen anymore. Besides, the Bureau moves me around a lot and that helps."

"Why do they do that?"

"Sometimes I work on special cases."

"How special?"

"The kind that doesn't earn you many friends."

Mason knew from Blues that the one cop other cops never liked or trusted was the cop from Internal Affairs. He assumed the same was true for the FBI. Kelly had gone back to the Bureau to prove they were wrong about her. Having been judged, she now judged others. He wondered whether her judgment was tempered with mercy born of her own experience or whether it was hardened by a desire to get even. Dennis Brewer couldn't be happy to have Kelly involved in Fish's case, especially if he had leaked Rockley's ID.

"Sounds like the FBI version of Internal Affairs."

"Let's leave it at that. I've got to get our equipment installed in Fish's house before he makes that phone call in the morning. Are you going to be there?"

"Wouldn't miss it. Before you come over, you might want to take a look at this," he said, reaching into his shirt pocket and handing her a flash drive.

"What's on it? Photographs?"

"Yeah. Consider it a welcome-home present."

She flipped the drive over in the palm of her hand. "Not of us, I take it."

"I'm saving those for my website. These are more interesting. Your partner Dennis Brewer is in one of the shots. He's got a couple of playmates. I was hoping you would tell me who they are."

She looked at him, her voice even, barely interested. "Just because we're both FBI agents doesn't mean he's my partner. Where were the pictures taken?"

"Outside a bar in Fairfax called Easy's. Not far from where you picked Blues and me up last Friday night. Two of them were sitting in a car across the street from the bar. Brewer was backing them up. Either you were backing Brewer up or maybe he's one of your special cases. Which is it?"

"Who took the pictures?" she asked, ignoring his question.

"Who took the picture of Blues outside Rockley's apartment?"

"That's on a need-to-know basis and you don't need to know."

"I have a lot of needs. That's one of them."

"I can't help you with your needs."

"Sure you can, especially if that will help with your needs. I need to know who took Blues's picture and you need to know who took the pictures of Brewer and his playmates. We need the same thing."

"The difference is, I already know who took your pictures. If they were taken outside that bar, it had to be you or Blues."

"Then why ask?"

"Confession is good for you. It builds rapport and trust with those to whom you confess. Cooperation follows confession and the next thing you know you're actually telling the truth. I'm just helping you find your way," she said.

"Then help me with this," Mason said. "Someone tipped off Rachel Firestone that the corpse in Avery Fish's car was Charles Rockley. The Star wouldn't have printed her story without corroboration from the FBI or Justice, both of which officially declined to comment. Somebody confirmed the ID off the record. Was it you?"

"I was holding the ID back from the police while we tried to make a deal with you. Why would I leak that information?"

"What about Samuelson?"

"Be serious. He doesn't go to the bathroom without double- checking the Justice Department manual."

"Who else knew about Rockley?"

Kelly pursed her lips, ran through her mental list and shook her head.

"Let me help you," he said. "That leaves Samuelson's boss, Roosevelt Holmes, some DNA database jockey at Quantico who confirmed the match, and Dennis Brewer."

She gave him a flat look that said she'd gone deaf. "Leaks are impossible to prevent and harder to trace."

"Might be easier to trace this one if you start with who else was tipped off. A blackjack dealer at Galaxy named Carol Hill sued Rockley and Galaxy for sexual harassment. Rachel Firestone wasn't the only one who got the tip. Carol's lawyer, Vince Bongiovanni, got one too."

The flicker in Kelly's eyes told Mason he'd gotten her attention. "We talked to Rockley's employer and found out about the lawsuit. How do you know that Bongiovanni was tipped off?"

"He told me. He knew that I represented Fish and he hoped I'd find out something that would help him with Carol Hill's case."

"What's the point of telling him about Rockley?" Kelly asked.

She'd made it clear that Brewer wasn't her partner. When she asked him about the pictures and the leak, he wouldn't be her friend either.

"Ask Dennis Brewer. Tell him he could use a good confession. If he turns you down, I'd watch your back, Special Agent Holt."

Kelly kept her cool as she slid out of the booth, pulled her coat over her shoulders, adjusting her scarf and pulling on her gloves. He watched as she walked away, head up, shoulders square, people making room for her as she passed.

CHAPTER FIFTY

A GUY WITH HUMVEE-SIZE shoulders bulled his way to the bar, empty bottles in each raised hand. Mason followed in the big man's wake, resting one foot on the rail at the base of the bar; thinking again about the deal Fish had made, not liking it any better. Fish had agreed just to get even with Wayne McBride over the fifty thousand dollars McBride had scammed from him before resurrecting himself as Al Webb, casino manager. Revenge made people do stupid things.

Fish was walking into a minefield with no idea where the trip wires were buried. Though Pete Samuelson had promised to protect Fish, Mason detected in Kelly a coldness that made collateral damage an acceptable fact of life. Everyone takes their turn in the barrel. She'd had hers. Fish would have his. It was a side of her that Mason hadn't seen before, and it made him realize he couldn't ask for her help. He was naked, any control over his life having vanished when Vanessa Carter knocked on his door a week ago.

He leaned against the bar, conscious again of the music.

Myles Cartwright finished the set with a flourish on the piano, the sound cool and crisp, the drummer, bass player, and sax giving him room. The audience exploded with applause as the musicians took their bows. Myles said they were taking a break and would be back for another set. He felt a hand on his shoulder, heard a familiar voice, and turned around.

"Hey," Rachel Firestone said. "What does a girl have to do to get someone to buy her a beer?"

Rachel always stood out in a crowd. It wasn't just her red hair or her striking looks. It was the way she carried herself, telling the world to bring it on. It made her a good reporter and a better friend, though lately she'd been more journalist than buddy. He understood her ambition and the pressure she felt from her boss to prove that she was independent enough to follow a story wherever it took her, even one that got into his kitchen. The glint in her eyes made him uneasy. He smiled and took a step back, trying to figure out which hat she was wearing.

"Ask nice and offer to buy the next round." He caught Blues's attention and held up two fingers. Blues handed him two cold long-necked bottles, and Mason gave one to Rachel. "Are you working or just looking for a good time?"

"I'm meeting a friend."

"Anyone special?"

"Not for me. She's involved with someone else. Girls' night out."

"Which means I get off cheap. I could have been stuck for another beer."

"There's still time. She'll be here any minute. By the way, I didn't know you were open for business this late." Mason lowered the bottle from his lips, waiting for the shoe to drop. "I saw Avery Fish and Pete Samuelson walking out of here arm in arm. Two seconds later, I bumped into Kelly Holt. I haven't seen her since your days at Sullivan and Christen- son. I hear she's back with the FBI and that she's the liaison with the cops on the Rockley murder. She looks great, by the way."

"This is a popular place."

"Don't feel bad, Lou. I mean, what are the odds? You have a private, late-night meeting with your client and the government. I stumble across it. But it's not news unless you tell me what's going on. How else will I find out if you made a deal or were just getting drunk together?"

"You could find out from somebody else."

"There's always that," she said. "But, I'm off the clock. Don't make me work for my beer or for my story."

"You're never off the clock and you'd never take a story you didn't work for." He couldn't tell Rachel about the deal Fish had made, but he could aim her at Dennis Brewer. If he didn't give her something, he'd be reading about his meeting in tomorrow's paper. "Step into my office," he said, motioning toward his booth.

"Not bad for a branch office," Rachel said as they sat down.

"Low overhead. Look, you know I can't talk to you about any conversations we may have had with the government."

"Yet."

"Or maybe ever. There's no story here. Let it go."

"Lou, do I look like a complete moron? You and your client meet with the Assistant U.S. attorney who's prosecuting your client for mail fraud and the FBI agent handling the investigation of a murder in which your client is the prime suspect. You do all this late at night in a bar, and that's not a story?"

"My office is upstairs."

"Then what were the four of you doing in this booth? Buying a round of drinks to celebrate? I saw Fish and Samuelson when they left. When I said I bumped into Kelly, I meant that literally, and it wasn't an accident. She said she was glad to see me, but believe me, I know when a woman means that. And she didn't."

Mason gave her a hard look. Not to change her mind about what she'd seen. That wasn't possible. But to let her know he was serious.

"I can't talk about the case, Rachel. It's that simple. If you write a story about seeing us together, people's lives could be in danger."

Rachel leaned forward, her elbows on the table, her chin in her hands, deciding whether to believe him. She nodded and straightened.

"Then tell me something that I can give my editor when I tell him that I can't write this story."

"How do you feel about a trade?"

"As long as it doesn't involve sexual favors, I have an open mind."

"When did you raise your standards?"

"When you were born male. What do you want?"

"You got an anonymous tip about Charles Rockley. The Star wouldn't have run the story without corroboration. The FBI and the Justice Department officially declined to comment. Who corroborated the story?"

"You know I won't reveal my sources."

"I'll settle for a place. Keep the name to yourself."

Rachel leaned back against the booth, thinking and nodding. "Okay. Now tell me what you've got to trade."

"Another anonymous tip.

"And what tip would that be?"

"That an FBI agent may be freelancing."

Rachel's eyes widened. "You give me a name and a reason not to think you're blowing smoke up my skirt, and I'll make that trade."

"I'll do better than that. I'll give you a name and pictures," Mason said, reaching into his coat pocket and fanning the photographs Blues had taken in an arc across the table. He shoved the FBI agent's toward her. "His name is Dennis Brewer. I don't know who the others are."

Rachel picked up the photograph, studying the image. "What makes you think Brewer is dirty?"

"The company he keeps. These guys have short tempers and bad manners."

"Where should I look?"

"Anyplace but the FBI."

"That leaves a lot of ground to cover. Can't you do better than that?"

Mason hesitated. He only had one lead to give her and it could threaten Fish, him, and her. But it was the only card he had to play. He needed help that he wasn't going to get from Kelly.

"This could be dangerous. Two people are already dead."

Rachel didn't flinch. "One of them is Charles Rockley. Who's the other one?"

"Johnny Keegan. Guy was a bartender at the Galaxy Casino."

"I saw that story. It sounded like a robbery gone bad. What's the connection between Rockley, Keegan, and Brewer? And why didn't you tell me this sooner? I should be kicking you in the ass for that instead of bargaining with you."

Mason had to give her something to work with even if it risked leading her back to him and Judge Carter. She couldn't do her job in a vacuum, and the story would leak eventually, whether from the cops or the FBI.

"Keegan was having an affair with a blackjack dealer named Carol Hill. Carol is married to an unpleasant guy named Mark. Rockley knew she was fooling around and figured to take his turn. Carol wasn't interested. Rockley pushed harder and she sued him and Galaxy for harassment. What I don't know is whether Brewer is mixed up with Rockley or Keegan. And I didn't tell you because I don't know which side you're on these days—mine or your paper's."

"That's a cheap shot!"

"But accurate. I liked things the way they used to be."

She took a deep breath. "Okay. No. It's not okay. You're using me to find the connection between these guys and I don't like being used."

"Then let it all go. Enjoy your night out on the town, forget about it and forget who you saw here."

Rachel shook her head. "Like there's any chance of that."

"I know. It's what you do. What about our trade?"

Rachel scooped up the rest of the photographs, stacked them like playing cards, and dropped them in her purse. She looked squarely at Mason, her eyes narrow and cautious.

"The FBI officially declined to comment about Rockley, but not everyone there is quite so official."

Mason reached across the table, his hand on her wrist. "Who was it?"

She delicately removed his hand. "I'd sooner give up my virtue than give up a source."

"You gave up your virtue years ago."

"But I've never given up a source and I'm not starting now."

CHAPTER FIFTY-ONE

Mason followed Rachel from the booth back to the bar. Myles Cartwright and the rest of the trio, sans the sax player, were back onstage, easing into a gentle number that would pull the crowd along like a lazy current before shooting the rapids. Chatter receded into the background as the music swept the room.

Rachel raised her arm, waving toward the entrance. Mason couldn't see who she was waving at but assumed it was her friend. He was glad she'd finally arrived because now he could gracefully bow out. The day had been so long that he would have to check the fossil record to reconstruct what had happened before lunch.

He glanced around for Blues to tell him he was leaving, not paying attention as Rachel and her friend embraced. When he looked back at them, Abby was standing next to Rachel, her cheeks flushed, her eyes wet from the wind, and her mouth an expectant half-moon.

"Hey," he said, instinctively taking her hand.

"Hey, you," she answered, covering his with hers.

It was what they'd said the first time they'd met. He'd taken her hand then as well, not giving it back until she told him he'd have to feed her if he didn't. Since then, it had become their special way of greeting one another reserved for the end of a hard day, or after they'd been apart or had a fight. It was code for Let's pick up where we started.

"Whew," Rachel said. "I didn't realize how late it was. I'm sorry, but I've got an early day tomorrow. I've got to get going."

Mason and Abby traded grins. Mason looked at Rachel, about to apologize for questioning her loyalty. He opened his mouth and she shook her head, telling him to forget about it.

"Okay, then," Rachel said, clapping her hands. "Am I good or what?"

"Very good," Mason answered.

"The best," Abby said.

Mason led Abby through the crowd, up the back stairs and to his office. He closed the door and turned on the light. Abby turned it off, leaving them bathed in the glow of yellow streetlights and purple neon shimmering through the large window overlooking Broadway. She slipped her arms around his back, her face against his chest.

"I'm sorry," he murmured.

"Me too," she said.

"Overs?" he asked, invoking the playground plea for second chances.

"Over and over," she said, nudging him to the sofa, knocking files and a crumpled sweatshirt and sweatpants to the floor.

They made love and, afterwards, lay tangled together as much by the narrow reach of the sofa as by their fear of letting the other go. They whispered more apologies and explanations.

Abby said that she had told Rachel what had happened Saturday night at the Republican Party dinner and about Mason's phone message that morning. Rachel said that Mason would probably end up at Blues on Broadway if he was working late and offered to go with her so she wouldn't look desperate if he didn't show up.

She told him that Senator Seeley fooled around, that his wife knew it and was suspicious of all the women on his staff, especially her after she'd made the mistake of hugging Seeley on camera on election night. Since then she had kept her boss at arm's length, telling herself that nobody was perfect, that the work was important and she needed a job. None of the excuses made her proud, she admitted.

She had invited Mason to the dinner to discourage Seeley and reassure his wife and should have told him so. More than that, she should have told him how much she missed him—that though she didn't want to live in his violent and desperate world, she didn't want to live in her world, where he was only a distant image.

Mason stroked her face, lacing her hair around his fingers. He wanted to tell her that he had until Friday to stop a blackmailer from destroying his career and Vanessa Carter's; that he wished he'd stayed at the dinner so that he and Lari Prillman wouldn't have been shot at; and that if he lost her again he wouldn't care about blackmail or bullets. He was afraid that if he pulled her back into his world her love would finally drown in his dark water. Instead he told her he was sorry about everything, cloaking his sins in vague regret.

"Rachel told me about your client, the one named Fish," she said.

He laid on his back, cradling her to his side, her head on his chest, his arms tense even as he held her. "It's complicated, but I'll get it worked out."

"You're in it, aren't you?"

"I'm his lawyer."

"But you're in it like your other cases. You're in trouble. I can tell by the way you hold me, like you're afraid to let go." She raised her head, searching his face.

He breathed deeply, letting it out slowly. "It's complicated," he repeated, watching her reaction, waiting for her to pull away.

She put her head down again. He felt a tear on his chest. "I called Mickey after I got your message. He'll be here in the morning. He'll help."

Mickey Shanahan had worked for Mason until Abby took him with her to Washington. He had been part office manager, part scam artist, and part wingman, covering Mason's flank while Blues took Mason's back. Abby had recruited Mickey by appealing to his ambition to work in politics. Her pitch disguised her maternal instinct to protect him from the dangers of working for Mason. Now, she had brought Mickey home.

"You didn't have to do that."

"You had a hole in your heart," she told him, pressing her palm over the scar on his chest. "The surgeon fixed it. Now I have one," she said, moving his hand to her heart. "I need you to fix mine."

He answered her with a kiss that promised to fix them both. They slept under an afghan he kept in the closet for those nights when he couldn't make it home. He rose before dawn, stiff from their close quarters, careful to cover her as she curled into the space he'd left. He picked his sweats off the floor, slipped them on, and sat behind his desk, watching her sleep.

Confession soothed her soul. Making love eased her heart. Commitment bound her to him. It may be enough for her, but it wouldn't be enough for both of them unless he could give the same to her. Overs. A clean slate, he said to himself. He couldn't keep his promise to Abby as long as he and Judge Carter were exposed to a blackmailer. Time was running out and he was not close to a solution.

Confession might be his least bad and only option. A blackmailer depended on the victim's fear of exposure. Take that away, and the blackmailer is out of business. Could he do that? he wondered. Could he sacrifice Judge Carter and himself? What if he could protect the judge, take the fall himself? Would he do that? He found the answer in the gentle rhythms of Abby's sleepy breathing.

Abby stirred, rolling onto her back and pulling herself up on her elbows. Groggy, she swept her hair off her face, focusing on him across the room.

"Is that you or the boogeyman?"

"Just me. I gave the boogeyman the night off."

"What time is it?"

Mason looked at the clock on his desk. "Five-thirty."

"Ugh. I hate five-thirty. Make it go away."

He reached for the lamp on his desk, the light enough to make them both blink. "It worked. It's five thirty-one."

"Swell. I've got a breakfast meeting with the senator."

She gathered her clothes, dressing with nonchalance as though they were an old married couple, and kissed him, neither noticing their sour morning breath.

"Tonight," she said. "Dinner, enchanting conversation, and a real bed."

"I'll bring the conversation. You bring the bed."

"Deal. I love you," she said and left.

He turned on the rest of the lights and saw his calendar for the day. Dinner—Samantha Greer—birthday.

"Shit!" he said, snatching a dart off his desk and flinging it at the board hanging on the back of his door, missing the bull's-eye by a wide margin.

He shoved his chair away from the desk, swiveling and stopping in front of the fax machine sitting on the credenza behind him. A five-page fax from Lari Prillman lay in the tray. It was her telephone records, the call made from her office Saturday night circled and starred. Next to it she'd written a note. Cell phone. Stolen. What now?

CHAPTER FIFTY-TWO

THE FBI HAD converted the phone in Fish's kitchen into a government party line, the kind where the person on the other end didn't know he'd been invited to the party. Everything Fish and Sylvia McBride said would be recorded, the text simultaneously appearing on a laptop computer as Pete Samuelson, Kelly Holt, and Mason used headphones to listen. A scruffy technician, his FBI identification tag hanging from a chain around his neck, double- and triple-checked the connections before giving Samuelson and Kelly a thumbs-up.

An order signed by a federal magistrate judge permitting the government to wiretap Fish's phone lay on the kitchen table, partially obscured by the morning paper, one corner held down and stained by a coffee mug. Mason flinched when he saw the order, instinctively recoiling at the tool the government had so often used like a crowbar to break into his clients' lives. He picked it up, reading the dry prose that blessed the raw invasion of Sylvia McBride's life, the government's allegations of reasonable cause accepted as gospel.

Dropping the order on the table, he turned to Fish, motioning him into the living room.

"Are you sure you want to do this?" Mason asked him when they were alone.

"What choice do I have? They've got me by the short hairs and, even at my age, the short hairs can still hurt."

"There's always a choice. Some are harder than others."

"Not this one. That bastard partner of mine got into my shorts for fifty grand. He played me like I was buying a time-share, then made me cry at his funeral. Now the FBI is going to help me balance the books and give me a pass on my indiscretions. That's not a choice, my friend. That's an opportunity and America is the land of opportunity."

Kelly Holt appeared in the doorway between the kitchen and the dining room. "Let's get going."

Fish left him as Mason lingered for a moment, glancing at the mantle above the fireplace where he saw Fish's tallit and tefillin. The tallit was a prayer shawl worn by Jews during religious services. The tefillin were two small black boxes with black straps attached to them. Some Jews wore them while reciting morning prayers, one box strapped on their head, the other strapped to one arm.

"Don't worry," Fish said, looking back at him. "I prayed for both of us this morning."

"Did God laugh when you mentioned our names?"

"No. He said quit complaining."

Mason followed Fish into the kitchen. Kelly handed out copies of a photograph of Sylvia McBride taken as she got out of her car in a parking lot, an office building behind her. The picture was stamped with the date it had been taken a month earlier. The sky in the background was cloudy, the pavement asphalt, her car black. Dressed in gray, she was late fifties, early sixties; slender, almost shapeless; her indistinct brown hair cut short. Though the picture had been taken from a distance, the zoom lens had captured her plain face, free of expression, her flat countenance giving nothing away. Only her eyes showed any life, though her gaze was guarded. She was practically invisible.

Mason slipped headphones over his ears, the soft pads muting Samuelson's last-minute instructions to Fish, who listened patiently, patting Samuelson on the shoulder as if to say, Relax, sonny, and watch me work. Fish was wearing a green warm-up suit that made him look like an overripe bell pepper, but his face was calm, his eyes sharp.

Sylvia answered on the third ring, saying hello in a voice that had the husky resonance of cigarettes and booze. If she wasn't five years older than Mason had guessed from her picture, her life expectancy was at least that much shorter.

"It's Avery Fish. How are you, Sylvia?"

She missed a beat in her reply, the hesitation enough to make Samuelson break a sweat. "After all these years. I thought I recognized your number on my caller ID. I'm fine, Avery. My God, it's been what? Ten years?"

"Give or take, but what's a decade between old friends? Right?"

"Nothing at all. It's good to hear your voice. It's been too long."

"I should've stayed in touch more. I still miss Wayne. It's been a long time."

"Me too," she sighed.

"You remember how he used to imitate my voice, call you up and pretend to be me?"

"It made me so mad," she said with a laugh. "The two of you were always playing jokes on me."

"What have you been doing?"

"After Wayne died, I moved up here to be with my sister because she had cancer. I was her only family except for a son and a stepson. Neither one of them had time for their mother. After I buried her, I thought, 'Well, Sylvia, this is God's way of telling you to start over.' So I did. I went to work nine to five. Took some getting used to, but I did it."

"I don't blame you a bit. I should have started over too."

"I saw you on television. I'm sorry for all your troubles."

"Yeah. I made CNN. How about that?"

"I saw it. You could lose a little weight, Avery. It's not good for you being so heavy."

"Don't worry. I've got no appetite these days."

"Keep fighting."

"I have to. I'm innocent, Sylvia. I had a few unhappy customers like any businessman, and the government is making a federal case out of it."

"CNN said they found a body in the trunk of your car."

"Bad luck. His and mine. I had nothing to do with that."

"I believe you, Avery. You wouldn't hurt a flea. I hope it all works out for you. It was nice to hear from you, but I'm going to be late for work."

"Sylvia, give me another minute," Fish said, adding a touch of desperation. "I need a favor and I don't have anyone else to ask."

"I work at a call center now," she said, her voice stiffening. "Eight hours a day of customer service. It's very boring, but no one comes to me for favors. I told you, Avery. I started over."

"The government has frozen all my bank accounts, but I've got a lot of cash they don't know about. It's for my grandkids. It's too much to leave in a suitcase under my bed. I need to move it, clean it, until this is over."

"I can't help you. I wouldn't know how and I don't want any trouble."

"Don't worry. My phone isn't tapped. I've got a guy who checks it every day. No one is listening."

"I'm listening. And, I'm not interested."

"Sylvia, you remember the money I gave you when Wayne died? It was my cut from the last deal we did."

"I remember. Wayne didn't leave me much. I'm grateful for what you did, Avery. But that doesn't mean I owe you."

"I don't mean it that way. You're right. You don't owe me a thing. But I've got more than twenty times that to move. I'll give you a cut and you can buy your own call center."

Mason listened as Sylvia hacked—clearing the phlegm from her throat, making way for the bait and hook Fish had tossed her.

"Even if I wanted to, I wouldn't know how to do it. Wayne always took care of the money."

"Then bury it in your backyard and dig it up when I'm dead. Just promise me you'll get it to my grandkids. You can take whatever you think is fair for your trouble, but I've got to move the money in the next couple of days. I've got a hundred grand hidden at home. The rest is in a safety deposit box under a phony name. The feds have me under twenty- four-hour surveillance. I can't go near the money. You and Wayne are the only ones I could ever trust with something like this, and he's dead. Will you at least think about it?" His question hung unanswered. "Sylvia? Are you there?"

"I'm here."

"Well?"

"I've got some sick days saved up. I'll think about it," she said and hung up.

CHAPTER FIFTY-THREE

"WHERE'S THE MONEY?" Fish asked.

Kelly lifted an aluminum briefcase onto the kitchen counter, snapped open the locks, and raised the lid, revealing neatly wrapped bundles of hundred-dollar bills packed tightly together like tiles. Fish elbowed Samuelson out of the way to get a closer look.

"Old money?"

"Heavily circulated, nonsequential serial numbers," Kelly said.

"You can trace that?"

"Completely. Don't get too ambitious. You've got enough problems as it is."

Fish laughed. "You don't have to worry about me, Miss Holt. You've already put me out of business. It's my former partner who's got ambitions."

"You think Sylvia will call back?" Samuelson asked.

"She'll call, and when she does, you better have the rest of the money," Fish answered.

"Hold on," Samuelson said. "It was hard enough to get the hundred thousand. You don't really think we're going to come up with another million and stick it in a safety deposit box for you to play with?"

"Actually, that would be another one million sixty-seven thousand. I told you that nobody believes exact numbers. And that's what you'll do if you want this to work. What's the combination?" Fish asked, snapping the briefcase closed and thumbing the numbers on the lock.

"You aren't serious?" Kelly said.

"I have too much respect for money to joke about it. I told Sylvia that I had the hundred at home. How's it going to look if she shows up here and I don't have it?"

"You think she'd do that?" Samuelson asked.

Fish rolled his eyes at Mason and let out an exasperated sigh. "Amateurs," he muttered. "What do you think she's going to do? Ask me to mail it to her?"

"There's no way we're leaving this money here with you," Kelly said.

"Out of the question," Samuelson added.

Fish picked up the phone and began dialing. Sylvia's number flashed across the laptop screen. Samuelson snatched the phone from his hand, ending the call before Sylvia could answer.

"What in the hell are you doing?" Kelly demanded.

"I'm calling Sylvia to tell her I threw the money out with the trash and she can forget I ever called her."

"You do that and our deal is off!" Samuelson said. "You'll die in prison."

"Fine," Fish said, his hands clasped beneath his belly. "So I'll die in prison. You think this house isn't a prison? No wife, no kids, no grandkids. At least in prison I'll have someone to talk to. Now get out of my house!"

Samuelson looked at Mason, pleading. "Talk to your client."

Mason shook his head. "You put him up to this. If he can't deliver the money to her, the deal blows up. There's no way for him to know if Sylvia is going to call back, show up, or send someone in her place. You can park someone here to babysit him and the money but that could complicate things if someone knocks at the door."

"What are we supposed to do?" Kelly asked. "Trust him? He's a crook!"

"Then get a receipt for the money or pick someone else," Mason said.

Kelly motioned Samuelson into the living room while the technician gathered his equipment. Fish poured himself a cup of coffee and read the paper. Mason stared out the kitchen window, trading glances with a blue jay bobbing on a sapling's narrow branch.

"Okay," Samuelson said when they came back five minutes later. "We're going to install surveillance cameras and microphones throughout the house. That money walks out of here, we're going to know about it."

"Isn't it supposed to walk out of here?" Mason asked.

"Well, yeah," Samuelson managed. "But not without us knowing it."

Fish waved a hand at Samuelson. "First I'm a snitch and now I'm a movie star. I don't want anybody seeing me naked."

"We can't make any room in the house off-limits," Kelly said. "I'm sorry."

"Tell you what," Mason said. "Keep a camera on the briefcase at all times. That's all you need to worry about. The man is entitled to some privacy."

Kelly looked at Samuelson, nodding. "Okay. We'll wire the house today," Samuelson said.

"Good. Now give me the combination," Fish said. Samuel- son scratched the numbers on a piece of paper, handing it to Fish, who glanced at them and handed the paper back. "This is just seed money. Sylvia and Wayne won't take my word about the rest of the money. They'll want to see all of it before they take any chances."

"How are you going to pull that off?" Samuelson asked. "You already told her you can't go near the money."

"I can't, but he can," Fish said, pointing to Mason. "I'm going to give him my power of attorney and the key to my safety deposit box."

Three copper canisters labeled Flour, Sugar, and Salt sat on the kitchen counter against the wall. Fish opened one that said Flour, reached in, and pulled out a plastic bag caked in white powder. He unsealed the bag and removed a key, handing it to Mason.

"It's for box number 4722 at the U.S. Bank branch at Fifty-first and Main. I've had it for years. It's under the name of Myron Wenneck."

"I can't believe we didn't find that key when we searched your house," Kelly said. "Or that the police didn't find it when they did their search."

"Who's going to look in the flour?" Fish asked. "You're policemen, not cooks."

"You've got a safety deposit box under a false name?" Samuelson asked. "That's against federal bank regulations."

Fish gave him a sheepish grin. "What are you going to do? Arrest me again? I can't open a new box. They'll see the signature card when Lou takes them into the vault to show them the money. If the box doesn't have a history, we don't have a story."

"I don't want you involved," Kelly told Mason. "I'll get an agent about your age and build. Sylvia won't know the difference."

"I've been on TV as much as Avery has. She'll know it isn't me before my double gives her one of my business cards. I've got to do it or it falls apart."

"There has to be another way," Kelly said, looking hard at Mason. "You'll end up a witness in the case against Al Webb or Wayne McBride—whichever name we charge him under. Once you're on the stand, who knows where the questions will go."

Kelly's comment and the piercing look she gave him were packed with warning, as if she somehow knew which questions he didn't want to answer. He glanced at Fish, who was dissecting Kelly's words and the mask she was wearing. Fish turned to him with narrowed eyes and a thin-lipped smile that said, Watch your step, boytchik.

Mason nodded. "I've got an alternative. My legal assistant, Mickey Shanahan, just got back in town. Fish can vouch for him and he can go to the bank."

"Swell, but what about the money?" Samuelson asked again. "My boss is going to think I'm out of my mind."

"You're the government," Fish said. "Print the money."

Mason looked at his watch. He was supposed to be at Vince Bongiovanni's office to swap information about Ed Fiori and Charles Rockley.

"I've got to get going. Let me know when you hear from Sylvia."

CHAPTER FIFTY-FOUR

KELLY SAID, "I'LL walk out with you."

The sky was half clouds, half sun; the air held a tentative chill, ready to give way if the sun won the battle with the clouds or hold on if the contest went the other way. The breeze started and stopped as if it couldn't make up its mind either.

They stood on the front porch. Kelly stuffed her hands under her arms to keep them warm.

"I think your client may have gotten the wrong idea."

"Which wrong idea? The one about the government helping him out of a jam?"

Kelly smiled. "Not that one. I think he's trying to figure out a way to steal our money."

Mason spun toward her. "Between the federal and state charges, the man could spend the rest of his life in prison. Despite what he says, he's got an ex-wife, kids, and grand- kids he wants to reconnect with when this is all over. Besides, he's not that stupid. You're going to have cameras and microphones everywhere except up his ass, plus you'll probably evict the neighbors across the street so you can spy on him in person."

"We don't evict them. We rent from them. And, it's not about being stupid. It's about habits—bad ones. People don't change. He's a con man. We just waved a boatload of money under his nose. He wasn't kidding when he said he has too much respect for money to joke about it. Only it isn't just respect, it's greed and the charge he gets out of running a con. He can't help himself. Plus, he wants to get even with his ex- partner."

"Those are exactly the reasons you wanted his help. He's good at what he does and he's highly motivated. I'll bet that's a quote right out of the FBI recruiting manual," Mason said, jabbing a finger at her.

"First page," Kelly said, slapping his hand away. She looked up and down the street, Mason following her eyes.

"All clear?"

"Habit," she said. "I like to see trouble before it gets here."

Kelly stared at him again, this time her face open. She was ready to listen if he was ready to talk. He wasn't, not until he understood her agenda.

"If you're sending me a message, I need a translator," Mason said.

Kelly did a slow circuit of the porch, poking her head around the corners of the house, coming back to Mason, who was standing at the top of the steps.

"Your client may be a con man, but I don't think he killed Charles Rockley."

"Did you tell that to the cops?"

"Detective Cates blew me off; made some noise that the Bureau should stick to catching terrorists and leave the street crime to the cops."

"I've met Cates. He's a wonderful conversationalist."

"Typical macho cop. Confuses his dick with his gun and probably can't fire either one. He likes Fish for the murder because they don't have a better choice. He doesn't care that there's no connection between Fish and Rockley. Or that Fish is too old to have taken Rockley down, let alone cut off his head and hands. Rockley was killed by a professional or a psychopath and Fish doesn't qualify for either, but Cates sees it the way he wants it to be."

"Rockley was in the FBI's database, which means he either had a record or he was a spook. I talked to his prior employers and they couldn't wait to have him back. That doesn't fit."

Kelly furrowed her brow. "Where did you get his employment history?"

Mason told her part of the truth. "From Galaxy's lawyer, Lari Prillman. Tell me who Rockley really was."

Kelly folded her arms, dipped her chin to her chest, and did a slow half turn in place. Straightening, she clasped her hands behind her back and answered him.

"His real name was Tommy Corcoran. When he was in his twenties, he was a grifter—ran small-time cons. He had a mean side and did time for sexual assault. That's how he got into our database. After he got out, he picked up a new identity and stayed off our radar until someone handed him his head."

"Wait a minute. You mean to tell me that Wayne McBride is masquerading as Al Webb, skimming money from Galaxy Casino, and Tommy Corcoran, a.k.a. Charles Rockley, is also working at Galaxy? And the FBI can't connect those dots?"

"Believe me, we tried. McBride worked the Midwest. Corcoran operated strictly in New Jersey. There's nothing to connect them until they show up in Kansas City. Then there's Johnny Keegan."

"What do you have on Keegan?"

"Just what I got from Detective Griswold. Why was Keegan holding on to your name and phone number when he was killed?

"I don't know. I've never heard of him," Mason said, holding both hands up. "The guy was in enough trouble to get killed; it's no surprise he needed a lawyer. Don't tell me he had a secret past too."

"Not that we've found."

"Which gets us back to my client being innocent. Griswold seems like a reasonable guy. Maybe you can convince him not to charge Fish?"

"Are you certain you want me to do that?"

Mason took a step back. "Why wouldn't I?"

Kelly dropped her arms to her sides, her hands on her hips. "Because Griswold might start asking himself the same questions I've been asking myself. Like why was Blues checking out Rockley's apartment before I told you that Rockley was the dead man? And why were you and Blues talking to Mark Hill and taking pictures down in Fairfax? And why were you talking to Vince Bongiovanni about Carol Hill's sexual harassment case? And why do you want me to investigate another FBI agent?"

Mason saw no point in telling her that Griswold was already asking him enough questions to make his shoes tight. "Was Brewer the leak?"

"I'll deal with Brewer. Answer my questions."

"It doesn't work that way. I answer yours, you answer mine."

Kelly crossed her arms. Mason smiled. She tapped her foot. He smiled again. "Fine," she said, not meaning it. "You first."

"Fair enough. Here's what I know. Carol Hill sued Rock- ley for sexual harassment. Somebody killed Rockley and hid his body in the trunk of my client's car on the same day we were supposed to make a deal with Pete Samuelson. Your pal Brewer breaks the news to Samuelson about the dead body just as we're about to ink the plea bargain. Samuelson shits his pants and says no deal. Samuelson and his boss change their mind and invite us back last Friday to make a new deal. Suddenly, Brewer is out and you're in."

"I don't need the history lesson."

"Wrong. History is written by the winners and this case is still a jump ball, so pay attention. Friday morning you tell me about Rockley. Friday night, Blues and I find Carol Hill's husband, Mark, in that bar in Fairfax. He tells us that his wife was having an affair with Keegan. Mark leaves and runs his pickup into a car parked across the street. Two guys are in the car; one jumps out and clocks poor Mark. The other guy gets on the phone and Brewer shows up two minutes later. We head for home and you nearly rear-end us."

"Tell me, Lou. Did you think if you said it fast enough and cute enough, I wouldn't realize you hadn't answered any of my questions? I've got a picture of Blues outside Rockley's apartment taken on Thursday and I don't think he was selling encyclopedias door to door. I didn't tell you about Rockley until Friday morning. Eight hours later, you had tracked down Mark Hill. How did you manage that?"

"I'm good at what I do."

"You're not that good. Carol Hill's lawsuit is a private arbitration, not a matter of public record. You couldn't have known about it unless someone told you and I didn't. Vince Bongiovanni didn't tell you because you wouldn't have known that he represented Carol until after you found out about her case. And that's not the kind of information big companies like Galaxy give to strangers, especially lawyers."

"It doesn't matter how I knew."

"It does to me if it means you're connected to all of this by something other than Avery Fish."

"I don't have any connection to Carol Hill, Charles Rock- ley, Johnny Keegan, or the Galaxy Casino."

"But you do have a connection to the Dream Casino. That's what the Galaxy was called when Ed Fiori owned it. You didn't represent him either. But, you were there when he died."

Mason was dancing as fast as he could, but Kelly was a step ahead.

"Ed Fiori is ancient history."

"There is no such thing as ancient history. The past is always waiting there to bite us in the ass. I did some digging after we found out about the sexual harassment case. Fiori was Vince Bongiovanni's and Carol Hill's uncle. Galaxy bought the casino from Fiori's estate. Bongiovanni was the executor. He accused Galaxy of fraud and sued to set the sale aside, only the case was thrown out. Maybe the two of them set Rockley up so they could get even with Galaxy."

"None of which has anything to do with me."

"Then why won't you answer my questions?"

"I did. You just didn't like the answers. It's your turn. Was Brewer the leak?"

Kelly blew her exasperation away in a fog of frosted breath. "You are beyond salvage. You know that? Beyond salvage."

"So sell me for scrap, but tell me about Brewer first."

She took a smaller breath that calmed her. "I don't know. Proving that Brewer was the leak is almost impossible unless Rachel Firestone has him on tape and agrees to give it up."

"Rachel will never give up her sources."

"Then I'll probably never know if Brewer was the leak."

"Which makes us even. You don't like my answers to your questions and I don't like your answers to mine."

"You always get in over your head. You can't help it any more than Avery Fish can resist trying to steal the government's money. I can't keep my eye on both of you. Talk to me before it's too late," she said.

Mason tried staring her down, but there was more steel in her eyes than in his. He would have settled for a smart-ass comeback, but he didn't have one.

All he had was a twisted gut he was about to choke on. He walked away without answering, not stopping until he reached his car. He opened the driver's door, lingering for a moment, looking back at her. It was still early, the street quiet. He ducked behind the wheel, fired the ignition, and drove away wondering if it already was too late.

CHAPTER FIFTY-FIVE

VINCE BONGIOVANNI MADE enough money suing corporations to build a building with his name on it, complete with corporate logo and slogan—Doing the People's Business. The logo was a golden eagle in flight holding silver scales of justice in its beak and was positioned above the entrance at an angle to reflect the sun off the eagle's shiny wings and bounce it again off the silvery scales. It was a not so subliminal message to potential clients to stop by and pick up their money.

The building was located at the intersection of Rockhill Road and Brush Creek Boulevard, east of the Plaza. The Nelson-Atkins Museum of Art loomed over its shoulder to the north. The Kaufman Foundation, devoted to education and entrepreneurship, sat across from it. The Stowers Institute, dedicated to curing cancer, rose on the opposite corner. The University of Missouri at Kansas City occupied the fourth corner of the intersection. Bongiovanni said that his building was dedicated to justice and was, therefore, a perfect complement to his neighbors.

His firm was on the third floor, the bottom two floors rented to other lawyers in pursuit of justice as their clients defined it. His private office would have accommodated three or four of Mason's, the artwork alone worth more than Mason's annual gross.

Mason tried not to be jealous, remembering his Aunt Claire's admonition not to be a prisoner of his possessions. Still, he conceded a twinge of envy, noting how well things had gone for Bongiovanni and wondering if he could have done the same had he stayed with the law firm he started with when he graduated from law school, a small group that had also grown rich representing plaintiffs. He'd left that firm in a dispute over ethics, though with the passage of years it was hard to remember the details or summon the passion of that moment.

Ancient history, he told himself, though Kelly had been right when she said there was no such thing as ancient history, if the phrase was supposed to mean that the past was dead and buried. Life was much more of a loop, colliding with the past, than it was a straight line running away from it.

Bongiovanni showed him into his private office, motioning him to a chair, taking the one opposite Mason, who declined his offer of an espresso. Wynton Marsalis's Magic album was playing on the sound system, speakers and components invisible, riffs, rhythms, and melodies layered like a canopy above them. A CD case lay on the table. Mason couldn't tell if it was for the music or something else, remembering the CD that had been stolen from Lari Prillman's safe. Bongiovanni was using it as a coaster for his coffee cup.

"Might as well get down to it," Bongiovanni said. "I need help with Charles Rockley."

Rockley's history as a sex offender would blow the lid off of Carol Hill's case, especially if Galaxy knew about it, ending any doubts about Carol's credibility and hoisting Galaxy onto the liability hook. Bongiovanni would smack Galaxy in its corporate face with that evidence. It would also put more pressure on Vanessa Carter to reopen the hearing before issuing her ruling. That realization was like twin screws on a vise around Mason's neck. But it was all he had to give Bongiovanni. If he got a tape of his conversation with Ed Fiori in return, it might be worth the risk.

Mason nodded. "Maybe you should reconsider settling the case."

"I told you before. We aren't interested in anything but Judge Carter's decision."

Bongiovanni had described Carol's case as a toss-up, yet neither of them would consider settling it. Mason's information about Rockley would only harden their determination to make Galaxy suffer.

Bongiovanni picked up his coffee cup, giving Mason a good look at the CD case. Mason had boxed himself in. He had to give Bongiovanni something, and the truth about Rockley was all he had.

Bongiovanni tapped a corner of the CD case on the table in a failed effort to match the beat of the music. Mason winced, each tap like a needle piercing his skin. He bit his tongue to keep from licking his lips, unable to take his eyes off the CD, desperate to know if he was on it, his past about to collide with his present.

"You all right?" Bongiovanni asked. "You look like you've got the DTs."

Mason forced a smile. "Late night, early morning. I'd like to get a look at what you found in Ed Fiori's office."

"You keep telling me that and I keep wondering why. It couldn't involve Carol's case since Ed has been dead for three years and she's only worked at Galaxy for a little over a year. So it has to be something personal to you. I did Ed's legal work or farmed it out so I know he never retained you. Which means your business with him wasn't of the sort you normally did. How am I doing so far?"

"I'm not a jury. You don't have to convince me."

Bongiovanni smiled. "Uncle Ed was an interesting guy. Some days he was good and other days he was bad. He liked to play around the edges. That must be where the two of you did some business—around the edges, I mean. Whatever it was, you figured it died with Ed, but you couldn't be sure and you've spent all this time waiting for the other shoe to drop. This case comes along and gives you the chance to trade some information for peace of mind. That about it?"

"What difference does it make?"

"Makes all the difference. Peace of mind doesn't come cheap. I hope you've got something worth it."

Kelly Holt had made the connection between him and Ed Fiori, though she hadn't filled in all the gaps. It wouldn't be long before she found her way to Judge Carter. Bongiovanni had a completely different piece of the story. If he sensed it would help him in his private war against Galaxy, he'd keep pushing until he too found his way to Judge Carter and the blackmail scheme.

He had to beat both of them to the finish. He felt like he was being chased by a pack of dogs and was throwing fresh meat over his shoulder to spur them on. He took a deep breath and tossed Bongiovanni another morsel.

"Charles Rockley's real name was Tommy Corcoran. He had a record for sexual assault. If you can prove Galaxy knew that, you could end up with the casino and the rest of the hotel."

Bongiovanni whistled. "Brother, you do deliver the groceries. How do I prove that?"

"Subpoena his records from the FBI."

"I'll need a witness to testify."

"Forget about the witness. Go to Lari Prillman. She'll convince Galaxy to settle. You can call a press conference, declare victory, and embarrass the hell out of them."

"Look around you, man! You think I give a shit about splitting another fee fifty-fifty with Uncle Sam? When Ed was killed, he was in debt up to his eyeballs. Those bastards at Galaxy bought the loans on the casino and the hotel before Ed was in the ground. Then they foreclosed. I tried to pay off the loans, but they wanted the properties, not the money. My aunt was left with nothing. I sued them and lost. I told my aunt I would take care of her, but she was ashamed to take money from me. She stroked out a few months later and will spend the rest of her life in a nursing home drooling into a cup tied under her chin. So I'm not going to send them a fucking settlement offer. I'm going to send them a subpoena."

Mason began to reach for the CD but pulled back when Bongiovanni picked it up and walked to a cabinet next to the bar. He pressed the cabinet door and it popped open revealing his sound system. He removed the Wynton Marsalis disk and inserted the unmarked one. It was Eric Clapton singing a blues number that matched Mason's mood. Bongiovanni turned to him, grinning wide.

"Ed's office was wired for sound. He had a button under his desk he pushed when he wanted to activate it," he told Mason. "I told him to get rid of it, reminded him what happened to Nixon. But it made him feel like one of the big boys. Wouldn't give it up, but I guess he finally took my advice."

"How do you know?"

"Like I told you before, I got to Ed's office as soon as I could after he was killed. I went through everything."

"Were you alone?"

"Just me and Ed's secretary. She was the one who really knew where everything was and she helped me collect all his stuff, including the tapes. I took the tapes home and listened to them. I sue a lot of powerful companies and people. Some of them take it personally. A few of them threaten me. I transferred the tapes to CDs just in case I might need them one day to level the playing field. I went back through them yesterday and you aren't on any of them. The last tape was made a week before Ed died. According to the newspaper stories, you would have been there during that last week. Whatever went down between the two of you stayed between the two of you."

Mason knew that was supposed to make him feel better, but it didn't. "What happened to Fiori's secretary?"

"She landed on her feet. Galaxy hired her and she ended up as their HR director. Her name is Lila Collins. The world is round, huh?"

CHAPTER FIFTY-SIX

THE WORLD MAY be round, Mason thought as he drove back to his office, but so were bullets and he felt like he'd just taken a slug between the eyes. There was absolutely no reason to think that Ed Fiori had lost interest in his surreptitious taping system at the same time Mason had shown up asking for an off-the-books favor.

Lila Collins was the link between Ed Fiori and Al Webb; between Mason strong-arming Vanessa Carter to release Blues on bail and the blackmail net that had dropped on both of them.

Timing was everything. Al Webb had given a CD to Lari Prillman to hide in her safe at the same time she was defending him and Rockley in Carol Hill's lawsuit. Turning the corner from Forty-seventh Street onto Broadway, Mason realized that timing was everything unless the timing didn't work. Vanessa Carter had been blackmailed after the arbitration had ended but before someone had broken into Lari Prillman's safe and stolen the CD.

Lari had told him that Al Webb had given her the CD for safekeeping at the outset of the hearing and that she hadn't taken it out of her safe since then. If she was the only one with the combination, how did the blackmailer get it out of the safe to use it in the phone call with Vanessa Carter, and why would the blackmailer have put it back in the safe?

The most logical answers to those questions were that Lari Prillman had lied to him and that she was involved in the blackmail scheme. Mason wondered whether she hated the prospect of losing the case enough to blackmail the judge. Vanessa Carter had told him that the blackmailer was a man. Lari could have used a device to change her voice. Or, maybe the blackmailer was working for her.

He reconsidered the burglary, remembering how cavalier Lari had been when they arrived at her office and found the door unlocked. She hadn't hesitated to walk in and would have continued down the hall into the arms of the thief if he hadn't stopped her. Perhaps she knew there was nothing to be afraid of even when the shooting started, though her posttraumatic stress had seemed genuine.

The thief knew about the CD and that it was kept in the safe. The thief was able to pick the lock on the office door, crack the safe, and shoot in the dark well enough to scare but not kill him and Lari. He made a mental list of likely burglars. There weren't many who fit that job description.

Al Webb knew about the CD but didn't strike Mason as having the necessary skill set to pull off the job, although he didn't have to be a second-story man. Webb had sat next to Lari at the Republican Party dinner the night of the break-in. He'd left early. Lari could have given him the key to her office and the combination to her safe. If she had, she wouldn't have taken Mason to her office until she was certain Webb was gone. If she'd simply screwed up their timing, Webb could have come up with a more graceful exit strategy than attempted murder.

Vince Bongiovanni knew about Fiori's tapes and may have known that Lila Collins had kept some of them for her own use, copying them onto CDs as he had. Assuming that Bongiovanni was willing and able to steal the CD, he would have blackmailed the judge to rule for his client, not against her.

Dennis Brewer was the only person Mason could think of who could have pulled off the robbery, especially after Mason and Lari interrupted him. Maybe there was more on the CD than the conversation between Fiori and Mason. Maybe Brewer was being blackmailed as well. Otherwise, Brewer would have just gotten a search warrant. Mason added another item to his to-do list: Check out a connection between Brewer and Fiori.

While he was at it, he'd try to answer a few other questions that kept rolling around inside his head. The FBI had intercepted an e-mail with the picture of Blues outside Rockley's apartment attached to it. Who had sent the e-mail and who had been the intended recipient? Why did Johnny Keegan have Mason's name and phone number on him when he was killed? Why did Rockley's killer choose Fish's car? What was so important about the outcome of Carol Hill's case that was worth the risk of blackmailing Judge Carter?

Mason had sought answers to these questions from Detectives Griswold and Cates, Samantha Greer, Kelly Holt, Carol Hill, Mark Hill, Vince Bongiovanni, Al Webb, and Lari Prillman. He'd been stonewalled, lied to, or duped with half-truths and artful omissions. All of which meant one thing. He had yet to talk to the right person, someone he could dupe with half-truths and artful omissions. Lila Collins was his last chance.

CHAPTER FIFTY-SEVEN

MASON STOPPED FOR a moment as he reached the top of the back stairs to the second floor above Blues on Broadway. There were three offices along the hallway. Blues used the one to Mason's right. The door was open, the office empty. The lights were on, Coltrane humming in the background.

Mickey Shanahan had lived in the office on the other side of the hall until Abby had lured him to Washington, D.C. He had originally rented the space for his own public relations firm, which had proved to be more fantasy than fact. Blues let him work off the rent by tending bar until Mason put him to work. The door to that office was propped open by a suitcase. Mickey was back but nowhere in sight.

Mason's office was at the end of the hall, the door closed. The mail slot in the center of the door, usually stuffed by this time of day, was empty. Mickey was probably sitting behind Mason's desk, feet up, balancing the day's take-in fees against the bills marked Past Due. Mason picked up his stride, pushed open the door to his office, and stopped, rooted to the spot.

Mickey was seated behind Mason's desk, though his feet were firmly on the floor, the unopened mail piled in front of him. Blues stood behind him, watching the traffic on Broadway. Both men looked up, though they offered neither a greeting nor an outstretched hand. Their faces were silent and long, their eyes now aimed at the woman sitting in the chair opposite Mickey, her back to Mason.

He recognized Vanessa Carter's erect bearing even before she rose and turned around. She removed the dark glasses she was wearing, revealing a purpled right eye swollen half shut.

"We are running out of time," she said.

"Who did this?" Mason asked, taking two steps toward her.

"I don't know. He was waiting for me inside my garage when I came home last night. He'd unscrewed the lightbulbs. It was dark. I didn't see anything. He grabbed me, hit me, and told me."

"Told you what?" Mason asked.

"That I was running out of time."

Wounds inflicted by guns, knives, or bare hands eventually healed, scars the last remnants. The wound that often didn't heal was to the psyche, to that inner sanctum where people took refuge from the vagaries of a harsh and uncertain world; fear of another attack became a daily rite marked by a tremor or a tic. Vanessa Carter was no different. The tic had wormed its way into her cheek, her facial muscles twitching like she'd been short-circuited.

"Did you call the police?"

She clenched her hands together, pressing them against her middle, biting the words. "We both know I can't do that. You have to stop this."

Mason looked at Blues and Mickey, searching them for answers, finding none. He took a breath. "I'm working on it."

It wasn't a lie, but it wasn't the truth either because the statement implied that he was making progress or that he had a plan; that a solution was in sight. None of that was true. Instead, the walls were coming down around him—and her—and he had no better idea of what to do about it than to sacrifice himself, an option that had as much appeal as throwing a virgin into a volcano to keep it from erupting.

"I can keep an eye out," Blues volunteered.

Judge Carter looked back at him, a tremor creeping into her voice. "I would appreciate that. I'll be at home until this is over."

It was another concession to her circumstance that she made reluctantly, her pride in being self-sufficient another casualty. She walked slowly down the hall, disappearing one step at a time.

Mason wiped his dry erase board clean, laying out the facts as much for him and Blues as for Mickey. Taking it from the beginning forced him to organize the story chronologically, highlighting the gaps in what they knew and underscoring the questions that had to be answered.

The first case Mickey had worked on for Mason had been the one in which Blues had been charged with murder. Mason and Blues hadn't told him about Judge Carter, seeing no reason to involve him. Hearing that part of the story for the first time, his eyes widened and he shifted uneasily in Mason's desk chair.

"You're in deep shit," Mickey said when Mason had finished.

"Is that what the politicians say in D.C.?" Mason asked.

"No. They say this is no time for politics, which means every man for himself. Do we have a plan?"

"Not exactly. Everything begins and ends with the casino.

Carol Hill, Charles Rockley, Johnny Keegan, Al Webb, Lila Collins—they all worked at Galaxy. Lila is the only one who worked for both Ed Fiori and Al Webb. She's the common denominator and the best bet to have found Fiori's tapes. There's no connection between Avery Fish and Charles Rockley, but there's a big connection between Al Webb and Avery Fish."

"What about a link between Rockley and Webb?" Blues asked. "Rockley is really some punk named Tommy Corcoran. Webb is really a con man named Wayne McBride who committed murder to fake his own death. The feds are investigating him for skimming from the casino. He had to have help. My money is on Rockley. Their relationship goes south, maybe because of Carol Hill's lawsuit. Webb pops him and stuffs him in Fish's car."

"Doesn't work," Mason said. "Fish's car is the last one Webb would have picked because it opens up his past."

"What about Dennis Brewer, the FBI agent?" Mickey asked. "Where does he fit in?"

Mason shook his head. "I can't get anything out of Kelly about Brewer or about whose e-mail the FBI intercepted with the photograph of Blues attached to it."

"No wonder Abby called in the cavalry," Mickey said.

Mickey was lean and lanky. Gone was the spiked hair and soul patch of his early twenties. In their place was the buttoned- down, close grooming of a Capitol Hill staffer. Mason was glad that Mickey's grown-up look hadn't suppressed the cockiness that he brought to the table.

"What did she tell you?" Mason asked.

"Just that you were in trouble—for a change, she said. She didn't know the details but said it had to do with Avery Fish. What do you want me to do?"

"I need a fresh pair of eyes to look at all of this. I down loaded the arbitration file to my PC. Start with that. I'll be back this afternoon."

"What about me?" Blues asked. "I'm tired of sitting on the sidelines."

"I thought you were going to keep an eye on Judge Carter," Mason said.

"That's a nighttime gig. Nobody is going to bust down her door in broad daylight. Besides, she got the message last night. No need to repeat it this soon."

"Okay. In that case, get back to Mark Hill. See if he forgot to tell us anything."

"I may have to motivate him. You got a problem with that?"

From anyone else, Blues's question would have carried a trace of humor, but he didn't joke about violence. It was a necessary tool to be applied selectively but without regret. He wasn't asking Mason's permission. He was just making certain that Mason knew.

Mason let out a long breath. The walls were crumbling down and he was tossing some of the bricks. It was ugly, dirty, and wrong, but so was the mess he was in. He could argue the fine points of whether the ends justified the means until he was buried under the last brick. Even before he answered, he knew that he was breaking another of his Aunt Claire's admonitions—if you're in a hole, quit digging.

"We need answers. Do what you have to do."

"What about you? What are you going to do?"

"I'm going to try my luck at the Galaxy. See if I can get Lila Collins to blow on my dice."

CHAPTER FIFTY-EIGHT

Mason liked dropping in on witnesses unannounced, preferring their unrehearsed answers to the ones prepared for them by their lawyers. It had become almost impossible to do that since Corporate America had become Fortress America. Visitors had to sign in under the watchful eyes of armed security guards while being videotaped for posterity. If the object of your affections didn't return your devotion, you weren't getting in.

Lila Collins had no reason to see him. If he gave her a truthful one, she'd have less reason. She would tell Al Webb, who would call Lari Prillman. Lari would bite his head off for trying to talk to her client without her knowledge. He would accomplish nothing more than to encourage them to build their wall a little higher.

Galaxy had gone to the mattresses like so many other businesses, cordoning off its business offices with armed guards and locked doors. Mason walked past the guards without stopping to ask where they kept the loosest slots.

It was just as well. Even if he could get past Galaxy's security, Lila's office was the wrong place to talk about Ed Fiori's tapes. He needed a private place for their meeting, somewhere she would feel comfortable enough to open up. If she had the tape and was involved in the blackmail, she wouldn't tell him even if he spirited her to a tropical island. If she knew about the tape but wasn't involved, she might talk if he could push the right button. It could be fear, greed, or jealousy. It could even be moral outrage, though Mason considered that a long shot.

He didn't know what Lila looked like so he couldn't hang around the blackjack tables hoping she'd walk by. She wasn't listed in the phone book, so he couldn't park his car in front of her house and wait for her to come home from work.

He wandered through the maze of craps tables, blackjack dealers, and video poker machines, past the slots, the cashiers, and the twenty-four-hour buffet until he reached the lobby of the adjoining hotel and called Vince Bongiovanni.

"Is Carol Hill still hiding out in your suite at the Galaxy Hotel?"

"She went home last night," Bongiovanni said.

"What about her husband?"

"She kicked his ass out."

"Where did he land?" Mason asked, hoping to get a lead for Blues.

"On a bar stool would be my guess. Why the interest?"

"I don't like guys who beat up women, but that's just me. I need a favor," Mason said and explained what he had in mind.

"Consider it done," Bongiovanni said. "I'll call Carol first and then the desk clerk at the hotel on one condition—I get whatever you get. Understood?"

"Consider it done."

Mason waited five minutes before asking the desk clerk, a smiling young woman whose name tag said she was Brandi and her hometown was Laramie, Wyoming, for a key to Bongiovanni's suite. She handed him the key and wished him hot dice and good hole cards.

There was a basket of fresh fruit on a table in the living room of the suite. Mason grabbed an apple, realizing that he'd missed lunch. He ate as he inspected the living room, bedroom, and bath, indulging his paranoia in a search for hidden microphones and cameras, wondering whether Bongiovanni or Galaxy was more likely to have installed them.

Despite his claim that he had advised his uncle to get rid of his taping system, Mason wondered if Bongiovanni had given in to the temptation. As for Galaxy, surveillance was its central nervous system, the best way to watch for card counters, cheats, and others who threatened the house's edge. Al Webb may have wanted the suite badly enough to bug it, hoping for leverage that would force Bongiovanni to sell. Such an acquisition strategy made sense for someone who would also blackmail Judge Carter.

After checking the lamps, the buttonholes on the sofa, the phones, and the vents, Mason was fairly certain the place was clean. Nonetheless, he couldn't shake the feeling that history was about to repeat itself when he heard the knock at the door.

Mason's plan relied on simplicity, deception, and surprise. If Vince Bongiovanni had done his part, Carol Hill would have by now called Lila Collins and invited her to the suite to talk about settling her case. The ruse would get him private face time with Lila and he would dazzle her with his charm and clever cross-examination. She'd melt at his feet and spill her guts—or not. Still, it was a simple plan and he was working on the fly.

The instant he opened the door the man who had decked Mark Hill outside the bar in Fairfax belted him in the stomach.

Mason had a split second of recognition before he lost his breath and his legs. The man grabbed him by the throat, forcing him to backpedal into the living room, where he dropped Mason onto the sofa. Still doubled over, Mason glanced up as another man swept through the suite before joining his partner. Mason recognized him as the passenger in the car Hill had sideswiped. They hoisted Mason to his feet, frisked him, pulling his shirt out and grabbing his wallet.

"He's clean—no weapons, no wires," the first one said, tossing Mason's wallet to a woman who had materialized behind them.

"He's alone," the other one said.

"Wait outside," the woman told them.

Mason took a few tentative steps, letting the spasm in his gut subside and rubbing his throat until he could walk upright and breathe at the same time. The woman studied his driver's license before throwing his wallet back to him. He caught it, circled her, and retrieved a bottle of water from the bar.

Her midnight-black hair was cut short, her spiked bristles better suited for someone twenty years younger. She had olive skin, heavily made-up dark eyes, and a mouth pulled back in a barely amused smile. Her thin body was taut like a switchblade, ready to snap open at a feather touch. She was wearing body-hugging black slacks and a matching long- sleeved top that clung to her spare frame, sharpening her hard edges.

"What do you want, Mr. Mason?" she said.

"I want to talk to Lila Collins. Let me know when she gets here."

She raised her hands from her hips, palms up. "That's me," she said as she retrieved an employee identification badge from her pants pocket, holding it up for him. The photograph and the name matched.

"Why the warm welcome?"

"I was being careful. You tried to set me up."

Mason tucked his shirt in. "Should have worked."

She smiled. "Carol Hill and Vince Bongiovanni would burn us down if they thought they could get away with it. They wouldn't negotiate a settlement and they forced us to go through arbitration. Now, while we're waiting for the judge to decide her case, she calls and says she wants to meet with me—no lawyers—to kiss and make up. Look at me, Mason. Do I look like someone who would fall for that?"

"I didn't know what you looked like. It's a casino. I took a chance."

"And you shot craps. Bongiovanni may have inherited this suite, but he and everyone who uses it still have to check in. After Carol called, I checked with the hotel to make certain she was still registered. The desk clerk said she left last night and that Bongiovanni had called to say that you would be using it this afternoon."

"Those two guys," Mason said, rubbing his belly. "They do sensitivity training for your employees?"

"They do what they're told, which includes waiting for me to tell them when and how far to throw you out."

"Sit down," Mason said, gesturing to a chair as he sat on the sofa. "Don't be in such a hurry. What do you know about me?"

It was an open-ended question. He wanted to see where she would start.

She sat across from him. "What I read in the papers and watch on TV, plus what the police have told me."

"Flatter me.

She laughed. "It's nothing to brag about. You're a lawyer defending that guy, what's his name? Fish? What kind of a name is that?"

"The kind his parents gave him."

"Then tell him to change his name. People do it all the time."

She was keeping it light now, throwing him curves or clues with her crack about people changing their names.

"You run into that a lot? People changing their names?"

"I'm in human resources. I check references for a living. Some people make up their entire lives."

He remembered Bongiovanni's astonishment at the ease with which Mason had gotten detailed references from Rockley's former employers. Lari Prillman had had similar success with Keegan's. He made a mental note to ask Lila if she'd checked Rockley's and Keegan's references, saving the topic for later.

"What else do you know about me?"

"I know that lately when one of our employees dies, your name comes up."

"You mean every time one of your employees is murdered, my name comes up. I assume that some of them do die of natural causes."

"Not in the last week," she said. "Charles Rockley was found in the trunk of your client's car and Johnny Keegan was trying to get ahold of you when he was killed."

The story about Rockley had been all over the news. The bit about him and Keegan hadn't been reported. He wondered how she knew. His surprise must have registered on his face. She recovered quickly.

"The police said something about Johnny having your phone number. They asked me if he had hired you. I told them I didn't know."

Mason added her use of Keegan's first name to her list of casual admissions. "How well did you know Johnny?"

She shrugged, forcing nonchalance. "I try to get to know all our associates. Johnny was a nice guy, worked hard, did a good job."

Keegan's affair with Carol Hill wouldn't have earned him a merit raise. Lila had to have known.

"Did that include sleeping with Carol Hill?"

She stiffened. "I don't know what your arrangement is with Bongiovanni, but I'm not going to give him another club to beat us over the head with by talking to you about Carol's lawsuit."

"You didn't have to come here to tell me that. You could have called Carol and cancelled the meeting. Why didn't you?"

"I wanted to know who was using the suite."

Mason shook his head. "I don't think so. You recognized my name when you got it from the desk clerk, and you knew you weren't going to talk to me about Carol's case. So why did you come, and why did you bring the Gold Dust Twins with you?"

"It's my job to know what's going on with my employees. You went to a lot of trouble to get me here instead of calling me on the phone for an appointment. I wanted to know why, but I wanted to make certain it was safe to find out."

Her explanation was reasonable and, more importantly, it was all she was going to tell him at the moment. She wasn't under oath and she didn't trust him. If he pressed her too hard, she'd whistle for her attack dogs. He'd have to take what she gave him, hoping to box her in. He decided to verify what Bongiovanni had told him before he drilled down to the critical questions.

"I want to talk about something I don't think you'd want to discuss at your office or over the phone. I met Vince Bongiovanni through my investigation of Charles Rockley's murder. He told me about this suite. I asked him to set up this meeting. It was the only way I could think of on short notice to speak with you privately and safely."

"Why would Bongiovanni help you?"

"Because I promised to tell him everything I found out about Carol Hill's case."

"Did you really think I would talk to you about that?"

Mason smiled. "Not a chance, but I can't help what Vince might have thought."

Her bony shoulders relaxed and she chuckled for an instant. "Lawyers screwing lawyers. I like that. Okay, what's so secret that you had to play spy games with me?"

CHAPTER FIFTY-NINE

"Ed Fiori. You used to work for him?"

She nodded.

"How long?"

"Five years."

"Were you working for him when he was killed?"

She nodded again, this time more cautiously.

"That's why you recognized my name," he said. "It wasn't because I represent Avery Fish."

"I never met you before today."

Her answer was another dodge and he let it slide. "What did you do for Fiori?"

"I was his secretary."

"Which meant what?"

She straightened in her chair, arms folded across her chest. "That was a long time ago. Why are you interested in that now?"

"I'm going to write his biography."

She rose and turned toward the door.

"Okay," he said, holding up a hand. "Take it easy. I'm not going to write his biography."

"Mr. Mason, do you know what a director of human resources does all day? Deals with other people's bullshit. I'm not interested in yours."

She had come to the suite knowing it was a setup, cautious enough to bring two goons along but confident enough to leave them outside the room. He'd kept her off balance, gotten her to laugh, and picked up some tantalizing hints, but he wasn't going to chitchat her into submission. He played one of his hole cards, mixing it with a bluff, remembering Fish's lesson that a con works because the mark wants it to whether she knows it or not.

"What if someone at Galaxy was blackmailing Judge Carter into ruling in your favor on Carol Hill's case? Is that a human resources issue that interests you?"

She stood next to her chair, gripping its high back. "I thought you didn't want to talk about Carol's case."

"I don't. I'm working on an old case involving Ed Fiori. There may be some splash back on Carol because she was related to him. Vince Bongiovanni says you helped him clean out Fiori's office after he was killed. Is that true?"

She hesitated, sifting what he'd told her, gauging her reply. "I was there."

"Fiori taped a lot of his conversations," he said, treating it as a fact, daring her to deny it. "You knew that, didn't you?"

"He was a careful man."

"Careful enough to tell you about the tapes and what was on them?"

"Careful enough to know who he could trust."

"Did he trust you?"

She looked him full in the eyes, her own slightly moist with a flash of memory that suggested they'd had more than a professional relationship. "Yes."

"What happened to the tapes?"

"Vince took them."

"All of them?"

Before she could answer, the door to the suite blew open, banging hard against the wall.

"What the fuck is this?" Al Webb marched into the living room, trailed by the two thugs. Webb was hot, the smooth, honeyed manner he'd shown Mason at the Republican Party dinner gone; his eyes were narrow slits, chest puffed up, shoulders flared back. Lila bolted from her chair, color rising in her neck, the words not coming. Webb pounced again. "I said what the fuck is this?"

"It's a private meeting," Mason said. "And you aren't on the guest list, so get out."

"I run this goddamn casino and this hotel, Mason, and I'm going to throw your ass out of it."

"Every square inch except this suite. You don't own it and I didn't invite you in. That makes you a trespasser. Vince Bongiovanni doesn't give frequent-defendant discounts, and I don't think he'll make an exception for you."

Webb aimed a finger at Lila. "Go on. Get back to the office." Lila ducked her head, her confidence evaporated, the two goons grinning as she walked past them, both of them following her out into the hall. Turning to Mason, he said, "You keep showing up where I don't expect you. Why is that?"

"Somebody's bad luck."

Webb took a deep breath, calm descending on him, the craft of the con man clicking in. "Don't make it yours. What did you want with Lila? And don't lie to me because she won't."

Mason didn't know whether she would, but he wasn't willing to take the chance. He also didn't want to say any thing that would make Webb resist the bait that Fish was about to dangle in front of him. If Webb were suspicious of Mason, he'd be even more suspicious of Fish.

"I've got a case that involves Ed Fiori. Lila used to work for him. I wanted someplace private to talk with her. Vince Bongiovanni told me about this suite. I asked him if I could use it. I was afraid Lila wouldn't meet with me if she knew what I wanted to talk about so I asked Vince to have Carol Hill call her and say she wanted to meet with her to settle her case. Lila showed up with her entourage. One of them belted me hard enough to renumber my ribs. She and I were just getting acquainted when you showed up."

Webb smiled as if he'd already known that was what happened, renewing Mason's suspicion that the suite was bugged and confirming his decision not to lie.

"Fiori, huh?" Webb asked. "Wasn't he the guy that owned the casino before Galaxy bought it? He's been dead for what, three years?"

"Long before you came to work here. Too bad you never got to meet him. He was an interesting guy."

"The dead don't interest me, Mason, because they don't gamble."

"So you won't be interested in me, because I don't gamble either."

"Then I guess there's not much difference between you and a dead man," Webb said.

"If you don't count breathing."

Webb looked around the suite, walked to the door, and closed it. He took his time coming back into the living room, stopping to examine the fruit basket, polishing an apple before setting it down. He ambled over to the windows, gazing at the full parking lot.

"You know," he said at last, "that story you told Lila about working on a case involving Ed Fiori is pure bullshit, but I liked that you told it so well. You made it believable. That's talent. Then, you didn't lie to me. That's judgment. Those are two important qualities in a man. Now what's all this about someone at Galaxy trying to blackmail Judge Carter?"

Mason had taken a chance throwing that comment at Lila, hoping to shake her up. He expected her to press him for details. Instead, she let him change the subject to Fiori's tapes. He had a sudden image of Webb and Lila scamming him. Lila's job was to draw him out, find out what he knew. Webb would then burst in like a jealous husband at the first mention of blackmail. Only Webb cut them off before they got into any of the details. Maybe Lila wasn't involved and Webb didn't want her asking any questions. Everything in this case had at least two sides and everyone had at least two faces. The permutations were making him crazy, reminding him not to trust anyone.

"Just talk."

"Just talk," Webb repeated. "Who's doing the talking? Bongiovanni? That's the kind of rumor he'd spread. He probably hopes it gets back to the judge and makes her rule in his favor just to prove there was no blackmail."

"Can't help you. Client confidentiality."

"Yeah, yeah, yeah," Webb said, waving his hand at Mason. "Everything is confidential until you need something that's more important than keeping the client's secrets secret. Believe me; I know how you lawyers work. Anyway, from what I read in the paper, I would think you've got your hands full with Avery Fish's case."

Webb was back in full huckster mode, his voice silky, his manner ingratiating, and his outburst at Lila the impetuous act of another man. He dismissed

Mason's blackmail claim, more interested in talking about Fish. Mason wondered whether Sylvia McBride had already spoken with Webb, pitting Webb's greed against the prospect of exposing his real identity. He knew that Webb was playing him, probing for anything that would help him measure the odds. Mason decided to give him something he hadn't read in the papers, knowing that inside information was the hallmark of credibility.

"The prosecuting attorney and the U.S. attorney have ganged up on my client. They think he murdered your late employee, Mr. Rockley. They've offered to dismiss the federal charge and not seek the death penalty if he'll confess to Rockley's murder."

"Sounds like the framework for a deal," Webb said.

"Not this time," Mason answered. "My client had nothing to do with Rockley's murder and the police have no evidence that he did except that the body was found in his car. That won't get them a conviction. He'll never take a deal that makes him look like a killer. The state will have to back off on the murder charge and we'll beat the federal charge."

"Seems like quite a risk. Your client could go to jail for the rest of his life."

Mason understood Webb's concern. If Fish was willing to make a deal, Webb couldn't trust him. If Fish wouldn't deal, his proposition to Sylvia would have more credibility. He invoked Fish's appeal to Sylvia about his grandchildren.

"My client is at an age when any prison sentence is likely to be a life sentence. If he pleads to murder one, he never gets out. If he pleads to murder two, he does fifteen years, which is the same thing. If the state drops the murder charge, the U.S. attorney says he won't make a deal on the mail fraud. There are enough counts in the federal charges that they add up to a life sentence if he's convicted. So, there's no deal he can make that keeps him out of prison. His only real concern is his four grandkids. All he cares about is making certain they are taken care of."

"Do you do estate planning as well as criminal defense work?"

Mason shook his head. "Not me. I leave that up to bean counters."

"Mr. Fish must have a lot of money to protect if he can afford you," Webb said.

"One thing you learn in my business is not to ask questions about how much money your client has or where he got it. All I care about is that he has enough to pay me. The rest is none of my business."

"Another honest answer," Webb said. "It's trite but true. We all have a price, don't we?"

"We are a nation of buyers and sellers," Mason said with a tight-lipped smile, his eyes locked on to Webb's.

"So, then. That brings us back to this business about blackmail. You wouldn't answer my question before when I didn't offer you anything in return. That was rude. I suppose that makes me the buyer and makes you the seller."

"It's trite but true," Mason said. "There are some things that money just can't buy."

"That doesn't mean they can't be bought though, does it?"

Mason looked at him. "No, it doesn't."

"Then name your price."

History was repeating itself. Webb was standing a few feet from Mason, his suit jacket open, a smartphone clipped to his belt.

Mason eased out of his chair, closing the distance between them, flashing his take-me-home-with-you smile. Webb grinned until Mason's hand shot out, clamping Webb's lips together. Mason shoved him against the wall while he yanked the phone from Webb's belt. Pressing his forearm against Webb's neck to pin him in place, he tapped the audio record app icon and listened to his conversation with Lila followed by the one he had been having with Webb. He pressed erase and turned it off.

"You figure it out," Mason said, releasing his grip and dropping the phone to the floor.

CHAPTER SIXTY

As Mason pulled out of the Galaxy Casino parking lot, a Lexus pulled alongside, the driver tapping lightly on the horn. He turned and saw Lila Collins behind the wheel, signaling for him to follow her. Mason let a couple of cars cut in front of him but kept her in sight as he called Detective Griswold.

"Homicide. Griswold speaking."

"It's Lou Mason. How many murders have you solved today?"

"Counting the ones committed by your client—one. Forensics found fibers on the plastic wrapped around Rockley's body that match fibers from Fish's house."

"Big deal," Mason said. "The fibers were already in the trunk when the body was put in there. I'd have been surprised if they didn't find some. That would have made it look like he cleaned the trunk."

"Could be Fish kept the plastic in the house before he used it to wrap Rockley up. Either way, it adds to the body of evidence. You got something for me, or are you just lonely?"

"Did you talk to Lila Collins about Johnny Keegan?"

"Collins? Yeah. She's the HR director at Galaxy. Gave us the usual employee-of-the-year crap."

"Did you tell her that Keegan was trying to get in touch with me?"

"No. Did she tell you that?" Griswold asked.

"Yeah. Is that enough to get your feet off your desk?"

"And my ass back to the casino," Griswold said, hanging up.

When Griswold interviewed Lila again, she was certain to tell him about Mason's blackmail inquiry and Ed Fiori's tapes, but Mason couldn't help that.

He had to know who was telling him the truth. At least he would get another shot at Lila before Griswold did.

She led him to Berkley Riverfront Park, a landscaped strip on the south bank of the Missouri River that drew kids, couples, and kites in nice weather but was deserted on a cold, blustery Tuesday afternoon in February.

She parked her car, got out, and walked down a footpath toward a grove of trees that provided shelter from the wind and witnesses. Mason waited until he was certain they were alone and then followed her. When he caught up to her, she was clutching her coat tightly around her thin frame, her collar bundled around her face.

"I don't have much time," she said. "Webb will be all over me when I get back."

"Why are we here?"

"Because I work for a piece of shit and we weren't finished talking."

Anger in the ranks was a powerful motivator, strong enough to make people take chances they would ordinarily avoid, especially when they'd just been humiliated. It also made them vulnerable, especially when caught in a lie. His suspicion that she and Webb had stage-managed the scene in the suite faded.

"I just talked to Detective Griswold. He didn't tell you that Johnny Keegan was trying to get in touch with me. How did you know that?" She turned her back to him. "Griswold is on his way to the casino to question you. Tell me and maybe I can help you."

She faced him, her thick makeup streaked with tears. "Boy," she said, wiping her face with her coat sleeve. "I can really pick 'em. Ed Fiori was married. Never ever promised me he was going to leave his wife and marry me, but I didn't care. Then Johnny comes along. He really could light up the room. I knew he saw other girls, but it didn't matter. Last week he asked me if I knew a good lawyer. I remembered you from when Ed got killed. Then I saw you on TV about Avery Fish and Rockley, so I gave him your name."

"Did he say why he needed a lawyer?"

She shook her head. "Just that he needed the name for a friend."

"Did you know that Webb had bugged Bongiovanni's suite?"

"That prick!" she said, renewed anger stemming her tears. "One minute he's practically making love to you the way he talks; the next minute he cuts you open."

"Why do you stay?"

"My shrink says I have low self-esteem. That's why I choose relationships that don't have a chance. Makes me a perfect HR director, huh?" she asked, laughing at herself.

"I don't know. You're tough on the outside, soft on the inside. That's not such a bad combination."

"You think?"

"Yeah, I think. You're going to have to tell Detective Griswold about Johnny, and he's going to ask what you and I talked about."

"What do I tell him?"

"The truth. Anything else will get both of us in more trouble. I just want a head start on Griswold. When we were in the suite, you didn't say anything when I told you that someone at Galaxy may be blackmailing Judge Carter. Why not?"

"Because I'm not stupid. I don't know anything about that and I don't want to know. That's out of my league. I was going to tell Mr. Webb and let him handle it."

"And now?"

"Maybe I'll tell Detective Griswold and let him handle it. What do you think?"

That was the last thing Mason wanted her to do, but it was the only thing she could do. He'd put her in this situation and he'd have to deal with the fallout.

"I think you should tell the truth. You said you spend a lot of time checking references. Did you check Charles Rockley's and Johnny Keegan's?"

"Of course I did. That's my job. They checked out fine."

"What about Webb's references?"

"His too. If they hadn't checked out, they never would have gotten the jobs. The Gaming Commission ran checks on them too."

"How did you do it? By telephone?"

"What do you think I did? Hop on a plane?"

"Easy, Lila. I'm not the piece of shit you work for," Mason said, changing subjects. "Did Ed Fiori ever talk about me?"

"He liked you. He told me how you stood up to him and how loyal you were to your friend—the one that was charged with murder."

Mason knew he might not get another chance to ask her about the tape. He shivered, though not from the cold. "Did Fiori have me on tape?"

Her eyes widened. "That's what this is all about, isn't it? You and your friend and Ed. You must have asked him for help with your friend's case and now you're worried it's all going to come out."

Mason had tightened the noose completely around his neck. He'd just told a woman he hardly knew enough to figure out what he'd done. On top of that, he'd pointed Detective Griswold at her like a heat-seeking missile, and instructed her to tell Griswold everything. If that wasn't enough, she worked for Mason's number-one suspect in the blackmail scheme. She'd probably also tell Webb as well if he yelled at her loudly enough or asked her sweetly enough. It would have been quicker if he'd thrown himself under the wheels of a bus.

"My friend was innocent," Mason explained, to salvage something of his reputation with Lila. "Ed helped me prove that."

"I'll bet he helped you a little too much."

Mason nodded. "A little too much. I need to know if Ed taped our conversations."

"I'm sorry. I don't know. He never let me listen to the tapes."

"Webb showed up before you could tell me whether Bongiovanni took all of the tapes after Fiori died. Did he?"

"I don't know that either," she said as a ripple of cold wind wound through the trees. "Ed hid them in different places. I checked everywhere that night, but I don't know if I got them all before the FBI got there."

"The FBI. They were there too?"

"It was crazy. I was scrambling around looking for the tapes. Vince was hollering at me and packing everything I found into a couple of briefcases. One of the security guards called and said two agents were on their way to the office. Vince got out of there in a hurry."

"What did the FBI agents want?"

"They tore the place apart. I asked them for a search warrant. They said they didn't need one since Ed was dead. I didn't know what to do."

"Was one of them a big guy, built like a linebacker?" Mason asked, struggling for a better description of Dennis Brewer, kicking himself for not having a copy of his photograph.

"That description covers a lot of ground. But I made them show me ID. I remember names for a living and I remember theirs too."

"Was one of them Dennis Brewer?"

"Yeah," Lila said. "He was the big one. The other one was a woman."

Mason sucked in his breath. "You remember her name?"

"Sure. Kelly Holt."

Despite the cold, Mason felt a surge of heat sweep across his face. More than one piece of his past was bearing down on him.

"Did they find any more tapes?"

"I don't know. They kicked me out. I would have called a lawyer, but Vince was the only one I knew and he ran for daylight as soon as I told him the FBI was on their way."

Mason had drawn a dotted line between Brewer's name and Fiori's name on his dry erase board. He was ready to replace it with a solid line and add another one for Kelly and Al Webb.

"Have you seen Brewer hanging around the casino, maybe talking to Webb?"

She took her time, squinting and concentrating as the wind pelted her eyes. "I don't think so. Not him. The other one, the woman, I'm pretty sure I've seen her around the casino a couple of times. In fact," she added snapping her fingers, "I'm positive I saw her in one of the bars with Mr. Webb. She was wearing dark glasses like she was hungover or hiding. It was maybe six in the morning. I'd come in early to catch up on some paperwork. I walked by the bar and did a double take, but I kept my mouth shut."

"When was that?"

"A month or so ago, something like that." She looked at her watch, her olive skin pale in the clouded light. "I've gotta get back. I shouldn't have followed you. That was stupid, really stupid."

Mason put his hands on her shoulders. "I'm glad you did."

"Yeah. I'll put you down as a reference when that asshole fires me."

Mason waited until she'd been gone five minutes before he took the footpath back to his car. When he got there, a gray Crown Victoria was parked next to his. Kelly Holt stood next to it, leaning against the driver's door.

CHAPTER SIXTY-ONE

Mason's Aunt Claire once told him that the world depended on both man-made and natural law. Man-made laws were elastic, adapting to special circumstance, acknowledging changing times or bending to clever argument. Natural laws were immutable, a gift of God or nature, depending on whether one's compass pointed to faith or common sense as true north. The law of gravity was her favorite because, without it, everything on earth would hurtle into space in a cosmic instant.

Despite Detective Griswold's innuendo, Mason considered the possibility that Kelly would bend the law—cross the line—as unlikely as God turning the gravity switch off in a fit of divine vandalism. Yet, as Mason walked toward her, he half-expected to be launched into the void by the centrifugal fling of a suddenly off-kilter planet.

From the moment Dennis Brewer had whispered in Pete Samuelson's ear about the body in Fish's car, Mason had suspected that Brewer was somehow stirring the pot. He'd been there when Rockley's body was found. He'd been there when Mason and Blues had braced Mark Hill at the bar in Fairfax. He had the skill set to break into Lari Prillman's office and safe and then escape under cover of darkness and gunfire. And, he was tied to both Ed Fiori and Al Webb.

Mason now knew that the same could be said about Kelly Holt. She'd had nothing to do with Fish's case until Blues was photographed outside Rockley's apartment. When Blues had predicted that another FBI agent was backing up Brewer that night in Fairfax, Kelly had been that agent. She was no less qualified than Brewer for the black bag job at Lari Prillman's office. Lila Collins had placed her at the casino immediately after Fiori's death and again, only a month ago, with Webb. And, she had persistently deflected Mason's inquiries about Brewer, certain that Mason wouldn't consider the flip side of the coin.

Brewer was an anonymous face with a badge and a gun and wouldn't be the first good guy who turned out to be a bad guy. Mason couldn't yet tie it all together, but if he kept bulling his way through the maze, he was confident that he'd nail Brewer and that the rest of the pieces would fall together. He would take his well-deserved lumps for what he'd done to Judge Carter, but the laws of man and nature would put everyone and everything where they belonged.

If Kelly was dirty, if she and Brewer were in this together or if she was in it alone, he didn't know what he would do. Even if he wanted to turn a blind eye, he couldn't. If she had Fiori's tape and she wasn't corrupt, she would have confronted him by now, maybe even arrested him. If she was corrupt, if she had the tape and was sitting on it, she was a threat to him that he couldn't tolerate.

He blinked, testing his sight and his mind, making certain neither was hallucinating. Kelly was real. Standing in the cold, hands thrust in her pants pocket, the butt of her gun visible under her arm as her open jacket flapped in the wind.

"Friend of yours?" Kelly asked when Mason came close.

"Who?"

"The woman you were talking to. The one you followed into the parking lot and then down the path. The one you gave a five-minute head start to before you came back to your car."

"Oh, that woman. Her name is Lila Collins. She's the HR director at Galaxy. I called her and told her I wanted to meet with her. She suggested the park since it was close to the casino."

"It's a cold day in the park. What's wrong with her office?"

Mason shrugged, ignoring the pin Kelly had stuck in his story. "I guess she wanted some fresh air."

"She know anything?"

Mason followed his gut instinct to tell her what she would find out soon enough from the cops or on her own. The rest of his gut told him not to tell her another word more.

"Johnny Keegan had asked her for the name of a lawyer. Didn't tell her why. She'd seen me on TV and gave him my name. I called Detective Griswold and told him. He's going to follow up with her. That's one mystery solved. How did you find me here?"

"I called your office. That Mickey is very protective. I practically had to fax him a copy of my badge. He told me you'd gone to the casino. I drove over to find you and saw you leaving. I was going the opposite direction. By the time I got turned around, and caught up, you were turning into the park. I saw the two of you get out of your cars and decided to wait."

"You should have called me on my cell phone."

"Then you should have given me the number, bonehead," she said with a smile.

Mason's suspicion retreated for a moment in deference to his stupidity and her charm. Her story made sense and he wanted to believe her, though he knew it was just as likely that she had another reason for coming to the casino.

"Point taken," he said, writing it down on a slip of paper and handing it to her. "For future reference. What's up?"

"Sylvia McBride called Fish back. She's coming in town tomorrow and wants a look at Fish's safety deposit box. It's set for three p.m. at the bank."

"What about the hundred grand?"

"She told him that someone would pick it up tonight."

"At Fish's house? Isn't she worried about surveillance?"

"She is and that's why it won't happen there. He's supposed to stuff it in his coat, go out to dinner tonight, get a table, and go to the bathroom. When he comes back, the coat will be gone."

"That's a lot of money to stuff into a coat."

"Not really. A million dollars in hundred-dollar bills only weighs forty-four pounds. A hundred thousand weighs a little over four pounds. I sliced an opening in the liner of Fish's topcoat and dumped the money in. The coat is a little lumpy, but on him, everything looks lumpy."

"What restaurant and when?"

"An Italian place in Overland Park called Cinzetti's. It's a big buffet-style place. People are always up walking around. He's supposed to be there at seven.

The place will be packed. No one will notice a thing. It's a smart choice. Webb must have told her about it."

"Once Fish leaves his house with that coat, I want the surveillance cameras and microphones pulled. We agreed to that only so long as the money was in the house."

Kelly smiled. "I'm one step ahead of you, Counselor. I already gave the order. We'll have our equipment out of there before Fish gets home from dinner."

"Who's going with Fish for the drop?"

"I'll be there. Having dinner like everyone else," she said. "Are you okay with that?"

Mason swallowed his doubts, knowing that suspicion infected everything and that being right mattered less than believing that he was right.

"Works for me. I've already got two dinner dates tonight."

"Take my advice. Don't break either one of them. Leave this to me."

"Who's handling the safety deposit box?"

"Fish offered up Mickey, just like you told him. Said he was grooming him to take over the business. There's no connection to you. Sylvia went for it."

"I better get back to the office and brief him. Are you going to cover the bank too?"

"Not by myself. Dennis Brewer will be there too. Tell Mickey that Brewer wants to meet with him in the morning to get him ready. He'll be at your office at nine."

They studied each other in a face-mask standoff, neither giving any ground. "Did you ever talk to Brewer about who leaked the identity of Rockley's body?" he asked her.

"I told you before," she said. "I'll take care of Brewer. Just trust me."

CHAPTER SIXTY-TWO

SINCE ABBY MOVED to Washington, Mason hadn't had many dinner dates and he'd never had two for the same night. Double booking had not been a problem for his social calendar.

He was supposed to meet Samantha Greer at eight o'clock. It was her birthday and their dinner her only celebration. Standing her up would turn her birthday party into a pity party she would spend staring into the bottom of a bottle.

His relationship with Abby had been revived—again— last night and there was more on the menu tonight than dinner. If he broke their date to keep Samantha company, they would be back to Code Blue.

Being in two places at once with two different women didn't bother him nearly as much as wanting to be at a third place instead—Cinzetti's. He wanted to see who walked out of the restaurant wearing Fish's hundred-thousand-dollar coat.

It was past five as he drove across the Paseo Bridge, taking the south side of the downtown loop, and exited on Broadway before heading south again. The evening rush hour was picking up. People were heading home to families, dinner, and must-see TV. It was a life he'd never had, though one he now thought about having with Abby. He could be late for their dinner, but he couldn't miss it. He called Samantha Greer first.

"Glad you called," she said. "We're shorthanded and I just caught a homicide. Dead body in Troost Lake. You know what I don't get? Troost Lake is on Paseo, not Troost. Why don't they call it Paseo Lake?"

"Why do they call it a lake? It's barely a pond."

"You've got a point. Some birthday present, huh? Not the kind of stiff I was looking for tonight," she added with a bitter laugh. "Rain check?"

"Sure, Sam. Happy birthday."

Fifteen minutes later, he was sitting in his office with Blues and Mickey, laying out the day's events.

"So, I'm supposed to show Sylvia the money in the safe deposit box; then what?" Mickey asked.

"Then you say nice to meet you, enjoy your stay in Kansas City and don't forget to try the barbecue," Mason answered.

"What if she tries to make a withdrawal?" Mickey asked.

"Get out of the way," Mason said. "That's the FBI's problem."

"What if Kelly or Brewer try to make a withdrawal?" Blues asked. "From what you've said, the two of them might end up fighting over the money."

Mason looked at Mickey dead-on. "Duck and get the hell out of there. Any luck finding Mark Hill?" he asked Blues.

"I've checked his job, the bar in Fairfax, and a few other places. No luck, but I've got a feeling where he is."

"Where's that?"

"Thin air, man. That cat is gone. I can feel it."

"Vertical or horizontal?"

"Flip a coin, you ask me. Either way, he isn't coming back."

Mason drew a red circle around Mark Hill's name on the dry erase board, adding Gone? Where? beneath his name.

"If I was you," Blues said, "I'd pin the blackmail label on Webb. Rockley's dead, Keegan's dead, and Judge Carter is still getting pressured. Webb is the only one left at Galaxy who has a stake in what happens."

Mason nodded, putting the tag under Webb's name in large blue letters. "What about you, Mickey?" Mason asked. "Any epiphanies from reading my file or did you just search the Internet for clues and come up with all the answers?"

Mickey laughed. "I haven't had a good epiphany since I went to Washington, but I have found a better way to get what I'm looking for than the Internet. It's called the staffers' network. I've been seeing a woman who's a staffer on the

Senate Judiciary Committee. She has a cousin who works at the FBI. By tomorrow, I'll have a rundown on Charles Rockley, a.k.a. Tommy Corcoran, and Al Webb, a.k.a. Wayne McBride." "Whatever happened to privacy and government security? Don't you have to have security clearances to get that kind of information?"

"There are no secrets in our nation's capital—just people who know them and people who know the people that know them. D.C. is the ultimate upstairs/downstairs world. All the politicians are busy running for reelection while grunts like me work the information black market finding the stuff that helps them win or lose."

"Makes me feel better about paying my taxes." "I did see one thing in your file that may be kind of interesting," Mickey said. "This Sylvia McBride works at a call center, right?"

"Right. But you've been in D.C. too long if you think working at a call center is interesting."

"No, man," Mickey said. "Check this out. Senator Seeley is on the telecommunications subcommittee. A lot of companies are shipping their call center operations overseas because it's cheaper to hire someone in New Delhi to give bad customer service than it is to hire someone in New Jersey. The committee staff is investigating because outsourcing jobs to foreign countries has become a real voter hot button."

"What's that got to do with us?"

"Bongiovanni made a big deal out of the fact that you got Rockley's employers to give you detailed references for him over the phone. You said Lari Prillman was able to get references over the phone for Johnny Keegan."

"So?" Blues said.

"So," Mason explained, "employers won't talk about their ex-employees anymore because they're all afraid of getting sued. What are you getting at, Mickey?"

"Okay," Mickey said. "Here's how it could work. We know that Rockley and Webb had fake IDs. That means they've got to use fake references too. When someone calls the phone numbers for the fake references, the calls are answered at Sylvia's call center. The operator knows what to say and the caller thinks he's getting the straight story. Pretty slick, huh?"

Mason came out of his chair, flipped through his file until he found Rockley's employment application. "Look. His prior employers are in three different states. How would that work?"

"Simple. The calls go through a router set up in the area code for the phone number. The equipment doesn't cost much, especially if it's not handling a lot of calls; doesn't even require an office. You call a number in Ohio and it gets routed to Sylvia McBride's call center in Minneapolis. She gets a readout that tells her the name of the company being called so she knows who she's supposed to be when she answers the phone."

"But I talked to a different person on each call."

"So she's got a few people working for her. No big deal."

"Easy enough to find out if the phone numbers are legit," Blues said. "Use a reverse directory to find out who owns the numbers. If it's not the companies on Rockley's application, I'd say Mickey's got it nailed."

"Where do we get a reverse directory?" Mason asked.

"Now that's what the Internet is for," Mickey answered. "If you don't mind spending a few bucks and getting a lifetime of spam." He opened the browser on Mason's desktop, did a search for reverse directory, and pushed his chair away from the monitor. "Pick any site you want. Plug in the phone numbers you're interested in and your credit card."

It only took a few minutes to confirm that each employer on Rockley's application was the owner of the phone number Rockley had given for them.

"Shit," Mickey said. "It seemed like a great idea at the time."

"Still is," Mason said. "All you need for a phone number is an address and a place to put the phone or the router to handle the calls. If you're in the fake identity business, that's just overhead. Can you use the reverse directory to check out addresses?"

"Sure," Mickey said. "Put in an address and you get a phone number that goes with it."

"Fine. Try some addresses close to the ones on Rockley's application. Start calling until someone answers. When they do, ask them about their neighbors."

"What about Fish?" Blues asked. "I'm supposed to keep an eye on Judge Carter."

"And I'm supposed to have dinner with Abby," Mason said. "We're both going to be late. I want you inside the restaurant with Fish and Kelly. I'll be in the parking lot."

"How's that supposed to work?" Blues asked. "Kelly will ID me in a heartbeat."

"I'll do it," Mickey said. "I can make the calls in the morning. Kelly and I have never met so she won't recognize me. Just give me a description of her and Fish and I'll get lost in the crowd. You guys wait outside. I'll call you when the money walks out the door."

"Then what?" Blues asked.

"Follow the money," Mason said.

CHAPTER SIXTY-THREE

THEY TOOK SEPARATE cars and drove different routes so they wouldn't arrive at the same time. Mason called Abby from the car, assuring her that he would be at her place by eight. She promised to chill the wine, not able to disguise the worry in her voice. It was nothing, he told her—a late appointment. Hurry, she said. He'd picked the wrong night to be late.

Cinzetti's was in Overland Park, the biggest city in Johnson County, a sprawling suburban enclave on the Kansas side of the state line that divided the metropolis between Kansas Jayhawks and Missouri Tigers. The restaurant occupied a large slab of the parking lot in an upscale strip mall on the west side of Metcalf Avenue, faux Roman columns flanking the entrance.

Blues was driving a BMW, a car that fit his personality as uncomfortably as a promise fit a politician. Both couldn't wait to get out of them. He preferred his pickup truck, but the BMW was a thank-you from a twentysomething trust fund baby who had gotten in too deeply with a drug dealer until Blues had separated them. When Blues turned the gift down, the grateful heir dropped the keys, title, and registration on the bar and walked out.

The BMW was perfect for surveillance in Johnson County, where driving a car worth more than the average person made in a year wasn't bragging—it was expected. Blues had backed into a parking place along the far row of the lot, giving him a clear view of the front and both sides of the restaurant and easy access to the street.

A service road separated the rear of the building from the back side of a row of shops, the door to each illuminated by halogen lamps that bathed the road in purple-white daylight. There was no place to park, and the only inconspicuous place from which to watch the back door of the restaurant was a rectangular alcove big enough for a soda machine between two of the stores. Mason drove slowly past as a man wearing a white kitchen coat kicked the door open, dragged two black garbage bags to a nearby Dumpster, and tossed them in before lighting a cigarette and watching Mason go by.

The alcove was deep and dark enough to swallow Mason when he made his way there after parking his car. The kitchen door was propped open, a triangle of light spilling onto the asphalt, garlic breeze escaping the kitchen and seasoning the air. He leaned against the rough brick wall, checking his watch, waiting for Mickey's call.

Follow the money, he'd told Blues before they left his office. It was an axiom made famous in political scandals that served equally well in solving crimes. Whether it was the money Webb was skimming from the casino, the money Kelly had hidden in Fish's coat, or the money Bongiovanni wanted from Galaxy, all he had to do was follow it. When it stopped moving, he'd have his answers.

Mason's cell phone rang. "What's happening?" Mason asked.

"The coat is moving," Mickey said.

"Who has it?"

"A white guy, mid-thirties, wearing khaki pants and a gray sweater. He's headed for the front door."

Mason called Blues. "Khaki pants, gray sweater and a hundred-thousand-dollar coat coming right at you."

"I've got him," Blues said. "Only he's not carrying or wearing a coat. He's banging on the door of a minivan. Someone opened up, he got in, and they're taking off. Here come Fish and Kelly. She's patting him on the back. He's squeezing her ass. I'm on the van."

"Shit!" Mason said, punching the buttons on the phone again. "Mickey! Where the hell are you?"

"Here, boss. How we doin'?"

"Lousy. The guy didn't have the coat when he got outside. Could he have passed it to someone else?"

"I don't know. There was a table full of women wearing red hats. They all got up at the same time as he did and I lost him. He could have handed it off to someone and I wouldn't have known it."

"What's the next thing you saw after the women got out of the way?"

Mickey waited a moment before answering. "Not much. Just a busboy carrying a garbage bag."

Mason peered at the back door to the restaurant just as the man in the kitchen coat emerged with another garbage bag, adding it to the top of the pile in the Dumpster, looking both ways before he went back inside. A moment later, a sedan pulled up alongside the Dumpster. One of Lila Collins's bodyguards—the one who had gut-punched him at the hotel—got out, grabbed the garbage bag, and tossed it into the trunk of the car.

Mason crouched on the ground, pressing himself against the base of the alcove as the car eased past. He stuck his head out far enough to read the license tag on the car, repeating it until he was certain he wouldn't forget it.

His car was parked too far away for him to follow the sedan. He doubted the bodyguard would take the money to the casino since video cameras recorded everyone who came or left. His best bet was to trace the tag on the car. He called Blues again.

"Are you still following the van?" Mason asked him.

"Yeah. They're taking their time, stopping for all the yellow lights."

"Write the plate number down and let them go," Mason said, explaining what had happened. "You know anyone who can run a couple of plates after hours?"

"After hours costs extra."

"The guy who charges extra, does he owe you for anything?"

"All my people owe me. That's why they're my people."

"Then tell him he's paid up if he gets us names and addresses tonight."

Mason checked his watch. He had fifteen minutes to make it to Abby's apartment. He'd be late but not too late. He called and told her he was on the way, the relief in her voice enough to warm them both.

A long line of cars was stacked up almost the length of the parking lot waiting to turn onto Metcalf. Mason decided to look for another exit on the west side of the strip center. He drove back down the service road past the entrance to the kitchen and into the drive around the outer edge of the store fronts. He turned left away from the traffic, trailing a few other drivers who'd adopted the same exit strategy.

The driver of the car in front of him had a change of heart and turned around, his headlights framing a man and woman standing in the darkened entrance of a vacant storefront. Kelly Holt and Dennis Brewer were wrapped around each other like braided snakes.

CHAPTER SIXTY-FOUR

Mason turned his head from them and drove past as if he hadn't noticed a thing, resisting the temptation to speed away as that would surely draw their attention. He glanced in his rearview mirror, wondering if they had recognized him or memorized his license tag.

He held his course, turning out of the lot, crossing into a residential neighborhood, and losing himself in the winding streets. No backup cars appeared behind him or cut him off, his cautious meandering giving him cover and time to think.

When he'd first met Kelly, she had recently left the FBI after becoming involved with another agent who'd turned out to be on the take. Her lover had been killed and she'd been suspected of being corrupt as well. Though she was eventually cleared, the suspicion and her lover's death were enough to make her quit. Now she was back with the FBI, involved with another agent, both of them with too much to explain. She reminded him of a woman who kept marrying alcoholics and complained that all the good ones were taken, not realizing that she was the one who was making the same mistake again.

He remembered her differently, as beautiful, brave, and unfairly accused. It was who he wanted to see and, at the time, who he had wanted to love. She'd walked away from him then; Mason had believed that she had too many wounds to heal to make a permanent place for him in her life. Now he realized he just wasn't her type. He checked his bitterness with the knowledge that she might think otherwise if she knew about Judge Carter. If he was going to step on the toes of people with clay feet, he'd have to start with himself.

The side street he'd chosen led him into a subdivision. He didn't think Kelly or Brewer was following him and he doubted they had backup for that purpose. Whatever they were up to, they had to be doing it on their own. Still, he didn't want to take any chances. His cell phone rang as he made another unnecessary turn.

It was Kelly Holt. "Where are you?"

"Just leaving my office."

"For a guy with two dinner dates, you're getting a late start."

"Lucky for me, one of them cancelled."

"Cancel the other one. We need to talk."

"Call Mickey and make an appointment. I've got a busy day tomorrow. Maybe end of the week."

"Stubborn and stupid could get you hurt," she said.

"Then you should be right there with me."

"It was you!"

"Yeah," he said softly, dropping any pretense. "And it was you too."

"It's not the way it looks."

"Like the song says, who should I believe? You or my lying eyes?"

"It's complicated," she said.

"I've hung too many things on that hook and I don't have room for anything else."

"Don't do this."

"Too late. We already did," he said and hung up.

His cell rang a moment later, this time Rachel Firestone's name was displayed on the screen. He'd turned her loose on Dennis Brewer the night before but doubted that she'd found out more in the last twenty-four hours than he had found out in the last twenty minutes.

"Where are you?" she asked.

"That seems to be everyone's favorite question. What happened to hello?"

"What's the matter? Are you lost? Who else is looking for you?"

"You're the only one that matters. I was lost until you found me. Any luck with Dennis Brewer?"

"You know what happens when a reporter starts asking if anyone knows whether an FBI agent might be dirty? Phones start ringing and none of them are mine. The publisher doesn't like hearing from the U.S. attorney."

Mason had met the publisher, David Phelan, a passionate man who was rumored to have ink in his veins instead of blood. "Roosevelt Holmes called David Phelan?"

"And demanded that the paper kill my story and that I turn over my notes and sources or get ready to tell the grand jury why I won't."

"What did Phelan tell him?"

"He told Roosevelt to go fuck himself. Then he told me that I better be right or I could go fuck myself too. Am I right?"

"It's looking that way. There are still a lot of loose ends."

"That's why I was calling you. One of them may have just gotten nailed down."

"Which one?"

"The reporter whose desk is next to mine covers the cops. All he does is listen to the police scanner waiting for something to happen. A little while ago, he picked up a report of a dead body and went to the scene. He called in and told the editor to save him some room for tomorrow's Metro section. I overheard the editor's end of the conversation. The editor asked if the victim had been identified, and then he repeated the name out loud. That's when I called you."

"Who was it?"

"Mark Hill."

He caught his breath. Blues had been right. "Where was the body found?"

"Troost Lake. Meet me there?"

He exhaled slowly. "Yeah," he answered, thinking of Samantha Greer's birthday celebration while not looking forward to calling Abby.

"Remember," she said, "it's on Paseo, not Troost."

"I know, and it's not really a lake either."

CHAPTER SIXTY-FIVE

ABBY HUNG UP in the middle of Mason's explanation. Right after he told her that a key witness had just been found murdered. She wasn't interested in the details or why he had to go the scene instead of reading about it in the paper like everyone else. He knew why but couldn't tell her because she didn't give him the chance and it wouldn't have mattered anyway.

If she'd let him, he would have told her that a case is a living, breathing organism conceived in conflict. It is a wild, uncontrollable adolescent while the facts are being fleshed out by the rule of unintended consequences. As it matures, lawyers may rein it in with pleadings and tactics and courts may squeeze it with orders until it surrenders its last gasp, but those days were weeks or months away. Tonight, he had no control over it. All he could do was hold on.

Troost Lake was a triangle of brown water lying between Twenty-seventh and Twenty-ninth Streets, the long leg of the triangle parallel to Paseo. The full name of the street was The Paseo Boulevard, though Mason had no idea what the north–south artery had done to earn that formal distinction.

The lake was a quarter mile east of Troost Avenue, both the lake and the street the legacy of a Dutchman, Benoist Troost, one of Kansas City's earliest physicians and civic boosters. Defeated for mayor in 1853, he had organized the city's premier newspaper in 1854 and helped found the Chamber of Commerce in 1857. Mason read the doctor's abbreviated biography on an historical marker near the south end of the lake well behind the yellow crime scene tape that kept him away from the cops working Mark Hill's murder.

Mason doubted anything would be named after him, though, given a choice, he preferred a couple of kids to a strip of concrete or a muddy patch of water. Troost Lake may have been named to memorialize the good doctor, but it had become a favorite burial ground for dead bodies owing to the terrain and the demographics. The Paseo was elevated above the lake and the surrounding trees provided additional good cover. The area was part of the urban core where too many people saw violence and death through eyes dulled with repetition. Outrage succumbed to resignation as the city shrugged its shoulders.

Rachel met him, wearing a sheepskin coat and a muffler knotted at her throat. The night had turned damp, moisture seeping through his jacket with the cold. He shifted his weight from side to side to keep warm.

"What do you think?" she said.

"Samantha Greer is working the case. That's her over there," Mason said, pointing to the right angle of the triangle. It was the heaviest wooded corner of the lake, least likely to give up its victims until fishermen returned in the summer. "I can't get close enough to talk to her."

Mason felt a hand on his back and turned around. "How about I take you a little closer?" Detective Cates said. "Sorry," he said to Rachel.

Klieg lights mounted on ten-foot stands illuminated the site where Hill's body had been found, warming the water enough to boil a ground-hugging fog. A forensics team moved slowly across the invisible grid they had laid down over the scene, lifting each square by its roots, shaking and sifting it for evidence. A diver in a glistening black wet suit waded out of the water, carefully pinching the butt of a gun between two fingers. An ambulance waited at the north end of the lake, its back end open and ready to receive the body.

Samantha Greer stood with hands on her hips, watching her people work. She nodded as they reported to her, took notes, and resumed the position.

"Wait here," Cates told Mason when they reached the yellow tape.

Cates ducked beneath the tape, walked over to Samantha, and tapped her on the shoulder. She turned and looked at Mason, listening as Cates spoke. When he finished, she brushed her hair with her hands and made her way to Mason, keeping the tape between them.

"Happy birthday, Sam," Mason said.

"And I don't feel a day older. You wouldn't be here if you didn't already know it was Mark Hill, so who told you?"

"A reporter at the Star picked it up from the police scanner, checked it out, and called it in to his editor. Rachel Fire- stone overheard and called me."

Samantha looked past Mason at Rachel, who waved and smiled. Samantha ignored the gesture.

"Why did she call you?"

"She's working Avery Fish's case."

"I read the article," Samantha said. "Big help."

Mason ignored the dig. He wanted to find out what he could as quickly as possible and get out of there so he could salvage the evening with Abby.

"I told her about Carol Hill's lawsuit against Rockley and Galaxy. She thought I'd want to know about Mark Hill."

"You think there's a connection between the deaths of Rockley and Hill?"

"Hill smacked Carol around. Rockley came on to Carol. She didn't like either one of them. Makes Carol a suspect."

"Women don't generally mutilate bodies or drag them to lakes in the middle of the night. When they kill someone, they leave them where they fall."

"Then again," Mason said, "Hill could have killed Rock- ley for harassing his wife and somebody killed Hill to balance the books. Give me enough time and I'll come up with plenty of options."

"All of which will conveniently point the finger away from your client for killing Rockley, huh?"

"That's one way to look at it. In fact, that's a pretty good way to look at it. How did Hill die?"

"Bullet to the brain."

"Did he do it by himself or did he have help?"

"Coroner says it's too early to tell."

"Time of death?" Mason asked.

"Somewhere in the last twelve to twenty-four hours."

"Talk to your client. Tell him he better be able to account for his whereabouts," Detective Cates said.

Mason turned to him. "What's the matter? Didn't you hear Detective Greer say that Hill's death points the finger away from Avery Fish?"

"I make a point to keep bullshit out of my ears," Cates said. "The way I see it, your client could have killed Hill just so we'd look somewhere else on Rockley. Bring him downtown tomorrow morning. Don't make us come and get him."

"Sam," Mason said. "You can't be serious."

"Rockley isn't my case, Lou. Hill belongs to me unless it turns out they're related. If they are, Cates and Griswold will take it. Right now we don't know one way or the other. Either way, we're going to need to talk to Fish. Might as well make it tomorrow morning."

Dennis Brewer was meeting with Mickey at 9 A.M. to prepare him for the tour of Fish's safety deposit box. Mason wanted to sit in on that session, which shouldn't take more than an hour.

"We'll be there at eleven," he said.

Mason told Rachel what he'd learned, thanked her for the tip, and declined her offer for a late dinner, telling her he was already late for dinner with Abby. His cell phone rang again before he reached his car. He let it ring while deciding whether to answer it or throw it in the lake, choosing the former when he saw Blues's name on the screen.

"What do you have?" Mason asked him.

"One address for both cars at Lake Lotawana. Place is owned by someone named Ernie Fowler. Got the phone number too."

"I'll bet the rent money that Ernie Fowler's phone is answered at Sylvia McBride's call center in Minneapolis."

"One way to find out," Blues said. "Call him."

"What if he doesn't answer?"

"Then we knock on his door."

"I was thinking of something more discreet. Besides, have you ever tried finding an address at a lake?" Mason asked. "You practically need a guide."

"I've got one. This BMW has a GPS system. I've already punched in the address. It's only twenty-four-point-thirty miles if we pick the route for the fastest time and the most use of freeways. Damn, being rich is a fine thing."

"Pick me up at the office," Mason said. "Ten minutes."

CHAPTER SIXTY-SIX

TROOST LAKE WAS an oversized pond, home to no one. Lake Lotawana was the real deal: a pastoral haven far enough from Kansas City to feel like you left. Mason didn't expect to find any bodies floating there, but that didn't make him feel any better about making the trip. The case was swallowing him whole, the dark water lapping against his chin. He had an image of Abby turning her back as the water closed over his head.

The first twenty miles were easy. They took Highway 71 south, picked up I-470, and got off at Colbern Road. A handful of quick turns later, they were on Lake Lotawana Road, passing the Lake Lotawana Police Department, which served and protected the two thousand people who lived in homes surrounding the lake, according to the brightly lit sign outside the station.

"Look at that map," Mason said, pointing to the GPS screen. "The lake looks like Italy and we just crossed the border from France. Ernie Fowler's house is south of Rome.

The way this road curves around, we are going to have to knock on his door. There's no way we can get there without being seen."

"You want to see his house from the outside in or the inside out?" Blues asked.

"I'll settle for outside. My breaking-and-entering days are behind me."

"Too much conscience is a bad thing for a man in our line of work," Blues said.

"Maybe I need a new line of work. What about the lake? If we can find a boat, we can check the house out from the water."

"I've got a pair of night vision binoculars in the trunk. But I didn't have room for the boat."

"We can borrow someone's boat," Mason said. Blues looked at him, eyebrows arched. "We'll put it back and I'll leave gas money, all right?"

"Need a new line of work, my ass."

Lake Shore Drive circled Lake Lotawana. Side streets named with single letters led from Keystone to the homes at the water's edge, the entrances to each flanked by long, curved brick walls that gave way to a split-rail fence, the fence connecting to the brick wall at the next side street. The wall and fence added an air of privacy to the residential area though they wouldn't keep anyone out.

Ernie Fowler's house was on L Street. They drove south on Keystone along the west flank of the lake, pulling onto the shoulder just beyond the entrance to L Street, not wanting to risk that someone was watching from the house for any unexpected traffic.

"Let's see how close we can get without being shot at," Blues said.

They took their time, Mason letting his eyes adjust to the darkness, Blues scanning the street with his night vision glasses. The street was laid out in a T shape with houses on both sides of the vertical leg and a row of houses on the horizontal bar at the top of the T. These were the lakefront houses and Fowler's was at the south end, cut off from his neighbors by a row of evergreens grown to privacy heights.

There were no streetlights and all of the houses were dark, late February not a popular time at the lake. The houses were spread apart, divided by mature stands of trees.

Like the others, Fowler's house was dark on the front, though they could see a glimmer of light through the front windows coming from the back of the house. The sedan and the minivan were parked in the driveway. The hoods of the cars were still warm, as was the hood of an SUV that was parked in front of the house next to Fowler's. Back in the car, Blues studied the GPS screen.

"There," he said. "The next road over is M. Let's hope somebody left their boat in the water."

M Street was laid out in the same fashion, the houses blacked out. There were no cars on the street or in the unattached carports. Blues picked the empty carport for the house at the top of the T, giving him a straight shot to Keystone. He backed in, unscrewed the bulb in the car dome light, and grabbed his night vision binoculars.

The yard behind the house was deep and wide open before reaching a forested tree line and sloping gently down to the water. Wooden stairs had been cut through the trees, leading to a dock where they found an aluminum fishing boat with its motor lifted out of the water.

"Just what we're looking for," Blues said. "Won't be too noisy or noticeable. No running lights either. That's even better."

"The god of the slippery slope is smiling on us," Mason said.

"Hey. No one is making you do this but you. I could be home with my feet up watching SportsCenter, you just say the word."

Mason took a deep breath. "You'll be the first to know. Let's go."

Blues kept the boat quiet, revving the engine barely above trolling speed. They crossed to the east side of the lake before turning north, hugging the eastern shore until they were directly across from Fowler's house. A light was on inside the room adjoining the deck, probably the den or kitchen, Mason guessed. The light was bright enough that they could make out the shapes of people standing on the unlighted deck.

"How far away are we?" Mason asked Blues when they cut the engine.

"Five hundred yards, give or take," Blues answered, studying the deck through the binoculars. "Looks like a party. Kelly and Brewer are there. I don't recognize the others."

"What's Fowler's phone number?" Mason asked, opening his cell phone.

"You sure you want to call right now? What if Fowler has caller ID? What are you going to say after you say hello?"

"You're right. Give me the glasses."

He adjusted the focus, capturing Kelly, Brewer, and Al Webb huddled at the deck rail. Even in the green glow of the night vision, there was no mistaking them. He swept the deck to see who else was there. The driver of the sedan stared back at him through his own binoculars, which he quickly lowered, rushing to Webb's side and pointing at the boat across the water. Webb snatched the glasses from him and looked for himself.

"Shit!" Mason said, ducking into the bottom of the boat. "We're busted. Get the hell out of here!"

They'd been seen, though there was no way to know if they'd been recognized, the distance and darkness in their favor. Blues started the engine and flattened himself against the seat, steering with one hand while watching the bow rise as the boat picked up speed.

The shape of the lake worked against them. Webb had a perfect view of their escape. If they cut back across the lake to M Street, he would know where to find them and would probably get there before they did. If they continued on their present course, they would have to get out on the east side of the lake with no way to get back to the west side and their car other than a walk that would take the rest of the night. He made his choice, angling the boat hard toward M Street.

Mason tied the boat to the dock and followed Blues to the line of trees at the edge of the backyard. They listened for the sounds of another car or anything else that didn't belong on a deserted street but heard nothing.

"Be quick but don't hurry," Blues told Mason, pointing toward the car.

They cracked the doors and slid in, closing them as quietly as German engineering made possible. Blues started the ignition, keeping the headlights off, just as a car skidded to a stop at the entrance to the street, blocking their exit. The bodyguards from the Galaxy Hotel got out carrying guns. They signaled to each other, pointing at the BMW, the only other car on the deserted block. The added shadow of the carport made it impossible for them to see Blues and Mason inside the car, though the engine was running.

The brick wall and split-rail fence bordering the entrance to the street, together with the car parked in the intersection, had Blues and Mason bottled up. The fence was the obstacle of least resistance, though the odds were good that they would be shot before they got that far. They would be even easier targets if they tried to escape on foot.

"I don't suppose BMW equips these cars with guns," Mason said.

"Nope," Blues said. "Should have brought my pickup. Got a nice shotgun on the rack be the perfect equalizer for these boys."

"Any ideas?"

"Ever play bodyguard pinball? Car doors make great flippers. When we get close enough, I'll floor it. Stay down and be ready."

When the bodyguards reached the end of the driveway, Blues shifted into drive, letting the BMW roll out of the carport. The bodyguards took aim and inched forward, lined up so that they would be on each side of the car as it passed.

In the same instant Blues stomped on the accelerator and hit the high beams, blinding the bodyguards. Mason and Blues flung the car doors open as they sped past, catapulting both bodyguards into the air before they could fire a shot.

Blues jammed on the brakes and they got out. Neither bodyguard was conscious, though both were breathing. Blues picked up their guns and their wallets, taking their driver's licenses. He ran back to the lake and threw their guns into the water. When he came back, he handed Mason their driver's licenses.

"These names mean anything to you?" he asked Mason.

The one who had worked Mason over at the hotel and picked up Fish's coat was Bud Tenet; his partner was Frank Naughton.

"No, but with the phony IDs in this case, these probably aren't the names their mamas gave them."

Mason rifled their pockets until he found the keys to their car and a cell phone. Blues parked their car alongside them while Mason used their cell phone to call 911 and report that there were two drunks passed out on M Street.

They passed the Lake Lotawana police station as a cruiser pulled out, siren sounding and lights flashing, an ambulance right behind it. They were northbound on Highway 71 when Mason's cell phone rang. It was Kelly Holt.

"How was dinner?" she asked.

"Nice and quiet."

"I'm glad to hear that."

"Really?"

"Really. See you tomorrow," she said.

CHAPTER SIXTY-SEVEN

BLUES PARKED THE BMW behind the bar, avoiding potholes as if he had radar. Driving back, they had dissected the possible explanations for what they'd witnessed. Both Kelly and Brewer could be dirty or both could be working undercover; or, only one of them may be on the take while the other was trying to bring him or her, and Webb, down. They exhausted the evidence and gave up, declaring themselves a hung jury of two. The only verdict they reached was that they couldn't trust either one of them.

"So what about Fish?" Blues asked. "Why did Rockley's killer dump the body in the trunk of his car?"

"Either it was a coincidence, and I don't believe in coincidences, or the killer knew there was a connection between Fish and Webb and wanted to take advantage of it."

"How?"

"I don't know. Once the body was identified, the cops would look for a connection to Galaxy since Rockley worked there and was in the middle of a sexual harassment suit. After they made the connection between Fish and Webb, they'd have to take a hard look at Webb."

"But they haven't made the connection," Blues said. "You told me that the cops are only looking at Fish."

"Griswold made some noise about Mark Hill, but that's over since Hill was killed. Now they want to talk to Fish about that murder too."

"The feds must not have told the cops about Webb."

"You're probably right," Mason said. "Pete Samuelson and Kelly both said they had to protect their investigation. They wouldn't tell the cops that Webb is really Fish's old scam partner because the cops would go after Webb and Webb would figure out why. That would blow the lid off their investigation."

"Only people that would know all of that have FBI Agent printed on their business cards. You thinking Kelly or Brewer killed Rockley?"

Mason shuddered at the image of Kelly hunched over Rockley's body, sawing away at his neck and wrists. Whatever she may have become, he couldn't accept that she was a killer. It was easier to imagine Brewer as the butcher.

"Not Kelly—maybe Brewer. Someone at Galaxy must have tipped off the FBI that Webb was really Wayne McBride. Maybe it was Rockley and that's why he was killed. Or, maybe it was Johnny Keegan and that's why he wanted to hire me. Either way, Brewer knew that Pete Samuelson was going to use Fish to close the loop on Webb."

"Guys like Webb would give up their grandma to make a deal," Blues said.

"Or their silent partner, especially if he happens to be an FBI agent."

"So Brewer kills Rockley to slow down the investigation and cuts his head and hands off to slow it down even more. I can buy all of that, but why would Brewer dump Rockley's body in Fish's car?"

"Sends a powerful message to Webb to keep his mouth shut," Mason said.

"Remind me about your plea negotiations on Fish's mail fraud charge. When did the U.S. attorney demand that Fish help them with the investigation of Webb?"

"Officially, not until after they found Rockley's body in the trunk of Fish's car," Mason said. "Up until then, we were just trading dollars and days. But I think Pete Samuelson was about to make the pitch when Brewer walked in and dropped the hammer. What's your point?"

"Webb killed some dude and used the body to fake his own death. He got away with it until he started skimming from Galaxy. Rockley or Keegan tipped off the FBI that Webb was really McBride. Now, they don't just want him for stealing. They want him for murder. They set up a reunion between Webb and Fish hoping that Webb will tell Fish all about it so they can make the murder case against Webb."

"But if Fish is convicted of Rockley's murder, he makes a lousy witness against Webb," Mason said. "That's why Brewer left Rockley's body in the trunk of Fish's car—to frame Fish and ruin his credibility as a witness against Webb."

"Makes sense for Brewer to kill Rockley, but it doesn't make sense for him to leak the identification of the body. It was going to come out in a few days anyway.

"Actually, it does," Mason said. "Rachel wouldn't have run that story without corroboration from two sources. She already had it from one source when she went to Brewer. He gave it to her because it was going to come out anyway and he knows the killer wouldn't do that. At the right time, he'll probably admit to being the source."

"Maybe so. But the whole thing makes my hair hurt. Most people don't plan so carefully when they kill someone unless they're a serial killer or a pro. Usually, it's all about hot money, hot blood, or hot pussy. They shoot first, then do something really stupid and get caught. We're trying too hard to make everything hang together."

Mason let out a sigh. "You got any better ideas?"

"The FBI got my picture when they opened up somebody's e-mail. Had to be Webb's. When I was checking out Rockley's apartment, one of his neighbors told me that someone else had been asking around for him. Could be that was the cat that took my picture and e-mailed it to Webb. We find out who sent that e-mail we might find out something worth knowing."

"I imagine one of your people could hack into Webb's computer, but that's going to take time," Mason said.

"We won't have to do that if Lila Collins does it for us," Blues said.

"That's taking a big chance. You think she'd do it?"

"You said she loved Ed Fiori and she hates Al Webb."

"I'll call her in the morning," Mason said.

"Morning may be too late. Call her now."

"I don't have a phone number for her."

"Got a name, don't you? That's enough for my man that ran the license tags," Blues said. He flipped open his cell phone, punched in the number, and explained what he needed. "I hear you, brother man," he said before hanging up.

"Done?"

"Gonna be done. The tags were on his account. This one is on yours. He'll leave you a message on your cell phone. What about Judge Carter? What are you going to do about her?"

Mason shook his head, looking at his watch. It was just past midnight, Wednesday morning.

"I'm about out of options. She's going to issue her decision on Friday. We're caught in the middle of a clusterfuck that's getting us no closer to the blackmailer. If I don't come up with something better, I'll go public with what I did, take the responsibility, and do my best to cover for her."

"They'll punch your ticket, you know that."

Mason smiled at Blues. "Yeah, well. I can always tend bar for you or write mysteries like every other lawyer who burns out on the practice."

"I was you," Blues said, "I'd study up on mixing drinks."

CHAPTER SIXTY-EIGHT

IT WAS CLOSE to 2 A.M. when Mason knocked on Abby's door. He hadn't called because he didn't want to give her the chance to tell him not to come over. He would have come anyway, adding one more offense to his charge sheet. She didn't answer and he knocked again, uncertain whether she was asleep or too angry to open the door, though both were possible. He knocked again as she unlocked the door.

She was wearing washed-out jeans and a sweatshirt. Her hair was matted from sleep and her eyes were puffy. A lamp was on in the small living room. She leaned against the doorframe, holding the edge of the door in her other hand.

"I'm sorry," he said.

"I don't know what that means."

"It means that I'm sorry I'm late and that I screwed up our evening."

"Now I know what it means. Good-bye."

She started to close the door and he caught it with the flat of his hand. "Abby, give me a break. Let me explain."

"You mean there's more?" she asked, running one hand through her hair, dropping her arms to her sides.

She was angry, but not in the volcanic style of their past fights. She was too subdued, as if she'd said good-bye before he got there. The prospect that he'd already lost her drained the blood from his heart.

"Yeah. A lot more."

"If it's about attorney-client privilege or cases that have a life of their own or any of the other bullshit you eat and drink to justify your life, I'm not interested."

"What are you interested in?"

"Nothing anymore, really. Except for one thing. What's so much more important than us?"

"It's complicated," he began, stopping when she raised her hand.

"I've heard that one too. Try the truth, which, in my experience, is usually pretty simple."

"Okay, then. I'm in trouble."

"That's not new either. I figured that out. That's why I asked Mickey to come home. What I can't figure out is why you make this so hard. I'm not a little girl to be protected from the truth. If you want me in your life, you've got to put me in your life."

Mason nodded. "If you'll open the door, I'll let you in."

Abby smiled weakly. "God, I hate it when you do the charm thing. C'mon."

They sat across from each other, Abby's bare feet curled beneath her, Mason's elbows on his knees. He told her everything that had happened since Vanessa Carter had walked into his office a week ago. She listened silently, neither berating nor excusing him for what he'd done to secure Blues's release from jail three years ago or the lengths he'd gone to over the last seven days to keep it secret.

"Mickey is running down some leads, but none of them have anything to do with the blackmail. It's the elephant in the room. I can't talk to anyone about it."

"Sure you can," Abby said. "You said it yourself. Go public. Take the blackmail away from the blackmailer. Even if you keep the lid on it this time, there's no way for you to ever know if someone else isn't out there with the same information. You'll never be free. Trust me; I know what it's like to live that way."

Mason looked at her. When they first met, she had confessed a secret she had carried since she was a teenager that nearly cost both of them their lives. The guilt and grief she carried with her secret added weight to her burden. She had shed some but not all of that baggage since moving to Washington.

"I'll probably lose my law license."

"Is that all you are. A guy with a law license?"

He laughed. "On a good day. I may go to jail. How do you feel about a boyfriend with a record?"

She walked over to his chair, pulling him up to her, arms around his back. "I don't want a boyfriend with a record. But I can live with a man who made a mistake and set it right."

Two hours later, she lay sleeping while he stood in the kitchen dialing Lila Collins's phone number. Blues's contact had left an anonymous message on his cell phone, apologizing for the delay and explaining that it took longer than expected because Lila's number was unlisted.

"It's Lou Mason," he said when she answered, her voice thick with sleep.

"It's the middle of the night. What do you want?"

She listened as he explained, telling her it might be dangerous, that she didn't have to do it and he'd understand if she said no. When he finished, she made a promise that should have reassured him but didn't.

"I'll go to the office now and call you as soon as I get something."

CHAPTER SIXTY-NINE

MASON WENT HOME, knowing that he wouldn't sleep while waiting for Lila to call. Clutching his cell phone, he paced the first floor of his house. The Kansas City Star hit the driveway at five-thirty. The air was icy and still when he went outside to pick it up, the plastic wrapper crackling as if it might crumble. He brought the paper in, glanced at the headlines, and tossed it onto the kitchen table, his face stinging from the cold.

At six, he changed into athletic shorts and rowed eight thousand meters, his cell phone lying on the floor alongside the flywheel. His time was slow, his technique sloppy, but he didn't die and the phone didn't ring. Afterwards, resting on the hard seat, he listened as his ragged breathing slowly steadied. Hunched over the slide, he worried about the reasons Lila might not have called, none of which made him feel any better, his anxiety competing with his concerns for what else the day would bring. There may be fifty ways to leave your lover, but there was only one way to come clean.

He remembered a conversation he had had with Fish about Fish's life of crime. Atonement, Fish had said, required that you apologize to those you've wronged and ask for their forgiveness. It wasn't enough just to ask for God's forgiveness, though Fish did so each year on Yom Kippur, the Jewish holiday of atonement. He preferred confessing to God rather than to people because, he said, God was more understanding—wouldn't send you to jail and would never hire a lawyer to get even.

Mason had little experience with prayer but enough with people to accept Fish's comparison, especially regarding Vanessa Carter. She was desperate to keep the remnants of her reputation intact. Mason had to tell her what he was going to do in advance so that they could get their stories straight since part of what he would admit would be a story. That was the only way he could protect her from the blackmailer.

He and Fish would be at police headquarters at eleven to meet with Detectives Griswold and Cates. Samantha Greer would probably be there as well. When they were done with Fish, he would lay it out for them. It would be out of his hands after that.

Working it out in his mind revealed another problem. What he considered a confession of a past crime, the police would hear as an admission to obstructing their investigation into the murders of Charles Rockley, Johnny Keegan, and Mark Hill. They wouldn't be wrong.

Mason had tried without success to prove that the blackmail and the murders were tied together. The cops had the resources to prove he was right. If he had told them about the blackmail sooner, they may have run with that angle instead of zeroing in on Fish.

He was back to the conflict of interest that should have caused him to resign as Fish's lawyer, another reason he would be disbarred. Once he laid the story out for the cops, he'd have no choice but to quit. Not even Fish could talk him out of that, though Mason wouldn't give him the chance. The good news for Fish might be that if the government took down Al Webb, he wouldn't need a lawyer any longer.

He wiped the sweat from his face, draping a towel around his neck and following Tuffy into the kitchen. She pawed the back of his leg while he made her breakfast; Tuffy's impatience was a comforting part of their daily routine. He scratched the back of her neck as she dipped her head to the bowl when his landline rang.

"Good morning," Vanessa Carter said when he answered. The magisterial timbre she usually brought to their conversations had been replaced by a brittle bravado.

"I was about to call you," he said. "How's your eye?"

"It's black, yellow, and ugly. He called again this morning. He wants to see a draft of my opinion by the end of the day."

"How are you supposed to get it to him?"

"He gave me the address for a website and a password that is only good for one use. Once I post the opinion, I can't get back on the website."

Mason twisted the ends of his towel around his throat. "How would you rule if it wasn't for all of this?

"The evidence cuts both ways, but I can justify a ruling for Galaxy."

"But that's not the ruling you think you should make, is it?"

"No, it isn't. I believe Carol Hill is telling the truth."

"What do you want to do?"

"I want to do what's right. No one would think twice if I rule in Galaxy's favor. But if I do, Galaxy will own me forever and they'll steer every case to me knowing that I have to rule for them again. I can't live that way and I'm afraid of what they'll do if I rule against them. You're my only hope."

Mason let out a long sigh. "Write the opinion the way you think you should. Write another version finding in favor of Galaxy and post it on the website. That will buy us a little time."

"Have you found the blackmailer?"

"No."

"Then I can't do that. Even if I rule for the plaintiff, he'll be able to use the draft opinion against me. He'll ruin me or kill me. At the moment, I don't know which would be worse."

"He won't do either. I'm going to tell the police that I'm the one being blackmailed."

"You? How does that solve anything?"

"I'll tell them what I asked Fiori to do three years ago; that Fiori taped our conversation and the blackmailer found the tape. I'll tell them that the blackmailer contacted me and threatened to go public if I didn't pressure you into ruling for Galaxy."

"I don't see how that helps me," she said. "What about the tape of my conversation with Fiori?"

"A friend of mine, Rachel Firestone, is a reporter for the Star. She'll run the story. Once it's public, you withdraw from Carol's case and say that you'll decline any more cases in which Galaxy is a party. The blackmailer will lose his leverage. He's got nothing to gain by exposing your tape."

"What if he comes after me again? He was in my garage the last time."

"The police will provide protection for you and so will Blues. And I'll take the heat. Consider it my apology."

"You know what this will mean for you?"

"I'll get a good lawyer."

"I thought you would find the blackmailer and stop him. I never thought you would have to do something like this."

"Neither did I," Mason said.

CHAPTER SEVENTY

Dennis Brewer was on time. They met in the office Mickey used as his living room, sitting on folding chairs around a card table. Brewer was all business, slipping a transmitter the size of a flat aspirin into the collar of Mickey's shirt and a tiny receiver into Mickey's ear with practiced ease. He explained that they would have Mickey under surveillance at all times and would use the transmitter and receiver to coach him as well as to record his encounter with Sylvia McBride.

Finished, he handed Mickey two bank forms. One was a signature card confirming that he was authorized to use the safety deposit box registered in the name of Myron Wen- neck, the alias Fish used to hide his ownership of the box. The second was a register signed and dated by owners of safety deposit boxes each time they used them. It bore two signatures of Myron Wenneck showing he had been in the box twice in the last six months. There were blank lines on either side of both signatures.

"Sign the signature card and then sign the access card three times," he instructed, handing Mickey three different pens and pointing to lines on the card above and below where Fish had signed Myron Wenneck's name.

Mickey looked at Mason.

"I thought Fish was going to execute a power of attorney," Mason said to Brewer.

"This is simpler," Brewer replied. "We'll backdate Mickey's signature on the signature card by six months and date the register so it looks like he's been in the box before. Different pens will make it look like he signed on different dates. When he asks to be let into the box this afternoon, it will look like business as usual to Sylvia McBride."

"You can do that?" Mickey asked.

"We're the FBI," Brewer answered. "All you have to do is show her the money. Let her count it if she wants to, as long as it's all back in the box when you leave. Walk out together and go your separate ways. Got it?"

"Got it," Mickey said.

"Good," Brewer said.

That was it. There were no silent exchanges between Brewer and Mason filled with accusations or suspicions. They didn't spar with one another and neither of them dropped hints about what he knew or thought he knew. Mason had found more hidden meaning in fortune cookies.

"Brewer doesn't give much away," Mickey said after Brewer left.

"What's he going to do?" Mason asked from the doorway, watching Brewer show himself out. "Grill us? He's got to play it cool."

"Maybe he didn't kill Rockley and maybe he isn't in bed with Webb. Maybe he's just doing his job."

"Or maybe he's just very good."

"Not as good as we are," Mickey said. "I called the businesses that should be next door to the companies that Rock- ley and Keegan claimed they worked for. Guess what? None of Rockley's and Keegan's former employers exist. They're all fake."

"That means you're right about Sylvia's call center," Mason said. "She's in the phony ID business."

"Except Keegan's name wasn't phony, just his employment records. I got a call this morning from my girlfriend. Her friend at the FBI hit pay dirt."

Mason returned to his folding chair. "Give."

"You remember you told me that Sylvia McBride had a sister in Minneapolis?"

"Yeah. The one she went to live with after her husband supposedly drowned."

"Her name was Olivia Corcoran. She was married to Tommy Corcoran's father. That made her Tommy's stepmother. Tommy's aunt Sylvia gave him a new ID as Charles Rockley. Johnny Keegan was Olivia's son by her first marriage. He didn't need a new ID since he'd never been arrested. Aunt Sylvia only gave him a phony résumé."

Mason whistled. "How many laws were broken getting us that information?"

"None," Mickey said. "Our friend's job includes running checks through the FBI's database. She ran Corcoran's name and came up with his bio. There was an obit for Olivia Corcoran that listed Tommy, Johnny Keegan, and Sylvia McBride as her survivors. But here's the weird part. She couldn't get into the rest of Corcoran's file or the file on Wayne McBride and his alter ego, Al Webb."

"Why not?"

"She doesn't have clearance for national security matters."

"Since when is skimming dough from a casino a matter of national security?"

"It isn't," Mickey said. "But dealing in phony IDs could be, especially if the IDs are sold to people that blow up buildings with airplanes."

CHAPTER SEVENTY-ONE

Mason called Lila's office phone and cell, but she didn't answer. He tried again as he was driving downtown to meet with the homicide detectives with the same result.

She would call as soon as she could, he told himself. If she could, he added, getting the sick feeling that he got while a jury was deliberating and his gut told him that he'd lost even before the jury took a vote. It was a toxic blend of fear, frustration, and outrage coated with a paralyzing layer of helplessness that was an all-too-accurate barometer of the verdict. All that was left was second-guessing. If anything happened to Lila, he'd be answering those questions the rest of his life.

Mason told Fish to meet him in the parking lot across from the Jackson County Courthouse a little before eleven. They walked the long block to police headquarters together, keeping their chins tucked against the cold as Mason told Fish what he'd learned about Al Webb and what had happened at Lake Lotawana.

"Wayne—a terrorist?" Fish said, using Webb's real name. "I don't believe it!"

"I'm not saying he's a terrorist. I'm saying that he and Sylvia are in the fake ID business. If they sell to underage college kids who want to buy beer, that's one thing. If they sell to terrorists, their FBI file gets stamped Top Secret. That's all I'm saying."

"Unbelievable," Fish said, shaking his head.

"Don't forget. He got started by killing some poor bastard just so he could fake his own death and Sylvia helped him pull it off."

"And what's this all about?" Fish said, waving at the entrance to police headquarters. "Who is it I'm supposed to have killed this time?"

"Mark Hill. Carol Hill's husband."

"Why not? I haven't not killed someone in a week. I might as well not have killed him too."

Detective Griswold met them in the second-floor homicide bullpen.

"Thanks for coming down," he began. "But turns out we don't need to talk with Mr. Fish."

"Did you make an arrest?" Mason asked.

"No," Griswold said. "But the coroner fixed the time of death as Monday night between six and midnight."

"I was home," Fish said.

"We know that," Griswold answered.

"By myself," Fish added.

"We know that too. I had a meeting this morning with Kelly Holt. She's the FBI's liaison on Rockley's murder. I told her you were coming down to talk about the Hill case. She made your alibi. Said they had you under surveillance and you didn't leave the house Monday night. Sorry for the trouble."

Fish lifted his hands in protest. "Trouble? What trouble?

I'm delighted to be your guest, especially considering it was such a short visit. C'mon, Lou. I can't afford to pay you to stand here and kibbitz."

"You go ahead," Mason told him. "I'm going to stick around for a few minutes."

Fish crooked a finger at him. "A word," he said, taking a few steps away. "What's going on?" he whispered when Mason joined him.

"Nothing's going on. I've got another case to talk about with Griswold. That's all."

"It wouldn't be that business with Judge Carter, would it?"

Mason pursed his lips. "Nah. It's a new case—armed robbery."

"Such a terrible liar you are, boytchik. Don't be stupid."

"I'll do my best," Mason said, forcing a grin.

"Remember one thing. The mark never feels the hook until it's in too deep."

"Don't worry. Griswold will take the bait."

Fish studied him, a sad smile spreading across his jowls. "Of course he will, boytchik. Of course he will."

"Someplace quiet we can talk?" Mason asked Griswold.

"Sure. You've seen our deluxe private conference rooms. How about one of them?"

Mason followed Griswold to the interrogation room. Griswold stood at the open door, waiting for Mason to take a seat.

"You want an audience or is this private?" he asked Mason.

Mason had imagined that this moment would include Detective Cates and Samantha Greer, Cates relishing it while Samantha suffered through it with him. Now that the moment had arrived, he didn't need either of them to make him feel worse. He took a deep breath and shook his head.

"You'll do. Close the door."

Griswold sat across from him, hands in his lap, a curious glint in his eye. "I'm all yours."

"Did you follow up with Lila Collins about Johnny Keegan needing a lawyer?"

"I did. She said Keegan told her he needed a lawyer; didn't say why, and she gave him your name. Just like she told you. I didn't get anything else out of her."

"She worked for Ed Fiori when he owned the casino. You remember him?"

"I remember. It was called the Dream in those days," Griswold answered. "Fiori went out the hard way. You and your buddy Blues were there, if memory serves."

"We were there."

It went like that for more than an hour. When it became clear what Mason was doing, Griswold interrupted to give him a Miranda warning, making him sign a statement that he declined counsel. Griswold teased the details out of Mason, who didn't want to appear too eager to confess. He wanted Griswold to believe that Vanessa Carter was innocent, and nothing undermined a witness's credibility more than being too prepared, too rehearsed.

"I've got a problem here," Griswold said when Mason finished laying it out. "You asked Fiori to put the arm on Judge Carter to get Blues released on bail. He says okay. She releases Blues. Looks like she's got as big a problem as you do. But you keep telling me she didn't know what was going on. You understand my problem here?"

Mason knew his story would fall apart if the blackmailer went public with the tape of Fiori and Judge Carter. He was counting on the blackmailer staying private once the leverage of the tape was gone. Disclosing it would only increase the risk the blackmailer would be caught, getting him nothing in return.

"Fiori told me he never made the call," Mason said, improvising a detail he hoped would close the deal, especially since Fiori couldn't contradict him from the grave. "Judge Carter confirmed that. She said she made her decision to grant bail strictly on the merits. That's why I couldn't pressure her to rule in Galaxy's favor. She told me the blackmailer was my problem, not hers."

"Rockley could have been part of the blackmail scheme— trying to save his ass and instead got himself killed by whoever was running the show. Who do you like for the blackmail?"

"Al Webb is the only one left," Mason said. "Rockley and Keegan are dead."

"Which reminds me," Griswold said. "I talked to Lila Collins again. She told me the same thing she told you about Keegan. He said he needed the name of a lawyer to give to a friend so she gave him your name. If you're involved in this blackmail scheme, that could have been enough to get Keegan killed."

"I've thought of that."

"You should have come to me sooner," Griswold said. "Now you're looking at attempted bribery, extortion, corruption of a public official, and obstruction of justice. Not what I'd call a good day, Counselor. What happened, you get a conscience transplant?"

"Something like that," Mason answered. "What now?"

Griswold let out a sigh. "It's not every day that a member of the bar walks in here and hands me his nuts. I've got to talk to the prosecuting attorney. In the meantime, I'd hire a couple of lawyers. One for you and one for your client."

The morning cold had stiffened with blunt gusts of wind, each one like a hard right hand. Mason took the blows with out feeling them as he walked back to his car. For an instant, he thought he saw Fish waiting for him in the parking lot. He hurried toward him, waving and calling his name, ready to tell him what he'd done until he realized the old man he saw was a bum scouring the asphalt for lucky pennies. Confession was supposed to be good for his soul. He hadn't known it would also cloud his vision.

CHAPTER SEVENTY-TWO

MASON TRIED LILA'S numbers again. When she didn't answer, he drove to the casino and surveyed the parking lot until he found Lila's car in the section marked off for employees. He kept going, not stopping until he found a side street just off the casino grounds and out of range of its ubiquitous video cameras. If Lila wouldn't answer her phone, he'd have to flush her out. He called Galaxy's main number and asked for Al Webb.

"It's Lou Mason," he said.

"What can I do for you that you shouldn't be talking to my lawyer about instead of me?" Webb asked.

"You're blackmailing Judge Carter. I don't think you want me to talk to your lawyer about that."

Webb laughed. "We're back to that, are we? Why would I blackmail Judge Carter over a lousy sexual harassment claim? For which the casino has ample insurance coverage, I might add. Sorry, not interested."

"The last time we talked you were interested enough to ask my price for telling you what I know."

"You're confusing two different commodities. I'm not interested in talking to you about whether I'm blackmailing Judge Carter because I'm not blackmailing Judge Carter. If someone else is, or if someone like that two-legged turd Vince Bongiovanni is spreading a rumor that I am blackmailing her, that's information I would gladly pay for."

"In that case, I've got something you want and I'm ready to do business. When can I meet with you and Lila?"

"Lila? What's she got to do with this?"

"I'll tell you when we get together. I can be at your office in ten minutes."

"Won't work," Webb blurted. "Lila's not here. She called in sick. You and I can make a deal without her."

"You can, but I can't. No Lila, no deal. Call me when she's feeling better," he said, reciting his cell phone number.

Mason had a good view of the main road leading into the casino parking lot. He was parallel parked in a row of cars similar enough in color and style that his didn't stand out. He could sit there the rest of the day and wait for Lila or Webb to drive by, except he didn't have the rest of the day.

Mickey was due to meet Sylvia McBride at the bank branch on Fifty-first Street in an hour. Mason had promised Fish he would wait with him at Fish's house until Mickey and Sylvia finished their business. He took a long look toward the casino parking lot. It was impossible to choose winners and losers from the handful of people he could see coming and going or tell if Lila was among those leaving. His cell phone rang as he put his car in gear.

"Seven o'clock tonight," Al Webb said.

"With or without Lila?"

"She'll be there."

"Where?"

"Lake Lotawana. Ever been?"

"Nope, but I hear that it's nice and quiet this time of year."

"Can't beat it," Webb said and gave Mason directions to the house on L Street titled in Ernie Fowler's name. "You think you can find it?"

Mason listened closely but didn't hear any sarcasm that meant Webb knew Mason had found the house once before.

"How hard can it be? See you at seven."

CHAPTER SEVENTY-THREE

PETE SAMUELSON WAS at Fish's house when Mason arrived, accompanied by the technician who had set up the equipment for Fish's phone call to Sylvia McBride. Samuelson and the technician were seated at the kitchen table, the technician tapping keys on a laptop computer and adjusting the sound on a pair of speakers. Fish was standing behind Samuelson, looking over his shoulder at the computer screen.

Samuelson looked up as Mason walked in. "You're just in time," he said. "We thought Mr. Fish might be able to help us with this. We're tapped into the bank's closed-circuit monitors and the transmitter and receiver Mickey is wearing."

"You don't call ahead for an appointment with my client anymore? You just show up. You forget that he has a lawyer?"

"We didn't forget," Samuelson said. "We don't have to tell you and we don't need your permission. It's all in the deal Mr. Fish signed. He belongs to us. You're welcome to stay, but don't interfere."

"It's all right," Fish said. "They haven't asked me to confess to anything else and I have no secrets left anyway."

Mason didn't like it but knew that didn't matter. It would be a problem for Fish's next lawyer, something he would have to wait to explain to Fish.

"Who's covering the bank?" Mason asked.

"Kelly Holt is inside the bank with two other agents. Dennis Brewer is in a van across the street," Samuelson said. "Plus we've got backup in the parking lot. That money isn't going anywhere except back in the vault."

"That's her," Fish said. "That's Sylvia."

A small, slender woman wearing a winter coat and gloves appeared on the screen, the high angle of the camera distorting her image. She was in the lobby of the bank. Mason looked at his watch. It was 2:45 P.M.

"She's early," he said.

Fish smiled. "Like I told you—either early or late, but never exactly on time. Watch what she does. She'll take a tour of the lobby."

"What's that she's carrying?" Mason asked.

Samuelson leaned into the screen. "Bring that up," he told the technician, who enlarged the picture.

Sylvia was carrying a large shopping bag adorned with images of famous books. She set the bag on the floor next to a round countertop where customers could fill out deposit slips.

"Get me inside that bag," Samuelson instructed the technician, who cycled through the bank's cameras until he found the one that was directly over the countertop, zooming in until the contents of the bag were visible.

"Books," Mason said. "It's a bag of books."

A man entered the picture, but the overhead camera didn't capture his features. Sylvia picked up the bag and the two of them walked toward the desk nearest the vault holding the safety deposit boxes. The technician switched cameras again, this time getting a head-on view of Mickey and Sylvia.

"Where the hell is the volume?" Samuelson snapped. "Why can't we hear what they're saying?"

"I'm on it," the technician said, his fingers racing across the keyboard. He put on a set of headphones and twirled the dials on the speakers. "Either the transmitter is dead or she's jamming it."

Samuelson picked up a two-way radio. "Brewer, Holt," he said. "We're calling it off. The audio isn't working. We've got no ears."

"I know," Brewer said, his voice audible to all of them. "We're not getting anything either. But you can't call it off. She'll know it was a setup and we're finished. Besides, we've still got the cameras."

"There are private viewing rooms inside the vault. No cameras in there," the technician said. "We'll be deaf, dumb, and blind if they use one of those."

"The kid is with her," Brewer said. "He's our eyes and ears."

They stared at the computer monitor. Mickey was signing the safety deposit box register.

"This is my call," Samuelson said. "It's off. Arrest her."

"For what?" Kelly asked. "She hasn't done anything. They're in the vault now anyway. I'll take the responsibility."

Samuelson turned pale, his bald head beading with sweat. "Agent Holt, I'm ordering you to call this off."

"I don't take orders from you. Call your boss. Let him decide if he wants to blow up this investigation."

Samuelson slammed the radio onto the kitchen table, whipped out his cell phone, and marched into the living room. Fish, Mason, and the technician watched the monitor, the camera trained on the inside of the vault. Mickey opened the safety deposit box, removed it, and carried it into a private room with Sylvia behind him.

Mason watched the timer at the bottom of the screen tick off five and half minutes until the door opened again. Mickey returned the safety deposit box and locked it. He went back to the private room and came out again carrying Sylvia's bag. She followed, closing the door behind her. Samuelson returned just as they exited the vault, sporting a paler shade of pale with matching stooped shoulders.

"Did you reach the U.S. attorney?" Mason asked.

"He was in conference," Samuelson said. "I told his secretary it was urgent. She said she'd mention that to him."

Sylvia stopped at the countertop again, buttoning her coat and pulling on her gloves. Mickey stopped alongside her, setting the bag on the floor. Samuelson started to speak, but the technician cut him off.

"I got it," he said, switching to the overhead camera, zooming in on the books.

"Thank God," Samuelson said.

"God doesn't play these games," Fish said. "But He likes to watch."

CHAPTER SEVENTY-FOUR

THE BANK'S CAMERA followed Mickey and Sylvia out the door before losing them to the street.

Samuelson grabbed the radio. "Brewer, do you have them?"

"Big as life. She's getting in a minivan. The kid is waving good-bye."

"Follow her," Samuelson said, "just in case."

"We're pulling out now," Brewer said. "She's northbound on Main at the traffic light. It just turned green."

"Maintain radio contact," Samuelson said. "I want to know every turn she takes."

"Relax, we've got her," Brewer said an instant before screaming, "Look out, you crazy son of a bitch!"

Samuelson held the radio at arm's length, the sound of crying tires and crunched steel making his hand shake. He pulled the radio back to his mouth.

"Brewer! What's happening? Holt, what the hell is going on?"

Kelly's voice broke in over the radio. "Some asshole ran a red light and broadsided Brewer's van."

"Is anybody hurt?" Samuelson asked.

"I don't think so," Kelly said.

"What about Sylvia McBride?" Samuelson asked.

"She got away. I've got to go before Brewer takes out the guy who hit him. You better get down here."

Samuelson raced out of the house. Mason followed him, Fish telling him he would be along in a few minutes. By the time Mason arrived, the intersection was clogged with police, tow trucks, and an ambulance. The contingent of

FBI agents was gathered on the sidewalk in a tight circle surrounding Mickey. They stood outside the entrance to the bank watching the cops work.

Dennis Brewer and Kelly Holt peeled away from their group when they saw Samuelson approach. Mason caught up to them in the middle of the street.

"I thought you said no one was hurt," Samuelson said to Kelly.

"The other driver claimed he had a seizure that made him black out and run the light. The cops called an ambulance to take him to a hospital to get checked out."

"What a mess," Samuelson said with a deep sigh. "At least the money is safe."

"Well," Kelly said. "Not all of it."

Samuelson blanched. "What do you mean, not all of it?"

"I mean Sylvia took a little over eight hundred and fifty thousand. It was all she could fit in her bag and still cover the top of it with a few books."

"You're kidding me!" Samuelson said. "What the hell was Mickey doing?"

Kelly smiled. "He packed it up for her. The kid would make a good sacker at a grocery store."

Mason shot a look at Mickey, who raised his cuffed hands in greeting. He started toward him when Kelly put her hand out. "You'll have to wait here," she said.

"What for?" he demanded.

"Where's Fish?" she asked.

"On his way," Mason said. "I'm going to talk with Mickey."

"No you're not."

"I'm his lawyer," Mason said. "You can't stop me."

"We have a rule, Counselor," Kelly said. "We don't let suspects talk to one another until we're done talking to them separately."

"Suspects? What the hell are you talking about?" Mason asked.

"I told you that Fish was going to try to steal the money. You didn't believe me, and you let him suck you and Mickey into his scam."

"Have you gone completely nuts? Exactly how were any of us involved in stealing the money?"

"Mickey said Fish called him on his cell phone while he and Sylvia were in the private room. He told Mickey there had been a change in plans and that he was supposed to let Sylvia take as much of the money as she could stuff into the bag."

"That's the dumbest thing I ever heard. Fish didn't make that call. Samuelson and your technician were with us the entire time. They'll tell you that. Pete, tell her," Mason said.

Samuelson shook his head. "We were set up in the kitchen, but I was in the living room trying to reach Roosevelt Holmes when Mickey and Sylvia were in the vault. I'll call the tech and ask him if Fish left the kitchen," he said, stepping away.

Mason said, "Mickey's story doesn't make any sense."

"That's exactly why I don't want you talking to him. If that's his story, I'm going to make him stick with it. At this point, all three of you are suspects."

Samuelson rejoined them. "The tech said Fish was in the kitchen the entire time Mickey and Sylvia were in the vault so he couldn't have made the call. He also said Fish left the house right after Mason did. He should be here by now."

"Then where is he?" Kelly asked, hands on her hips, her chin aimed at Mason.

"How the hell am I supposed to know? Look, either arrest me or get out of my way," Mason said, glaring at Kelly, needing both hands to count the different faces she had shown him.

Kelly returned Mason's heat, her chest heaving slightly. Samuelson stepped between them, pointing a finger at Kelly.

"You don't have probable cause to arrest Mason. You do have enough to take Mickey in for questioning, but if you deny him his right to counsel, nothing you get from him will be admissible in court. Plus, Mason knows I told you to cancel the operation and that you blew me off. What do you think he'll do to you when he gets you on the stand? On top of that, he'll make me testify that this was the second time today that you disregarded my advice. If you would have listened the first time, there wouldn't have been a second time."

Kelly's eyes now blazed on Samuelson, but he didn't back down. She'd pulled rank on him when he told her to call off the operation. Now he'd outflanked her with a deft maneuver that forced Mason to reconsider his appraisal of the assistant U.S. attorney. "What about Fish?" she asked Samuelson. "Do we have your permission to take him in for questioning?" Samuelson nodded, ignoring her sarcasm. "Absolutely, based on Mickey's statement that Fish called him and told him to let Sylvia have the money."

Kelly said to Brewer, "Tell one of the other agents to work with the police on an APB for Fish. I want him found fast. Tell the others to take Mickey to the detention center at the Federal Courthouse." Turning to Mason, she said, "You can talk to him there. With any luck, we'll have Fish in custody by then and save you a second trip."

"See you there," Mason told her. He crossed the street to the sidewalk, stepping into the circle of FBI agents who cut him off from Mickey. "Back off," Mason told them. "I need to speak with my client."

The agents exchanged looks with Kelly and Brewer, who were watching from the middle of the street, then widened the perimeter around Mason and Mickey, giving them space without giving them a way out.

"What the hell is this?" Mickey asked, lifting his cuffed wrists. "Fish called me and said there'd been a change in the plan. He said I was supposed to let her take the money."

"Keep your voice down. I never gave Fish your cell phone number. Did you?"

Mickey's face reddened. "Shit! I am too stupid to live."

"We'll see," Mason said in a low whisper. "They're going to take you to the Federal Courthouse. I'll get there as soon as I can, but I may have to send someone else for a little while. In the meantime, don't answer any questions and don't try to win any votes."

Mason called his Aunt Claire from the car and gave her a quick rundown on what had happened.

"Can you go the Federal Courthouse and hold Mickey's hand until I can line up someone to represent him?"

"Of course. But, aren't you going to be his lawyer?"

Claire had raised him to do the right thing, often telling him that recognizing it was a lot harder than doing it. It was the single highest virtue in her world. He had yet to tell her that he wouldn't be representing Mickey or anyone else for quite a while because he had fallen short of her standards. He owed her an explanation in person, not over the phone.

"There may be a conflict of interest with my representation of Avery Fish. I'll call B. J. Moore. He's almost as good as I am," Mason said, hoping the joke would distract Claire. She didn't laugh. "You've got enough to do. I'll call B.J." "Thanks." "Lou," she said, a fresh concern in her voice. "Is there anything else?"

She was his aunt, not his mother, but she had a mother's intuition, sensing when there was something else. She often told him that she could see it in his eyes or hear it in his voice. Sometimes, she said, she could just feel it.

"Yeah. I'll tell you about it as soon as I can." "I'll be here," she said.

CHAPTER SEVENTY-FIVE

THE SUBCONSCIOUS MIND was the brain's buried treasure. It was where memories, dreams, and other evanescent flotsam and jetsam lay hidden until synapses short-circuited, allowing a particle of past knowledge to escape and pop into one's head. Sometimes a song lyric became lodged against an ear, looping over and over. Sometimes it was the starting lineup of the 1963 Dodgers. Sometimes it was a scene from a movie.

As Mason drove away from the bank, he had such a moment, flashing on another scene from Animal House, the one where a member of the fraternity takes a freshman pledge to the grocery, throwing items over his shoulder to the pledge, who tries to keep up, catching as many as he can, until he is finally overwhelmed and slides to the floor in surrender. The frat boy doesn't care whether the pledge catches a single thing. He just wants to keep the pledge's hands full.

Mason felt like the pledge when he realized that Kelly was throwing as many things as possible at him so that he couldn't keep up with her. He was certain that Mickey was telling the truth about the phone call and he was equally sure that Fish hadn't made the call. The combination was enough to get Mickey arrested and an APB issued for Fish, both of which would tie Mason up long enough that she and Brewer could finish what they'd started—whatever that was.

He focused on the call he knew Fish had made to Sylvia McBride setting everything in motion. Kelly had been there and had heard Fish reminisce about how his late great friend Wayne could mimic Fish's voice well enough to fool Sylvia. Fooling Mickey, who barely knew Fish, would have been easy.

Kelly could have obtained Mickey's cell phone number simply by flashing her FBI badge and invoking the Patriot Act.

All of which made Kelly and Webb, nee McBride, partners in a bank robbery. Hardly a matter of national security and hardly worth the risk. But there it was. Kelly had set him, along with Fish and Mickey, up to take the fall for the robbery.

Along the way, Rockley, Keegan, and Hill had been murdered and Judge Carter had been blackmailed. As the day wound toward dusk, Mason couldn't get away from Al Webb as the trigger man. Rockley and Keegan must have turned on him, or given him reason to think they had, and he killed them. Mark Hill must have gotten drunk enough to go after Webb to avenge his wife's honor and met the same fate. Webb also had to be the blackmailer despite his protest that he had nothing to gain since the other likely candidates were dead and the blackmailer was still pushing Judge Carter's buttons.

The pieces didn't fit perfectly together, but criminals were not models of rational behavior. While economists contrive mathematical models to explain what rational people should do, real people persist in their refusal to act as predicted. The models fail because they are stripped of the emotions that drive people to buy high and sell low. Or, in the case of blackmailers and murderers, sell out and kill often.

The rational thing for Mason to do was to get Mickey released and spend a quiet night with Abby. By the time Fish turned up, he'd have a new lawyer in place for him as well. But there was one other thing left on his day's agenda. He was to meet Al Webb and Lila Collins at the house at Lake Lotawana. He had a feeling they wouldn't be alone when he called Blues and told him to meet him there.

That evening, as he was on the way to the Lake, Rachel Firestone called him. "What did you do to Vanessa Carter?" she asked.

He knew that she wouldn't have asked him the question unless she'd already talked to Detective Griswold or to Judge Carter. Griswold wasn't a talker and Judge Carter wouldn't have been either except that Mason had told her he was going to give the story to Rachel.

"What did she tell you?"

"An absolutely unbelievable story about you, Blues, and Ed Fiori. She said that you asked Fiori to pressure her into releasing Blues on bail when he was charged with murder; that she didn't know anything about it and released Blues anyway. She says that Fiori taped his conversation with you and somebody at Galaxy ended up with the tape and is using it to blackmail you to blackmail her to rule in Galaxy's favor in Carol Hill's sexual harassment case. Jesus Christ, Lou," she added, out of breath. "You can't make that up."

"She didn't make it up. It's true."

"In case you forgot, I covered Blues's case. Judge Carter granted bail for Blues, then she quit the bench without saying boo to anybody. When it happened, I asked you why she released Blues and then quit and you said you didn't know."

"I lied," Mason said. "I'm sorry."

"That's it? You lied, you're sorry."

"I couldn't tell you then. I was going to tell you today, but I haven't had a chance."

"Judge Carter said you told her that you were going to give the story to me. She figured you had already talked to me and wanted to make certain that I knew she hadn't been blackmailed then or now."

Mason knew the story would erase any doubts Rachel's editor had about her loyalty and commitment to the paper. If there was an upside to his predicament, that was it.

"She's telling the truth. Print the story. I've already told the police. The prosecutor is probably preparing an indictment with my name on it."

Mason parked on the side of a gas station across the street from the Lake Lotawana police department and waited for Blues, who pulled up just before seven, driving his pickup, signaling Mason to follow him. Mason fell in line behind the pickup, trailing Blues onto a service road that disappeared into the woods far away from any houses. Blues got out of the pickup and slid into the passenger side of Mason's SUV.

"I called you an hour ago," Mason said. "Where have you been?"

"Peeking in people's windows. I figured we're headed into trouble and I like to see it before it sees me."

"Kelly told me the same thing a few days ago."

"I thought we might be back after our last trip out here so I looked at some maps. The house Webb is using is on L Street, which T-bones into a long, narrow cul-de-sac. This service road feeds into a bike path that comes out at the opposite end of the cul-de-sac from Webb's house. Since no one is home at the other houses, it was easy to get close without being seen."

"What did you find out?"

"Lot of lights on in that house. Webb was there."

"What about Lila Collins? Dark hair, thin, mid-forties."

"I saw two women. One of them was older, late fifties, carrying a bag with both hands like it was real heavy."

"That's Sylvia McBride. The money she stole from the bank is in that bag."

"The other woman was younger. Could have been Lila, but I couldn't see her face too well. Sylvia and Webb had to hold her up like she was sick or drunk."

"What did they do with her?"

"Last I saw, they took her out on the deck and down a set of stairs and locked her in a storage room underneath the deck."

"You've got to get her out. Webb is expecting me at seven. I'll keep him occupied."

"There's another problem," Blues said.

"I know. Sylvia. I'll have to play that by ear. Maybe Webb will keep her out of sight."

"She's not the problem. Avery Fish is. He showed up just as I was leaving."

Mason slammed his hand against the steering wheel. "Damn! Kelly was right. Fish was in on the robbery. He told me that the mark never feels the hook until it's in too deep. He was talking about me. I let that old man con me. I don't believe it!"

"How do you want to play this?"

"I'll knock on the front door. You rescue Lila."

"You got another plan after I rescue Lila or am I going to have to come back and rescue you too?"

"Might as well. I'd hate for you to feel left out."

CHAPTER SEVENTY-SIX

Fish's rental car was parked in front of the house. Mason opened the driver's door looking for any hint that Fish was there for a reason other than to split the pot. He found a receipt on the floor from a sporting goods store that Mason had passed on the highway. According to the time printed on the receipt, Fish had made his purchase less than an hour ago. The timing bothered Mason as much as the description of what Fish had purchased—a box of .38 caliber ammunition.

When Mason rang the bell, Webb opened the door wide enough to see who was there. Mason shoved it all the way open and walked past Webb into a large den with a vaulted, wood-beam ceiling. The sofa, chairs, tables, and rug had a fresh, barely lived-in look. The whole place had the feel of a safe house, not a home.

The far wall was all glass, opening to the deck. The kitchen was to his right. There was a darkened hallway to his left that he assumed led to bedrooms.

He didn't see Sylvia, Fish, or a bag full of money. He took a slow pass around the den, luring Webb to follow until he had a view of the lake and Webb's back was to the deck. It was the best he could do to make certain Webb wouldn't see Blues.

"Where's Lila?" Mason asked.

"I told you," Webb said. "She's ill. She didn't come to work today."

"Then why was her car in the parking lot?"

"She got sick yesterday. She couldn't drive so I took her home."

Mason knew he wouldn't get anywhere trading lies with Webb. He had to buy time until Blues could free Lila.

"Then we've got nothing to talk about. I'll just go to the police, tell them about your blackmail scheme, and you can do business with them. Of course, you can't blame the cops if they're more interested in the three murders you committed and the money you robbed from the bank."

"I thought you were only obsessed with blackmail. Now I see that you are completely out of your mind. I didn't blackmail the judge. I didn't kill anyone and I don't know anything about a bank robbery."

"Killing Rockley and Keegan makes a certain amount of sense if they were about to give you up. You might catch a break on Mark Hill if you claim self-defense. But I think you're screwed on the bank robbery."

"Blackmail, murder, and bank robbery. Who do you think I am?"

"I know who you are," Mason said, walking down the hall leading to the bedrooms. "Fish! C'mon on out and bring Sylvia with you."

The first door down the hall opened and Fish stepped out. Sylvia McBride was next, turning on the hallway light. She darted past Fish, barely giving Mason a glance as she joined her husband. The color had drained from Fish's face and his breathing was labored. He lumbered past Mason, bracing himself with one hand against the wall. Mason caught him by the elbow.

"Are you all right?" he asked.

"Never better, boytchik."

Kelly Holt followed Fish, a gun in one hand, the bag of money in the other.

"Hello, Counselor," she said. "Like they say in the movies, put your hands up."

"You were in this all the time," he said, raising his hands.

"From the beginning. Now let's join the others," she said, directing him with the gun.

Fish sat in a chair barely big enough to contain him, one hand on his chest, sweat pooling in the folds of his cheeks and neck. Sylvia stood next to Webb. Two shadows appeared on the deck and Webb quickly unlocked the sliding door, pulling it open as Dennis Brewer shoved Blues into the den, his gun inches from the back of Blues's head.

"Facedown on the floor; hands behind your back," Brewer said to Blues.

Blues looked at Mason, shaking his head in apology, and laid down. Brewer holstered his gun and pressed his knee against Blues's spine, lashing Blues's wrists with plastic cuffs. Finished, he stood and pointed to Mason.

"You're next," he said and then repeated the procedure.

"Put them downstairs with Lila," Kelly said.

"What about him?" Brewer said, pointing to Fish. "Should we cuff him?"

"What for? He's harmless," Kelly said. "Put him with the others."

"Why don't you kill them and get it over with?" Webb asked.

"Because," Kelly said, "having four bodies turn up at this house may not be in our collective best interests. We'll get rid of them, but not here and not together."

Brewer marched them down the deck stairs and deposited them in the storage room with Lila Collins, who lay on the floor unconscious, knees to her chest, her head on one arm, the other covering her face. The floor and walls were bare concrete. The deck provided the ceiling. The room was empty except for them.

A single bulb hung from the ceiling. Brewer turned the light on long enough to make certain the cuffs on Mason and Blues were secure, then shattered the bulb with the barrel of his gun, leaving them in the dark as he locked the wooden door behind him.

Mason felt his way to Lila, sitting next to her and bumping her gently until she moaned softly.

"They drugged her," Blues said.

"You were supposed to rescue her."

"I had her in my arms when Brewer showed up. He didn't give me a chance."

Mason sat next to her. "Lila. Lila, wake up."

"Let her be," Fish said, his words and breath coming slowly. He had slid to the floor and was propped against the wall, legs stretched out in front of him. "Sylvia said she'd come out of it soon."

"I'm glad the two of you had a nice chat. What in the hell are you doing here?" Mason asked him.

"I came for the money," Fish said.

"All of it or just your cut?"

"All of it."

"Too greedy. If you'd been satisfied with your cut, you'd still be upstairs with them instead of downstairs with us."

"Is that what you think, boytchik? That I helped them steal the money?"

"Mickey said you called him while he was in the vault with Sylvia and told him to let her take the money."

"You were with me. You know I didn't make the call. Wayne must have imitated my voice. The whole thing was actually very nicely done. I especially liked the car wreck. I'll bet anything that other driver walked out of the hospital the first chance he got."

"If you weren't involved, how did you know Sylvia would bring the money here?" Blues asked.

"After Lou told me that Wayne was using this house, it was a good guess. I thought if I could get them to give the money back, it would settle my account with the government."

"Did you really think they would just give it to you?" Mason asked.

Fish laughed, gasping at the effort. "Even I'm not that good of a con man. I had a gun. But that Kelly Holt took it away from me."

Mason felt a surge of affection for the old man, mixed with guilt at having been so quick to condemn him. "You did good, Avery."

"Well, boytchik, doing good is something new for me. I thought I'd give it a try while I still had the chance," Fish said, struggling to get the words out.

"Take it easy. We'll get you out of here."

"Of course you will," Fish rasped. "Such a good lawyer I've got."

Blues felt his way along the wall until he came to the door, feeling the lock in the dark. "Damn," he said. "Can't pick the lock from this side even if I could see what I was doing. We're stuck here until they come and get us."

The sliding door overhead opened and two people walked across the deck and down the stairs.

"Won't be long," Mason said as he and Blues backed themselves against the wall opposite the door.

CHAPTER SEVENTY-SEVEN

Brewer and Kelly opened the door to the storage room, shining powerful flashlights in their eyes. Hands behind their backs, Mason and Blues ducked their heads, unable to avoid the blinding glare. Though only a few feet away, they couldn't see Brewer and Kelly well enough to attack them even if they were foolish enough to try.

"Time to go for a ride," Brewer said.

"Lila is still out and Fish needs help getting up," Mason said. "Take off our cuffs and we'll move them."

Brewer shined the light on Fish. His chin lay on his still chest and his open eyes didn't blink at the bright light.

"This one doesn't need any help," Brewer said. He poked Fish with the toe of his shoe then pressed the flashlight against Fish's cheek, the temperature hot enough to sear his flesh. Fish didn't flinch.

Kelly set her flashlight down, pushing Brewer's away, and knelt at Fish's side, feeling for a pulse. "He must have had a heart attack. He's dead."

"Natural causes. We caught a break," Brewer said.

Mason closed his eyes, seeing Fish in his living room, his grandchildren tugging at his ankles, his bitter daughters pulling them away from him. He heard Fish telling him that all he wanted was another chance with his family. It was enough to make Mason forget the odds. He opened his eyes, lowered his shoulders, and launched himself at Brewer with a piercing, guttural yell.

Leaping over Fish's body, he caught Brewer in the belly, the two of them tumbling through the doorway and onto the frozen ground. Mason landed on his back like an overturned turtle, cuffed hands beneath him. Brewer was quick to his feet but was knocked flat an instant later when Blues flew into him like a linebacker blindsiding a quarterback.

Brewer made it up on all fours, shaking the cobwebs from his head. Blues was about to kick him in the ribs when Kelly fired a shot at his feet. Blues whirled around toward Kelly, measuring his chances.

"The next one goes in your knee, Bluestone," she said.

Brewer staggered to his feet, gathered himself, and walked up to Blues. Without a word, he slammed his fist into Blues's solar plexus. When Blues folded up, he hit him hard in the back of the neck with a two-handed blow, dropping him in the grass. He took a step toward Mason, drawing his gun.

"Not yet," Kelly said. "Get Webb and his wife out of here and don't forget the money. Somebody may have heard that shot and called the police."

"What about them?" Brewer asked.

"Leave that to me, darling," Kelly said.

Brewer kissed her hard on the mouth. "You are something else, Agent Holt."

Mason and Blues managed to sit up as Brewer went back in the house.

"Stay where you are," Kelly said, pointing her gun at them when they started to stand.

"Is this what you meant when you told me things weren't what they looked like between you and Brewer?" Mason asked.

"Keep your voice down," Kelly said, glancing over her shoulder at the house.

"Afraid the neighbors will hear?" Mason asked.

"For once in your life, just shut up, Lou!"

One by one, the lights in the house went out. A moment later, Brewer, Webb, and Sylvia climbed into the car parked in the carport. Brewer gave Kelly a final wave before they drove away.

When their taillights disappeared, Kelly walked over to Mason. "On your belly."

"No thanks. You're going to have to look me in the eye."

"That's the way you want it?"

"That's the way I want it."

"Fine by me, but it's harder that way." She stuck her gun in her waistband, took the handcuff key from her pocket, and wrapped her arms around Mason. "Been a while since we've been this close, Counselor," she said as she unlocked his cuffs and handed him the key. "You take care of Blues and I'll check on Lila."

Mason looked at her, not trusting her or his eyes. She patted him on the cheek and he grabbed her wrist.

"Whose side are you on?" he asked her.

"Mine."

CHAPTER SEVENTY-EIGHT

Blues prowled through the house to make certain no one had stayed behind. He and Mason carried Lila and Fish inside and laid them down in separate bedrooms.

Back in the den, Mason and Kelly stood facing one another. Mason saw a woman he once thought he'd loved, a woman whose life he'd saved and who had saved his life. Still, he didn't know her and wasn't certain whether he even recognized her.

"Let's have it," Mason said.

Kelly ran her hands through her hair like she was trying to pull off a mask. Nothing changed except her features softened with weariness and relief.

"The FBI asked me to come back a few years ago. They'd been burnt by too many agents who had been bought by drug dealers or foreign governments. They told me my background would give them an edge."

"Because you had had a partner who was dirty and that made you suspect as well?"

"The higher-ups wanted someone they could send in to work with agents who were under the microscope. Even though I was cleared, they made sure I still had a bad reputation when I came back. I played on that by looking the other way, dropping a hint that I was open to something extra. If the agent reported me, we backed off. If the agent invited me to the party, we ran out the string."

"Why go back? Why put yourself through that?"

"When my partner went down, he took part of me with him. I wanted that back."

"Was Brewer one of the bad boys?"

"Very bad. We tried to nail him a few years ago, but we couldn't get anything solid."

"Was that when the two of you raided Ed Fiori's office right after he was killed?"

Kelly nodded. "Brewer claimed he was working a confidential source inside Fiori's organization, but we suspected he was on Fiori's payroll. We had heard a rumor about Fiori's taping system and, when Fiori was killed, Brewer said he wanted to check out whether his source was incriminated on the tapes."

"And you wanted to know if Brewer was on the tapes," Mason said.

"There was no informant. Brewer was after the same thing. There were only a handful of tapes left when we got there and Brewer wasn't on them. Fiori's nephew, Vince Bongiovanni, had gotten there ahead of us and taken most of the tapes. When we asked him for the tapes, he said he had destroyed them out of respect for his uncle's memory."

Mason almost asked her if she had found the tape of his meeting with Ed Fiori, but let it go. It didn't matter anymore since his confessionals with Detective Griswold and Rachel Firestone.

"Bongiovanni told me he kept the tapes. I have a feeling he may have used some of them to settle a few of his cases," Mason said.

"Comes as no surprise. My bosses in D.C. thought Al Webb and Brewer would be a good match. I hadn't worked with him since Fiori died. We were both assigned to the investigation. He was already working on Fish's case. Brewer came on to me and I didn't discourage him," she said, looking away. "I just pretended he was someone else."

Mason took a deep breath. He didn't want to ask who but was glad she didn't dismiss her relationship with Brewer with a goes with the territory nonchalance.

"Brewer reached out to Webb," Kelly continued, "and let him know he was available at the right price. Webb low- balled him and Brewer threatened to bust him on the spot. Then Webb came up with the conversations between Brewer and Fiori on a CD and Brewer took the money."

"Did Webb get the CD from Bongiovanni?" Mason asked.

"I doubt it. Webb and Bongiovanni hate each other. Webb must have found a secret stash of Fiori's tapes that we had missed. That's when Brewer asked if I wanted in. He said if we got the tape, we could level the playing field with Webb and become his partners instead of his employees. I told him yes."

"Webb gave the CD to his lawyer for safekeeping," Mason said. It was a guess, but he made it a fact. Kelly didn't deny it. "Which one of you stole it?"

"You're lucky it was me. Brewer would have killed you and Lari Prillman."

"Did Webb cut you in?"

"He wasn't happy about it, but he did."

"That's a lot just to nail an agent that's in the bag for a guy skimming from a casino."

"Skimming and bribery are crimes, Counselor."

"So is selling fake IDs to terrorists," Mason said.

CHAPTER SEVENTY-NINE

KELLY'S EYES WIDENED. "What do you know about that?"

"I know that Sylvia McBride uses her call center as a front for phony IDs. I know that she supplied IDs to her husband, Wayne, so he could become Al Webb and to her step- nephew, Tommy Corcoran, who became Charles Rockley. Johnny Keegan was her nephew. All he needed was a résumé. I know that the FBI's files on the family are off-limits on the grounds of national security. The rest is just a matter of connecting the dots."

"One thing the terrorists learned from nine-eleven was to be patient," Kelly said. "They want to set up sleeper cells in this country. That takes more than fake IDs; it takes complete covers—job histories, residential histories, family histories. More than that, they need people to front for them whose names and skin color don't match a Homeland Security risk profile. Sylvia and Webb were running a nice little ID scam. They hooked up with a Saudi Arabian charity and took the operation international."

"Why did you drag Fish into all of this?" Mason asked.

"We needed him to set up the bank robbery."

"Why not just give Sylvia and her husband the money?" Blues asked.

"I told you that Webb wasn't happy to have Brewer and me as his partners. Webb's overseas partners were even less happy. They demanded proof that we really had changed teams. We couldn't blow up a building for them and we don't kill people. Then Fish fell into our laps when Rockley was murdered. His connection to Webb was too good an opportunity to pass up. Our charity sponsors liked the bank robbery."

"Who leaked Rockley's ID to Rachel Firestone?" Mason asked.

"The initial leak came from outside the Bureau, but Brewer confirmed it. He figured it was coming out soon enough anyway. I chewed his ass out if that makes any difference."

"Not much. Who took Blues's picture outside Rockley's apartment?" Mason asked.

"Johnny Keegan. When Rockley disappeared, Webb sent Johnny to look for him. He took Blues's picture with a camera phone and e-mailed it to Webb. We were monitoring Webb's e-mail. That added to the pressure on Fish to work with us because it made him look guilty."

"Fish didn't kill Rockley; Webb did. So why would Webb send Johnny to look for Rockley?" Mason asked.

"Webb didn't kill him or Johnny. Like I told you, Webb didn't trust many people, but he trusted those boys because they were family and he needed them for his operation. Plus, Brewer and I can alibi him for both murders."

"How do I know you're not covering up for Webb in the name of national security?" Mason asked.

"You're just going to have to trust me. In any case, the robbery did the trick. Webb is taking us to meet his contact."

"I'm glad everything worked out so well for you. Too bad I can't say the same thing for Fish," Mason said.

"Fish had a heart attack. That wasn't our fault. He should have stayed home."

"That's an easy out," Mason said. "All you cared about was your investigation. If someone gets hurt or dies, you toss that off as collateral damage."

"You should know, Counselor. You're pretty good at that yourself. You're the one who dragged Lila into this case. Webb caught her on his computer. It didn't take much to get her to tell him she was doing a favor for you."

Mason felt a flash of heat in his face. Kelly was right about Lila. He could add her to the list with Vanessa Carter. He was about to pay his debt to Judge Carter and would have to find a way to make it up to Lila.

Kelly's cell phone rang. She looked at the screen, ignoring the call.

"Brewer?" Mason asked.

"Yeah. We don't have much time." Kelly stood up. "Get up and hit me," she said, pointing to her chin.

Mason stood, his arms at his side. "I'm not going to hit you."

"Look, if you don't hit me, Brewer and Webb aren't going to believe that you escaped without my help. You're right about one thing. This investigation is more important than me or you or any other collateral damage. I'm going underground and tracing this ID network as far as it goes. I can't take the chance that my case falls apart because you don't have the stomach to hit a woman."

"Get out of my way," Blues said, pushing Mason to the side and dropping Kelly with a hard left hand. "You people talk so much it makes my head hurt."

Mason helped Kelly onto the sofa, cupping her chin in his hand until her eyes focused. The right side of her face was red and swelling fast. There was a trickle of blood at the corner of her mouth. He wiped it with his sleeve. She draped her arm over his shoulder and pulled him close.

"I want you to know something," she whispered.

"I know. It could have been Brewer instead of you."

"Not what I mean," she managed. "That night in Fiori's office, I found some of the tapes. Brewer was in another room. I took them with me to listen to later. You were on the tapes talking to Fiori about Blues and Judge Carter. There was also a call from Fiori to the judge."

Mason stared at her, unable to move. "It was you?" he finally said. "You were the blackmailer. Was that another chip you tossed onto the table for Webb?"

She shook her head and sat up, rubbing her jaw. "I wouldn't do that to you. I burnt the tape after I listened to it."

Mason heard voices for the second time that night. This time it was Vanessa Carter telling him that they had a problem, followed by Fish reminding him that the mark never feels the hook until it's in too deep. Fish had warned him, but the hook was in too deep for Mason to understand.

"Why did you do that?"

"Blues was innocent. The judge was already compromised. It didn't matter and I didn't want you to end up as collateral damage."

"Why tell me about it now?"

"I saw the look on your face when I told you about Brewer's tape. Besides, this way you'll know that I'm not as bad as they will say I am. Now get out of here."

CHAPTER EIGHTY

MASON DROVE FISH's rental car, with Fish's body lying in the backseat, to Fish's house. The charge of mail fraud and the suspicion of murder would be buried with his client. Mason wanted more for him than that. He wanted Fish's daughters to believe their father had died peacefully in his own home, his debts paid in full, their memories of him not tainted by murder. That meant finding Charles Rockley's killer. Though Fish had no connection to the murders of Johnny Keegan and Mark Hill, Mason's gut told him they were dominoes that fell when Rockley's body hit the ground.

Blues followed in his pickup with Lila, awake but still groggy, riding shotgun. They were surprised that a police car wasn't parked in front of Fish's house after the APB had been issued for him.

They sat Fish in his easy chair, expecting that his body would be found in the morning by the housekeeper or perhaps by one of his daughters. His death would be classified as unattended, requiring an autopsy that would reveal his body had been moved after he had died. There would be questions to answer, but no crime had been committed.

After another trip to Lake Lotawana to pick up his SUV, Mason took Lila home. She rejected Mason's apologies, insisting she'd known what she was getting into and making her own apology for getting caught.

"I would have gotten away with it," she said, "if I had quit after I found the e-mail Johnny sent to Mr. Webb, but I kept poking around. Mr. Webb had an e-mail folder for travel. He had made a reservation for Johnny to go to New York and then make a connection to Saudi Arabia."

"When was he supposed to leave?" Mason asked.

"Last Saturday," she said. "The day after he was killed. The weird thing about it was it was a one-way ticket. Johnny was leaving and he wasn't coming back."

"Why were you so curious?"

"I know this makes me a real bitch, but me and Johnny had been spending time together again. He said he was finished with Carol Hill, but he didn't tell me he was leaving. It made me wonder if he told her."

It made Mason wonder too. It was after midnight when he left Lila's house. He called Samantha Greer on her cell phone.

"Things are going crazy around here, Lou. What do you want?"

"Did you get a ballistics report yet on the bullet that killed Mark Hill?"

"Yeah, why?"

"Do me a favor. Check for a match with the bullet that killed Johnny Keegan."

"Do you know something I should know?"

"Carol Hill was cheating on her husband with Keegan. Her husband was beating the crap out of her."

"That I know. Carol may have killed her husband for beating her, but why would she kill her lover?"

"Because he dumped her for someone else and he was leaving the country on a one-way ticket," Mason said.

"What about Rockley?" Samantha asked. "You think she went for the hat trick?"

"Carol says he raped her."

"Even so, I don't see Carol cutting him up."

"She didn't. I'm betting Keegan did. He knew about the connection between Fish and Webb and dumped Rockley's body in the trunk of Fish's car to throw suspicion at Fish."

"I don't know what you're talking about. What connection between Fish and Webb?"

"It's complicated. Ask the FBI."

"We're being overrun by the FBI at the moment and the lab doesn't open until seven o'clock. It'll have to wait till morning."

"What's with the FBI invasion?"

"You won't believe this. The bank robbery was an inside job. The two agents—what were their names? Brewer and Holt—set the whole thing up. The feds released Mickey and want our help catching their agents. We cancelled the APB on Fish. Be sure you tell him."

"Thanks. I'll do that."

"One other thing," Samantha said. "Griswold told me about your come-to-Jesus session. You didn't leave him much choice. He had to take it to the prosecuting attorney."

"I know. Any word from Ortiz on what he's going to do?"

"Ortiz doesn't have much choice either. Hard to give a criminal defense lawyer a pass at the same time a couple of FBI agents make the Ten Most Wanted list. Are you going to be all right?"

"It's no hill for a climber. Call me in the morning when you get the ballistic results."

CHAPTER EIGHTY-ONE

Mason parked across the street from Carol Hill's house just as the morning sun was burning the horizon. He'd managed a few hours of sleep, enough to sort out what he thought had happened. If he were right, this would be his only chance to hear it from Carol.

Lights came on inside the house at seven-thirty. Carol opened her front door and a puppy bolted outside, sniffing the crisp air. She was wearing a robe and slippers and padded down the driveway to pick up her newspaper. Mason waited until she was at the curb before he got out of his car.

"Nice morning," he said to her.

"I wasn't expecting company," she said. Her hair was tangled from sleep and her eyes were puffy from having just woken up.

"I don't blame you. I've got a busy day and wanted to be sure I caught you. It's about Johnny Keegan."

She clutched the unopened paper to her chest. "What about him?"

"I talked to Lila Collins. She and Keegan were close, but you knew that." Carol's eyes narrowed and she nodded. "Anyway, turns out Keegan asked Lila to recommend a lawyer and she told him about me. That's why he was carrying around my name and number when he was killed. Small world, huh?"

"Yeah. Real small."

"Remember the other morning when we met at Vince's suite at the Galaxy Hotel, I asked you if Keegan told you why he needed a lawyer and you said he didn't?"

Carol retreated a few steps toward the house. Mason kept pace with her, the puppy scampering between them. She nodded her head again.

"Lila told me that Keegan was leaving the country and not coming back. I was wondering, did he tell you that?"

"He said he didn't want to go, but Webb was making him."

"You offered to go with him, but he said no, didn't he? Did he tell you that if he was going to take anyone, he'd take Lila?"

"If he wanted that skinny bitch, he could have her. It made no difference to me."

"It will make a lot of difference to the police," Mason said. "For starters, it means he didn't need a lawyer. So he must have known someone who did, someone he wanted to help out even if he was dumping her. And, it means he was the second guy you put out for who crapped on you."

"I don't know what you're talking about," Carol said, swallowing hard and glancing at her front door. "I have to go." She turned away, but Mason grabbed her arm.

"The police are going to compare the bullets that killed Keegan and your husband to see if they were fired from the same gun. When they get a match, they're going to drive down this street and knock down your door."

"What do you want?" she asked, her face trembling.

"I want to tell Avery Fish's daughters that their father wasn't a killer."

"I can't help you," she said, pulling her arm free.

"Sure you can. Tell me if I've got it right. Let's start with Charles Rockley. You and Vince cooked up your lawsuit to get even with Galaxy—maybe you even set poor Rockley up. Then everything came apart when Lari Prillman exposed your affair with Keegan. You were afraid Rockley was going to get away with it."

Carol's face turned red, her mouth turning down. "He raped me!"

"That's your story. The jury might even believe you. Trouble is you waited so long to kill Rockley that it looks premeditated instead of in the heat of the moment. Especially since you cut off his head and his hands and stuffed him in the trunk of Avery Fish's car."

She dropped the newspaper, covering her face with her hands, her body convulsing. The tremors passed and her arms fell to her sides.

"I didn't cut him up," she murmured.

"Was it Keegan?"

She nodded, barely moving her head. "He said he'd seen it done on The Sopranos and it would make it impossible to identify the body."

"Why did he put the body in Fish's car?"

"He said he'd seen Fish on TV. The guy was already in trouble. He said that would really throw the cops off."

"Did he leak Rockley's identity to the press?"

"That was Vince's idea. He said it would put the heat on Galaxy and it might help with my case."

Mason wasn't surprised that Carol had told Bongiovanni what she'd done. That explained why Bongiovanni had been so quick to assure Mason of Carol's innocence, claiming that he too had received an anonymous tip and offering to work with Mason. No doubt Bongiovanni would refuse to testify against Carol, claiming that anything she said to him about Rockley was protected by the attorney-client privilege.

"When Keegan told you he was trading you in for Lila Collins and leaving the country, it must have been too much to take. I'll bet killing him was a little easier after you had your first murder under your belt. Then, when your husband kept beating you, you knew just how to make him stop."

The puppy nipped at her slippers. She scooped him up, stroked his neck, and held him to her breast, her eyes red but dry, a fresh defiance straightening her spine.

"They were shits. All three of them. They looked at me and all they saw was tits and ass. Well, they won't see any of that anymore. Johnny said you're supposed to be the best. Will you help me?"

Mason picked up the newspaper. Rachel's story was on the front page above the fold. He tucked the paper under his arm as a convoy of police cars turned the corner. Detectives Griswold and Cates got out of one car, followed by Samantha Greer in another. A half dozen uniformed cops began securing the scene.

"I almost wish I could," Mason told her.

He walked away as Griswold read her rights to her.

CHAPTER EIGHTY-TWO

Kelly Holt had destroyed Ed Fiori's tapes. Vanessa Carter had blackmailed Mason with a lie that she was being blackmailed. She didn't want his money. Instead, she wanted to do to him what he had done to her, and he had obliged, ruining his career with a confession that shielded her from the fallout. He thought back over the last eight days. She had played him perfectly. Fish had taught him that a con worked best when the mark wanted to believe it. Mason not only had feared that he would one day pay the price for what he'd done, he knew that he should. He was low-hanging fruit and she had picked him clean.

The judge's voice message said that she was filling in at the Jackson County Courthouse. Mason found her there, clothed in a black robe, sitting on the bench, dispensing justice.

The courtroom had the latest in technology. The judge's bench and the counsel tables were equipped with computers.

The court reporter used a computer to produce a real-time transcript that also fed into a computer in her office so she could monitor proceedings even if she wasn't in the courtroom.

The county had just installed an experimental voice- activated system to back up the court reporter. The court reporter or the judge or the lawyers could turn it on when they argued matters at the judge's bench outside the hearing of the jury. The system recorded what was said and instantly converted it to a transcript.

It was motion day, which meant that lawyers were lined up, taking their turns to be heard on various motions in their cases. The low hum of conversations among the lawyers waiting for their cases to be called disappeared when Mason walked in and took a seat at the rear of the courtroom. The other lawyers were all in uniform, wearing dark suits and starched shirts. He was dressed in jeans and a striped shirt. No one sat near him. No one talked to him. They looked away, resuming their conversations. He didn't exist.

He waited until the last group filed out. Judge Carter nodded at the court reporter and her bailiff, telling them they were excused.

"Mr. Mason," Judge Carter said.

Mason rose and approached the bench. She looked down on him from her perch, her face radiant, her black eye healed, not noticing when he pressed the button for the voice-activated court-reporting system.

"Your eye," Mason said. "You told me the blackmailer confronted you in your garage and hit you."

"That was more persuasive than telling you I had an allergic reaction that inflamed my eye," she said with a wave of her hand. "I had to keep you motivated. That's why I kept moving up the blackmailer's deadline."

"You lied about everything."

"I lied? Were you lying when you told the police and that reporter what you did to me?"

"You weren't being blackmailed. It was all a scam to get even with me."

"I worked my entire life to be here, in this courtroom, and have the respect of the people who appear before me. Look at what I've missed because of you. The change in technology alone makes me feel like a child on her first day of school. I don't understand how any of it works. But, this is my house," she said, pounding her gavel, "and you took it from me because you weren't a good enough lawyer to represent your client like everyone else does—according to the rules. Well, I took it back. Call it what you want, but I call it justice."

"What made you think you could get me to turn myself in and cover for you at the same time?"

"You did. Look at you. Look at the people you represent. Look at the risks you take for them. You can't wait to fall on your sword. All I did was sharpen the blade. You are excused, Counsel."

The court reporter opened the rear door of the courtroom and raced to the computer at her desk. The bailiff followed close behind her, the two of them scrolling down the monitor, studying the transcript of the judge's and Mason's conversation.

"What's the meaning of this?" Judge Carter demanded.

"There's no mistake," the court reporter told the bailiff. "It's the same as on the computer in my office."

"Judge Carter," the bailiff said, one hand on the butt of his service revolver. "We have a problem."

CHAPTER EIGHTY-THREE

THE DAY AFTER Fish's funeral, Mason received a phone call from one of Fish's daughters. She read to him a letter she'd received from the United States attorney, Roosevelt Holmes. The letter commended Fish for his exemplary and selfless cooperation with an important Justice Department investigation. Holmes wrote that for reasons of national security he regretted that he could not share the details with the family but added that the mail fraud charge against Fish had been officially expunged. She asked Mason for details of what her father had done. Mason explained that he was subject to the same constraints, but said that Fish had done the right thing and that was all that mattered.

Carol Hill pled innocent to the murders of Charles Rock- ley, Johnny Keegan, and Mark Hill. She claimed that Keegan had killed Rockley, out of jealousy; that her husband had killed Keegan, because he was jealous of Keegan; and that she didn't know who killed her husband. Vince Bongiovanni hired a dream team of defense lawyers to represent her. They kicked him off the team after they interviewed Mason and he told them that Bongiovanni had helped cover up Carol's guilt.

Samantha Greer confided to Mason that Carol had a decent chance of getting off. Carol blamed two of the murders on two of the murder victims. One key witness, Al Webb, had quit his job at the Galaxy Casino and left town without a trace. Mason was the prosecution's other key witness, particularly concerning his conversation with Carol immediately before she was arrested, and, according to the prosecuting attorney, he had less credibility than a dead politician.

The police caught a break when the pistol they recovered in Troost Lake proved to be the weapon used to kill both Mark Hill and Keegan. The gun had been wiped clean of any prints. The registration was traced to Ed Fiori and had been included on the list of personal property prepared by Vince Bongiovanni in his capacity as executor of his uncle's estate. Carol claimed she didn't know anything about the gun. Her lawyers persuaded Carol to accept the prosecutor's offer to plead guilty to second-degree murder in the deaths of Keegan and Hill. As part of the deal, she agreed to testify against Bongiovanni for his role in the cover-up of the murders. Charges were dropped on Rockley's murder, which remained classified as unsolved.

Patrick Ortiz decided to defer any decision on whether to prosecute Mason or Judge Carter until after the State Bar Disciplinary Committee reviewed their cases and forwarded its recommendations to the Missouri Supreme Court, which would make the final decisions. If the state disbarred Mason, the Federal Courts would do the same.

Judge Carter avoided the entire process, voluntarily surrendering her law license, and was disbarred. The prosecuting attorney let her plead guilty to a misdemeanor charge of theft by deception. She paid a fine and left town.

Mason appeared before the Supreme Court represented by his Aunt Claire. She argued passionately on his behalf, emphasizing the difficult burdens of criminal defense lawyers and highlighting that Mason had taken responsibility for what he'd done. She urged the court to allow him to keep his license and practice under her supervision for a period of two years. The court took his case under advisement, promising to issue its decision within four to six weeks.

Mason spent the next four weeks in limbo as the last of his clients drifted away and the phone stopped ringing. He sold his house because he needed the money. None of the neighbors helped him pack, though a few stopped in at his garage sale asking how soon he'd be gone. Emptiness grew inside him as he sealed each box of belongings, sorting through what he would keep and what he would give away, surprised at how little he wanted.

Claire kept telling him that change was invigorating and that he should embrace it. He replied that he would take it slowly, having made it a rule to hold hands before embracing. Tuffy took a final trot around the house, sniffing her favorite spots one last time. Mason rented an apartment overlooking Brush Creek on the Plaza.

Abby offered to take a leave of absence from Senator Seeley's staff, but he convinced her to stay on the job. Sensing that his notoriety was a liability to her in high-profile Washington circles, he declined her invitations to visit and kept their telephone conversations short. His feelings for her hadn't changed, but his capacity for their relationship was, like his future, uncertain.

He kept up on the search for Dennis Brewer and Kelly Holt through Samantha Greer and Rachel Firestone. Eventually, the FBI told the police they no longer required their assistance. The news coverage subsided until one day in March when Brewer's body was discovered in a shallow grave in Detroit. An FBI spokesman said there were no leads or suspects and that the money taken in the robbery had not been recovered. There was no word about Kelly. Mason tried reaching Roosevelt Holmes and Pete Samuelson, but neither returned his calls.

By the time the Supreme Court decision arrived, his mail had dwindled to a trickle of bills and promotions so the official- looking envelope was easy to spot when the mail carrier shoved it through the slot in his office door. The envelope landed in the center of the floor and he stared at it from behind his desk.

He had brought Tuffy with him to the office to give her a break from confinement in the apartment. She was lying on the sofa. When the mail arrived, she climbed down and sniffed it.

"You open it," he told the dog, who looked up at him, her tail wagging.

Mason opened the envelope and skipped to the last paragraph of the decision, knowing that's where the ruling would be set out. After reciting the undisputed facts, the court cited Mason's duties as an officer of the court, the corrosive effect of his conduct on the legal system, his determined efforts to keep his actions secret, and that he had only come forward when he had been duped into doing so. In light of all that, the court said, there was no alternative. He was disbarred.

Standing in the middle of his office, the court's order dangling from his fingertips, he turned slowly around, surveying the law books lining his shelves, the empty spaces where he used to stack client files, and the dry erase board where he dissected the puzzles that were his cases. Abby's words echoed in his mind. Is that all you are? Some guy with a law license? It was time to find out.

"C'mon, dog," he said. "Let's go see what's shaking."

NEWSLETTER SIGNUP

If you'd like to receive an email letting you know when Joel's next book will be released, sign up at www.joelgoldman.com/newsletter/. Your email address will never be shared and you can unsubscribe at any time.

REVIEW THIS BOOK

Thanks for adding *Final Judgment* to your library. Readers depend on readers to recommend good books and authors depend on readers to generate positive word-of-mouth for their books. If you liked *Final Judgment* I hope you'll leave a review on Amazon and Goodreads, even if it's only a few words. It will make a big difference and I will be very thankful.

LET'S CONNECT

Joel enjoys engaging with his readers. Drop by his website, www.joelgoldman.com, to find out more about him and his books. Read what he has to say about the writer's life on his blog, www.joelgoldman.com/blog and join him on Twitter at www.twitter.com/joelgoldman1 and on Facebook at www.facebook.com/joelgoldmanauthor. Check out all his books at www.Amazon.com/author/joelgoldman. And watch videos about Joel and his books at www.youtube.com/user/joelgoldmanwriter.

ABOUT THE AUTHOR

Joel Goldman is the author of the Edgar and Shamus nominated Lou Mason thrillers, the Jack Davis thrillers and the Alex Stone thrillers. He lives with his wife and two dogs in Leawood, KS. He was a trial lawyer for twenty-eight years. He wrote his first thriller after one of his partners complained about another partner, prompting him to write a mystery, kill the son-of-a-bitch off in the first chapter and spend the rest of the book figuring out who did it. And he never looked back.

Made in the USA
Middletown, DE
17 March 2015